ST

STAGE FRIGHT

GARRETT BOATMAN

With a new introduction by
WILL ERRICKSON

VALANCOURT BOOKS

Stage Fright by Garrett Boatman
Originally published by New American Library in 1988
First Valancourt Books edition 2020

Despite extensive searching, the Publisher was unable to identify
the artist or copyright holder of the cover painting. Anyone with
information is invited to contact the Publisher at
info@valancourtbooks.com.

"Paperbacks from Hell" logo designed by Timothy O'Donnell.
© 2017 Quirk Books. Used under license. All rights reserved.

Published by Valancourt Books, Richmond, Virginia
http://www.valancourtbooks.com

ISBN 978-1-948405-65-2 (*paperback*)

Also available as an electronic book.

All Valancourt Books publications are printed on acid free paper
that meets all ANSI standards for archival quality paper.

Cover design by M. S. Corley
Set in Dante MT

INTRODUCTION

T HERE'S NO WAY YOU MISSED THAT COVER. Not a chance. In the annals of paperback horror, the sight of a keytar-jamming skeleton decked out in a stage costume that would've made *Theatre of Pain*-era Mötley Crüe jealous is one to be cherished. Celebrated. Turned into a blacklight poster sold at headshops everywhere. Caught in mid-jump, at the height of jammin' rock 'n' roll mania, our skeletal muso is about to lay down some serious tuneage guaranteed to blow the minds of his teenage fans.

Anyone who is familiar with the genre or who has read my and Grady Hendrix's *Paperbacks from Hell*, well knows that skeletons and skulls were de rigueur for cover art during this era: an easy signifier for readers eager to lap up grue and ghast-liness, a hint, a promise, of the macabre mayhem inside.

Throughout its heyday of the excess-is-best Eighties, horror fiction was often adorned by our bodily architectures stripped bare and depicted in a full range of activities that we humans often enjoy while alive, like frisky cheerleading (Jack Ketchum's *The Girl Next Door*) or driving a K-car (Richard Lay-mon's *Resurrection Dreams*), from dancing like a court jester and playing a flute (*Piper* by Rutherford and Robertson) or for the young-at-heart, riding a tricycle out of a midnight netherworld straight at you, potential book buyer with an extra $2.95 burn-ing a hole in the pocket of your jeans (*Tricycle*, natch, by Russell Rhodes, this last I believe to be solely responsible for my horror paperback obsession). The Eighties—you had to be there.

And believe it or not, in the 1980s there were a few humans who actually enjoyed playing the keytar, basically an electronic keyboard strapped around the body like a guitar. New Wave and prog rock bands alike embraced this new synthesis of instruments, using it to highlight how technology was beginning to infiltrate and define our daily modern lives—whether we wanted to hear A Flock of Seagulls or The Human League over and over on our radios or not.

The regrettable thing about these covers is that they so often simply do not depict anything to be found inside the book itself. Is there a keytar-jamming madman within the pages of *Stage Fright*, the 1988 paperback original from first-time novelist Garrett Boatman? There is not. There is a lot of stuff going on there, stuff that also would have made a bad-ass paperback cover image (marauding raptor? Underwater zombies? Undead jellyfish? Check, check, oh and check). But this is the book you now have in your hands, thanks to the fine fellows of Valancourt Books, and I'm here to tell you that while there is no keytar of any sort to come, there is much Eighties-style enjoyment to be had.

Born in Columbus, Georgia, Garrett Boatman's family settled in New Jersey. *Stage Fright*'s mashup of horror and science fiction comes from the author's lifelong love of the two genres, reading his way through the Jersey City Public Library starting at age 10. ("Savage, gothic, noirish place to grow up," he quips about Jersey City. Sounds wonderful!) Boatman soaked up the "monster kid" vibe of his era, watching Creature Features and Chiller Theater shows on television and devouring genre fiction from *Lord of the Rings* to Lovecraft. Also an influence: "The violence, overall grayness, and brown pall of industrial smog" of N.J./N.Y.

After college, Boatman taught for a few years—he told his students horror was his religion—and figured since he was reading so much of it, he'd try his hand at his own book. *Stage Fright* was his second attempt, written longhand and then polished on an IBM Selectric. It took him two years. In a move of brilliant simplicity, Boatman simply called up Signet Books and asked to speak to an editor, of course, because "they published Stephen King." An editor actually came to the phone and asked Boatman what he had, and it was a 700-page science fiction novel called *Death Dream*. Boatman sent in the manuscript, got a meeting, where the editor-in-chief told him books with "dream" in the title didn't sell, and decided it'd be a better fit for the brand-new horror imprint called Onyx—once the title was switched to *Stage Fright*.

Onyx was the horror and thriller imprint of New American Library, which was created at the time NAL became a division of Penguin Group. They published many a classic vintage paperback by the era's big names, well-known and loved titles from the likes of David J. Schow, Rex Miller, Michael Slade, and British giant James Herbert. Lesser-known works like *The Breeze Horror* by Candace Caponegro and *Manstopper* by Douglas Borton were also popular (and remain so, as both have positive reviews online). Quite of few of these works were adorned by some spectacular cover illustrations, like John Shirley's *In Darkness Waiting*, Hugh Zachary's *The Revenant*, and Nancy A. Collins's *Sunglasses After Dark*. At the time, *Stage Fright*'s art was just another commission; to this day the author has no idea of the artist's identity.

Boatman would have preferred the skeleton on the cover to be playing "an SG like Tony Iommi," which makes more sense for the genre. "Looked more Merry Pranksters than horror," he says now of the too-bright costume adorning the skeleton, and he asked that its colors be toned down to look more horror-appropriate: "We'd sell more copies," he said, knowing what a publisher wants to hear, "if it was dark." Editor and art department agreed. Onyx had *Stage Fright* on the shelves in July 1988, and it sold well, he did some signings in bookstores . . . and the paperback horror crash happened a short time later. He wrote more books, but they went unpublished, and three decades passed. Searching his name online, Boatman discovered a small coterie of fans of his novel—which had become a much sought-after collectible—and then *Paperbacks from Hell* featured that Merry Horror Prankster on its cover, and here we are.

The main conceit of *Stage Fright* is a future technology called MDIT, for "microwave dream-imaging transmitter," explained in the book's second chapter. Invented in the early Nineties, it is not perfected till Izzy Stark, a rock star who comes along in 1998 and masters what is known as "dreamies," which are movies made from, surprise surprise, the creator's dreams, which other people can then partake in as a thrill-ride. The instrument he uses is called a "dreamatron," natch. His girlfriend Helen, a psychology student, hips him to a drug called taraxein, being studied by her abnormal psych professor, Casper Nösberger. Made from the blood of schizophrenics, taraxein causes various states of derangement in subjects.

To say this piques Izzy's interest is an understatement. Already obsessed with dreams and visions, nightmares and altered states, all in the service of story, Izzy is determined to experiment with taraxein and find out how it can take his already masterful dreamies to the next level. It's just that the next level turns out to be murderous, and woe betide anyone who stands in his way of achieving his ultimate creation: *"A dreamie spun from schizophrenic nightmares! A 'new wave' of dreamies! And, once more, the name Isidor Stark hailed as an innovator, as a prodigy, a genius!"*

In an interview with the horror and occult blog Nocturnal Revelries, Boatman expands on the real-life history that inspired *Stage Fright*: "In the 1950s, researchers at Tulane University discovered a protein antibody called taraxein in the blood of schizophrenics that caused schizophrenic behavior when injected in monkeys." What? I had never heard of this, and this seems like the kind of thing I'd have heard of! Boatman continues: "Administered to inmate volunteers from the Louisiana State Penitentiary, taraxein produced schizophrenic episodes that lasted up to half an hour, presumably until the body's defense mechanisms defeated the invading substance. Hmm, I thought. From the blood of schizophrenics. Now there's an idea." (Today it seems taraxein is considered "possibly nonexistent" according to Wikipedia, but don't let that stand in the way of a good story!)

Colorful, vividly-drawn set pieces of splattery gore and nightmare visions will satisfy genre fans, particularly the opening scene, where it's most important. I also appreciated Boatman's sensitive handling of Izzy's elderly neighbors, one of whom is struggling with Alzheimer's and who is most comfortable watching old black-and-white classics like *Them!* and *Creature from the Black Lagoon*. Alas, this man's lifelong habit will set the stage for one of the best, most horrific sequences herein. Of course no horror novel about a deranged pop star would be complete without a cast of his fans: here, teenagers hang out in a garage, drinking and drugging and trading cringeworthy insults while hoping to score tickets to Izzy's ultimate show, "Inferno."

"I'm obsessed with how technology influences human and social evolution," Boatman says about the origins of the dreamatron. He also says, and this did not surprise me, "I was at David Bowie's 1974 *Diamond Dogs* concert at Madison Square Garden, the whole mind-blowing extravaganza stuck with me." Boatman envisioned a pop star that could offer his own twisted drugged-out visions straight into the frontal lobes of his audience. This literally sets the stage for *Stage Fright's* over-the-top climax, an OD of pure Eighties horror, of Boschean creatures and young bridge-and-tunnel stoners colliding in a concert hall that's about to collapse.

All right kid, got your ticket, we gotta search you, no glass containers, no cameras or metal objects . . . Oh, and watch out for the floating undead jellyfish. Enjoy the show!

Will Errickson
May 2020

WILL ERRICKSON is a lifelong horror enthusiast and creator of the *Too Much Horror Fiction* blog. With Grady Hendrix in 2017, he co-wrote the Bram Stoker Award-winning *Paperbacks from Hell*, which featured many books from his personal collection. Will resides in Portland, Oregon, with his wife Ashley and his ever-growing library of vintage horror paperbacks.

For that ol' sidewinder
my dad
Richard Garrett Boatman
with love and appreciation

PARADISO

This is indeed no dream!

—Poe

I

Izzy Stark was King of the Genre. What happened
didn't have to happen, but it did. All we can do is ask
ourselves *how?* and *why?*

> —Quentin Hughes
> *Izzy Stark: Shooting Star*

The eel-gray water of the Hudson River slapped hungrily
against the hull of the police boat as it nosed through the fog.
Already the soup made visibility poor; another hour out here
and they would have to find their way back by radar. Across
on the Jersey side, the high-rise condominiums, office towers
and hotels that had sprouted along the Hoboken-Jersey City
waterfront over the past dozen years loomed like titans rising
from the mists of creation. The setting sun, shining between
two of the buildings, reflected blood-red off the tops of
the World Trade Center towers visible above the cluster of
high-rise apartments of Battery Park City. Downriver in the
harbor, where the fog was building more rapidly, the Statue of
Liberty was already lost from sight and the foghorns and buoys
sounded eerily across the water.

The police boat was responding to a boater's frantic call.
Something he had seen in the water.

"Coming up on the Twenty-second Street pier," Selznick
said, squinting shoreward.

Frank Price followed his old drinking buddy's gaze and, sure
enough, the long, rectangular bulk of a pier loomed out of the
fog into the river on their left.

Charlie, the third member of their party and the tub's
helmsman, stuck his head out of the pilothouse and yelled,
"See anything yet?"

"Not yet," Price yelled back. "Won't be long now."

Won't be long if we run into an incredible amount of luck,

he thought, considering they had to guess the location allowing for a half-hour of drift since the report. A floater drifted about as well as a log. Would've made things a lot easier had the boater stayed with the corpse and kept in radio contact.

Looking down into the murk—and some slap-happy environmentalists said it was getting better!—Price wondered how anything could live in it at all. Not that he minded taking a dip in the Hudson; he had even swum all the way around Manhattan two summers in a row when he was younger. Hell, he didn't mind the gunk that caught on your regulator, or the oil that worked under the collar of your wetsuit so that you had to use a grease solvent in your shower, or the tar that caked on your mask, or the nasty habit corpses had of popping out of the inky blackness into the white beam of your lantern. He was going on fifty and had been diving in the Hudson in the line of duty for twenty-three years. He had dived in the East River and Harlem River too, in daytime and at night: it didn't make much difference down there. He dived for murder weapons, drowning victims, and dumped bodies. And in all that time, in all those hundreds of man-hours spent underwater, he had never been afraid.

Until now.

Lately, the river had gone sour. People around the docks and aboard small craft had, over the past two weeks, been mysteriously disappearing. Boats found drifting or tied up at their moorings empty, stereos left blasting, showers running, lights blazing, drinks unfinished. And, more sinisterly, in some instances, there had been signs of struggle: broken furnishings, scraps of torn clothing, and blood.

Price had seen a few of the boats and had talked to those who had seen others, and in every case, not a single body had been found, neither above nor below the water.

Then, two days ago, police officers Lorenzo and Mueller vanished from their boat without a trace after going out on a routine search for two stiffs in a Dodge that had gone off the end of a pier. Price had seen their boat too, had seen the blood, and unlike the other boats from which people had disappeared, had seen the bullet holes. At least one of the cops had fired his weapon; the slugs dug out of the deck and the pilothouse were .9 mm, same as police issue.

The TV and the papers were having a field day with the whole mess. A few reporters hinted that the disappearances and presumed homicides were drug-related, others called them the actions of a group of crazed mass murderers. Neither explanation made much sense to Price. Mass murderers, sure! That was obvious—but where were the bodies? If they'd been dumped into the river, he'd have certainly found one or more of them by now. In all, between two and three dozen people had disappeared, probably more when you considered how the derelicts that hung around the waterfront had been thinning out.

Price shivered as if an icy tendril of fog had found its way under his wetsuit to touch his spine. He had a bad feeling out here on the river tonight. Or maybe it was just a residue left over from his dreams. Since Lorenzo and Mueller, he had been having nightmares.

He was night diving, looking for a body. His underwater lantern punched an incandescent hole through the enveloping blackness. He went down and down through the dirty river water, feeling as if eyes were watching him. The bottom came into view. He searched, his lantern gridding the darkness. Time ran out, but no corpse. He started up.

When he broke the surface, something bit into his leg, breaking through the wetsuit and puncturing his calf. Price stuck his head back into the water and saw, in the white beam of his lantern, the bloated, dead faces floating up from the depths, the horrible dishpan hands stretching toward him.

He grabbed for the dive knife strapped to his ankle, but one of the dead caught his arm, bit into his wrist. The grinding of teeth against bone was excruciating, but not as painful as the incredible cold that blossomed around the bite.

Then the lantern was lost, its beam spiraling down into the inky depths, and teeth were tearing into his throat, his arms, his legs . . .

Price wiped the sweat from his face with his hand, then worked on the rubber diving gloves. "Pass me the pole," he said.

Selznick passed him the pole.

It was twelve feet long and topped by a wicked-looking grappling hook. Price didn't care to use the hook in front of people—live people, that is—but out here in the fog, using the hook kept him out of the river. It wasn't as easy as a civilian might think to fish a floater out of the water, not without splashing in and securing a harness about the body and using the hoist. Even then, sometimes the bastard bobbed and tugged so hard it seemed it was wrestling with you. And when you were in the water, sometimes it would roll and pull you under. Price knew the silly—but nonetheless real—terror that came from having a floater's arm suddenly slap over you and force you down.

A job's a job, he told himself. Somebody has to do it.

"There!" he said, pointing to a mass of something that detached itself from the fog.

Selznick squinted and grunted and scratched at his withering plot of yellow-red hair. Then he saw it too.

"Slow up, Charlie," he called up to the pilot.

It didn't look like anything yet. It might have been a mass of seaweed bobbing on the tide, or a bundle of old clothes. The slow chug of the engine dropped to idle. The boat nosed toward the dark smear ahead.

Perhaps it was a breeze cooling the sweat on the back of Price's neck as he peered through the mist, but a cold chill swept through his veins.

Go home, he told himself. It's nothing but a bag of garbage . . . a pile of old clothes . . . Go home . . .

Then the smear sprouted limbs—bloated, sausage-like appendages that stuck out like inflated balloons.

"Looks like our baby," Selznick said, rubbing his sizable beer belly as if troubled by gas.

Price grunted. Baby was as big as a walrus. He passed the pole back to Selznick. "Looks like I go in."

"Yeah, well, don't piss in the water." Selznick's stab at humor came out flat.

Price zipped the front of his suit and worked the hood over his shaved head. In his business, hair got in the way. Then he pulled on his tank as Charlie cut the engine and Selznick readied the grappling pole to snare the floater and hold it in place until he could get into the water.

Price liked the new yellow suits, liked the idea that he'd be easier to spot in case something fouled up. He didn't like the notion of fish nibbling out his eyes. Nor did he find appealing the thought of getting hung up on something down there and turning to Jell-O inside his suit, eventually swelling up so much he would split a seam. He wondered about that: could a wetsuit contain the bottled-up pressure once the corpse bloated? The image he conjured was almost comical, but not quite—not when the face on the blimp figure was his own. He had handled enough corpses to know the feel of their jellied, waterlogged flesh. Sometimes, they were so saturated with river water and so badly decomposed the flesh came off in your hands. And when you had the corpse on deck, gases had a nasty way of leaking out. On warm, humid days the police tub smelled like the inside of a used coffin. He didn't look forward to going in.

The boat drifted alongside the corpse, and the floater bumped silently against the hull. With an experienced twist of the grappling pole, Selznick snared it by its shirt.

The body floated facedown, its long, matted hair spread like seaweed around its head. On the fat, bare arms that stuck out of the sleeveless sweatshirt were what once must have been tattoos, though they were so stretched and pocked with decay it was hard to tell what they depicted.

Price clamped his teeth around the regulator's mouthpiece, adjusted his mask, attached the tether (the river's currents could be swift), and dropped backward over the side into the water next to the body.

Price completed the loathsome job of securing the corpse into the harness then swam for the ladder and hauled himself, dripping, over the bulwark as the thing was winched from the water and lowered to the deck.

The stench hit him when he removed his regulator. Water streamed from the corpse, more water than could be attributed to its wet clothes; it was as if the floater were a hole-ridden barrel and the water was pouring from those holes.

Now that the thing was on the deck, he could see just how large it actually was. The male Caucasian had been big even in life—well over six feet and fat, long-haired and bearded. The remains of his blue jeans bulged with bloated meat. He wore a pair of work boots, probably steel-toed. Biker, Price guessed. They had made the right choice using the hoist.

Price was pulling his hood over his head when Charlie's scream sledgehammered into his brain. He whirled in time to see the impossible happen. The corpse, still streaming water from the many holes in its torso, was rising, hauling itself hand over hand up Charlie's leg.

Charlie's face had gone white. His mouth was still open, but the scream had played out. The aging police-boat pilot went down under the weight of the creature. Before they toppled to the deck in a heap and the bloated, rotting corpse, horribly animated, plunged its teeth into Charlie's throat, Price saw by the fading sunlight the lambent, fish-pale eyes that shone from the pocked and noseless face like twin moons. The pilot clawed at the thing's face, and strips of cheesy dead skin peeled off under his nails. The teeth clamped down on Charlie's throat, holding on like a pit bull. The sounds of cracking bone and gurgling were loud in Price's ears. He still held his hood out in both hands, as if offering it in supplication to the floater.

The thing dropped its burden. Charlie slumped to the deck. The creature began to rise, struggling to its feet. The sweatshirt, deteriorated from God only knew how long a stay underwater and stretched taut over the inflated torso, split up the back. Price was still too shocked that his nightmare was coming true, but Selznick sprang into action, snatched up the grappling pole, and swung it in a whistling arc at the floater's head.

Incredibly, moving supernaturally fast despite its size and advanced decomposition, the creature wrenched the pole from Selznick's grasp and hurled it clattering across the deck. It came to rest against the pilothouse. Then the thing grabbed Selznick and slammed him to the deck like a rag doll. The veteran officer's head caromed off the oak planks. The *crack* of splintered bone split the air.

The corpse rose from its second slay. Its dead eyes glowed with unnatural life. Its teeth and beard and rotting lips ran red with Charlie's blood. Its eyes met his, and Price dropped to his knees, yellow hood shaking in his hands. His dream had come true! Only, instead of in the water, it was happening on the deck of the police boat. Just like with Lorenzo and Mueller!

Unless I'm dreaming now!

His mind clutched at the thread of sanity as if it were a lifeline.

Looking more than ever like a balloon figure—a balloon that stayed fat despite its many holes—the floater stepped over Selznick's corpse. Its belly sloshed gelatinously where it bulged from its torn sweatshirt. Price tried to stand but tripped over his feet and went down heavily. He rolled without looking, glimpsed the dead, ruined face bending over him. The stench was overpowering.

Propelled by terror, he rolled until he slammed against the bulwark. He scrambled to his feet. The monster bore down on him, hands big as catcher's mitts outstretched, fingers working eagerly. Even though it had decomposed, the thing's nails had grown.

Price threw himself over the rail. The cold black water received him, closed over his head. His wetsuit buoyed him up almost instantly, and even as he bobbed to the surface, sputtering and gasping, he struck out, swimming for all he was worth away from the boat and the carnage on its deck.

But the boat was in his way! He had leapt from the wrong side, and he and the boat were drifting with the current at the same speed.

A huge bulk splashed into the water beside him. Something grabbed his arm. A hand that smelled of seaweed and rot closed over his face. Nails dug into his cheek and throat.

The floater pulled him around, drew his face closer to its own, its dead breath mingling with his. The kiss of its teeth was ice.

When Price stopped kicking, the floater released him and, slowly, began drifting cross-current toward the Manhattan docks now invisible behind a blanket of fog.

On the deck of the police boat, the corpses of the mutilated officers rose, blood streaming from their wounds, shambled to the rail and pitched themselves overboard.

Price, drifting face down in a spreading red tide, air bubbles escaping from the holes in his throat, stirred. When he came to, awakening into the consciousness of the dead, he was consumed by an overwhelming thirst that all the water in the Hudson couldn't quench.

Quentin Hughes blinked as the house lights came up, and he experienced the curious sense of dislocation that always accompanied the return to reality. His elbow joints cracked as he straightened in the faded red velvet seat that had seen better days, and took in the audience, his brown eyes recording.

Around him, fans were stretching, grins appearing as their eyes met their neighbors'. The theater was packed. Typical for a Friday night. The two persons seated immediately in front of Quent wore *Floaters* masks—jelly-eyed, bloated, decomposed faces copied from two of the riverlogged dead that peopled Izzy Stark's latest cult classic. To his left and two rows ahead, a tall, bullnecked, shaved-head man wearing a black wetsuit, which had to be hot in the small theater, emulated Frank Price. All the way in the front, a group of role-playing teenagers doubled as their favorite members of the street gangs that would ultimately save Manhattan in Stark's opus.

Audience participation.

That was why Quent preferred catching the midnight show in Greenwich Village to attending a Loew's in New Jersey.

Abruptly, the audience broke into a heady collective murmuring, and so began the ritual of sharing the experience. Quent switched on his belt-buckle tape recorder to catch the reactions of the ghouls sitting in front of him.

"Was it as good as last time?" the leather-jacketed creature said to his date.

"Wow!" A female voice. She blew out her latex cheeks and goggled her egg-yolk eyes for emphasis.

They got up and started for the aisle.

Be easy to take that one out of context, he thought, clicking off the recorder. Time to get moving. But he waited another moment. As usual after a Stark dreamie, his member was semi-erect. Unlike a lot of young bantam cocks who stood to strut their stuff as soon as the lights came up, he gave his body a minute to compose itself, then headed for the aisle, flicking up the soiled seats as he went.

The floor under his sneakers made sticky noises from the spilled soda, and the smell of greasy popcorn was pervasive. The theater doubled as a movie house, though tonight the only screen the audience needed was the linings of their eyelids.

In the lobby, he walked slowly, buoyed among the outgoing stream past the crowd waiting behind fraying velvet ropes to take in the late-late show. All the freaks were out tonight, the grue addicts, the hardcore fiends. These were the real night people: the leather boys, the glamour girls in glitter, the ghouls in whiteface—a tradition inspired by Stark himself when he chose to wear it for his live performances of *Dreamquest* and *Vampirophile*.

Outside, the night was balmy, the cigarette-strewn sidewalk gritty and as sweet as ripe garbage with the sweaty life of urban youth. The ingoing line stretched down the block. A stunning, punked-out whiteface caught his eye, and she, noticing his gaze lingering on her, smiled back, her teeth fluorescent white against her black lipstick. A skinny, breastless girl in an official *Floaters* T-shirt depicting a watery scene with a caved-in head and a bloated clawlike hand showing above the surface, told a bearded bum asking for money where he could shove it. Farther down, in the doorway of a novelty shop whose windows were stuffed with the standard paraphernalia—real-looking lumps of plastic horse hockey in candy boxes labeled "Road Apples," phony newspapers with mock headlines, rubber chickens, whoopee cushions—stood a group of older fans.

"He's so cute! I could just eat him alive!" a bleached blonde proclaimed to her friends in front of a guy whom, from his frown, Quent assumed to be her date.

"Yeah?" boyfriend said. "He wouldn't touch you if you came on a bed of coke!"

Quent smiled at the unintended *tout entendre*, as did the

blonde and her friends, making the boyfriend madder. Quent paused a moment to look back at the marquee, at the tall black letters that spelled FLOATERS.

On the corner a T-shirt vendor had set up shop on the hood of a parked car.

"All sizes! Popular colors! Ghoul green, putrid purple, yuck yellow! All your favorites, sickies! Show the world who you love!"

The hawker held up a T-shirt—that symbol of pop stardom since the mid-sixties. The shirt was black with a portrait in white of a youthful, boyishly serious face. The chalky complexion and longish white hair gave the portrait a ghoulish, albino appearance, and though the face was smiling, the eyes, airbrushed in red, made the portrait look devilish. Izzy in whiteface: the Pale Prince of the Undead image he had cultivated the first couple years of his stardom.

Quent stopped, seizing on a thought: *T-shirt . . .* symbol of stardom.

"How much?" he asked the vendor, knowing that prices varied from night to night and from customer to customer, depending on how the vendor sized you up.

"Nine bucks."

Quent took the T-shirt from the vendor and looked into the blood-red eyes.

"Hey, you buying?"

Smiling, Quent handed the T-shirt back. "Sorry. Too rich for my wallet."

"Well"—the vendor allowed himself to look disappointed, then lowering his voice and leaning toward him—"how about . . ."

But Quent was already rounding the corner.

T-Shirt—Symbol of Stardom.

I like it, he thought as he hurried off to catch a PATH train back to Hoboken. An article was starting to gel. Maybe he could make a buck out of it.

2

Like the early motion pictures, or "flickers" as Edison's were called in the 1880s and '90s before the industry moved to Hollywood, dreamies had their origins in New Jersey. Thomas Edison, who developed the kinetoscope in his laboratory in West Orange, New Jersey, and who saw motion pictures' chief value as that of an educational tool, would scarcely have believed the spectacular feature-length color films that proliferated in the second half of the twentieth century. Imagine, then, the amazement of the Wizard of Morris Plains had he lived to see the rise and sudden popularity of dreamies by the end of the century.

The dreamatron, the "magic" machine that made it all possible, was the brainchild of Dennis Mann, at the time a graduate student at Princeton. As Mann himself stated in a 1992 interview: "The technology was all there; I was just lucky enough to have found a way to put the pieces together before somebody beat me to the finish line."

Four scientific developments made during the '80s enabled the dreamatron to become a reality: digital recording, bubble memory, soundless radio, and a better understanding of brain function.

Digital recording had, of course, been in widespread use since the 1970s.

Bubble memory was on the drawing boards and in limited use in some computers for years, but not until it became economically feasible to mass-produce the bubble pak more cheaply than floppy disks were the miniaturized laser reading head and other peripherals available to the lone inventor.

Soundless radio grew out of hearing-aid technology developed in the early 1980s. Scientists discovered that, since the brain is both a transmitter and receiver, sound waves, broadcast through a transmitter at 2.4 Hz., could be picked up directly by the brain, bypassing the ear entirely. This fact opened up wonderful new possibilities for the deaf. The principle was soon found to have more commercial applications.

In 1990, Sony Corporation came out with the Soundless Walkman, touted as the "ultimate head music," revolutionizing the portable-radio industry. Boom boxes and headphones and millions of home stereo systems became obsolete practically overnight.

But it was Mann's interest in brain function that tied it together. If the brain site governing hearing could pick up an electromagnetic signal at 2.4 Hz., then wouldn't the sites governing taste, smell, sight, and touch respond to other frequencies? At first it seemed that five amplifiers would be needed to correspond with the five senses, but Mann solved that problem by programming one amplifier to alternate between the five frequencies at a rate of five hundred pulses per second, which the brain perceived as simultaneous: it was the first dream-imaging transmitter.

Mann saw, at once, the advantages the MDIT would have in the rock video market.

In 1991, Mann amazed the nation with a new spectacle when he toured the U.S. as the opening act for the rock group Jest. He stole the show with a forty-minute series of three shorts—a fantasy, a horror, and a science fiction. Who can forget the awesome aloneness of the survivor adrift in his space boat, knowing it might be years before someone picked up his feeble SOS?

As Mann anticipated, a new generation of music videos hit the market featuring every type of dream sequence imaginable, from the comic to the pornographic to the horrific.

In 1992, the first feature-length dreamies appeared. The new industry was not without its geniuses . . .

—Custler's Popular History of the Dreamies

*

The fear kept him from screaming. And the knowledge.

The fear that, if he moved any part of his body other than the big toe of his left foot, the monster snoring beside him, whose massive, hairy arm pinned him to the dank earth, would wake and tear him to ribbons. And the knowledge that it was just a dream.

As usual, the dreamer experienced the dream twofold, as if he were two distinct entities. His viewpoint was, at once, that of the Victim, pinned against the ground by a great shaggy beast that reeked like a garbage truck on a hot day, and that of the Watcher, the noncommittal, reasoning perspective, the voyeur who viewed the Victim from a point above and to one side—from the wings of the theater of sleep.

The dream was vivid. Spanish moss hung from the branches overhead. Despite the general gloom, he discerned the bristling red-brown hairs that pelted the arm lying like a log across his chest. Less than two feet from his face, lay the bony head of the snoring monster. Its nostrils flared. The grinding of its teeth was like the rasping of metal files.

If he turned his head he knew he could look directly into its long black ear, into the wax-encrusted auditory canal. But he wasn't going to turn his head. He wasn't going to move any more than he had to in order to breathe. (Funny how, even in a dream, you had to breathe. Old habits—waking habits—die hard.) He wasn't even going to blink if he could help it, until he could get his big toe to move. If he could jerk his big toe, he would wake up and escape right out from under the monster's arm. Trouble was, the toe wasn't responding. Every other nerve and muscle in his body was on the verge of spasming— his right ear itched, his nose itched, a cough was accumulating in his throat like a ball of dust, his left foot was threatening to cramp—but he couldn't feel his big toe at all. It was if someone had snipped the nerves that connected the toe to his brain.

Could it be that he didn't want to wake up?

The excitement of the dream experience lay not in the moment of tooth and claw, but in the anxious moments leading up to the explosion of action. The suspense—the *danger*—was everything.

He was far-traveled. Most dreamers only tentatively explored the upper waters, but he, a frequent and intimate traveler in the dreamworld, dived down to the nether depths. He thought of the dreamworld as an ocean—far vaster than any on earth—an ocean of sea that connected with oceans of space. For the experienced and patient dreamer, the ocean led anywhere and everywhere. From a distance, he had glimpsed vast Cthulhu in a sea off Aldebaran. He had conversed with Poe on the nature and uses of melancholy in a bar at the world's end; he remembered the poet's sad, sometimes impassioned, monotone, tolling, tolling, tolling . . .

He concentrated on his toe. Only the toe existed.

And Mr. Beastie, you dummy!

No, only the toe. The rest of him was frozen solid. The beast's snoring was deafening.

His left foot suddenly cramped, curled into a knotted ball of pain that made him grunt.

The snoring faltered; the arm shifted.

His toe jerked.

The monster's roar catapulted him awake.

"Ouch!"

"Huh!"

"You kicked me."

Isidor Stark struggled to hold on to the exquisite and fleeting terror of the dream, but a voice summoned him.

"Iz? Are you all right?"

The dream slipped away like an exhaled breath. Where and when came together—in bed with Helen in the middle of the night. She was going to spoil it even before his heart rate slowed and his breathing returned to normal.

"Cramp."

"Want me to rub it?" Her hand found him under the covers and strayed over his hip and up his side.

Instead of answering, he turned over and made sleepy noises, hoping she would take the hint. He lay there, thinking of his dream till he slipped back into the subterranean waters, secure in the knowledge that it was just a dream and anticipating the next danger.

The blank screen of Quent's word processor stared at him. It was the same old Apple his father bought him when he graduated high school. Its memory and capabilities weren't as awesome as the new computers, but hooked up to the Epson printer behind it, it was more than sufficient for his freelance work.

If he were practically minded, he would be on the staff of

some major stereo-equipment magazine, getting a steady paycheck as a tech writer, or even a brochure writer at an advertising agency. But he had tried that nine-to-five shit for a year and a half after college and had found it numbing. In college he got used to having a different schedule every semester and being different places different days, after which the New Jersey-New York subway commute was as constricting as a straitjacket.

His desk was the kitchen table which faced the wall to the right of the window. Behind it hung a big cork bulletin board shingled with notes. When Quent ate, unless he held a sandwich in one hand and cleaned copy with the other, he took a television break and caught a few minutes of whatever was on.

There had been a time, during the months following his resignation and headlong leap into freelancing, when a few minutes turned into whole movies, but he was getting better.

Soft blond morning light pouring through the kitchen window called him to get up and go for a walk. Leave the typing for later. The city sounds of traffic and birds chirping and kids yelling and half a dozen different radios rocking and rapping were a siren song. He compromised by rolling his swivel chair over to the window.

The sky was a clear, tranquil blue. Billowy white clouds drifted overhead. A latticework of grape vines formed a canopy over the yard below. The backyard vineyard was the pride of his landlord, Mr. Romero, whose family occupied the first two floors. The leaves were yellow now, the harvest over.

Two quick raps at the door.

Quent went into the living room and opened up.

"Good morning," he said to the short stocky man with the thick arms and stock of bushy gray hair.

"'Morning, Queent," the old man returned, rolling the *r* and elongating the vowel in his name. Mr. Romero's eyes were clear this morning, dark, sparkling brown surrounded by porcelain white. He hadn't started on the cognac yet. By afternoon, he would be as mellow as an alley cat on a boiler room roof, and by night, his eyes would be as veined as marble. "Bring you your mail." He handed Quent the small sheaf of envelopes.

"*Una copa?*" Mr. Romero held up his thumb and forefinger

in a gesture that some might interpret as meaning a little bit, but that Quent knew meant a shot glass—more specifically, a shot of *coñac*—Spanish cognac, homemade stuff Mr. Romero's brother sent from northern Spain, nearly two-hundred-proof, lethal. And all Mr. Romero's shot glasses were double.

"More of the family recipe?"

Romero's dark eyes twinkled. "Ah, *si! El*—a—" Reaching for the English, but not coming up with it, he supplied what he knew: "*Es el mejor coñac en La Coruna.*"

"Well, maybe I'll take you up on that, but later." Quent indicated his computer. "Work first."

"*Bueno.*" Mr. Romero clapped him on the shoulder. "No work too hard."

"I won't."

When Mr. Romero left, Quent turned his attention to the envelopes. The top one was from the National League of Abortion Rights. The next was an advertisement for a correspondence course with the American Writer's School. ("Yes, you, too, can turn rejection slips into cash!") One by one, he pitched his mail into the kitchen can. Then did a double take when he read the name on the third envelope.

Isidor Stark.

Quent grinned. "Well, I'll be dipped in shit, tarred, feathered, and fed to an alligator—he answered me!" He tore open the envelope, slid out the letter.

Dear Quentin:

Hey! How're you doing, old buddy?

It's good to hear a voice from the past. By the way, I liked your article on T-shirts and stardom. So that's it, huh? My success can be measured by the number of T-shirts my fans buy? That's fine with me, so long as they keep buying.

If you can make it, why don't you stop by for lunch Saturday. Say, eleven-thirty?

The letter was written in a slanted, careless hand, and there was an air of spontaneity about it that made him think Izzy had actually been glad to hear from him. Izzy flattered him. They were not old buddies. Though he and Izzy had both attended high school at the Hoboken Academy for the Arts, they hadn't become chummy—if you could call it that—until their senior year, when Quent, as a reporter for the school paper, interviewed Izzy after a synthesizer performance.

Izzy Stark didn't give interviews, and Quent hadn't been sure if the man would even remember him. The letter didn't say whether the King of the Dreamies was interested in giving an interview or not, but at least it was an opening.

He pitched the remaining envelopes onto the table without looking to see who they were from, set Izzy's letter beside his machine, and flopped into the chair behind the computer.

"Oh, the freelance life is the only life for me! Yippy ti yi yippi yi yay!" he sang, keying in the words, which splashed across the screen in glowing letters. He admired his handiwork, then deleted it.

Well, this is something to celebrate, he told himself. Maybe I should go down and take Mr. Romero up on his offer. Maybe have a coffee and brandy under the grapevine. Looks like a glorious day!

He looked at the Apple's lit screen and at the open folder beside it and sighed. Pushing Izzy's letter away, he positioned his fingers over the keys and said, "Giddyup, Ol' Paint!"

The peach trees had grown this past summer. Though their trunks were spindly, the saplings had shot up and bushed out at the tops. There were four of them in a line near the hedge on the right-hand side of the yard.

Next year we'll have peaches, Helen thought, looking down at the yard from her bay window. Her mother had told her, soon after Helen and Izzy planted the infant trees two years ago when they bought the house, that it would take three years and severe pruning before the trees would bear fruit.

All the way in the back of the yard, running from the detached clapboard garage on the left to the hedge on the right, her hybrid thornless roses still showed three or four big white and red flowers, though the dark leaves were beginning to yellow. The roses had come with the property. "Maybe they'll deter someone from jumping over the wall," Izzy said the first day they looked at the house. Thornless bushes didn't seem like much protection. Still, Helen couldn't imagine anyone wanting to drop over a ten-foot wall into bushes of any sort. The rest of the flat, well-manicured yard, from the driveway to the peach trees, they had kept clear. "For croquet!" Izzy said. And during that long first summer at their new house in Weehawken atop the Palisades overlooking the Hudson, where life was planets different from their cramped existence in their old three-room apartment in Hoboken, he actually purchased a set and they played often on warm afternoons and cooling evenings. The peach trees were no more than fat twigs guarded from their occasional wild strokes by curls of chicken wire. This summer they hadn't played once. And when May and June went by with Izzy seldom emerging from his studio except to eat and sleep and half the time falling asleep down there working till all hours of the morning, she stopped suggesting it.

Helen let the curtains fall into place. Izzy had his studio in the basement and she had hers here on the second floor. She turned her head, looked back into the room, and smiled. She couldn't say she didn't have company. Besides Ingrid, the big spider plant that hung in the center of the bay window, there were other, unnamed plants—philodendrons and begonias and purple hearts and cacti and succulents and (not much at conversation, but a steady companion, which her mother claimed was over sixty years old) the rock plant on her smoked-glass desk.

The room itself was special. It was *her* room. And everything in it—except the bay window and the window seat in which she sat—had been picked out, painted, hung, decorated, and furnished by *her*. It was, at once, her studio, botanical garden, sewing room, and study. Occupying the corner to the right of the door was a rattan chair with a floor lamp arching over it where she liked to curl up and read on those evenings Izzy didn't come up for air. Two easels occupied the center of the room—one big and one small—both holding partially finished watercolors. The big painting was of the roses, the rear wall, and the backs of the houses on the other side of the block. The smaller watercolor depicted a scene from Izzy's *Dreamquest*. She was doing it from memory, letting her own imagination help shape the work, rather than simply copy Izzy's version. Her style was different from his, her medium better suited to the diffuse sunshine of April on a rainy day.

Looking at the two unfinished works, she felt guilty. A couple of her art teachers, as well as Izzy and, naturally, her mom and pop, had told her she was talented and she guessed she was. But she didn't have Izzy's obsessive drive to make the big time. To her, watercoloring was an escape, like reading a novel.

The bay window and the tufted-leather window seat were a gift from Izzy. She'd always wanted a house with a window seat; her grandmother's South Jersey home had one where she loved to sit and look out on the big holly tree. Izzy kidded when they'd bought this house. "Sure you want it? It doesn't have a window seat."

Then one day after visiting her parents, she came home and there it was! Just like that! Magic! Izzy had the old window removed, the hole enlarged, and a big beautiful bay window installed. He flashed his grin at her. "Like the room any better?" She did. They christened the window seat that night, making love on the leather cushions in the dark, with only the starlight of a clear, moonless night by which to see each other.

She returned to the book open on her lap: *Superstar Breakdown: The Rhinestone Road to Million-dollar Tears*. The book listed a number of celebrities who OD'd, presumably either because of the pressures and loneliness of being at the top, or as a result of wild life-styles. She'd picked it up thinking it might shed some light on what was happening in her relationship. But, no, Izzy was in no way like these lonely, fragmented people who couldn't cope with success, destroyed when economics no longer moderated their vices. And he wasn't insecure and tragic. When Izzy was working—which was most of the time—he was whole, complete unto himself: all will and artistic genius. Though he said he needed her, more and more he sought her company (or her body) only when he was "taking a break." She should have known the book wouldn't apply to him, but, somehow, it was preferable to think that his sexual cooling the past year was due to his fame and increased productivity than to what she saw as the alternative—that he might be falling out of love with her.

She was being silly. She couldn't be mistaken after all these years. Izzy loved her, she knew that. It was his work—a phase he was going through. This was his Golden Age, the peak of his youthful creative juices. And this house, this reclusive life-style, was what he'd been working for all along. Not for the freedom to lounge and indulge in idle chatter, not to vacation, to sun and surf, to tour the museums and restaurants of the world—but for the freedom to work.

And work and work.

She set the book aside on the window seat and covered it with her school notebook, feeling guilty trying to analyze Izzy. From the small inlaid table that served the window seat, she picked up a textbook, intending to read until Izzy got up. She set the book on her lap and opened to where the dog-eared bookmark stuck out of the pages.

"Like your outfit."

Izzy, in a loose-fitting white cotton jumpsuit, his hair still wet from the shower, stood in the doorway. Sometimes he could walk like a cat. The outfit he referred to was her black lace negligee. It was ankle-length, but slit all the way up to her matching panties exposing her left leg. She had hoped he would notice. "Morning, sleepyhead."

"Nope, wide awake!"

He came over, kissed her, his mouth minty from his tooth-paste. He ran his hand appreciatively over the top of her thigh. He dipped under the book, probing the softness of her inner thigh.

"Now, now!" She squeezed her legs together, extracted his hand. "Later. I'm sure you're famished. What time did you come to bed last night?" She knew. The luminous hands of the old-fashioned alarm clock had swum into view: nearly three-fifteen. She kept the clock on her side of the bed because Izzy didn't care what time it was.

Izzy shrugged, so Helen continued. "How's work going?"

"Okay. I'd be finished if I didn't have to sleep."

"We've all got to sleep sometime."

"I suppose."

"Besides, you like to dream." That was an understatement. "You had a nightmare this morning. You kicked me."

"Did I? Where?"

She showed him a minuscule scratch that his toenail might or might not have caused. "There."

"Let me kiss it."

She let him. "You don't remember the nightmare?" she asked while his lips were bent to their healing task.

"Yeah," he said out of the corner of his mouth. He was now tracing little wet circles up her calf with his tongue.

You remember but you don't want to talk about it. Okay, I won't push it. That was another thing: Iz hardly ever shared his dreams with her anymore. There had been a time when he woke her up in the middle of the night to tell her about the wild dream he'd had; and she used to hate it. She never would have believed then, back in that cramped Hoboken apartment, that she'd miss his waking her up to tell her his dreams, but she did. You tell someone not to do something often enough, and sooner or later he's likely to take the hint.

As Izzy straightened, still looking down, the colorful, glossy pictures on the pages of the book open on Helen's lap caught his eye.

"What's this?" He picked up the book.

"My abnormal-psychology textbook," she said. "We're learning about schizophrenia. Those pictures are examples of how schizophrenia affects artwork."

Both pages were adorned with brightly colored pictures of cats—at least most of them looked like cats. The largest picture, which took up most of the left-hand page, depicted a group of cartoonish cats wearing bow ties and having a tea party. The four smaller pictures on the right, on the other hand, were each more bizarre and purely ornamental than the one before it. The last contained nothing of a face about it, but looked more than anything else like the ornate, geometrical patterns of a psychedelic poster.

"Louis Wain," he said, reading the name of the artist.

"Um-hum. The painting where the cats look like cats," she pointed to the tea party, "was typical of the work he did in the early 1920s. By the mid-twenties, he suffered a schizophrenic breakdown, and his paintings degenerated—or blossomed, whichever you prefer—into abstractions."

He preferred "blossomed." However unfortunate the artist's condition, the paintings of his latter period were inspiring, especially that last, fantastically ornate abstraction in which you could imagine whatever you wanted to imagine: a cat . . . or a monster!

What, Izzy wondered, would a dreamie made by a schizophrenic be like? Would a schizophrenic be able to maintain a story line? A plot with a beginning, a middle, and an end? Or would the audience experience the dreamie as a bombardment of disjointed, hallucinatory images and sensory impressions? Though he preferred the former—a story, particularly a thrilling and fantastic one—the latter idea fired his imagination. Bill it as a "psychodrama," he thought flamboyantly. A schizophrenic episode.

Wheels spun, possibilities jostled for his attention. The fans would love it. To feel what it was like to be crazy for a while, to experience the terror of being out of control, of being under attack by one's own mind.

He turned the page. As he looked it over and turned the next page, and the next, he surveyed an assortment of schizophrenic drawings and paintings: distorted faces peering through tangles of mushrooms and squiggly tentacle shapes; a bald-headed, pointy-eared woman with a beetle depicted scarablike on her tall forehead; flowers with flaming petals; a tree root with the head of a man . . .

"It says here that obsession with the self is typical of schizophrenics," he read. He leafed through pages detailing types of schizophrenia: simple, hebephrenic, paranoid, the subheadings read off.

"My abnormal-psychology professor is working on something you'll find interesting," Helen said. "He's conducting studies with a drug called taraxein."

"And why is that interesting?" he said when he saw that she was waiting for prompting, knowing from her smile that she was holding back some strange tidbit. Helen, too, knew the uses of suspense.

"Taraxein is made from the blood of schizophrenics."

"No!" But Izzy knew Helen preferred unusual facts to jokes. "Really?"

"Um-hum."

She turned a page, tapped the middle. Something she'd yellow-highlighted caught his eye, a single italicized word: "*taraxein.*"

"'. . . obtained from the blood of schizophrenics.'" He grinned. "The blood is the life," he affected in phony Transylvanian.

She summed up what little the text said about the exotic drug—or "substance," as the book referred to it.

"The substance has been around since the fifties. A doctor from Tulane Medical School first injected two volunteers from the Louisiana State Prison with taraxein. One had a brief catatonic-type reaction, the other a paranoid-type. But it doesn't last long. Something in a normal person's chemistry knocks out the foreign substance."

"Fascinating."

The fans'll eat it up!

Helen rose from the window seat. "How about some breakfast?"

"Sure." He closed the book and started to set it down on the window seat. The cover caught his attention and he studied it a moment.

He recognized the piece—a section of a painting by Hieronymus Bosch. Across the top of the painting, in the background, burned what looked like the ruins of bombed-out buildings. Across the middle plain in the lurid glow of the fires, demon night riders herded naked sinners like an army of slaves. Naked bodies strewed the earth. In the foreground rose a pair of giant ears, transfixed by an arrow and standing upright on either side of a great knife blade, the whole affair suggestive of two testicles and an erect penis. The giant ear/

knife combo was crushing a heap of naked bodies; arms, legs, torsos, protruded under the giant lobes. Closer to the foreground, demons and witches led more naked sinners around a huge, smoking bagpipe atop a round platform balanced on the head of a giant. The picture was a section of Bosch's *Gardens of Earthly Delights*. Izzy couldn't remember what the rest of the picture contained. He made a mental note to look it up.

Knowing well the signs of inspiration, Helen watched him study the cover of her book feeling a mixture of affection and frustration. "How do you want your eggs?" she interrupted at last.

Izzy looked up, saw her standing, laid the book on the coffee table. "Sorry. Great picture."

He slid his arms around her. She felt the warmth of his hands through the thin silk of her negligee.

"How about dessert first?" he said.

"Sounds good to me."

She met his kiss, and a coal that had cooled in the pit of her stomach while he had stared in rapt fascination at the cover of her textbook, herself noticeably forgotten, fanned into a flame.

But as they walked arm in arm toward the door, he stopped and looked back.

"Taraxein," he murmured dreamily. "What did you say your professor's name was?"

3

There were two signs on the once-white garage doors. There was also graffiti, of course—none of the garages and sheds lining the Jersey City alley had been spared the cryptic code of the walking brain-dead—but two signs had been put there by club members. One, on the right-hand door near the bottom so the lowlifes could see it, was a black skull and crossbones with the legend painted underneath

DON'T FUCK WITH MY GARAGE!

The other, on the left-hand door, higher up out of range of spray cans and painted in blood-red letters on the back of a one-way sign taken from the nearby intersection

SATAN'S FIFTH

Up in the loft that had been converted into a clubhouse, Todd looked up from the old Smith Corona at the sound of a dirt bike approaching from the next alley. Originally, two, three years back, when they'd spent their afternoons and weekends scouring the county on bicycles, they'd all wanted to be outlaw bikers, one-percenters riding hogs with thunder rattling between their legs. Even Jamie had caught the fever for a while, though he'd normally say he preferred to have four wheels and some steel around him on the highway. So far, only Deek had a bike and it was far from being a Harley.

Sitting on the sagging couch, Fred brought his long nose up from the Conan comic and glanced at the big double doors that swung outward over the alley. The bike stopped, revved twice, and cut off.

"Deek," he said, and dunked his nose back into the comic, returning to the high road of adventure and making it clear he wasn't going down to open the door.

Todd sighed, switched off the Smith Corona. "I'll get it." He started to rise. The polyurethane of the desk-chair wheels rumbled softly on the bare planks.

"Keep typing. I'll get it." Jamie called up from below.

Jamie had gone into the house to make some PBJs and sneak a few cans of his dad's beer. Not that Mr. K. minded if they drank a few. Last spring, when he'd needed help robbing bricks from a construction site to build a barbecue pit in his backyard, he had given them two cold six-packs for their help. "Just don't go home till you're sober boys," he'd said. "I don't want none of your parents shooting my kneecaps off." Yeah, Jamie's dad was all right. Todd wished his own parents were as cool.

The buzzer sounded three times. He went back to typing as he heard Jamie unlock the small access door built into one of the panels.

A moment later, Deek climbed out of the trapdoor and bent to take the tray from Jamie. Wearing scuffed, black bikers' boots and with his Conan-style haircut and his habitual black leather vest over his denim Lee jacket, Deek tried his best to look like a one-percenter, but despite the trappings, he had the baby-faced good looks cops loved to pick on. For that reason, he'd bought the vest a couple sizes too big at the bike show at the arena last year, saying he'd grow into it. That was about the time he started lifting at the gym. Now the vest fit fine, but he was going to need a new jacket if he kept up the bodybuilding. Jamie pushed his pear-shaped body through the hole and Deek returned the tray to him.

"*Heyyy,* amigos!"

Todd waved, went back to typing. Fred grunted without looking up from his comic.

Deek stopped in front of Fred, swiped the comic out of his hand. "Yo, bro, you want to shoot some hoops for some rice and beans?"

"Give me that!" Fred snatched for the book, but Deek danced away chanting, "Rice and beans, rice and beans. Let's shoot some hoops for some rice and beans."

"Didn't your mama feed you enough for lunch?" Jamie said, setting the tray of sandwiches and beers down on the milk crate they used for a coffee table.

"Naw, mon. Ate at the Roach Coach. No rice and beans, mon." Deek walked up to Jamie and held out his hand. "Hey, mister, can you spare some rice and beans? I got to have some rice and beans."

"Go fart in a closet," Jamie said cheerfully as Fred swiped his comic back.

"No ken fart in the closet without rice and beans." Deek eyed the tray, which held only three beers and three sandwiches. "Where's yours?"

"Right here." Jamie scooped up a sandwich and beer and walked away.

Fred, sitting right in front of the tray, was quick, and then there was only one beer and only one PBJ sitting lonesome on the tray.

"Take mine. I'm not hungry," Todd lied. But he had typing to do and would be heading home to dinner in a bit.

"No, thanks. Too fattening!" Deek said for Jamie's benefit, a big grin stretching dimple to dimple.

"Ummm!" Jamie retorted, tearing off a big juicy bite and gobbling it up.

Jamie wasn't fat, but nobody referred to him as a rail either. In truth, he was shaped like a bear cub and wasn't much taller than one. He had been fat in grammar school, until one time he was out for a few weeks and when he came back he was so skinny you could see his ribs when he changed his shirt at gym. Of course he'd gained some of it back—some people are fated to go through life pear-shaped.

"You playing racquetball Sunday?" Fred asked.

"Naw, mon," Deek said with his mouth full, the peanut-butter-and-jelly sandwich having found its way into his hands. "Gonna shoot me some hoops for some rice and beans."

"Seriously, Dickweed. If I come by to get you at eight-thirty, you going to be ready?"

"Man"—Deek ran a hand through his long black hair that was forever falling in a wave over his right eye—"that's too early to get up just to whip some white boy's ass."

"You wish, Fartbag," Fred said, though it was true: 8 A.M. was too early for Deek to get up on a Sunday morning. Whereas the rest of them went to school, Deek was a working dropout, busting his hump six days a week delivering auto parts.

Chomping away, Deek sniffed the air. "Hey," he said between bites, "that smells good."

"It was good," Fred corrected.

"There's no more?" Deek looked sad.

Fred shook his head. "Nope." He looked at Todd. "How do you feel, Todd?"

"Not bad. Pretty good weed," Todd played along. He, Jamie, and Fred had roasted a bone a half-hour ago.

Deek looked dejected. "Well . . ." he said, strolling in front of Fred, who, sitting in the busted-spring sofa, looked like a daddy longlegs. "Guess I'll have to smoke this all by my lonesome."

Fred's face, like his nose, was long and thin; his mouth was also thin and slit his narrow, acned face like an incision. He smiled as he eyed the plump white bone that appeared like magic between Deek's fingers. Knowing Deek, the pot would be smoother than baby's shit.

"Heyyyy! What time is it?" Deek asked.

"Cheeba time!" Todd and Fred said at once.

Decal flipped the joint to Fred. "Spark it up!"

"One roast bone, coming up," Fred said, fishing in his pocket for his lighter. He inhaled, exhaled, inhaled again, passed the bone to Jamie.

Jamie abstained and walked the joint over to Todd. "How's the copy coming?" he said, passing him the joint.

"Pretty good."

"Are you using twenty-six space columns?" Jamie said, looking over his shoulder at the copy that was quite obviously typed straight across the page.

"You want to do it?" Todd said testily, angry at himself for forgetting.

"Yeah. Why don't you get up and smoke and let me type?"

Todd grinned. "Deal." They traded places.

"So"—Jamie ripped Todd's sheet out and rolled in a clean one—"we're going to get the next issue out before the Dreamacon?" He set his tabs and pushed his black-framed Poindexter glasses up with a jab of a finger.

"With the two of us, how can we not?"

"You think so?" Jamie began typing.

"What can go wrong?" Todd stepped away to pass the joint to Fred.

"Me too, gringo!" Deek plucked the bone from Fred before it reached his lips.

"Lots of things," Jamie said. "The printer at school can break down and not get fixed until after the Dreamacon. Hell, this typewriter could break down, and then where would we be?"

"You worry too much. You keep it up and you'll go gray."

The joke was long-standing. Jamie's short-cropped hair was already speckled with gray, a family trait. Mr. K.'s hair—or so he'd told the boys—had turned gray when he was sixteen.

Deek downed the last of his beer, burped, jumped up,

clicked his heels, and farted. When he landed, he burped again.

"Jesh!" Fred exclaimed, jettisoning himself from the sofa and putting distance between himself and the spreading miasma. "You're a regular symphony."

"Thank you! Thank you!" Deek bowed and managed an encore. When he rose, he raised his eyebrows and put his hand over his mouth. "Oops!"

"Cut it out!" Jamie snorted. "Doesn't your mother ever feed you anything but rice and beans?"

"You're just jealous because you can't fart and burp at the same time."

"Jamie doesn't fart," Todd couldn't resist tossing in, and when Jamie gave him a look, "He gave it up when he was three."

"Cocksucker doesn't shit either." Fred carried the baton.

"Any word on the tickets?" Todd asked Deek before Jamie got pissed.

"Not for under two hundred bucks a seat."

"Jesh!"

Tickets for Izzy Stark's live Halloween concert were being handled by a few local radio stations. Fans had been invited to send in as many postcards as they liked; names were to be selected by random drawing. They had each sent in a dozen cards to WNEW-FM and had agreed that if one of them won, they all won. The concert had been announced simply as Stark's *Mystery Show* with no indication as to where it would be held or what it was about. Details to be announced.

"Man, if we could find out where Stark's performing and what the show's about," Deek said, passing the jay to Todd, "we'd have the hottest fanzine at the Dreamacon!"

"If," Jamie grunted over the typewriter keys without turning around.

"Yo, Todd," Fred said, leaning forward, elbows on his bony knees. "You're the dreamie critic for the school paper."

"Reviewer."

"Whatever. Can't you get your mitts on a few tickets from the school?"

41

"Way ahead of you, pal," Todd said, holding the pot smoke in as he passed the roach to Fred. "But it's a long shot."

"Life's a long shot," Jamie grunted.

"Yeah, only two things're certain in this world," Deek said, red-eyed and grinning.

"What's that?" Todd asked when no one else did.

Deek produced another joint, flicked it to Fred. "Deek's got the best cheeb in the city and Fred's one homely muthafucka!"

4

Thwock!

The arrow quivered in the bull's-eye.

They were in Izzy's basement. After a few minutes in the foyer—during which Quent pumped his old schoolmate's hand and they told each other how long it had been—Izzy led him across the living room, under an arch into the dining room, through a swinging door into the kitchen, and down a flight of stairs to the basement. Izzy reminded Quent of a kid who wouldn't think of entertaining his pals in his mother's living room when he could take them into his room and show off his favorite toys. Helen, Izzy's live-in girlfriend, was visiting her parents.

The basement was part studio: against one wall Izzy's customized dream machine gleamed pearl white, mirrored in the deeply varnished, hardwood gymnasium floor. And part rec room: beyond the dreamatron was an eight-foot sofa, and taking up a six-foot-long rectangle on the opposite wall hung a flat TV screen. Painted red, two shuffleboard triangles pointed at each other from opposite ends of the floor. Straight ahead down the shuffleboard alley, a well-stuffed archery target with a sheet of plywood behind it leaned against the oak-paneled wall. Some of the dazzle of the summery fall day outside got past the white curtains covering the small windows mounted high into the walls; recessed lighting completed the illumination.

The bow was a thing of beauty—a highly polished, powerful-looking recurve—and Izzy handled it as if he knew what he was doing. A quiver of arrows hung from a hook on the wall. Izzy took another, notched it, drew the fletches back to his cheek, and sank it into the bull's-eye beside the first.

Grinning, he turned to Quent. "I was into Robin Hood as a boy. I still can't split the arrow, but I'm working on it."

"You're not far off."

With his blond, blue-eyed looks and bow in hand, Izzy might have been Legolas slaying orcs at the Battle of Hornburg— minus the pointed ears. He plucked another arrow from the quill and offered it and the bow to Quent.

"Take a shot."

"I better not," Quent said, looking dubiously at the bow. "I don't want to put a hole in your wall."

"You'll notice the target's pretty big. Go on, take a shot."

Quent held his palms up defensively. "I haven't touched one of those since I was a kid in summer camp."

"Well, here's your chance."

Quent shrugged and took the bow. The wood was smooth as plastic under his fingers. He curled his fingers around the leather grip. He flashed on a scene from the *Odyssey*: Odysseus drawing the string of the bow that none of Penelope's suitors could bend. Though he was slightly larger than Izzy, he had a hard time keeping his arm from shaking as he drew the feathers back to his ear.

You're supposed to draw and release in one fluid motion, he told himself. Yet he tried to aim, wishing the arrow into the bull's-eye, and ended up sinking the shaft two rings off his mark.

"Not bad," Izzy said, but Quent was disappointed.

"Yeah, but I was trying to split your arrow."

Izzy offered him another arrow.

"Thanks, but no. My aim'll only get worse." Quent returned the bow to Izzy and walked over to the superstar's legendary machine. Though he knew there were really two of them—the dreamatron he performed with on stage, a twin to this one, was kept in a warehouse—he felt a shiver of excitement as he approached the gleaming white instrument. Actually, seeing the machine on which Izzy shaped his inspiration was more exciting than seeing the machine through which he broadcast the finished product.

The keyboard was ivory. The curved console, brushed chrome and mother-of-pearl. Though there are only five senses, there were eight access ports for multitrack recording and editing.

"Here, check this."

Izzy slipped into the white-leather chair and powered the machine. He hit a few chords on the keyboard. Being soundless, the music registered in Quent's brain, not in his ears. Izzy pressed a button, adjusted a slide lever, and the blank television screen on the nearby wall began to pulse with color—purple, red, and green—in time to the music.

Izzy turned the gain up, not enough to rattle Quent's kidneys, but loud, and launched into an old favorite from the early days of rock 'n' roll. "96 Tears." Question Mark and the Mysterians. Nineteen-sixty something or other. Quent recalled it had been one of the numbers Izzy performed as president of the Music Club back in the Hoboken Academy.

"I remember. Still into early rock?"

Izzy grinned, kept playing.

"Bom-bom bom-bom bom-bom," Quent imitated the organ's simple repetitive rhythm.

Izzy's grin broadened. He rocked into the final chords, building to an energetic finale.

"Bravo!"

Izzy accepted Quent's accolade with a bow of his head.

After they'd chatted a while, Izzy decided it was too beautiful a day to waste indoors and led Quent down the block to where Hamilton Place intersected Boulevard East. Here the spiked iron fence that ran along the Palisades separating Hamilton Place from a nasty tumble gave way to the low concrete wall of the pedestrian walk that continued north for blocks. To Quent's surprise, Izzy hopped the wall and led him down a path that zigzagged precipitously through tangles of bushes and mimosa saplings and across the ancient disused train yard where rusting rails glittered through the weeds to a crumbling concrete dock beside the river. Across the Hudson the Manhattan skyline spread like a panorama beneath the brilliant blue sky. Quent removed his shirt to take advantage of the summery day.

"Good idea." Izzy removed his own and rolled his pants legs to mid-calf. "Helen says I don't get enough sun."

Though the air had hardly stirred up on the Palisades, it was breezy enough out on the river to puff the sails of the lone white sailboat Quent saw amid the riot of motorized traffic. The combination of light and water and open space imbued the panoramic vista of the river and the Manhattan skyline with a feeling of clarity and depth that might have inspired a watercolorist.

"By the way," Izzy said, "I really liked the review of *Floaters* you wrote for *Vampirophile.*"

"You read that?" Quent was surprised. *Vampirophile,* the fanzine of the official Izzy Stark Fan Club and named after Izzy's dreamie of that title, had a relatively small circulation—no more than a few thousand.

"The editor sent me a copy. I think you're one of the few critics who understands my work."

Quent started to say he wasn't a critic, that he paid his rent—when he could—by hyping electronics for stereo companies, and that the *Vampirophile* article had earned him only four cents a word, but he let Izzy go on.

"You know, one critic claimed I was romanticizing—'paeanizing' is the word he used—street gangs by having them turn out to be too much for the baddies. But you understand what I was doing."

Quent shrugged. "What can I say? I'm a fan. I've seen all those old movies where the teenagers save the town."

"Exactly right." Izzy nodded, pleased, and Quent got an inkling of what it meant to an artist to have his work understood. What Izzy felt, he supposed, was a lot like the feeling he got when he received a check in the mail instead of a rejection slip. "That was the thesis behind the experiment," Izzy added after a moment.

"Do you view your dreamies as experiments?" Quent asked.

Izzy grinned. "You did say in your letter you wanted to interview me."

"My father taught me there's no harm in asking."

"No. No harm." Izzy gazed at him a moment, a lazy grin hitching one cheek farther back than the other, then said: "You know, I've turned down a lot of interviews. I haven't given one since *Rolling Stone*. What would you do with an interview with me?"

He's not saying no! Quent mentally crossed his fingers. "Pay my rent." Which was true, but he wished he could come up with something more clever.

"Would you sell it to *Vampirophile*?"

"You kidding? Your first interview in almost a year? I was thinking *Rolling Stone,* maybe *Time*."

Izzy seemed pleased with the answer. "Yes, I view all my dreamies as experiments. How could it be otherwise? In the dreamie art and science become one." Izzy smiled his deep-felt appreciation at the thought. "The machine is the science, man provides the art."

"I know it's the question every artist hates, but . . ."

"Where do I get my ideas?"

Quent nodded.

Gazing at the water glittering beneath his feet, Izzy mused. "The initial inspiration," he said, "often comes as a flash, an image or an idea, a character, a plot trick triggered by something I'm reading or hearing or watching. As for the rest . . . you know the saying: 'Ninety percent of inspiration is perspiration.' To an extent, my style dictates a lot of my 'inspiration.' " He drew quotation marks in the air.

"For example."

"A dreamer can learn a lot by studying paintings. For example: going back I don't know how long, artists have known that a little dash of red in the right place draws the attention to an area that deserves emphasis. Other things. If you want to make the viewer think of death as beatific, you show him a nonbleeding person dying. You emphasize the spiritual side of human existence, you would show the upward gaze of the eyes, the face, perhaps glowing with inner light. A little Gothic architecture wouldn't hurt. If you want to represent death as horrible, you emphasize the blood, the agony. One of man's worst fears—far more terrifying than the fear of getting shot or stabbed—is the thought of getting really opened up, of being so badly ruptured that you can't keep your insides from falling out."

"I see your point," Quent said, feeling queasy.

"In my dreamies, death is always violent. If the purpose of horror is to remind the viewer of his own mortality, then the most vivid way to point out that fact is to underscore it in red."

Quent's finger itched to switch on his belt recorder. It made him sick to be missing salable copy, but he refrained, not wanting to blow his chance at a big-time interview that could point his career in a whole new direction.

"That's why," Izzy went on, "I don't diddle much with goreless murder. Stranglings or drownings are fine, so long as the victim also gets chopped, sliced, diced, chewed, or busted wide open—just so the audience gets a strong dose of the red red juicy. In horror, the blood is the life."

The blood is the life! Izzy's fans would eat this up. The hell with the fans—editors would eat it up!

"Look," Quent hesitated, aware he was about to be boorish, "I've got this recorder." He tapped the silver buckle: tiny holes in the shape of a roadrunner were punched into its surface. "Some people collect stamps or autographs; I collect conversations. May I turn it on? I wouldn't publish any of it unless you gave permission."

Izzy grinned. "Sure, turn it on."

Quent did so, relieved at not having to rely on memory. "'The blood is the life!' Great line."

Izzy agreed. "Another way I get ideas when inspiration takes the day off is to go through checklists."

"For example?"

"Say I need a good monster, but something at least halfway original refuses to just pop into my head like magic. Well, I try a roundabout approach. I go through a checklist of weapons and see if I can match the monster to the weapon. Here, you play. Think of the methods the good guys used in all those old movies to kill the monster."

"Fire," Quent said. "Silver bullets . . ." He snapped his fingers. "Crosses, magic swords, holy water. Ashen stakes for the vampire, silver for the werewolf, lamb's blood over the door to ward off the angel of death in search of Egypt's firstborn, an atomic bazooka for the Giant Behemoth." A rush of images— black-and-white and Technicolor—flowed before his mind's eye.

Izzy was grinning broadly, obviously amused. "You do know your monster movies."

"Thank you. But tell me, what're your favorite weapons?"

"Easy: fire and silver. Silver, like you said, for the werewolf— that's a classic. Fire for everything else. Monsters hate fire."

Quent shook his head. "This is great copy. Your fans'd eat it up with a shovel."

Izzy laughed. "Not exactly pearls of wisdom."

"No. It's just . . . they're attracted to you and want to know more about you. You're a mystery to them."

"Look," Izzy said after a moment, "what would you say if instead of an interview, I asked you to write my biography?"

"Your—?" Quent couldn't believe he'd heard right.

"I like your style. I've known you since high school, and if someone's going to make money on this, I'd rather it be someone I know than a stranger. Solly, my manager, has been urging me to agree to a book. Two publishing companies have already approached him with big offers."

Quent was flabbergasted. He'd come here hoping for an interview and was now being offered the chance at a best-seller.

If you don't fuck up!

But he wouldn't. This was the break he needed. His technical background and knowledge of dreamies, plus the fact that he and Izzy attended high school together, would combine to produce a unique perspective on Isidor Stark. Sitting beside the Hudson with the breeze on his face, Quent thought he smelled money.

Izzy interrupted his whirling thoughts. "I see your wheels are spinning. Are you interested?"

"Interested? When do we start?"

"We already have." Izzy smiled and pointed at Quent's buckle.

5

Monday morning Izzy visited Helen's professor, Dr. Casper Nösberger, at his office.

Izzy hadn't been able to get the pictures of schizophrenic artwork out of his head all weekend. Their bizarre distortions of objects as common as cats and flowers, their simple but startling color schemes, and their dreamlike use of symbols, all spoke to him with the shocking clarity of a child's nightmare. He had read and reread the chapter from Helen's book and was repeatedly struck by the feelings of paranoia the pictures evoked. One thing he had read kept coming back to him: "Our own nightmares are the closest we can come to understanding a schizophrenic's hallucinations."

He was onto something big. He felt inflated, inspired, ready to burst with invention. It was a familiar feeling, though he hadn't felt it this strong since one night five years ago, when reading a vampire paperback wherein the novelist described the vampire's exsanguination of its victims in highly erotic language. It struck him that he could do the same thing in a dreamie simply by programming his machine to stimulate the brain's pleasure centers the same time it was tickling the amygdala's fight or flight response. From that erotic union of the undead and their hapless victims, he developed *Vampirophile* and the style that was to make his fortune and fame.

What he felt now was equal to the excitement of that past inspiration, and he wondered if his intuition was on the track of a new cult classic. Inflamed with ideas, he'd been too distracted yesterday to work on his Halloween show. Instead, he spent his creative time thinking of plots incorporating schizophrenic sequences. The idea was a natural for the mad-scientist trope. Even the name, "taraxein," sounded like something a mad scientist would concoct. Jekyll and Hyde in modern dress.

Or schizophrenic vampires!

49

According to Helen's text, the drug's effects lasted fifteen to forty minutes, then dissipated. The book didn't cite any side effects.

Nösberger, with his granny glasses and his longish trim of brown hair circling his bald pate, looked like a tall, skinny Ben Franklin.

"Schizophrenia," the doctor, seated behind his desk, was explaining, "is basically an altered state of consciousness. Whereas some altered states are achieved by chemicals taken orally or intravenously, schizophrenia and its accompanying bizarre visions and paranoias and states of elation and depression are a by-product of brain chemistry. Taraxein is a neuroinhibitor, meaning it blocks the flow of information in the brain, and, thus, screws up the thinking."

"How?" Izzy asked, intrigued.

"The accepted theory is that this neuroinhibitor interacts with the neurohormone serotonin. The taraxein converts this normal neurohormone, or neural transmitter, into a psychosis-producing agent."

" 'Psychosis' as in 'psychotic'?" Izzy said.

Nösberger nodded. Through his thick lenses his hazel eyes appeared smaller than they probably were.

"You know how taraxein research started?"

"Injected into the veins of prison inmates in the 1950s."

"Right. In the 1960s, the CIA allegedly experimented with the possibility of using taraxein to disorient the enemy. There was a rumor going around at one time that the Company spiked the drinking water of an encampment of South American rebels. Trouble is taraxein's schizophrenic effects wear off in a little while. But I understand from a colleague at Georgetown that the Company's still trying to come up with a long-lasting synthetic taraxein. It could be devastating to a ground force. Think of it, released from jets in a mist form, the troops below suffering from disorientation, hallucinations, catatonia—"

"Paranoia," Izzy said, seeing more possibilities for a dreamie—paranoid delusions, soldiers firing on their buddies, believing they're under attack.

"By the way," the doctor said, "taraxein does have one side effect."

Izzy's ears pricked. "What's that?"

"It's a minor, temporary effect: test subjects who take the drug for three nights running begin losing deep, rapid-eye-movement sleep by the second night, and if the drug is continued for a longer period, hallucinations begin to bleed over into waking time. In other words, he will dream less during his sleep period and show an increase in fantasizing or daydreaming when awake."

"Wow!"

Nösberger nodded, pleased with Izzy's reaction. " 'Sleep that knits up the raveled sleeve of care' is more than poetic sentiment. Wild, huh?"

"Yeah, wild." But Izzy wasn't thinking about sleep; he was thinking about hallucinations bleeding over into waking time and about recording those hallucinations on bubble pak.

Izzy told the doctor what he had in mind, how he wanted to volunteer for an experiment. After all, the professor was working with volunteers. When he suggested they conduct the experiment in his home so he could test the effects of taraxein on his dreamatron, Nösberger at first complained that they couldn't expect a controlled environment in his home, but then he agreed, providing Izzy sign a release form allowing him to later publish his findings.

"Tomorrow night, eight o'clock?" Nösberger asked.

"Tomorrow it is," Izzy agreed.

And so the bargain was struck—not between man and devil, but between two creatures of mortal clay who, typical of the species, lacked the foresight to see the consequences of their actions.

"That's it?" Izzy said.

"That's it."

Professor Nösberger handed him the small square of white paper. Izzy, seated behind his dreamatron, held it up to the basement's recessed lighting and inspected the rows of red-orange polka dots.

"Looks like blotter acid."

The professor nodded appreciatively. "My idea. Easier to refrigerate, takes up less space. Early experiments used injections or transfusions directly from the schizophrenics' veins."

Izzy returned the sheet to Nösberger, who produced a pair of children's plastic scissors from his briefcase and snipped two hits from one corner into Izzy's outstretched hand.

"It's concentrated," Nösberger said, and explained that two dots were equal to the amount of taraxein in a pint of a schizophrenic's blood. "Drink up!"

Izzy dialed the overheads down until only the eerie lights of the dreamatron console lit the basement, then popped the hits into his mouth, unable to suppress a qualm over the fact that he was eating someone's dried blood.

Izzy swallowed the spitball and checked to see if he'd inserted a fresh bubble pak. "How long?" he asked.

"As soon as it reaches the brain. Give it a minute or two." Nösberger took a seat on the nearby sofa and, stretching his long legs, made himself comfortable. Izzy powered up the CPU, punched the record button, and settled back.

The machine's automatic biofeedback unit activated. A tiny red light, alone near the top center of the console, began to pulse at a rate designed to aid in self-hypnosis. Izzy's breathing slowed. In seconds, his eyes closed, but the pulsing red light still registered through his lids. His eyes were rolling slowly under his lids and he was experiencing alpha waves at a rate of eight cycles per second, when he felt the first rush wash through his body. White sound, like crashing surf, filled his head, and through it ran riffs of a thousand melodies, instruments, snatches of old Pink Floyd, scraps from his father's keyboards, and fragments of the theme music he had composed for his dreamies. He felt detached, floating. His thoughts flowed like a stream overspilling its banks. Then, as if a manhole cover onto his subconscious mind opened, sights and sounds roared out. All was chaos, frothing motion, colored lights rippling pulsing changing, the cacophony of unseen crowds. His inner ear went on the blink, producing dizzying spatial distortions.

He brought the chaos under control, stilled his mind and

formed an image. He willed an apple. An apple appeared, glowed bright red. A hole appeared in its skin. Another. Worms with human faces squeezed slimy bodies out of the holes.

Pleased with his success with fruit, he decided to experiment with animal life.

Next door, Lois Carruthers turned off the hot water in the second of the two stainless-steel sinks before setting the plate in the dish rack and returning her latex-gloved hands to the soapy water in the first. Chet had suggested since he moved in with them that she get a dishwasher. But what for? What was she going to do with her time instead? Watch TV with her husband, Jason? He never watched the current shows anyway, always the same old science-fiction and horror movies, most of them black-and-white and as dated as the songs they used to perform.

And all the while his brain was drying up!

She rinsed a handful of silverware and dropped them into the rack with a clatter, then wiped her forehead with the back of her wet glove. It was a humid night, and warm, without the least flutter of curtain at the kitchen window. Not for the first time since reading the article in the *New York Times* magazine last month, she reflected on how the climate was changing with all the industry and construction and traffic growing in and around the metropolitan area. October was certainly a lot warmer now than it had been in her youth. It was a wonder the crabs and sturgeon in the river weren't caught parboiled.

And that stink isn't helping any! She wrinkled her nose at the yellow plastic garbage bin over by the refrigerator. She had asked Jason twice today to put the garbage out and he'd forgotten twice. Well, she wasn't going to do it for him. She did enough around here!

Lois let the water out of the sink, dried her hands and left the kitchen. In the living room Jason sat in his rocking chair watching a black-and-white movie on the old Sony Trinitron. Jason hit pause on the remote, freezing the picture. She had picked a bad time to come in: on the thirty-inch screen of the old but sharp-pictured console, a little girl sat horror-struck in the backseat of a patrol car, her eyes wide and staring as if she'd just seen something a mite worse than the devil.

As usual, Jason's grin was big and pleased to see her, and as usual, he motioned for her to have a seat on the sofa nearby.

"Come join me. This is a classic. *Them!* 1954. You remember. James Arness, James Whitmore, the giant ants?"

His hazel eyes were bright and enthusiastic, and though they were the same age, his face showed fewer wrinkles than hers. When he smiled, the few age lines he'd acquired became part of the smile so that his slender features appeared boyish and charming—in spite of his gray hair.

"I remember. I've only seen it a dozen times." She was exaggerating; she'd seen it only twice, but twice was enough. "I don't want to watch a movie right now. What I want," she spoke quietly, as though instructing a child, trying to conceal the peevish frustration she felt in spite of herself, "what I asked you to do, is for you to put out the garbage. Okay?"

"Okay." His smile was gone. He looked defeated, older too. Immediately she felt rotten.

Maybe I shouldn't be so hard on him. But it's not easy on me either!

He smiled as if to cheer her up, as if to say everything would be all right. She kissed him on the cheek and went into the bathroom as he scraped off in his slippers toward the kitchen.

When she came out, she saw him standing just inside the kitchen doorway looking around.

"Now what's the matter?" she asked, knowing already what the matter was.

He grinned sheepishly. "I came in here for something, but I can't remember what."

"The garbage, Jason. The garbage," she said, feeling the exasperation rise. She knew she should have more patience with him, but it was hard; his condition was trying, depressing. She went down the hall and out the front door without looking to see if he made it to the yellow Rubber Maid trash can before he forgot again.

They didn't have a porch, and she sat on the top step of

the stoop, as they used to call it back when she was a girl in Elizabeth.

We walk in quicksand, she thought. The difference between youth and age being when you're young you don't notice the quicksand as much. Not so many of your friends die that you notice. But when you get older and middle age starts looking like youth to you, and your friends and acquaintances start thinning out like your husband's hair, you start noticing.

She caught herself. You're getting as bad as Jason, she told herself. Going senile. Brain turning to pudding.

Worse than Jason, actually . . . Jason, at least, seemed to be taking it a lot better than she.

Jason's doctor had been straight with him—Alzheimer's. High blood pressure and hardening of the arteries were at the root of his senility. He was on medication, but he was getting worse. The doctor had prescribed what he called memory pills. They were still considered in the experimental stage and did not reverse Alzheimer's. They did enlarge the veins in his head so that his brain could receive enough oxygen to carry on normal storage and retrieval functions. Jason was supposed to take his medication no more than three times a day, but the effects weren't constant. His memory would peak for a while, and then start petering out an hour or so before the next dose was due. So, of course, Jason tended to overlap medications. His doctor had warned him that this was dangerous, but Jason had always been active and wasn't ready to give up thinking.

Which led to a second, deadly drawback: an overdose could result in death by causing the same veins to over expand and collapse.

Outwardly—and the irony of it made her heart bleed every time she thought of it—Jason didn't look a day over fifty-eight, though he turned sixty-eight last June, but his brain was deteriorating, the worm gnawing at the apple's core.

She sighed. Why was she thinking such morbid thoughts? Why couldn't she accept? Other people adjusted to old age and approaching death.

She got up and wandered around to the side yard, which was separated from her neighbor's property by a neat row of evergreen hedges. The perfumed scent of the honeysuckle blossoms that grew alongside the house in the summer was missing.

If you could just pass away in your sleep, she continued thinking despite herself, while you still had your health, it wouldn't be so bad. But most people didn't have any such luck. Death among the elderly was usually preceded by illness and the degrading breakdown of bodily functions.

Her thoughts stopped dead when a sudden noise startled her. She looked to her right in time to see a vision from her worst nightmare hop over the hedge and land in the yard not twelve feet from her. In that brief glimpse before she fainted, she took in the black eyes glittering like chips of obsidian, the hooked beak that opened and closed, and the too-small wings that rustled against scaly sides.

The garbage was out and Jason was back in front of the Trinitron, watching the movie from where he left off. With his movies his memory was on firmer ground. Not that he remembered the scenes from the beginning of the movie up until he'd hit the pause button, but from all the times he'd watched it years ago. That was the funny thing about his condition: the old days stayed with you, but the new seemed like a dream—one that was hard to remember when you woke up.

He was tilting his Rolling Rock to his lips when a weird thing happened. He came to the conclusion even before he forgot about it that his eyes—or perhaps his mind—was playing tricks on him. But for a second, for a flicker of the eye, he thought he had seen something in the movie that was definitely not in the original.

On the screen, the state troopers had found a country store deserted, wrecked, the storekeeper missing, a hole in the wall of the clapboard building big enough to drive a car through, and mysteriouser and mysteriouser, sugar all over the place. James Whitmore had gone back to HQ, leaving the second officer to hold the fort. The weird noise that signaled the presence of giant ants had started up and the trooper was drawing his gun, staring horrified at and backing away from something that was coming in after him—when it happened. From one side of the screen to the other, appearing, not out of the hole through which the state trooper was firing his revolver, but as if out of the wall beside it, flashed what looked like a two-legged dragon that was running instead of flying. A glimpse of taloned feet, of black-flashing eyes, and a feeling of intense malice, and it was gone!

His Rolling Rock slipped from his hand. The carpet saved the nearly full bottle from exploding, but beer splashed over his slippers. "Shit and go blind!"

Then he almost remembered. His eyes leapt to the screen, but the thought was gone, whatever it was, slipped through the sieve his mind had become. On the Trinitron, James Whitmore and James Arness were talking. Whitmore was blaming himself for the death of the officer he had left to mind the store and Arness was telling him it wasn't his fault.

Jason chuckled, picked up the bottle, punched pause, and went into the kitchen for some paper towels to clean up the mess before Lois came in.

"Ooh wee!" he chirped as he passed through the dining room. "Freaked yourself silly, didn't you? Gotta watch that, Jack, or you'll never see a hundred!"

Pedro Morales had wandered a long way from the Club Cubanos off Bergenline Avenue in West New York, his usual hangout. He was nearly sober, but he didn't want to go back to the shabby apartment he shared with Maria and Juan Junior, Maria's four-year-old by her ex. Junior would be crying and the TV would be squawking and he needed peace and quiet to think, because if something didn't happen in his life soon . . .

He shook his head self-pityingly, kicked a pebble. He didn't want to go home and he didn't have two bucks to buy another drink (it hadn't occurred to him how he was going to get home), so he ended up miles away wandering along the shore of the Hudson, sobering, tiring, wondering what to do with his life, and hearing only distant traffic, an occasional plane and water lapping the rocks for answer. A drink would have helped, but what he really needed was a shot of methadone. He licked his dry lips: they stayed dry. His tongue was dry too. On second thought, a cold Rheingold would hit the spot.

The monorail, which ran along the Hudson shore out over the water from Bayonne to Fort Lee, chose that moment to flash by, cutting a silver-and-white streak through the dark on its way to Hoboken, attended by the steel rumble that whooshed out of the distance and faded just as quickly. As it passed, its lit windows illuminated a crumbling concrete dock a short distance ahead. Pedro sat on the edge of the sea wall staring moodily into the glistening black water lapping below as he cooled and tried to get his head straight.

He lipped a Marlboro and was reaching for his Cricket, when he heard someone kicking up gravel, running toward him out of the dark. His immediate thought was he was about to be mugged, and he drew the 007 blade from his hip pocket, flashed it open, and turned to face whoever was coming.

The knife slid from his fingers when he saw what had interrupted his thoughts. The unlit Marlboro tumbled from his mouth as his jaw dropped. For an instant, Pedro thought it was someone from a costume party, but as the thing rushed onto the dock shrieking like a predatory bird, he saw it wasn't human. The legs bent backward at the knees—like a bird's.

The creature moved so swiftly and its appearance was so outrageous, Pedro caught only glimpses of his assailant before it struck. The hooked carnivorous beak, the taloned feet that made sparks as it charged across the concrete, the glistening scales that covered its body instead of feathers. The impression was a hideous mating of snake and bird. Pedro's brain was so flooded with what he was seeing, it didn't register the bellowing, hawk-like shriek that startled boaters on the river.

The impact knocked the wind out of him and slammed him into the crotch of the sea wall. He was barely aware he had shit himself, and though he had recently taken a leak, his bladder spasmed and let go.

Shuddering, his body out of control, Pedro tried to crawl away. But something sharp stabbed him in the back

"Ay, Dios mio!" he screamed.

Then the crushing weight, the knifelike instrument, was

gone, leaving only the lancing pain. And as he flopped over, turning to face his attacker like a cornered animal, raising a shielding arm in front of his face as much to keep from seeing the monster as to protect himself, he inhaled, and his breath fizzed wetly through the hole in his back.

Shrieking wildly, the thing hopped onto his chest, cracked ribs and pierced his abdomen and lungs, narrowly missing his heart. His breath labored. He felt himself drowning as blood flowed into his wounded lungs.

Looking past the arm he raised defensively, he saw the brutal head against the stars. Then its razor beak flashed downward, pierced his left eye, and took most of that side of his face away when it lifted its head.

Oh God! Not my eyes! Pedro's mind screamed, for his mouth could not.

Dying, more amazed than afraid now, and even that fading, he saw with his remaining eye the beak plunge again, felt his ribs break, his flesh rip free. Blood burbled from his mouth. It became impossible to breathe. His brain starved quickly for oxygen and mercifully shut itself off before a slashing talon pierced his heart.

As the body followed the way of the brain, the thing raked his corpse like a chicken scratching in a barnyard. Strips of clothing and flesh became indistinguishable as the dock was dyed a dark uniform red.

The lights came on automatically as Izzy rose from alpha into beta, the wave form of the waking mind. He was in the basement seated at his dream machine, feeling groggy and disoriented, as if he'd suddenly sobered from a good drunk.

On the sofa, Nösberger looked pale as he blinked at the light. "You've got some imagination, my friend." He shook his head incredulously. "That was some ride."

Izzy agreed. Involuntarily shuddering, he wondered at the intensity of the experience. Though the basement was air-conditioned, his T-shirt was soaked. He felt drained, distorted, his equilibrium off. Yet he was curiously elated, amazed at what he'd just experienced and excited over the possibilities.

The whole dreamie had sprung full-blown from his mind like Athena from the forehead of Zeus.

He cut the power, pushed his chair back, got shakily to his feet. "Wow!" He and Nösberger grinned at each other, at a loss for words. The trip had been shocking for him; he could imagine what it must have been like for the psychologist.

Extricating his lanky frame from the plush sofa, Nösberger rose, checked his watch. "About twelve minutes. That was a short one. Your metabolism must burn up the chemicals faster than normal."

Izzy grinned. "Does that make me a freak?"

Nösberger shrugged. "Not necessarily. Your metabolism's faster than normal." The professor stepped over to the dreamatron and looked down at the bubble pak visible in its Lucite port. "And it's all recorded?"

"It is."

"I'm going to see if I can get a grant to buy a dreamatron for my lab, though I'd better call it a 'thought imaging device' or some such."

"But will your average student volunteer be able to go into alpha and record?"

"I don't know, but that's the fun of getting grants to experiment with new equipment and new drugs." Nösberger said "equipment" as if he was thinking "toys."

"You might have to give them biofeedback training first," Izzy suggested.

"That's a thought."

Nösberger shook his head again, remembering. For a few minutes he had been that young man, had felt the terror of being pinned under a gigantic weight, his body punctured and bleeding, had felt what it was like for his lungs to fill with blood, knowing that the beak of the thing that reared over him shadowing the stars had just ripped out his eye and learning what it was like to look forward to the next stroke being the last. He was shaken—and excited. The power of the dreamie to evoke such diabolical imagery and sensory responses, especially in the hands of a master like Stark, was impressive. Coupled with the psychotic, hallucinatory imagery of the schizophrenic, it was mind-boggling. He understood perfectly well where Stark's thoughts were taking him, which was fine with him. He had, when Izzy first outlined his plans, imagined a paper for the *Journal of Abnormal Psychology*. But now, after experiencing the full impact of the combination of dreamies and taraxein, a book might be more appropriate.

Or a dreamie! Showing a dreamie composed of schizophrenic episodes at a meeting of the American Psychological Association would surely draw attention to his research and lure grant money his way!

They discussed the experiment awhile longer, Nösberger jotting notations in a notebook. Then, agreeing to a second experiment after the Dreamacon, Izzy saw the professor to the door and said good night.

Helen had gone up. He resisted the urge to go tell her about the experiment and went, instead, back down to the basement and sat at his dreamatron, intending to replay the bizarre experience he had recorded.

But as he sat staring at the play button, he broke out in a cold sweat. The experience had been so real! And, now that he thought of it, as bizarre and shockingly violent as the dreamie had been, it lacked the psychedelic texture or distorted faces of the schizophrenic artwork he had seen.

He popped the bubble pak out of the port, placed it in a drawer under the console. Tomorrow would be soon enough to review it. Not sleepy, yet not feeling like working and not wanting to be alone, he decided to make an early night of it and went up to the second floor, where he found Helen asleep. He stripped and quietly climbed in beside her. He lay there a long time, restless, his mind full of images of rending talons and jetting blood, his ears echoing with the screams of the dying young man, trying not to toss and turn, but unable to get comfortable. Finally, he gave up and went out on the balcony and watched the river.

A thin sliver of moon rode high over Manhattan. Out on the dark river, a boat horn sounded, and somewhere in the night a dog barked in reply.

PURGATORIO

Conscience seems to be silent in dreams, for we feel no pity in them and may commit the worst crimes—theft, violence and murder—with complete indifference and with no subsequent feelings of remorse.

—Jessen

6

The purpose of Horror is to scare the crap out of the audience.

—Isidor Stark
Rolling Stone

He was in the water—cold, dark, slimy water—and beneath the salt smell, the pungent reek of New York's million-gallon-a-day raw sewage bloated up into his face so that it was all he could do to clench back the vomit that boiled in his stomach, trying to force its way up his throat.

It was night. Through the fog he could see the lights of the cities on either side of the river, liquid firefly points of light outlining buildings and bridges, but the river was black.

He realized he was dreaming as the mucky water splashed in his mouth. For one thing, the currents were strong and he knew he should be swept swiftly downriver, knew the myriad lights on either side of the river's dark banks should be sliding past as he bobbed toward the sea. But the water slid greasily past and he remained where he was, treading water. For another, the river was never this quiet. The muted rumble of the highway traffic on either side of the Hudson and on the George Washington Bridge, as well as the dull roar of helicopters and foghorns—all missing. The water that slapped his face and his labored breathing (he had never been a good swimmer) were the only sounds.

Of course, he knew the dreamscape; after all, he had designed it—including the unnaturally quiet and, therefore, scarier river. And knowing the dreamscape so well, he certainly knew what these oily currents concealed.

Fear encircled his heart in viperish coils, battening vampiric fangs into his nerves.

This is wrong! he told himself, wondering at his trip-hammering heart. He was the master dreamer. He loved nightmares. He knew that the trick to survive, to keep your sanity in the darker realms of the dreamworld, was to keep your distance, keep reminding yourself that it's only a dream, the waking world is only a toe jerk away. But he was losing it, losing his detachment, his objectivity. He was buckling to fear. And once fear crept in, the nightmare had you—right in its clutches.

A sullen splash . . . like riverwater sloshing against a half-submerged log. But he knew precisely what it was. He was the dream's engineer, after all.

Still, he didn't want to name his dream. Knowing he was dreaming and knowing the power of suggestion in a dream, naming the thing might conjure it more quickly and gruesomely.

A hand grabbed his ankle, yanked him down. His head went under. Water poured down his throat, pushed its way up his nostrils.

Through the bubbles streaming from his mouth, a pale face emerged from the blackness—the dead, bloated face of a floater. With a horrible lurch of his heart he recognized the man. Though the features were distorted, puffy and soft with decay, the skin torn and hanging like pieces of water-logged white bread, the hair grown long and matted—still, he remembered.

The image floated back to him, superimposed over the face floating up from the depths, over the jaws that were opening, revealing yellowed, nicotine-stained teeth. He remembered the man's face writhing with terror as his throat flooded with his own blood and as the demon bird clawed him to a shocking smear.

He screamed as teeth sank into his shoulder, tearing flesh, scraping bone. The young man's teeth were sharper than they'd ever been in life.

7

"For Christ's sake! The man's probably still sleeping." Which was probably true, Chet Brown thought. It was only six, barely dawn, and the traffic on Boulevard East half a block away almost nonexistent. Like Lois, he wore a bathrobe and slippers. The grass was sopping with dew, his slippers were soaked, and at the moment, the cold spatter of wet grass against his bare ankles numbered among the more unpleasant sensations he'd experienced in his seventy-two years. The only ones who seemed happy about the time of day were the birds. Still, he was curious about the footprints.

"Be quiet, Chester, and let the officer do the talking."

The officer said nothing, but led them across Stark's lawn to the front door. Routine procedure following a homicide. When the young officer asked Lois if she had seen anything suspicious-looking the night before, she'd given him an earful.

"Suspicious? It was horrifying!"

Standing on their doorstep with the east paling behind him, the policeman looked as if he would rather be far away, as if he'd half-decided Lois was a bowl of Fruit Loops. But only half-decided, because every now and then, as Lois spilled her tale of a giant birdlike creature (a "goblin bird," she called it), his gaze narrowed and he asked for more detail. When she took him into the yard and pointed out the huge claw-like prints, the officer's eyes had widened. At Chet's prompting, the policeman confided that more of the same prints had been found on the dock below Hamilton Place where a young man had been killed.

Chet had worried about his old friends last night. He'd come downstairs and found Jason, face urgent, rewinding and fast-forwarding sections of a movie. Then Lois came running in, gasping, her eyes wild with fright, leaves and grass stuck to her hair and sweater. He'd known Jase and Lois Carruthers since before they were married nearly fifty years ago, back in the big-band era when the three of them had worked for the Louis Ames Band—Jason "Sticks" Carruthers on drums, Chet Brown on the alto sax, and Lois Heffinger the sweetest songbird ever to hail from Elizabeth, New Jersey.

The Stardust Ballroom. Newark. 1949.

He was best man at their wedding, and it was going on five years since he'd sold his house and real-estate business in

Brooklyn and accepted his old partners and best friends' invitation to move in with them. In all the years he'd known them, he'd never seen them so distraught. It had taken a half-hour and a tall brandy to get the story out of Lois. Last night, her tale of a goblin bird leaping the hedge and sprinting across the yard sounded like a hallucination. But now, after the policeman showed up telling them about a murder and after seeing the claw prints in their yard, he didn't know what to think.

The officer rang Stark's doorbell. After a minute he rang again, then knocked.

Stark himself opened the door. Surprisingly, though he was wearing his robe and slippers, the young man didn't look sleepy. Chet concluded he'd been up working. Stark had mentioned his Halloween concert the last time they spoke.

"Sorry to bother you, Mr. Stark, but we have a problem you may be able to help with," the patrolman said.

"There's been a murder," Lois said before the officer could continue.

"A murder?"

"Yes, sir," the officer said. "Right down there by the water." He pointed across the street to where the trees screened the river.

Chet thought that Stark, who stared where the policeman pointed, seemed to look a little green. Then he remembered the hour and wondered if he himself looked as bad.

The cop didn't offer any details of the homicide, except to say, "Messiest murder I've ever seen. Hey, ain't you . . . ?" He pointed at Izzy as the face suddenly clicked.

Stark nodded as the policeman shook his hand, the grisly murder momentarily forgotten.

Lois was impatient. "What about the footprints?"

"Footprints?" Stark looked at her, then at the officer.

"Would you step out here for a moment please."

Stark excused himself, not inviting them in, but leaving the front door cracked, as if too polite to close it in their faces. Minutes later, he reappeared dressed in sneakers and white jeans. Helen was with him, looking sleepy and wearing a robe and slippers. Lois led them around to the side of the house and pointed at the ground.

"As you see . . ." she began, but the rest of it was lost on Stark, who paled and whose mouth, Chet noticed, dropped open when he saw the trail of size-fourteen, triple-E bird tracks.

"What in the hell?"

"There are more in Mrs. Carruthers' yard." The cop pointed toward the hedge to which the tracks led. "And lots more around the body. As you can see, the prints start outside your basement window."

It was true. The first print was outside one of the small basement windows. It just appeared. As if whatever made it had hopped right out of the brick wall. And the prints were deep. The sucker that made them had some weight on him.

The sucker that made them . . .

Izzy marveled at the sight.

There's been a murder.

You've got some imagination, my friend.

The impressions were definitely birdlike, three-toed with a mark that could only be a cockspur—only the tracks were huge!

Izzy's mind rattled with conjecture. He imagined the impossible: that the monster he had created in his mind, the creature of his imagination, had taken on physical form and had left physical manifestations. He glanced across the street to where the thinning leaves were revealing more and more of the New York skyline, as if he expected to see the creature still lurking, watching its creator. He realized the absurdity of the thought. Dreamies existed only in the mind and in the bubble pak, as binary information to be recorded or played, not as living solid matter, free to run abroad and murder.

A more realistic explanation occurred to him. "A fan," he said, as if to himself.

"What's that?" the officer asked. They were all looking at him.

"I was just speculating. Perhaps it was one of my fans. They're not the most stable people in the world, and a lot of them like to dress up in costumes. Just go to a midnight showing of *Floaters* at the Eighth Street Theater in the Village and take a look at the fans in line, and you'll see what I mean."

The policeman rubbed his chin. "A fan."

"It was only a thought. It occurred to me because you'd be amazed at the things some of them will do to get attention. I've gotten tapes that sounded as if they were recorded at an orgy, a lot of nude photos—of men as well as women. Sorry to offend your ears, Mrs. C."

Her expression softened when he called her Mrs. C., as he had when he used to visit Jason. "They're not offended in the least," she said.

"And once I even got a jack-in-the-box full of laughing gas with a CO_2 cartridge to spray it in my face when I opened it."

"God." Chet shook his head.

Izzy grinned. "It could have been worse. My manager takes care of my fan mail now. I'll give you his number, if you like."

"Wait a minute!" Mrs. C. wasn't buying the idea of a fan running around, possibly committing murder, dressed in a Halloween costume, and neither was Izzy. The coincidence was too much—the slashing talons, the rending, blood-gorged beak, the gurgling screams, the three-toed footprints outside his basement window! But he had to stay calm, throw the policeman off track until he had time to think. "I saw it last night," Mrs. C. said. "It was no guy wearing giant chicken's feet either! It jumped the hedge and looked right at me. I thought it was going to kill me—there was murder in its eyes!"

Murder in its eyes!

You've got some imagination, my friend.

What I'm thinking is ridiculous.

"I think I will take that phone number, if you don't mind," the policeman said apologetically. "Just so the lieutenant knows I covered every contingency."

At breakfast Helen was inquisitive. "Did you hear anything? I didn't hear a thing. I was upstairs reading, and the window was open. And those footprints . . ."

Izzy answered with the briefest mumbled responses, then excused himself and hurried to the basement.

Sequestered in his studio, he powered up his machine, snapped open the drawer below the dreamports, and plucked out the bubble pak containing the results of last night's experiment. He switched on the giant TV screen and the tiny blood-red strobe. Colors—violets and reds and dark purplish blues—flowed like slow-motion lava. The strobe flashed like a dying star. His finger hovered over the play button. He was sweating, seized with an impossible notion.

Am I afraid of what I might see? But that's silly! There's a perfectly sane reason why I dreamed a creature that killed a man last night. I just haven't thought of it yet.

One way to find out.

He closed his eyes and hit the play button.

While Izzy reviewed the bubble pak, Helen went out to examine the bizarre footprints. The sun was higher now, the day brighter, warming. In the backyard, birds chirped merrily over Izzy's uneaten toast. His eggs she'd eaten herself. He wasn't hungry, had to work.

Something was bothering him. He had avoided her eyes, and when he met her gaze, it was with a phony smile.

A chill crept over her, became an ice cube on the back of her neck as she neared the tracks.

The footprints were more than a little scary, she thought, looking down at the humongous bird track right outside the basement window. The ground wasn't soft, but the prints were deeply indented, implying that, whether male or female, the killer was big. There were other footprints, but this was the one, the first one, that had a special fascination for her. It was the heart of mystery.

There's been a murder!

And Mrs. Carruthers had seen the killer. Poor woman. Why had the killer bypassed her and killed someone else? Mrs. C. was luckier than she realized.

Izzy switched off the machine, rubbed his eyes. His hands shook.

The material was only a few minutes. A swift night run, a feeling of tremendous animal power, a wild insatiable hunger that blossomed as he ran, culminating in an explosion of raw, incredibly savage violence. After that, before dissolving, the finale was pure bloodbath: the screams of the victim becoming choked gurgles, the shrieks of the beast. The sheer force of the violence left his nerves jangling, as if he'd been slammed against a wall.

An image stood out in his memory—a three-taloned claw ripping through flesh and ribs as easily as it ripped through the man's shirt. The foot was the same size and shape as the prints outside his window.

But that didn't make any kind of sense. How the hell could a fictional image, a transmitted thought, leave a footprint?

And a corpse!

No. He shook his head. It had to be the other way around. A fuzzy idea that had been forming suddenly popped into focus—he had picked up the thoughts of the killer! After all, some critics touted the dreamie as the closest thing to telepathy. How his dreamatron had operated in reverse, receiving instead of sending, he had no idea, but it made a lot more sense than believing a giant bird, hatched from his imagination, had stalked the neighborhood the night before and committed murder.

8

Whack!

Todd's racquet sent the ball flying low and straight into a corner of the outdoor racquetball wall.

Whack!

It ricocheted off the concrete, but failed to skim under Fred's long reach. Fred slammed it high when Todd thought he was going to smack it low, and with the sun in his eyes, Todd ran to get under the ball. He missed and the ball bounded into the chain-link fence.

A car honked as he retrieved the ball, and he looked up, vaguely hoping, as every young man does, it was a car full of beautiful women who wanted to take him for a ride.

The skinny one behind the wheel—the one with the small breasts and the wide mouth—was Fred's girl, Wanda. He'd once asked Fred what he saw in her and Fred had replied she gave good head. Her wide mouth did give that impression, but she talked a lot of shit and Todd personally considered her a total airhead. The other one, whom he had never before seen, was a full-bosomed, dark-haired beauty with the face of an angel. Smiling, she blinked at him like an owl.

Fred came up beside him. "Hey, Wanda! Come on in!" He pointed his racket at the gate in the chain-link fence.

"And have you wipe your sweat all over me?" she called over the idling engine. "Unn-uh. Just wanted to remind you I'm picking you up at seven. So be ready. And bring a date for Donna."

Wanda didn't wait for a reply, but peeled out. Still smiling and blinking, Wanda's big-breasted girlfriend—Donna? waved as the car sped away.

"Who was that?" Todd asked, watching the car.

"Wanda's cousin from South Carolina. Just flew in for a visit last night. Some gazuntas, huh?"

"Who's the date you're supposed to get for her?"

Fred grinned. "I thought maybe Deek would be free for the evening."

"Forget Deek." Todd tossed Fred the ball. "I'm sure he's got deliveries to make. Busy, busy."

They went back to the game, but Todd was distracted and Fred won fifteen to nine.

"What I saw was no guy in a fright suit."

Lois was adamant. And Chet was worried: if she truly believed what she saw last night was real, then she must have been hallucinating. She was depressed over Jason's condition, but this was something new. She didn't do drugs. Except for a sip of brandy or a little wine with her meals, she didn't drink. Menopause was in her rear view. Was she going through a breakdown? Some sort of hormone thing?

They were in the living room, Jason in his rocker watching TV, Chet on the sofa watching Lois pace. Her arms were crossed, her expression grim.

"Perhaps it was dark and the costume really good," he

offered, hoping she would concede this frustrating argument. Or, at least, accept the possibility that she had been fooled.

She wasn't buying it. "It opened its beak and I saw its tongue. I saw its eyes. And its legs were bent backward at the knee joints like a bird's, not forward like a person's."

Jason stopped rocking and massaged his forehead with an index finger, a habit as long as Chet had known him. It meant he was trying to remember something; he was doing it a lot more often. He looked up smiling and snapped his fingers. "A beak!"

"What're you talking about?" Lois looked at him impatiently.

"A bird! Some sort of weird-looking bird. I saw it too. I knew I had something to tell you." Jason looked pleased with himself and Lois looked relieved. She looked at Chet as if to say, There! What did I tell you?

"You saw it out the window?" Chet asked.

Jason's smile faded. "No, I saw it on TV," he said, and when Chet and Lois exchanged glances, he hurried on. "I was watching a movie last night—though I can't remember which one. Anyway, I was watching this movie, and all of a sudden, this monster—part bird, part lizard—at least it had wings like a gargoyle and legs sort of like an ostrich's . . . you know, bent backwards at the knees." He demonstrated with an index finger.

Lois rolled her eyes. "You saw no such thing, old man! You're repeating what I just described. God, please let me die before I get old."

"Lois!"

"Don't Lois me, Mr. Chester Brown. I won't be patronized."

Jase smiled at him as if to apologize for Lois' behavior, though it went without saying he didn't have to. The smile didn't fool Chet, though; it was about as cheerful as Emmet Kelly's. He felt like saying, You are old, Lois, count your birthdays without cheating. Instead, he counted to five, and just as he was on the brink of adding insult to injury, the animosity passed.

It hurt Chet to see his old friends, the friends of his youth,

losing control, falling apart at the seams. It hurt to see Jase look
at him shyly in the middle of a checkers game and ask which
color he was playing; they hadn't played in six months. And no
matter how jokingly accepting Jase appeared, it was a façade.
The slow deterioration was getting to him, wearing him down.
Though rare, there were moments that he let his deeper feelings out. Just the other week, Chet was at the breakfast table
reading the paper over a cup of coffee and Jase came in and sat
next to him, looking sad. "If I ever get senile," he said after a
long, weary sigh that got his attention, "I mean *really* senile,
just bump me off, kiddo." And he made his hand like a gun and
pointed it at Chet's chest and winked as the imaginary hammer
fell.

Chet knew he should count himself lucky to share his winter
years with his old partners and friends, but he was living in a
madhouse, treading water and getting nowhere: he and Lois
morosely waiting for Jason to slip over the edge, for the day
when he would no longer know who they were.

Still, he couldn't leave. They needed him, Lois and Jase.
They were his lifelong buddies, and more like family than the
two elderly spinsters last known to have lived in Duluth, who
were his next of kin.

"I'm going to go soak in a cool tub and sip a glass of wine,"
Lois said. Her expression had softened.

"Good night," Jason said.

Lois stopped and looked at him, and to Chet's delight, she
altered her course, came up behind Jason, and put her arms
around him and kissed his neck.

"Hey!" Jase exclaimed. "What'd I do to deserve that?"

"I love you, you know that, Old Man?" She looked down into
his upturned, grinning face. "And I don't think I've told you in
weeks."

"Months."

"Don't push it."

"You know, I worry about her," Jase said when they heard
her bedroom door close.

"Me too," Chet said. Despite his worries though, he wasn't
sad. The lightening of Lois' mood, however brief, let some sun

in, and Jase's memory pill was working pretty well considering. His eyes were clear, twinkling even, now that Lois had broken the ice that had been growing thicker between them the past few weeks. He hadn't faded off in the middle of a sentence in hours.

"You know, I saw it." Jase nodded as he slowly rocked.

"Did you?"

"Yeah." Jase looked him in the eye, as if trying to convince himself too. "Only I saw it on the TV, like I told you."

"You sure it wasn't part of the movie?"

"No. I mean, hell yes, I'm sure. I was watching"—he snapped his fingers—"*Them!* I remember now. Giant ants. Remember?"

"I remember."

"Well, I was watching the movie, and all of a sudden, this sort of a wyvern—you know, like the two-legged dragons you see in medieval illustrations?—loped across the screen."

Chet mulled this over a moment. "You a hundred percent certain you're not just repeating what Lois said?"

Jason chuckled. "Of course I'm not a hundred percent certain! I'm senile, remember?"

Jason's humor cut deeper than the sharpest satire; tragedy's edge was always keener when honed on irony. "Well, maybe you picked up a television image from something on another station. Or maybe an old signal from years ago. I've heard it happens."

Jase shook his head. "Then why did Lois see the same thing?"

"I don't know," he said. And he didn't. Unless, of course, Lois was right and Jase was repeating what she'd said.

Rocking slowly, Jase gazed down at the carpet in front of his feet. Momentarily, he looked at the television with a puzzled expression on his face. Then he brightened. "Oh, yeah. Remember this?"

"Yeah, I remember." Chet managed a halfway cheerful grin.

On the screen, a hooded murderer poured acid down the throat of the half-naked girl who should never have gone into the house in the first place. The gurgling scream that welled out of the Trinitron's speakers filled the room.

9

Helen woke just after dawn. The bed was heaving. Then she realized it was Izzy thrashing and moaning. His hands, held up before him, clawed at the dark, his legs scrabbled under the blanket, as if he were climbing ... or swimming ... acting out his dream.

Escaping, she thought, remembering she had learned in one of her psychology courses that the most common nightmare was the dream of being pursued. She wondered as she shook him what monster was pursuing him now, ready in the dream reality to sink its claws or fangs into him.

"Izzy! Iz?"

Still holding his hands in the air, he came out of it.

"Huh?"

"A bad one," she said, then realized when she touched his forehead just how bad: he was drenched, his skin clammy, and he was shivering. She put her arm around him and cradled his head, wiped his brow with her hand. And he came to her without protesting that he needed a few minutes to savor the dream, to record it while it was still fresh in his mind.

It was unlike Izzy not to enjoy a nightmare, not to thrive on the dream's roller-coaster adrenaline flow, the heightened perception that fear gave. But this made two nights in a row since the night of the murder that he had reacted violently to a dream. She wondered if it was the same dream and started to ask him, but though he was clammy, he still trembled and she decided he would tell her tomorrow if he wanted to.

Stark wasn't the only one to greet the dawn with nightmares. Twenty miles away in his Bayonne apartment, Dr. Casper Nösberger woke from the nightmare that had pursued him from one troubled fit of sleep to the next, leaving him drenched and exhausted when he finally gave up and piled out of bed at seven. In the dream, a young dark-eyed, dark-haired man was endlessly clawed to gory tatters. In the dream, it was as if he and the screaming young man were one, and he felt the agony of his ribs snapping, of talons puncturing his lungs, of his blood filling his throat, drowning his screams.

In the kitchen he keyed the automatic coffee maker for two cups, set a mug under the spout, tapped for cream and sweetener, and stepped onto his balcony while the appliance went to work. The sun was up, bright and warming. It was early for Nösberger. He was a night bird, taught afternoon and evening classes, preferably evening so he could spend the afternoon working in the lab and, again, half the night after classes.

Nösberger's balcony faced west, away from the glamour of the Hudson and the Manhattan skyline and toward the sleazier industrial charms of South Kearny and the Newark Bay. The sunlight glinted off the windows of cars, tiny with distance, on the New Jersey Turnpike.

The morning air cleared some of the cobwebs from his head, and he thought about the experiment the night before last that had caused the nightmares. But when he closed his eyes trying to recall the details of the experience, all he saw was a scything beak and a pair of cold, predatory eyes.

"That was some trip," he said, and went back in.

The coffee was ready. He set his mug on the breakfast bar to cool and turned on the portable television that stood at one end of the counter while he whipped up a Nutrient drink in the blender. The *whiiirrrrrr* of the machine drowned the small set. The picture cut from the anchorman to a dockside location. Recognizing the spot, he shut off the blender to hear what the voice-over was saying.

From the weed-grown shoreline with its Manhattan backdrop to the red-brown splashes on the crumbling dock, he recognized the scene at once. From the voice-over he learned a murder had been committed on the pier. The murder was not current, but had taken place Tuesday night at about the same time he and Stark conducted their experiment. Yesterday, he'd been so busy he hadn't seen a newspaper or watched TV. As he listened further, his eyes opened wide with disbelief as the picture shifted back to the studio and the anchorman explained that the police believed the killer to have been a maniac dressed in a bird costume.

The piece ended with a photograph of the victim. He recognized the glossy-haired Hispanic youth, though he remembered him as a bit older, his face fuller, in need of a shave, his hair longer and less neat. The station cut to a commercial, but Nösberger continued to gaze on that face through the camera eye of his memory. Something the news hadn't shown: the terror he had seen in those dark Cuban eyes.

Murder!

Bird tracks!

His coffee and his New You Nutrient drink forgotten, he called Information and asked for the number of the news desk at the local paper.

Todd was fashioning a paper airplane out of a syrupy "Jesus Loves You" poem one of the Holy Molies had written, when Jamie entered the office of the Ferris High School newspaper, *The Green and Gold,* with a storm cloud hanging over his head—which, for Jamie, was not unusual.

"What's news?" Todd greeted, knowing the expression annoyed Jamie. He used to ask, "What's up?" until they joined the newspaper staff, Jamie assuming the position of chief editor simply by taking over the work load and getting the job done. Jamie had decided on a career as an editor-writer. Todd kidded him that perhaps he could get a job with Penguin Books. Jamie didn't take offense; fat jokes rolled off his back like . . . well, like snowballs off a penguin.

"Another submission by Barbara Sullivan?" Jamie said, ignoring his question.

"How'd you guess?"

"There's some stinky verse on the wing that I can smell over here. How many paper planes do you have to make for her to give up?"

Todd shrugged and flew the plane. It struck Jamie in the chest and fell at his feet. "Not amused." Jamie stepped on it on his way to his desk. He stopped by the bulletin board, removed a few thumbtacks, and dropped a couple outdated bulletins into a wastebasket.

"Why so grumpy?" Todd asked.

Jamie sighed, looked at him. "Can't get the tickets."

Todd's chair scraped as he shoved back and stood, looking at Jamie with something like shock.

"Can't get . . . ? But you said—"

Jamie held up a plump hand. "I know what I said. Sometimes, positive thinking helps get the job done."

"What went wrong?"

"Mr. D. said Maloney wouldn't go for it."

Maloney was the principal, an old fart who probably thought spending the evening translating Cicero was having a good time. Mr. Dexter, the teacher in charge of the school paper, was a cool-enough guy, though his jokes were corny.

"Damn!" Jamie said. "I mean, how can I run a paper without funds? I mean, a *real* newspaper dishes out money for tickets so the sports and film critics can do their job. What does Maloney expect us to do? Interview people as they come out of the theater?"

"I think Maloney's been listening to the reports on dreamies."

"Naw." Jamie shook his head. "I think the problem was greed. We might have gotten away with one ticket to the Stark concert, but four?"

"Dammit!" Todd said, jamming his hands into his pockets. "I promised Donna I would take her."

Fred had been as good as his word about fixing him up with Donna. The four of them—Fred and Wanda and Donna and himself—had double-dated to the movies last night. Afterward, he and Donna had held an embarrassed conversation on Wanda's living-room sofa—her parents being out for the evening—while listening to the squeaking of bedsprings in Wanda's room. He learned Donna was a high-school senior and worked as a checkout clerk in a Piggly Wiggly back home in Florence, South Carolina. Her blinking-owl act was caused by the new pair of contacts she was breaking in. And she had never been to a dreamie. Finally, the certain knowledge of what was going on in the next room became too much for them, and he put his arms around her. She'd snuggled into him, so he kissed her, all the while heatedly aware of her ample breasts against his chest. He kissed her throat, his brain swimming feverishly in her perfume. He had his hand under her blouse, caressing her breast through the thin material of her bra, and was wondering what to do next when a much-rumpled Fred and Wanda came out of the bedroom and Wanda said he and Fred would have to leave because her parents would be home any minute.

Jamie stared at the bare spaces he had created on the bulletin board, as if thinking what to hang there. Todd knew him better than that.

"Hey!" he said, resuming his seat. "Why don't you let me take Donna up the clubhouse?"

Jamie snorted. "That's against the rules."

"Rules were made to be broken."

"Not this rule. My father made it, and you know how he is."

Todd nodded gravely. Mr. K. was a nice guy, until you stepped on his toes. But Todd felt like being stubborn. "Yeah, well, we smoke pot and drink beer in the clubhouse and I don't see you shitting bricks over that."

"That's different. It's easy to hide a joint. A woman's a little bigger. Anyway, be quiet. I've got to think." Jamie went to his desk and sat in his swivel chair, an old-fashioned Bank of England wooden chair with the seat carved to accommodate the human derriere, leaned back, folded his hands on his stomach, and stared grumpily at the wall.

Jamie was plotting, fishing for an angle to get tickets. Of course, they could wait for the drawing—all four of them had sent in to WNEW a dozen post cards apiece—but that was chancy, probably futile. Come on, Jamie, Todd thought. Jamie was always the guy with the answers. When everyone else was sweating over a problem—be it algebra or history or how to get tickets to Stark's upcoming *Mystery Show,* so long as it wasn't mechanical—Jamie plucked solutions out of his head the way magicians plucked rabbits out of hats.

Jamie once told him intelligence might depend on how fast the brain's neurons sped the electrical signals that made up info. "I'm just an old swifty," Jamie said, and Todd laughed. Not many people appreciated his friend's sometimes cornball humor, but when it came to homework or editing or new ideas for *Tentacle*, his neurons laid rubber.

Todd smelled the rubber burning now. As he watched his friend scheme, his lips pressed tight, his eyes, small to begin with, squinched like little pig's eyes behind his black-rimmed glasses, he thought of past schemes. Like the time Jamie came up with the idea that they pool their money and buy a dozen hot radios one of the neighborhood junkies was selling for a few bucks apiece, stash them in the garage until Christmas, and then hawk them on Thirty-fourth Street for twenty and thirty apiece. Or the time Deek uncovered six decrepit-looking fox stoles—the type that uses the whole fox, head and all, each fox biting the tail of the guy in front of him—in an abandoned building they were exploring. Deek had thrown them aside, looking for more obvious treasure, like a stash of cash. But Jamie gathered them up and stuffed them into a plastic shoe-store bag and sold the lot on Canal Street for fifty dollars to a bug-eyed Oriental with long hair and frayed pants' cuffs, who smiled and stated, in answer to Todd's question, that he wanted the stoles for a collage.

Jamie sighed disgustedly and pushed himself to his feet. "Come on, let's get out of here. I can't think on an empty stomach."

The Art Deco curio cabinet was tall, glass-fronted, and stood by the archway to the dining room. It was trimmed in bleached-blond oak, the door and the side panes were curved and beveled. Inside, the shelves were glass, and the population of ceramic, porcelain, jade, ivory, soapstone, tourmaline, plastic and glass was doubled by a mirrored back.

"I guess I'm a materialist," Helen said.

Quent considered this as he gazed at the ordered chaos behind the beveled glass. There were four jade dragons and beautifully detailed figures of Dresden china, and the center-piece of the top shelf was an Oriental carving, intricately wrought from ivory and detailing a bridge and a train spanning two precipitous mountain peaks, the whole nearly as big as a football. But among the gold doubloons were some wooden nickels. There were lots of shells, common as well as rare, a pictorial saucer on a plastic stand with "Puerto Rico" inscribed over palm trees, a copper-plated Statue of Liberty with "Atlantic City" on its base. Childhood mementos included a small porcelain doll on a lower shelf, one side of its head veined with yellow glue lines; a cardboard racing car colored red and yellow with crayons, flames decorating its nose and, on its hood, a silver rocket ship, as if the decoration might add the look of speed and thrust to the boxy shape. "Izzy made the car when he was seven," she said.

"Did he?" The car's black-crayoned wheels were held on by brass upholstery tacks that gave the look of hubcaps. "You know, I wouldn't say you were a materialist."

"No? What would you say?"

Her gaze made him warm; he looked back into the case. "You could afford to fill this cabinet exclusively with expensive items, yet you have five-and-dime stuff and boardwalk souvenirs. I would say you're a sentimentalist."

"Oh, no!" Helen covered her face with her hand for a second. "Sentimentality's looked down upon these days, isn't it?"

" 'Fraid that means you're outdated."

"I am though—sentimental, I mean." She turned the frosty glass of diet cola in her hands, her shell-pink nails tracing lines in the condensation. Her smile was bemused. "I still have my Communion dress, a stack of crayon-colored get-well cards my third-grade classmates sent me when I was out with the measles, my first doll."

He sipped his own cola and observed her over the rim of his glass. She was slim, but far from skinny, her breasts and her hips accentuated by her yellow cotton dress. Hers was an ethnic beauty, a Grecian beauty. Her eyes were dark lamps, her cheekbones high and the angle of their descent matched by her jawline, her nose straight, classical.

"Definitely sentimental," he said, lowering his glass. Her gaze brushed his, and again he felt a warmth flush through him that he was afraid would show on his face if he didn't look away, and again he sought refuge in the menagerie.

He realized what had happened: she'd opened the door and he'd gotten an instant crush on her—what teenagers called "love at first sight" but adults knew as "lust at first sight." He was amused, dismayed, and surprised at his sweaty palms and his quickened pulse.

Izzy was busy and would be up in a few, she'd said, ushering him into the living room. So he'd decided to interview her in the meantime, fill in some of the trials-and-tribulations stuff from the time between high school and stardom. His belt recorder was on with Helen's permission.

"What was it like?" he had asked her. "I mean, married life—before Izzy made it big?"

"We're not married."

"Right. But you know what I mean."

"My parents thought he was a bum. At least, my father did. Momma was undecided. You couldn't mention Izzy's name without Papa having something bad to say about him. They forgave him his shortcomings after he made it big," she added.

His gaze lingered on a picture he had glanced over before. The photo-portrait was small, the ornate, gilded frame dwarfing it. It sat on a middle shelf, not in a prominent position, but to one side, as if Helen liked to be able to look at it without it being conspicuous. The girl looked like a teenage version of Helen, only her hair was still long and she hadn't lost all of her baby fat.

"You?" He pointed.

"No, my sister, Maria."

"I didn't know you have a sister."

"I don't."

"Huh?" he said, then realized the next second how dense that made him sound.

Helen smiled sadly. "Maria died."

"I'm sorry."

"Don't be. It happened a long time ago." She looked at the portrait. Her smile was tender. Quent could tell that though years had passed, Helen hadn't stopped loving her sister. "Maria was fifteen in that photo. It was taken the year she died.

She was a year older than me." She was reminiscing now, the sadness gone from her smile, her eyes warm with nostalgia. "She was a live wire, that girl, a real tomboy most of the time. I had a hard time keeping up, but I tried. We were inseparable. I always tagged after her. Momma called me her shadow. Once, I got sent to summer camp without Maria and I cried for three nights."

He laughed at that.

"It's funny," she said, "that, after years of Maria being my older sister and me always trailing behind, always trying to make up the difference, I should pass Maria up and become the older sister. To me, Maria has remained pretty much as you see her in that picture—frozen in time.

"One day, Maria was working in the store with Papa. I wasn't there, but I've heard it so many times from my mother. Momma said Maria stopped after stocking a shelf and complained she wasn't feeling well. Momma told her to go upstairs and lie down, but Maria wanted to help get the stock unboxed for tomorrow. A few minutes later, her voice and her hands started shaking as if she had palsy. 'Call an ambulance, Papa. Something's wrong.' That's what Momma said she said. She put her hand to her head as if she had a headache, then she . . . Momma said she just fainted—just like that, dead away with no warning."

"God!" was all he could think to say when he realized her story was finished. He shook his head, imagining what a shock it must have been for Helen to hear her sister was dead, and how painful the weeks and months afterward.

Helen returned to the sofa. Quent came around and sat in the armchair kitty-cornered to her. His glass was empty, so he set it on the marble coffee table.

"Do you want a refill?" She started to rise.

"No, no." He waved his hand. "I'm fine, thank you."

She retired her own glass, half-full, to the table and settled back. "You know," she said, "what you said before about my being able to fill that cabinet 'exclusively with expensive items' was wrong. Izzy could, I can't. It's his money."

He was intrigued. So money was a problem! He hadn't

suspected that. Aware that she was revealing something personal about her life and at a loss as to how to proceed, he did something he wouldn't normally do: he switched off his belt recorder.

"He doesn't let you spend it?"

"Oh, it's not that. I can buy anything I want. But it's not the same, is it?"

Quent was impressed. Most women—most people, for that matter—would love to be rich and buy whatever they wanted, regardless of who was paying, and here was a woman who worried about who was paying the bill. "Obviously it's not to you."

"You know," she adjusted her dress and draped an elbow over the jelly-roll arm of the sofa, "I changed my major from art to psychology with an eye toward a career. I didn't know how long it would take Izzy to get his own career off the ground—not that I ever doubted he would—so I thought, meantime, I'd better prepare myself for a vocation. Funny thing, though—all the time I was working at the bank and then at the college, I thought mainly about two things: Izzy making it in his career and me making it in mine. I guess I was wishing us both free of shit jobs." Quent noted that from the way she said "shit," you could hear the quotation marks letting you know the word was not part of her normal vocabulary.

"I detect a note of resentment."

She spread her hands on her lap. "Not resentment. I'm appreciative, especially for the house"—her gesture encompassed her surroundings—"but I feel . . . not useless, but like I've lost direction. I still want a career, but I look at the job listings and see the twenty-to-twenty-five-thousand-dollar starting salaries for psychology majors. Compare that to the four-plus million Izzy's worth, and the whole idea of finishing my degree and pursuing a career is a joke." Her smile was a shrug—not bitter but ironic.

Before he could think of a response, the chimes sounded and Helen excused herself to answer the door.

"Nonsense!" Izzy smiled and shook his head. "You expect me to believe that my participation in an experiment in some way caused someone to get killed? Ridiculous! I know about the murder and the similarities with my dreamie. Now I'll tell you what I think happened."

Until a few minutes ago, Izzy had been pacing the floor, worrying, wondering why he wasn't enjoying his nightmares anymore. In last night's dream, there had been many floaters with him in the dark Hudson. And they weren't just drifting with the current; they were moving toward him through the oily water with the sluggish animation of the hungry dead. He hated to keep Quent waiting, but he wasn't ready for a question-and-answer session. He never reached a conclusion, though, for then Helen buzzed him on the intercom to tell him Dr. Nösberger was here and that the doctor said it was important.

When the doctor came downstairs, it was plain to see he was upset.

"What's the matter, Doc?"

Nösberger gushed the whole works: the news piece, his call to the reporter.

"What I think happened," Izzy said, "was the dreamatron worked in reverse last night. In other words, instead of my generating images, I picked up the killer's thoughts, what he or she was seeing and feeling."

Nösberger, sitting on the sofa with his hands clasped between his bony knees, his eyes round and staring at his thumbs, remained pensive for a minute.

"It's a marvelous idea," he said at last. "And certainly less incriminating than some of the notions that have crossed my mind." He grinned, guiltily Izzy thought. "But . . ." He rose and shrugged. "I've got to call the experiments off."

"Call them off!" Izzy jumped up from the arm of the sofa. "You can't do that! Don't you realize the implications of what I've just told you? Remember, the dreamatron was originally designed for recording dreams. There was no concentrated effort of will on the part of the dreamer to project images; the dreams were simply recorded. The technology's new. There's obviously a lot we don't know about it. Look, Professor," Izzy spread his hands, "if money's a problem, I could hire you."

Nösberger shook his head.

"You supply the taraxein and keep a journal. And think of this: a portable unit, the telephone of tomorrow, able to hook you up telepathically via satellite to anyone on the globe. How would you like a percentage of the copyrights on that action?"

Nösberger rose from the sofa, slapping his hands on his knees and pushing himself up. "The answer is no."

"You don't understand," Izzy said, his patience wearing thin. "Somehow, the taraxein must have altered my brain waves enough to make it possible for me to extend the range of the dreamatron, or"—he snapped his fingers as an idea occurred to him—"maybe it made me telepathic for a few minutes. I don't know. But we've got to find out."

Nösberger waved his hand as he shook his head: a visual double negative. "I'm sorry. *You* don't understand. I like my job. I'm very involved with my present research. I don't want to do anything to jeopardize it. Without my fellowship, I'm just a regular teacher, stuck to the grind of grading papers." The professor stared off into space for a moment. When he looked at Izzy again, his eyes were narrowed and a little haunted. "I keep seeing that young man die, all ripped to shreds. I keep thinking about the implications." Nösberger smiled nervously. "Maybe we can conduct some experiments at the lab later on where we can have tighter controls and I can monitor your brain waves." Nösberger started walking toward the stairs.

"That's just great," Izzy yelled behind him. He'd remained quiet, let the professor talk, hoping he would change his mind, but now his anger came bubbling out. "You make some wild paranoid connection and you want to cut off an experiment that might make telepathy accessible to the masses."

"That's a bit farfetched."

"So was the notion of flying or of walking on the moon. For that matter, so were dreamies. You're the straight doctor in the old movies who says: 'Some mysteries are better left unknown.' I don't agree!"

Nösberger had reached the stairs. "I'm sorry," he said. "It's too risky. I'll be in touch."

And he was gone.

Izzy went back to pacing. He no longer thought about Frank Price and his dreams of waterlogged zombies. He thought about "the implications," as the professor had put it.

He was onto something wild. There was no way the experiments were going to stop now.

No way!

10

The footprints were still there.

After Nösberger left, Izzy went upstairs and lunched with Helen and Quent, making small talk, all the while fuming at Nösberger's decision. When Quent left he went outside to see the tracks again. The talons of the birdlike prints had torn up the lawn. It hadn't rained since the night of the murder, and the tracks were clear. And so realistic!

He got down on one knee and examined the track in the afternoon light. In three of the talon impressions, he discerned the imprint of tiny scales.

He considered himself part scientist. After all, he had designed many of the modifications on his own machine. But, first and foremost, he was a dreamer—the King of the Dreamies, bar none—and his mind grabbed gladly for the impossible like some kid grabbing for the brass ring on some long-ago carousel.

To create! To birth matter from thought!

His head swelled to godlike proportions.

Creatively, the following day was a waste. The dreamie he'd worked on for over a month seemed trivial. With Halloween a week away there was no time to come up with a replacement dreamie, but the potential . . .

His skull could scarcely contain the ideas running through his head: picking up a killer's thoughts ... broadcasting a dreamie beyond its programmed range ... technical puzzles that cried out to be pursued. But more important to the artist in him were the subtle alterations taraxein had wrought in the fabric of the dreamie.

Where psychedelics produced pulsating patterns and a feeling of inexpressible illumination, a mystical sense of the cosmic, taraxein dealt with darkness and emotions of violence, of claustrophobic paranoia, of terror. As Nösberger had commented after their experiment, it had been "some ride."

Talons opening great red wounds, ripping flesh, cracking bone. The image of a face laid open. The stalk of an eye dangling from a lidless socket.

Izzy shook the image from his mind.

Retrieved it.

He had the experiment on bubble pak. It was a start. Make a hell of an opening. *In media res*. If he just had more taraxein to open up the crypts of his subconscious mind, he was sure he'd come up with amazing material.

As he paced up and down the shuffle board painted on the basement floor, his scalp crawled the way it did when he looked at a wasp's nest. His stomach bubbled acidly.

He decided to go for a drive.

He drove with the window open, his foot heavy and nervous on the accelerator. He took the Alfa Romeo on the Palisades Interstate and, risking a ticket, opened her up as much as he dared. Only the sensation of speed eased the tension in his guts. He turned off, went south on 9-W. The traffic was halfway light, mostly trucks, and he managed to zigzag in and out of it, which gave him something to concentrate on so he wouldn't have to think about where he was going. On Tonnele Avenue he made better time.

Izzy parked a block away from the college, telling himself that he did not intend any larceny, but merely to try to talk some sense into the doctor. On campus, he walked quickly, afraid Nösberger might see him from a window of the white-brick science building.

Nösberger's office was empty. The door was unlocked and the lights were on. Had the doctor stepped out for a moment? Was he even in?

He hurried across the office, opened the door to the lab.

"Hello?"

No answer. The lights were off. He switched them on, stepped into the room. He licked his lips as he scanned the workbenches, cabinets, chemistry apparatus. He scratched his shoulder. He itched all over, his palms were sweaty. Where would Nösberger keep it?

He started toward the nearest workbench, nervously resigned to working his way through the room's many drawers and cabinets.

Then he saw the small avocado-colored refrigerator on a counter near a sink and decided it would be the most likely place to store drugs. He opened the fridge.

And breathed a sigh of relief when he saw the squares of taraxein in the zip-lock bag. He wasn't going to have to spend the next half-hour going through drawers, after all.

Voices in the outer office.

He closed the fridge and ducked under a workbench. The lab door opened.

"Doctor?" A female voice.

"I guess he's not here."

A pair of female legs, visible from the hem of her green skirt to her pink sneakers, strolled into sight between the stout wooden legs of the workbench. Then a second pair, chubby legs in tight pedal pushers. The workbench didn't afford him much cover; if they were to walk around this side, they'd see him for sure.

"Probably stepped out for a moment," the first voice said. "Do you want to wait in the office? He won't mind."

His heart lurched. Go away! Get lost!

"No. It can wait till Monday. Coffee?"

The legs strolled away, a door opened and closed. Izzy scrambled out from under the bench, shot a glance at the door: he saw no movement through the frosted-glass pane. He darted for the fridge, grabbed the plastic bag of taraxein, stuffed it into his back pocket, slapped the lights off and left.

The hall was empty.

He hurried toward the stairs in the opposite direction, hoping no one would recognize him. An old guy in a blue suit and red bow tie carrying a briefcase waited in front of the elevator. Beyond the elevators, the men's-room door opened, and Izzy's heart leapt when he saw Nösberger's long head coming out.

The elevator door opened and he ducked inside, stepping to the rear and behind the bow-tied gentleman. Nösberger strode past as the door whispered shut.

Downstairs, a security guard got on as he got off, and Izzy said, "Happy weekend."

"You too." The guard smiled back.

He spent part of the evening with Helen going over his speech for the Dreamacon tomorrow and fidgeting through Episode One of a made-for-television extravaganza, fully aware that he had no intention of watching the remaining episodes.

He ended up in the basement holding a sheet of the red-brown blotter. It was eleven before he got the courage to put two hits in his mouth.

Almost immediately, his day-long anxiety relaxed. Moments later objects in the basement—his dreamatron, the sofa, the television screen—became edged with a silver light. He resisted the strong urge to work on his machine, not because he didn't want to, but because he was afraid. So he paced up and down the vibrating shuffleboard pattern painted on the floor.

At midnight he was still pacing. He was suffocating. His shirt was damp and his sweat had a chemical smell.

He went for a walk. The fresh air cleared his head. He went along Boulevard East on the Palisades' side and looked out at the New York skyline and at the lights of the river traffic.

He was walking along the observation area a couple blocks from his house where the sidewalk widened and coin-operated, telescopic viewers lined the low stone wall, when the hallucination hit. A fairy radiance outlined the coin-ops, the skyscrapers across the river darkened and began to pulsate and blur. The radiance was like purple chrome. The earth pitched drunkenly.

He turns, staggers. The boulevard traffic is doing it too—pulsating, rippling with dark purples and reds. Car outlines blur, become an impressionist kaleidoscope of movement. He closes his eyes, tries to shift his center of balance from his vision to his inner ear, where it belongs.

When he opens them, the boulevard is gone! Cars, taxis, the lighted lobbies of the apartment buildings across the street. Instead, there lies before him a smoky cobbled road lined on either side by crucifixes on which writhe blackening bodies starkly lit by the flames that consume them. Black and red and smoke everywhere. A Boschean hellscape.

His blood curdles, his scrotum shrinks at the horror.

They're calling my name!

Their blistering faces, their melting eyes, are turned toward him, and amid the crackling of flames and flesh, parched, sibilant whispers, calling him. A sere wind, the breath of flames, blows the words to him.

Isidor Stark . . . Isidor Stark . . .

And with his name, a curse.

Cracking lips name him as the progenitor of their anguish, call down on him and any progeny he might beget everlasting suffering. A curse that carries the certainty and weight of natural laws, of destiny.

He is blameless! He has hurt no one! He wants to shout at them that they are mistaken, but hearing his name slurred by the sizzling lips turns his bowels to water. Horror drives him blindly into the smoky, lightless night away from his accusers.

The voices grow faint. Darkness swallows the flickering fires. Monstrous shapes move in the darkness. Eyes like lanterns blind him as a beast, rearing and screeching, bears down on him. He is struck, lifted, flung.

He landed on the hood of a car. The bus driver was stepping out of the Number Twenty-three, at once swearing and asking was he all right.

Izzy ran all the way home and locked himself in the bathroom. He was undressed and in the shower before he felt the bruises on his arm throbbing or realized how lucky he was.

Letting the warm water sluice down his back, he thought about his hallucination. He couldn't recall the exact words of the curses, only their gist. But he could still hear their voices, sibilant with the dry-leaves rattle of death, harsh with anger. Blistering lips condemning, and promising . . .

Retribution.

II

The terrors did not end with the night's ghastly vision of burning bodies and his near-fatal encounter with the Number Twenty-three bus. Last night after his long hot shower, still unable to stop the shivering that rattled his soul as well as his teeth, he crawled into bed with Helen and lay awake, exhausted yet restless, afraid to sleep for fear of what he might encounter in the dream world, his eyes filled with a dancing ghoulish firelight and the beams of a speeding bus until dawn's gray light paled the window. Then he dozed, fitfully, alternately dreaming of flaming, faceless corpses and of bloated, decomposing floaters.

He woke stiff, head ballooning, tongue parched. Helen's side of the bed was empty. When he sat up, his left shoulder cried out in pain. With a sudden bass-drum slam of his heart, he remembered the bus.

In the bathroom, he examined himself in the vanity mirror. The damage wasn't as bad as he'd thought. The bruises on his left shoulder and his hip were purple and smarted every time that arm or leg moved, but they were the only signs of injury. He was lucky to be alive. Damned lucky!

He showered, hoping to clear his head under the cold water. But as he toweled dry, his skin crawled, a bloated nausea writhed eel-like in his stomach.

Back in the bedroom, he dug into the pockets of the pants he had been wearing when the bus clipped him, and came up with the rest of the square of taraxein from which he had torn two hits. Afraid after last night's bad trip, he bit off only half a hit, then lay on the bed with his eyes closed.

Within minutes, the nausea dissipated, his jangling nerves relaxed. He smelled bacon and then Helen was at the bottom of the stairs calling that breakfast would be ready in a few, and

94

he stuck his head out the door and yelled down that he was getting dressed.

It was while dressing that the new horror revealed itself, peeling back the mask of sanity and exposing the cadaverous face of madness beneath.

He had just put on a fresh pair of white jeans and was drawing on a pair of socks when his attention riveted on the back of his hand.

A rough circle of flesh was missing. Ligaments and two white bones showed through the gaping hole. The wound was bloodless, the surrounding flesh as gray and dead as the flesh of the floaters in his dreams. Then his eyes teared and he blinked and the hand was whole, just as pale, but white and traced with blue veins, not gray like cold dead stone.

It had been another hallucination, of course—the taraxein again. He was as sane as ever . . .

The turnout for this year's Dreamacon was huge and the sights and sounds of the loud, multicolored throng dazzling. The crowd was the same cross section of pop-culture aficionados—leather boys, space cadets, lounge lizards, and all the varieties and vulgarities in between—you'd encounter in lines outside dream palaces everywhere. Many in the throng, male and female alike, wore every type of makeup you could imagine, from eye shadow, to white face, to macabre and imaginative designs suitable for a Halloween masque.

The Best Costume Contest was held after dinner in a huge hall on the twelfth floor of the Newport Convention Center. Although some exhibits were still open and there was an all-night Horror Classic Film Festival going on down on the ninth floor, most of the Dreamacon crowd was amassed here. The stage—a broad, round dais in the center of the vast room—provided the crowd with a good view of the bizarre parade of fandom phantasmagoria. On two sides of the dais were the judges' seats. The judges were six: the Guest of Honor, Isidor Stark was one.

The Dreamer's face glowed with ruddy Dionysian health. Sitting on the stage, dazzling in white suit and gloves, he was washed with painted lights—purple, green, gold—so that he looked like a chameleon doing his trick.

Though he was feeling unusually good, he was restless, agitated. It had been hard to sit through the past hour of costume watching and there was a final hour to go—the judges' decisions and the awards ceremony. He glanced at his watch: five minutes to intermission. He'd agreed to grab a burger with Quent and Helen during the break.

Catcalls and whistles and a rising murmur proceeded the next group to mount the dais. The crowd was parting, and down the aisle strode a bevy of Venusian beauties: seven gorgeous blondes wearing high heels and golden swimsuits—fantasy space suits consisting of little more than bikinis with Flash Gordon epaulets. All tall, tanned, long-legged, and blessed with the grace and well-toned musculature of professional dancers. If they had been in a beauty contest, they would all be runners-up for one another. Two of them, heart-stopping twins, walked arm in arm. The purple, green, and golden lights bathed their bronzed flesh as they rose out of the throng and paraded across the stage, their movements fluid, hypersensual, seemingly unaffected, though so coordinated they had to be practiced.

The goddesses descended the steps on the far side of the stage with all the sensual majesty of a setting sun, and were replaced by a bunch of clowns in rubbery alien costumes with snouts and tentacles for faces. The soundless system launched into a cut from Euclid's new album. The music, stately and melancholy with soaring church-organ riffs, was incongruous with the aliens' slapstick antics on stage, as they began flailing one another with rubbery human arms they produced from suitcases.

Moments later, the house lights came up, signaling intermission, and Izzy stood, stretched, and excused himself.

On his feet, he felt alert, his senses preternaturally keen. Each smell—the whiffs of cigarettes and reefer that wafted his way, the aroma of hot dogs turning on the grill—seemed augmented, distinct, each sound amplified and discrete. Conversations around him seemed unnecessarily loud; a quiet remark twelve feet away seemed spoken at arm's length.

". . . What size bra would you wear? I mean, if you wore one . . ."

". . . Look, isn't that Isidor Stark?"

"Yeah. Shit! I stood in that autograph line for almost an hour. I could've waited and gotten it now . . ."

". . . You mean it's finished?"

"All gone. *Pffft!* No more."

"But it feels like more . . ."

He looked around trying to spot Quent or Helen in the crowd that was breaking up and drifting toward the concession stands, elevators, and rest rooms, but didn't see them.

"May I have your autograph?"

Dark-brown eyes twinkled beneath a mane of black hair. The short, muscular teenager was covered with tattoos: dragons on his forearms and serpents on his upper arms, the yellow skull with flaming red eyes on his chest glaring at him through the crisscross of rawhide thongs lacing his shaggy barbarian vest. A small stack of what looked like high-school newspapers were tucked under his arm. The kid held out one of these for Izzy to sign.

"Sure." Izzy took the newspaper—and almost dropped it!

Above the title on page one squatted a huge hairy spider . . . black with a yellow spot on its back.

Terror filled him, cold terror, as if the spider had already bitten him and the venom was just touching his heart. The poison-plump nightmare was only inches from his hands. Tiny eyes like black glass beads glittered in its ugly head.

Drop it! Stomp it! His thoughts were like the frenziedly shouted words of a bystander, but his hands wouldn't obey.

Then, without any blurring or overlapping of images like you see in movies, he was looking at a flat, two-dimensional pen-and-ink drawing of an octopus, slit eyes staring at him from the page, its long decorative arms coiled around the crumbling stonelike letters of the single word title.

Tentacle.

A fanzine! he realized. He'd autographed a number of them in line that afternoon following his talk on the Future of Dreamies. Simultaneously, he realized he'd just had another hallucination like the hole in the back of his hand. Afraid the hand hallucination might recur in front of his fans, he'd worn white silk gloves to match his suit.

He scribbled his signature across the blank white space beside the octopus and returned the fanzine to its owner.

"Thanks." The tattooed barbarian's expression, as he examined the signature, might have been that of an archaeologist discovering another Dead Sea scroll. Despite the jolt he'd just experienced, Izzy was pleased with the appreciation.

"Me too."

A second teenager, carrying an identical stack of fanzines and holding one out for him to sign, materialized on his left. The groomed hair, clear skin, and even pearly whites gave the kid that all-American look; the faded cords and the green-and-gold high-school sweater with the capital *F* on the back—presumably for the name of the school—labeled him as "normal," which made him a minority at the Dreamacon. A second, similarly clean-cut high-schooler—this one chubby and bespectacled and also carrying an armload of fanzines— appeared behind the first.

Trying not to look at the logo, Izzy signed the fanzines, then glanced at the chubby kid's copy before returning it. Near the upper left-hand corner was printed "No. 3" in a double circle. Below the title, he read: "Editors: Jamie Kern and Todd Anderson." And below that: "Artwork: Jose Cintron." Inside were three rather grisly cartoons: one with a beheaded corpse telling a hooded executioner, "You missed me," the others uncaptioned illustrations for stories. The drawings were done in a funky, graffiti style, the lines thick and sinuous, a style probably developed decorating his desk and the backs of test papers.

"Who's the artist?" Izzy asked.

"Me," the long-haired youth said.

Izzy turned to compliment him on his drawings, but his gaze was drawn to the skull face on his chest.

Had the eyes moved?

But, no, the flaming slits had no pupils; they would have appeared to follow him no matter where he stood.

"Something wrong?" The barbarian was looking down at his chest.

"No. Just admiring your tattoo."

"It's not a tattoo," the chubby kid said. "It's a decal."

"And the ones on your arms?"

"Decals," the barbarian said. "That's me: Decal, Deek for short. Pleased to meet you." He pumped Izzy's hand enthusiastically. "Tattoos're painful! And you get bored looking at the same pictures all the time. With decals you get a change of scenery whenever you want.

"That's Todd and that's the one and only Jamie Kern," the decaled warrior pointed first at the thin kid and then at the heavier one.

"Here comes the stiff," Jamie said.

Izzy looked and saw a gangling, dusty-haired youth approaching, carrying two pint containers of beer. A head taller than most of the crowd, the teenager was grinning, having already spotted his friends.

Deek hailed him. "You find the can, man?"

"Does an elephant have an A-hole?" the "stiff" said, and then did a double take when he saw Isidor Stark. His grin faltered only for a moment, then came back broader than ever.

"Fred here's our critic," Todd said, accepting one of the brews. "He can't draw or write, but his momma taught him how to read." And then to Fred, "We were talking about *Tentacle*."

"Good read, man!" Fred's grin stretched even wider when he looked at Deek. "But the artwork sucks."

Deek's dark eyes flashed under his black bangs. This was a sport he obviously enjoyed. He sniffed the air, wrinkled his nose. "Didn't your momma teach you to wipe your hole before you pull up your drawers?"

Fred elbowed Deek in the tit, making the skull on his chest wince; then, before Deek could hit back, he passed him a beer. "Crotch rot."

"Sperm Lips." Deek took the beer.

Jamie tucked his fanzines under his arm, produced a notebook and pen and asked, "Is there anything you'd like to say to your fans? We can print it in the next edition."

"It would boost our circulation," Todd said.

"Yeah," Izzy said remembering his encounter with the bus. "Tell them that only by facing the certainty of your own death does everything else fall into perspective."

"Great! Thanks." Jamie jotted.

"A present." Deek handed him a copy of *Tentacle*.

"Thank you. Good—"

He started to wish them luck but something was tickling his arm and he looked down and saw the plump black-and-yellow spider crawling up his arm.

He blinked, wished the hallucination away, but when he opened his eyes, it was still there.

It's real!

He slapped his arm.

But it was gone.

"Why don't you look at your hand?" a voice said.

Startled, Izzy looked to see who had spoken, but though a crowd had gathered around them, he saw no one who appeared to have addressed him.

He glanced at his hand. The back of the glove had a big red splotch on it.

His gaze jumps to Deek, to Todd . . .

Their faces are missing! Eyes, noses, mouth—gone! Instead, ovals of gleaming chrome molded to suggest human features occupy the front of their heads. The hair and flesh surrounding the ovals appear normal and there is no seam where chrome meets flesh. The mirrored surfaces reflect his own distorted features.

And now he realizes the babble around him isn't only from people talking. He is hearing the crowd's thoughts too, like a submersed murmuring beneath the chattering and laughter. He can't make out what they're saying, but he feels the vibrations in his head and the freezing heat of their collective malice.

The crowd's smiles—a moment ago eager, worshiping, stoned, impatient, insipid—are grown ominous, sinister. Tension charges the air, an electricity, static crackling, as if at any moment the walls will buckle and split from the pressure of too much noise, too many crowding faces . . . The eyes that meet his are intense, draining him.

He sees now: it comes to him in a flash of insight. Yes, that's it! They're draining me! Sucking me dry! He feels his life force ebb before the crowd's thousand-eyed stare. He might as well be a hobbit standing paralyzed under a dragon's hypnotic gaze, sapped of will and strength, unable to move. White dots swirl before his vision. His brain buzzes and hums.

He opens his mouth to excuse himself, trying to appear normal, outwardly cool, trying to keep his mind off his fear, to keep the crowd from seeing his confusion; but the skull on Deek's chest is grinning at him, eyes flaming, evil jack-o'-lantern crescents, leering at him. And as he stares, the smooth hairless flesh on Deek's chest moves, skin and muscle rising from the rib cage, pushes outward, as if the skull is growing from his chest. The skull-face bulges, expands, then suddenly shoves forward, straining the vest's rawhide thongs.

And then the mouth opens and a flap of intestine wags like an obscene tongue as it speaks, "You're meat, mutha-fucka!"

Izzy backs away, shocked, closes his mouth to prevent the scream from spilling out. Then he's pushing through the crowd. The air is stifling, the hall desert bright.

Quent materializes. There is no malice in his eyes, only concern.

Izzy mouths something like "Wait here, back in a minute," moves on.

He is more than halfway to the elevators when he crashes into a kid with bad teeth and a green Mohawk and they both go down.

Gooseflesh pops out all over his body, a cold hand grips his heart. He stares, not at the Mohawk-haired face of the kid, but at the head of a predatory fish.

Piranha! his thought whispers.

Yes, piranha. The mouthful of crooked teeth has translated into the serrated, carnivorous grin of the man-eater, the bottom teeth lengthening, jutting dagger-like from the lower jaw. The pale-green Mohawk above the sloped forehead has metamorphosed into a fish's fin, the dark-green shades into bugging fish eyes.

Hot blood pounds in his ears. He blinks. The vision remains. The mouth opens.

He is running, pushing through the crowd. Startled faces turn to follow. Then he's out of the thick of it, sprinting for the elevators, zigzagging around fans. He feels their gaze . . . draining him . . .

A small excited voice deep within tells him to stop running. He's had a hallucination, a flashback. He's being paranoid. His feet aren't listening.

Elevators appear, banks of numbers blinking on stainless-steel plaques above the doors. He stabs the up button.

Their gaze . . . draining . . .

An elevator arrives. He jumps in, jabs the button marked 14. The doors take an interminably long time to close. Fans standing before the elevators stop chatting to stare at him. Their faces darken. Crooked teeth grow over their bottom lips.

Stop it!

His vision dances, dims, brightens. He jabs the 14 again, tries to smile as if nothing's wrong. The doors whisper shut and he rides up the two floors to where he and Helen have their suite.

The elevator stops. The doors open. Two punked-out, bleached-blond, leather-jacketed space cadets block his exit.

Oh my God! He feels sapped. They're not going to let me out! They're going to get in and make me ride back downstairs where the crowd's waiting!

He pushes his way between them as they enter.

He turns a corner. His suite is on the left. Cursing the gloves that encumber his fingers, he fumbles for his key, feels the oval Lucite tab with the gold 1405 on it, pulls it out as he steps up to the door . . . and freezes!

The keyhole is bleeding!

He watches in fascinated horror. Red liquid trickles from the tiny slot, streams down the door, pools on the carpet.

Suddenly blood spurts from the keyhole, spatters the front of his white suit, his patent leather shoes. He backs away. More blood spreads from underneath the door, oozes from the top and from the seam between door and jamb.

He's running, hysteria pushing up his throat. He wipes at the blood on the front of his suit. A red stairwell door appears on his right. Quent will help me. He takes the stairs, his footsteps echoing off the tiled walls.

He bursts onto Twelve. Heads turn, follow his progress. Eyes burn cigarette holes into the back of his head. The blood reek from his suit permeates the corridor. Looking down, he sees his clothes, his gloves soaked red and dripping.

Across the hall is the entrance to an exhibit. He hurries through, avoiding eyes, not running because he doesn't want to attract attention.

Attract attention! That's a laugh! The convention's guest of honor, dripping blood!

He finds himself in the Hall of Dreamies, where scenes from his creations have been translated into giant floor-to-ceiling 3-D displays. A maze of startling alien worlds, worlds so shockingly vivid, so surprisingly detailed, it seems as if one might step into them and disappear off the face of the earth.

His fans' eyes are on him. He feels the heat of their gaze. The thousand-tongued voice of the throng maintains a continuous stream of babble around him, compounding his confusion and relentless fear. Faces blur by. He tries not to look, but sees the same conspiratorial smirk on face after face as the crowd parts. Paranoia battens vampiric fangs into his heart, leeches his life force. His vision swims, his legs about to give way.

He passes through what seems a veil ... and the crowd is gone. Flames lick the murky night sky.

Before him appears a narrow cobbled road, along which, on either side, roasting bodies writhe on crosses like the grotesque fruit of otherwise barren trees. Blackening tongues moan, whisper, insinuate his guilt. The lick of flame adds its own hideous voice to the cacophony. Beyond the crosses, a landscape of smoky darkness.

He claps his hands over his ears and flees down the cobbled road between the crosses. The garish torchlight dances greasily over the cobblestones. The stench of burning flesh chokes him. Then he is past the flaming bodies, bursting back into the light of the convention hall. Abruptly, the moans and rattling whispers of burning apparitions give way to the babble of the Dreamacon crowd.

He stops. A giant bars his way, nearly eight feet tall and glaring down at him with eyes that are a searing electric blue. He falls to his knees, helpless, uncomprehending. How can such an impossibility be?

He feels himself lifted by both arms ... Fear squeezes his heart. He is being lifted onto a wooden cross, bound, splashed with gasoline, set afire ...

Helen and Quent ... helping him to his feet, asking if he is all right. But he isn't listening: he is staring at the giant whose terrible gaze had driven him to his knees—the giant holographic statue of himself!

He looks back, sees that what he took for flaming bodies writhing on crosses are only the flame trees of desolate Phing, which, though not in Lovecraft's original, he'd added to *Dreamquest* for good measure.

Helen asks if he would like to lie down. He remembers the blood, looks down at his clothes expecting to see them drenched. Except for the smudges on his pants where he fell to his knees, his clothes are as white as when he'd put them on that morning.

I've been hallucinating! he tells himself, feeling relief and amazement. The blood, the crosses, the giant—all part of a bad trip.

Had it all been a drug-induced schizophrenic episode? Or had taraxein opened his metaphysical eye?

All around, fans were staring. Was there any mistaking the cold-blooded hatred directed at him? Could there be any doubt of the malevolence radiating from the crowd like energy waves? Was it possible to mask the sadistic rapture in their grinning lips, their smirking eyes?

He jammed his hands into his pockets, hoped the enemy wouldn't notice how badly they were shaking.

12

Helen sighed as she looked at the unfinished watercolor on the easel in front of the bay window. Earlier, she had tried to capture the ambience of the golden sunset light on the yellowing leaves of the peach trees. Sunset, with its piled cumulus clouds and rose-gold rays setting the autumnal leaves and the underbellies of clouds ablaze, had been baroque, more Titian than Turner. She had failed.

Actually, the painting hadn't looked half-bad with the sun's dying rays to illuminate it. Now, shadows collected on the canvas, the leaves seemed dull, lightless, more mustard yellow than the red-gold that had burned along the branches.

She reached out and stroked a variegated frond of the spider plant beside her and wondered: Is Izzy doing drugs?

Following his "publicity stunt," as he'd called his bizarre actions the previous evening, she had wondered if someone had slipped a hallucinogen into Izzy's soft drink. She remembered how his face used to look when he experimented with mescaline working up imagery for *Dreamquest*. Only last night his eyes were wild, frightened, as if he'd had a bad trip.

It wasn't until today that she had suspected he might be taking drugs on his own.

At breakfast he was talkative and hungry. He kept saying how good it was to be getting back to it and how he felt guilty not working over the weekend with his Halloween concert less than a week away. He wolfed down six slices of French toast smothered in syrup, two bananas, and a cup of coffee, kissed her neck and disappeared into the basement.

By contrast, he was quiet at lunch, picked at his food (she made tacos, one of his favorites), mumbled, not convincingly, "Okay," when she asked how the work was progressing. She tried to tell him about the pregnant woman who was due to give birth in space. Doctors explained on the morning news what dangers the fetus faced. She stopped when she saw he wasn't listening. As if he mistook her pause for the end of conversation, he smiled, said, "That's interesting," and disappeared into the basement.

She wished they could be off somewhere alone, just the two of them—no dreamatron, no concerts, no fans—for a while at least.

Vacation is the farthest thing from Izzy's mind as he chews three hits of the red-brown blotter. A minute or two later, he feels them kick in. The universe tilts. Sounds augment, echo, become discrete. The air in the darkened basement is spangled with a gossamer radiance that he can't see directly but shimmers in his peripheral vision. Objects—the bull's-eye, the sofa, the TV screen, his machine—are outlined with a ghostly radiance at once eerie and beautiful. The knots that have twisted his stomach all day loosen, relax, are gone. Gone, too, are the plaguing doubts, replaced by serenity and confidence.

He gazes at the photograph taped to his dreamatron just below the red blinking light. The photograph Quent took after the contest last night. There are five faces in the snapshot: the four fans—the tattooed barbarian and his vampire friends—and himself.

Which one? he asks himself.

He closes his eyes.

Eenie meenie miny moe!

He touches the photo, opens his eyes. He smiles. Ah, the perfect choice!

Todd had less than thirty seconds to find and turn off the alarm in the dark—or it was all over.

He'd let himself in with the key Jamie gave him. They'd passed by the front of the house and, except for the porch, all the lights were off. He banged his knee smartly on something. The clatter of a wooden milk crate falling over on the cement floor startled him. He listened, but it was hard to hear anything over his heartbeat.

The switch wasn't inside the access door where most people would have put it; it was on the side of one of the beams that supported the ladder to the loft, invisible from the door, even for someone with a flashlight. His hand slapped the switch first shot, clicked it off.

Turning, he bumped into Donna. She had followed him into the garage.

She giggled.

"Shhh."

She was a shadow, a vague, velvety shape that he saw more with his imagination than with his eyes, having spent a lot of time lately studying her proportions. He could smell her in the dark, her nearness. His heart thumped.

He put her hand on the ladder. "After you."

She giggled, started up.

He had a hard-on already, but when he reached out to help her and encountered her round bottom, exquisite flesh warm through her cotton skirt, he thought he would burst his zipper.

Deek was making a delivery, his Kawasaki winding in third down the long flat stretch of Grand Street that led to the hill that led up to the junction. Up there where Grand intersected with Communipaw were stores, houses, bars, a black discotheque, the Board of Education, and Lincoln High School. There he would, no doubt, run into noise and people and maybe a little traffic. But down here the nightscape was desolate. Whole blocks had been bulldozed for redevelopment. On a couple of the blocks stood the skeletal frames of new housing units; the remainder contained only the rubble of bulldozed bars and tenements. The area's rebirth was more than a decade behind that of the Montgomery Gateway Project to the north. Which was why he'd chosen Grand and Communipaw to get him crosstown instead of Montgomery—more lights and people on Montgomery . . . more cops.

The two ounces of sense he was delivering to a rich fart who lived in a big house over by Lincoln Park were tucked snugly inside his motorcycle boots. Three hundred for the ounce, another twenty for delivering . . . call it three and a quarter. Dude wouldn't bat an eye; he had money coming out the wazoo.

The whine of his engine carried eerily over the vacant blocks. He ran the red light at Johnson Avenue and was starting up the hill when he heard the thunder of approaching Harleys. He saw them from a distance, descending the hill in the opposite lane. He downshifted to second, wanting to take his time watching them approach and pass, possessed by the thrill and admiration and envy he always felt around a class-act hog. Then they were passing under a streetlight in front of the lumber yard and he saw their faces!

He hit his brakes, revved the throttle when he almost killed the engine from stopping too fast. Even though they were tiny with distance—they were still a couple blocks away and cruising—he made out the moon-pale skull faces beneath the gleaming helmets. It occurred to him even as he was spinning his bike around that they were wearing masks, but his sixth sense, his trouble detector, was telling him he might be better off taking a detour.

"Are you fucking kidding!" he screamed as an old lady peckerhead in a monstrous antique Buick—royal blue, white sidewalls, chrome bumper—ran a red light and sailed into the intersection.

He downshifted again, swerved to cut behind the car, and prayed the old fart didn't decide to test her brakes. He just made it around the big bumper, but his bike started going down and he skipped along on one boot trying not to go over on his face. He didn't, but the bike stalled.

He opened his mouth to curse the woman, but she looked back and he saw her face—or what was left of it. She had half a grin and one leering, bloodshot eye. The rest of her face looked as if it had been blown away by a shotgun blast.

I'm dreaming.

The Harleys' thunder blasted the night. They had sped up. Less than two blocks away, lamplight fell on chains and cycle chrome and gleaming Nazi helmets and bleached skulls that contrasted sharply with the blackness of eyeholes. The faces weren't masks . . .

He yanked the bike up, kicked the starter, and revved the throttle. Too much: it sputtered and stalled.

★

She was hot, so hot . . . She's boiling inside, Todd thought. So was he. There was a little light coming from the skylight and he could just make out her closed eyes, her parted lips, her heavy boobs rising and falling as she rode him, her plump thighs straddling his, her ankles hooked under his calves.

"Mmmm . . . so good!" she cooed.

Backlit by the skylight, her voluptuous shape presented a mind-boggling picture to his neophyte mind. Mesmerized, he watched her rise and fall, impaling herself on him.

He was having difficulty holding back, making it last. His cock underwent a minor spasm, quivering on the brink of orgasm.

"Stop!" she suddenly ordered in a loud whisper.

Stop? Now? He was boiling. His cock jerked, and too far gone to realize what he was doing, he rolled over on top, one hand behind her back, the other cradling one glorious buttock, and moaned as he spurted into her.

It took him a moment to realize she was trying to shove him off her.

"I said 'stop!' "

"Sorry," he said, confused, wondering what he'd done wrong.

"Get off. I lost a contact."

"What? Jeez!" He pulled out, reluctant to leave, his penis still throbbing with pleasure.

"I lost my contact," she repeated.

"Shit!" The chances of their finding a contact lens in the dark were phenomenally poor. If it made it to the floor it might even have fallen downstairs through a crack in the boards. He didn't mention the possibility to Donna, she was making enough fuss already.

Todd froze. Beneath him, he felt Donna tense. Thankfully, she kept silent.

Downstairs, a door had opened. It sounded like the door to the backyard, though he couldn't be sure.

The door closed.

Holding his breath, listening, he gripped Donna tightly, as if telepathically urging her to be silent. He didn't have to, though; she was still as stone.

Footsteps below . . . a shoe grated on concrete. A light beam stabbed through the cracks in the floor. Holy crap! Whoever it was had a flashlight! He became painfully aware of his nudity. The cot was all the way to the other end of the loft from the trapdoor. Maybe, if they stayed quiet, they wouldn't be noticed.

Footsteps on the ladder.

Donna's ripe body was no longer enticing as he devoutly wished they were both clothed. He pulled the rough army blanket over them as the trapdoor opened.

A light beam stabbed around, passed over them. Then it swung back and blinded Todd as he peered over the edge of the blanket.

He kicked it again, this time taking it easier on the throttle. The engine revved. He kicked it into second, popped a whining wheelie before he slammed it down and toed it into third.

The phantom riders were less than half a block away and closing. Their thunder shook the broad deserted street. He wanted to run flat out, but Grand Street was full of potholes. He hadn't noticed them so much in the other lane, but he was riding faster now and the potholes came up so often they seemed to be everywhere.

He came up fast on a big one. No time to swerve . . . He stood, knees bent, accelerated, yanked the front of the bike up and jumped, taking the bike with him. The rear tire cleared the crater and then some, both tires making contact with the asphalt and sprinting away. Fourth gear, fifth, zigzagging left and right around the holes. His concentration was intense, but he forced his body to stay loose, to flow with the bike. Blow your cool and you're a goner, man. He didn't know if he was dreaming, but he didn't want to stop and find out he was awake.

Back among houses now. The rubbled blocks gave way to brownstones, churches, trees. He risked a glance over his shoulder. In that blink his mind freeze-framed a tableau from hell: skeletal faces, some wearing mirrored shades, others staring hungrily back at him out of gaping sockets; chains spinning in the air, machetes hammers crowbars flashing.

He hooked a left onto Washington, leaned into the turn,

hardly slowing. His boot heel scraped asphalt. He hoped his pursuers couldn't make the turn as fast because of their heavier bikes. He glanced back as he shot past the old Bee Hive bank. To his surprise they were less than a half-dozen car lengths behind.

He hooked a right by the old post office atop its templed stairs, cut down the narrow, cobbled street that led to the docks where there were people and cars.

A spectral rider pulled alongside him and lashed out with a chain. Pain slammed up his left arm. He held on, the Kawasaki fishtailing on the cobblestones as he swerved away. He leaned forward, gave the bike full throttle as he hurtled suicidally ahead.

He shot onto the block-long wharf, a wide cobblestoned area lined with cars parked nose-in to the low sea wall. Half a dozen soundless radio stations attacked his brain at once. People scattered. Curses were hurled after him in Spanish. His phantom pursuers would slow down on the cobblestones ... he hoped.

An exit a block ahead looped back onto the streets. Dream or no dream, he intended to lose these suckers.

He downshifted, hit the brakes. A car chose that moment to back out in front of him. He swerved left, hoping the driver would be bright enough to back up far enough for him to get past in front of him. The driver wasn't. The car stopped and he looked right into the driver's wide eyes—a Hispanic youth about his own age—before he slammed into the red Chevy.

He was off the bike, sailing over the car, turning slowly in the air till he was facing a hazy night sky and dropping. He hit the top of the low sea wall, heard a loud *crack*. Awesome pain slammed through his back. He bounced off the wall, hit the cold dark waters of the Hudson.

He sank, came up sputtering. His left side was numb, his arm and leg wouldn't move. That side of his face felt dead. He was so frightened he felt like crying. He glanced at the row of faces on the sea wall. Surely someone would help him.

"Help!" He was drifting away from the wall, the current pulling him downriver.

They pointed and jabbered. Nobody jumped in.

"Help!" It was awkward keeping his head above surface, splashing around with one arm and one leg, his left side deadweight, pulling him down.

He heard a sullen splash behind him in the water. He had drifted too far for the sound to be the river slapping against the sea wall. Tiring, unable to do more than keep his head out of the water, he strained his hearing . . . Was someone coming to get him?

He heard the sound again: *splash . . . splash . . .* Something moving toward him in the water. He squinted into the darkness, but it was impossible to see. Fog wisped over the black water. He could no longer see the sea wall. In the harbor, a boat sounded its horn.

Again the sound, nearer, something slipping sluggishly through the water.

Then he saw the pulpy, waterlogged, decomposing face just under the surface an arm's length away.

His still-mobile right arm and leg went into overdrive trying to backpedal as he stared into the thing's dead eyes, at the same time thinking, Thank God, recognizing a face out of his favorite dreamie, *Floaters.*

I *am* dreaming!

Hands grabbed his vest. Another floater surfaced behind him. Teeth sank into his bare arm. It didn't hurt, though: it was his left, paralyzed arm.

A cheesy full-moon face floated into his blackening vision. He tried to punch it, but his arms were useless. The floater drifted closer, nuzzled its head under his vest, and sank its teeth into his abdomen, tearing away a big patch of flesh, then boring in again.

When he felt the cold river water pour into his belly, he lost his cool and sobbed.

Todd shielded his eyes against the beam. Then, as the light moved onto Donna, he saw the dim form that protruded through the open trapdoor, flashlight in one hand and what looked like Jamie's air pistol in the other. As the beam fell on Donna's face, he saw Jamie's mouth open in surprise and anger.

The flashlight clicked off and Jamie stormed noisily down the ladder.

The face forming on the pod underwent a sudden transformation.

Jason blinked. No, it wasn't a trick of his eyes. The face that had been twinning that of the woman who had fallen asleep was suddenly that of a corpse, bloated and too badly decomposed to tell if it was male or female. The visual image was so powerful, so repelling, he tasted vomit. He could smell the putrescence.

The movie was *Invasion of the Body Snatchers,* the original 1956 black-and-white version, and he knew damn well it didn't contain any scene like this!

The setting, too, had changed. Instead of a backyard garden, the TV showed a murky, black-and-white underwater scene. Now there were other bloated corpse faces in the water. They seemed to be clinging tooth and nail to a live boy. The kid was thrashing. A rotting cadaver's teeth gripped his throat. Horror distorted the boy's features. His eyes bulged. His mouth stretched in a silent scream . . .

Then the movie was playing again, the protagonist trying to wake up the sleeping woman, the woman waking up . . . changed.

13

Again, he finds himself dog-paddling in the black river water, cold, the current brisk, carrying him downriver toward the harbor. Only, instead of the ghostly, moon-pale fog, black smoke billows around him, blanketing the river and obscuring the stars. And in the blackness, red fires flicker, as if skyscrapers are burning. Or is it flaming crosses he sees through the smoke? Yes, vertical and horizontal intersecting lines . . . crucifixes rising from the water . . .

And voices—sibilant, leaf-dry voices whisper-slurring his name as if speaking through crisping lips.

He drifts closer. The crosses are empty, blackening beams behind crackling red veils. Still, the river reeks of charring flesh. And still the voices, accusing him, cursing him . . .

A worm of fear crawls through his intestines. The water is cold, but not as cold as the fear spreading through his body. Paddling softly, he tries not to splash, afraid the floaters of Frank Price's dreams will hear and come.

They'll come anyway, he thinks, it's inevitable. I wrote the script myself!

Up to his mouth in oily water, he decides that knowing the ending of this dream sucks. In spades!

A familiar sullen splash. Behind him . . .

He spins around, splashing noisily. He is sweating despite the cold. A dark shape floats in the water. Like a bundle of rags . . . He had made his audience think that by subliminally letting them see rags for a second, and so he thinks of it now. But he knows differently.

Other dark shapes on his left and right, another splash behind him. He is surrounded. He closes his eyes. He feels a hand on his leg, then teeth. As numb as the river water has made him, he feels those teeth sink into him. He doesn't feel pain, only a shocking sensation of intense cold, as if the river were warm compared to those teeth.

Hands close on his arms, his legs, pulling him down. Strong dead hands.

Panicking, he opens his eyes and sees the face of the thing ripping flesh from his arm with its teeth. The face is charred, peeling, hairless; blisters have formed on blisters; the eyes have burst open, boiled out of their sockets. The face seems familiar, but is burned beyond recognition. He screams and the river pours into his mouth.

As they bite and tear, the river runs red.

Dr. Casper Nösberger stood in his laboratory in front of the open door of the refrigerator. The taraxein was gone—all 250 hits.

Shouldn't have made the drug look so much like acid. Too many students willing to try anything to get high.

But staring at the empty space on the plastic shelf, he felt in his guts it hadn't been a student who'd removed the drug. The thief knew exactly what he was stealing.

An image came to him: Stark's face, contorted with anger when he told him the experiments were off. And on the heels of that, another image—the mangled, blood-crimsoned corpse of a Hispanic youth scattered about a concrete pier.

He rose, went around the desk, and fished in the top, right-hand drawer for the blue-and-white Date Log, compliments of Blue Cross, and turned to the inside front cover where he had jotted down Stark's address and phone number. He picked up the phone and placed the call.

Izzy opened the drawer.

Cut it out!

He closed the drawer again—the small, shallow drawer in the bottom right-hand side of the dreamatron under the dreamports. Was the stuff addictive? It certainly seemed like it. He'd done a lot of pacing in the hour since he'd finished his lunch of cereal and milk and came down to the basement. It was like a hankering for a bite of the hair of the dog that bit him. He was salivating—a moment ago his mouth had been dry—and his palms were sweaty and itchy.

Funniest thing. He grimaced as he scratched his palms through the silk gloves. Taraxein was heavy-duty stuff. Knock the socks off a sperm whale. Or maybe just off a dreamer . . . He considered the possibility that the differences in his brain chemistry might interact with the taraxein differently than it would with the brain chemistry of a normal.

Izzy touched the snapshot taped to the console of his machine. Satan's Fifth. He smiled. To think that he had actually believed he could just pick one of the kids on this photo and sic a monster on him and it would happen. That was crazy! He shook his head, his mouth a grin of disbelief. Yeah, just as crazy as his other delusion: that his fans were out to do him in. Pure raving lunacy!

But Saturday night and yesterday he had believed it, had believed all of it just as surely as he believed he was in New Jersey in America on the Planet Earth. He had felt almost godlike. At times it seemed he towered over people who came up to him. He hadn't slept much since the Dreamacon, he realized. That probably had a lot to do with his susceptibility to the altered perceptions the taraxein evoked.

He opened the utility drawer again. This time he pulled out and opened the zip-lock bag containing the stolen blotter. That much was real—he *had* stolen the taraxein. He must have been off his rocker. For someone who liked to keep a low profile, that was a pretty wild thing to do. He could see the headlines:

JEKYLL/HYDE SUPERSTAR STEALS DRUGS FROM COLLEGE

or worse:

KING OF GRUE EATS BLOOD OF SCHIZOPHRENICS

He snickered, shut up immediately, frightened, feeling the sudden wild pendulum swing over the line into insanity. The fright sobered him, shook him, made him look squarely at what had just happened.

Holy shit! As easy as that! He'd been rambling along, not looking out, and he'd slipped very quietly into the twilight zone. He put the taraxein away. Staring at the drawer, he saw it as if in cutaway view, the inside writhing with snakes.

I am addicted, he thought, running a gloved and trembling hand over his forehead. He was perspiring. He suddenly felt tremendously hot and agitated. He got up, paced. He turned on a radio station, current stuff, loud, repetitious; he wouldn't have liked it if he were listening—he wasn't.

He was losing control, skidding blindly back and forth over the dotted line that divided the lanes of sanity and madness. Yet even his saner side felt driven to pursue his experiments. The sensual texturing of the taraxein-influenced dreamies, the bizarre emotional and perceptual distortions, were, artistically, a gold mine. A dreamie that put the audience inside the mind of a schizophrenic . . .

He remembered something, stopped, looked at his hands. At least his delusions that his fans were out to get him and that he had the power to kill with a dreamie came and went, but his hand hallucination (and he knew it was a hallucination because when he washed his hands last night with his eyes closed so as not to look at the horror, he felt flesh, whole and solid) had persisted since Saturday.

He shook his head at the complexity and persistence of his delusions and hallucinations—not to mention his dreams! He realized he should have been keeping a notebook all along chronicling his experiences, but he wasn't one for writing. Besides, he had kept another, much better, kind of diary. Strolling over to his machine, he again looked at the small drawer, seeing it differently this time; besides the taraxein, it contained the bubblepak he had recorded his two experiments on.

He paced the shuffleboard. Something had happened the night of their first experiment, something unexplained and unintended. Something that smacked of the supernatural, if you were superstitious or got a rush off such things. Or of the paranormal, if you were more scientifically inclined, which he was. His theory that he had picked up the killer's thoughts and recorded what the killer had seen and heard still seemed more plausible than the alternative—that he had caused the guy's death. His own theory implied some sort of telepathy, and that in itself seemed ample reason to pursue his experiments.

But then the memory of the giant birdlike claw print outside his basement window loomed up like a specter and dashed his careful reasoning. He stopped at the end of the shuffleboard lane and sat at the bottom of the steps and rubbed his forehead.

He couldn't think. He was grateful he'd slept late. It was the most sleep he'd had in days. Still, being faced with a puzzle, an enigma his mind couldn't encompass, made his head ache.

"Time for a tour," he said, stretching. "Burn off some steam on stage."

He looked around. Man, he was getting sick of seeing these four walls. Though he generally hated to travel, he itched to get moving. Saturday night's show was to be a prelude. The real kickoff was going to happen in Motor City at the Convention Center, followed by Chicago, Los Angeles, Atlanta, Miami, and points between. His fame having recently spread beyond the U.S., he was also booked to play Tokyo, Sydney, Amsterdam, and London. He was taking Helen along. She'd always wanted to see the Opera House in Sydney.

Upstairs in the kitchen, the phone rang.

Rang again.

Helen had left a note saying she was going shopping with Mrs. Carruthers. He bounded up the steps, glad for someone to talk to, anything to get his mind off the taraxein.

It was Nösberger. His tone was cold, deliberate.

"I know you took my stock of taraxein."

"What?" Izzy said, surprised at the bluntness of Nösberger's accusation and offended even though the accusation was true.

"I understand the compulsion to pursue a line of investigation, but—"

"Professor—"

"—you've gone too far."

"Professor, what on earth are you talking about?"

"Look, Stark. I didn't call to play games."

"No? What did you call for?"

"To give you a chance."

"A chance?"

"Yes. And, frankly, I'm hoping you'll take it." Izzy didn't respond. Nösberger went on. "I want you to return what's left of the taraxein."

"Doctor, I—" Izzy wasn't used to lying; his palms were sweating through his gloves. A vein throbbed in his temple.

"Look!" Nösberger said when Izzy didn't continue. "I'll give you until ten tomorrow morning to return that taraxein to my lab."

"Or what? Assuming I had the contraband. You'll go to the police?"

"Yes. I will. And I caution you not to ingest any more of the drug. I've been giving thought to something we hadn't investigated."

Izzy grew attentive.

"You're a born dreamer, and as I'm sure you know, according to recent theory, a dreamer's brain chemistry is different than the average Joe's. The point is you might react differently. Maybe hurt somebody . . . or hurt yourself."

"Look, Doctor. You saw me on taraxein. Did I react any differently than any other subject you've worked with?"

"Well, no, but—"

"I have to go."

"Wait! Was there any instance of schizophrenia in your family?"

Izzy hung up.

14

That afternoon, Quent ran an errand for Izzy.

Following the costume contest Saturday evening, Izzy had looked up some fans he'd been talking with before deciding to pull his "publicity stunt" and had gotten Quent to take a Polaroid of himself with them. For reasons unknown to Quent at the time, Izzy had requested directions to the clubhouse they mentioned.

Entering the alley, Quent found the two dangling wires Todd told them about and touched their exposed ends together. A bell clamored loudly on the other side of the loft door above him. While he waited, he read the graffiti on the two-story clapboard garage; prominent among them were two legends: SATAN'S FIFTH in blood-red Gothic letters and DON'T FUCK WITH MY GARAGE, along with a black skull and crossbones with a snake around the neck and a slim dagger protruding from an eye socket.

Something else adorned the ancient, unpainted façade, something hung by a twist of wire on the loft door overhead. A black wreath. Had there been a death in Jamie's family? Quent wondered as bolts were thrown inside. He prepared to extend his condolences and offer to come back at a more appropriate time as a small access door swung inward, opening onto cool darkness.

"Hi! Come on in!"

Quent made out an indistinct shape that looked familiar; though the door was too low to see all of the face, the voice belonged to the tall fan named Fred.

Fred pointed to a square of light in the ceiling. A ladder of boards nailed across the studs led up to the open trapdoor. "Yo! It's okay!" he shouted up through the hole. "Just the East Precinct . . ." Fred's voice trailed off, as if his heart wasn't in the wisecrack. He sounded sad. Quent remembered the wreath.

Todd's intelligent face smiled down at him from the open trapdoor when Quent looked up. Todd turned and spoke to someone behind him. "It's that writer guy who took our picture with Stark."

Todd helped him through and shook his hand. It was lighter up here: a big plastic bubble skylight and a window onto the yard let in more sunlight than Quent remembered there being outside. Eight colorful fantasy posters, ranging from the grotesque to the sensual to the violent—including two Stark posters: a *Dreamquest* and a *Floaters*—lined the long side walls. Hubcaps adorned the spaces between the posters. The posters and hubcaps lent a medieval-hall effect to the loft, like banners interspaced with shields.

Jamie stood beside a scarred desk on which sat a small electric typewriter and behind which hung a bulletin board plumaged with papers in a variety of colors and sizes. Jamie's "Hello" sounded hollow, and as the teenager walked toward him, Quent saw that, despite the vague smile that had been added for politeness's sake, the young writer's expression was glum.

Death has been here, he thought. Mother? Father? Brother? "If I came at a bad time . . ." he said, offering his hand to Jamie.

"No, that's all right. Glad to see you." Jamie managed a smile that looked sincere enough, but he was preoccupied.

"Here, you can have the seat of honor." Todd indicated the side of the sofa that didn't have a torn cushion; the sunken seat on the other side looked as if someone heavy had sat there many years. Quent sat. Todd plopped himself on an arm of the sofa and Jamie pulled his desk chair over.

Fred perched himself on a milk crate, his legs so long his knees came up to his ribs. Downstairs in the dark, Quent hadn't seen Fred's eyes, but as the kid leaned forward, resting his elbows on his knees, Quent thought he looked like someone who hadn't slept in days, though he had just seen him, *sans* bags under his eyes, the night before last.

"There's been a death?" Quent asked Jamie, feeling foolish and callous saying it like that, but knowing he would have felt even sillier trying to avoid the obvious.

Jamie nodded.

"Deek," Fred clarified. "The guy with the Conan haircut you met Saturday."

"I remember." Quent recalled the gross insults Fred and the deceased traded Saturday.

"He bought the farm last night." Fred's voice had a bitter edge to it. A line creased one long cheek, showing the tension in his face.

The news was shocking, as it always is when the young die. The barbarian had looked to be in best physical shape of the lot. He had been a living, eating, dreamie-loving fan two days ago. Now he was dead. "How'd it happen?"

"Motorcycle accident," Todd said. "He would have wanted to go that way . . . if he'd wanted to go. Which he didn't."

"Motorcycle accident, shit!" Fred cursed.

Quent saw tears close to the surface. Again he recalled their comic ribbing. Their friendship probably went back years. He felt sorry for Fred. For all of them. He'd copped a dime of sense in the city, thinking it'd be just the thing to break the ice. This looked like a good time to spark up.

"Here." He tossed the small manila envelope to Fred, who looked like he would know what to do with it.

"Heyyy! Wow, man! Damn! I been down the river and to the park and *nothing!* Dry City! You read my mind." He broke the tape, opened the envelope, and smelled the contents. "Ummm, sense. Check it out." He passed the bag to Todd, who also gave it the sniff test, like one savoring the bouquet of a vintage cognac before imbibing. Todd returned the bag to Fred, who said, "Got papers?"

"No." Quent had figured a bunch like this, one of them would have papers. He was right. Todd tossed a pack of Zig-Zags to Fred. Jamie produced a lighter. Fred rolled three bombs out of the dime and, after tossing one to Jamie, lit the other. He inhaled deeply before passing it to Quent.

"Here's to Deek," Fred rasped, trying to hold the smoke in and talk at the same time.

"Hear, hear," Jamie seconded.

Todd and Jamie blew one and he and Fred blew the other, and by the time the bones were down to roaches, the tension in the place, the heavy pall of gloom, had lightened.

Deek had died of drowning, he learned. The incident was bizarre. After Fred and Todd jointly told him the details as they knew them, Fred speculated on what might have caused old Deek, who, he learned, was an ace dirt biker, to lose control like that. "Something must've went wrong with his bike. Throttle got stuck open; maybe his brakes went out . . ."

"Witnesses said he never slowed down," Todd added.

"Weirdest fucking thing, man," Fred said. "He was all bit up."

"Who said?" Quent was taken by surprise.

"I do." Fred looked Quent in the eye. "I was there when they fished him out of the river this morning. If he had been on land, I would have guessed he was attacked by dogs. One cop said it looked like the crabs had gotten to him, but shit, crabs couldn't have done that. His leather was shredded. Horrible way to go, huh?"

Quent had to admit that it was.

"Remember the time Deek got so shit-faced—"

"Yeah, yeah," Todd cut in on Fred. "Pissed right in the open window of a parked squad car."

Even Jamie grinned at this one. "I remember." He explained to Quent, "Car was parked right in the police parking lot behind the Montgomery Street Precinct."

Fred hooted and slapped his leg. "Chucked the empty in too!"

By the time they roasted the third bone, the mood in the loft had mellowed. The talk turned from speculation on what caused the accident and the mysterious bite marks to Deek himself, the man of action and surprises. Deek—according to the tales pieced together, at first by Fred and Todd, and then by Jamie, who became more and more talkative after the third bone—had done everything from riding his bike through Dead Man's Tunnel—a bad place to be when the trains passed through because there wasn't enough clearance on the sides for a person to survive—to breaking his leg trying to ride a guy wire from a train trestle to a telephone pole hanging from a hook attached to a pulley. It seemed he'd climbed up on the trestle, attached the pulley to the steel cable, grabbed the hook, yelled "Geronimo," and jumped. Halfway, the pulley came to a stop. Having reached the bottom of the cable's sag, he couldn't go uphill, so he jumped and broke his leg in the weeds below. In twenty minutes, Deek had taken on the proportions of legend, and his friends, at least for the moment and without being aware of it, were seeing the positive side—not the fact that Deek was dead, but the fact that his life, however brief, had been full. He hadn't been rich, but he'd had a good time.

Quent took out the folded white envelope that had been sticking up from his pocket and removed four orange-and-black tickets.

It took them only a second to realize what they were staring at.

No one spoke for a moment. Todd and Fred, leaned toward him. Jamie rose and stood beside him. All of them stared at the tickets as if they were fabulous jewels. All with a hand outstretched as if wanting to hold the fabled tickets to see if they were real. Black letters printed on orange—Halloween colors. MYSTERY SHOW, Saturday, October 31, Midnight, Row G, Seats 4 through 7.

"Holy . . ." Fred said.

"Wow," Todd seconded.

Jamie's mouth opened, but he didn't speak.

"Compliments of Isidor Stark." He handed the tickets to Jamie, whose mouth dropped even more. "He said to give his regards to his fans."

"Thanks," Fred and Todd said.

Jamie pocketed one, passed one to Fred and another to Todd. "And this one . . ."

They all stared at the ticket remaining in Jamie's hand. Ol' Deek, hell-riding daredevil of Satan's Fifth, illustrator, graffiti artist, terror of the alleys, fan extraordinaire, had seen his last dreamie.

Quent answered the phone on the second ring. He had been home an hour, long enough to have a Hungry Man meatloaf TV dinner and catch the seven-o'clock news. The weatherman was predicting blustery fall weather for Tuesday when the phone rang. It was Izzy.

"Oh, by the way," Izzy said after a few minutes of small talk, in which Quent did most of the talking after being asked how the biography was coming, "did you deliver the tickets?"

"Sure," Quent said. "They appreciated them. But here's the thing."

"What?"

"Well, remember the kid with the Conan haircut and the tattoos?"

"Decals."

"Yeah, well, he died last night. Pretty strangely too . . ."

When he hung up, Izzy stood for a long time, his hand on the phone, frozen in thought. Terror and excitement vied for first place among his emotions. Excitement won out. It came bubbling up, exploding to the surface like bubbles from an underwater demolition.

I did it!

I did it I did it I did it!

WOW!

He went down into the basement and locked the door behind him. He wanted to be alone with his wonder.

15

The evening passed uneasily for Helen.

Izzy had followed her into the bedroom and started stroking her and kissing the back of her neck, letting her know he wanted to make love. He told her he loved her and there was no lie in that. Only, she knew that wasn't why he wanted to make love, nor was it simply because he was horny, though that certainly turned out to be true. Something was bothering him, something he wasn't ready to discuss, and once again she wondered if he was doing drugs.

He was agitated, hyper. His voice was a shade higher pitched than normal, the way it got when he was excited about a new idea or pleased with a scene he'd just finished. His pupils were neither dilated nor red, but there was a feverish luminosity to them, and a crooked smile—almost a smirk—kept creeping over his face.

Afterward, he went down to the kitchen for a snack. When she came down minutes later, wondering how to broach the subject of drugs without dampening his creative processes and, frankly, fearing the slow erosion of the intimacy they'd shared in the early days of their relationship, he'd already descended into the basement, presumably to work. In his work, Izzy deferred all problems.

And when, hours later, Helen fell asleep after one, losing her place as the paperback she was reading slipped from her fingers, Izzy was still in the basement.

Working.

Cynthia Dorson stirred from her dreams. She opened her eyes and looked about to see what had woken her. Casper had gotten out of bed. The door was opening. She saw his tall shape outlined in the doorway.

"Casper," she said softly.

The door closed.

Oh, well, she thought, probably hungry after all that good sex we had last night. She wriggled under the sheets, feeling a wetness stir between her thighs. Her nose was too pugged and her cheeks too chubby for her ever to be called beautiful, but Casper raved about her body.

Dear Casper. Such a nice man. He took her interesting places: plays, the Cloisters, the Poconos, a motel in Scranton.

She was twenty-one and had never had a steady boyfriend. Dr. Nösberger was the first person, her parents included, who got honestly excited over her. And that flattered her to the point where she could believe she was in love, even if he was eccentric. She giggled into her pillow, remembering Casper's habit of putting on his underwear before getting out of bed.

"Accidents will happen," he'd explained when she asked. "If you go about with your John Thomas dangling, sooner or later you're going to lose it."

Smiling contentedly, Cynthia drifted back to sleep, oblivious to what was happening to "dear Casper" even now.

The auditorium was vast, the ceiling indistinct, like looking up into a cover of fog; the wall behind the last and highest tier of seats gray metal curving off into a similarly indistinct distance. The audience all looked the same—each dressed in black pajamalike outfits like Vietcong, and the face of each was a shiny chrome mask, vaguely suggestive of human features.

The broad stage was empty. The audience watched it attentively, silently, with their cold reflective faces; somehow, their blind stare was more terrifying than if they had eyes.

Nösberger beheld the scene as if he were looking on from a vantage point somewhere above the phantasmal audience. His vantage suddenly shifted, and he found himself gazing out at row after row of gleaming chrome faces. Their stare was chilling. He was now an actor in the dream, vulnerable. The audience was rising; slowly, orderly, they began filling the aisles, moving toward the stage. His hackles rose as he realized they were coming for him. He quit the stage, ran out the exit door backstage. Behind him, the thunder of feet moving across the wooden stage, not running, but as if they wore iron shoes.

He found himself running past lockers and empty classrooms. The hall lights were out, but enough pre-dawn light fell through the classroom windows for him to make out the rows of desks, the blackboard, and he realized with a jolt, as he ran toward the back of the school, hearing thunderous steps coming out of the audi behind him, that he was in his old high-school *alma mater,* James J. Ferris.

As he ran, barefoot and naked, down a long hall, he tried to make sense of the images that assaulted him. He sped past rows of lockers. A room number caught his eye—202. His old homeroom! Images of roly-poly Miss Tuscatano, his senior-year homeroom teacher and junior-year algebra teacher; of Mark Stevens and Dave Bentwell and Alice Haley and Lonnie DeDomenico and four or five other jokers whose names escaped him in the rush of the moment.

But he had just come out of the audi, and that was on the first floor! He reminded himself that he was dreaming.

Behind him came the *clank clank clank* of iron footfalls. Maybe they're zombies, he thought. Maybe they're not smart enough to put two and two together.

Oh, shit! What if they don't see at all but are homing in on the noise I make. Or maybe they're robots equipped with heat sensors.

He passed the art room, with its tiled floor spattered with paint droplets, descended the stairs to get to G Building. In G Building, well ahead of the sound of trampling on the stairwell, he burst through the doors into the pool area . . . and stopped.

A pale, cheesy light fell through the skylight, gloomily illuminating the huge tiled space that included an Olympic-size pool and bleachers for events. Salt wind blew in his face, whipped his hair. The pool heaved, an unnatural tide rolling end to end, sloshing water up over the bleachers and walls, the water pouring back down into the pool like surf withdrawing into the ocean.

The door to the locker room was on the other side. To reach it, he had to go around the pool. As he ran, the pool turned red, the smell of seawater took on a sharp coppery tang. He staggered as a wave crashed over him. The blood-smell cloyed his nostrils. His stomach churned.

Sprinting past the No Running sign at the deep end, he glimpsed a monstrous shape beneath the boiling waters. A single lambent eye followed his progress. Tentacles broke the surface, whipped through the air with a sound like lashing cables. Suckers latched onto his flesh and his arm went numb with excruciating cold. He wrenched loose and dove through the door into the boys' locker room. A tremendous *crack!* exploded behind his head as a tentacle took out a row of tiles above the door.

The lights flickered and buzzed in the locker room. Rows of lockers lined either side of the varnished benches. He slowed, afraid, confused. This was like no dream he'd ever had—it was so real! Gone was that sense of being the watcher, coolly observing, consciously aware that it was just a dream, that there was no danger. There *was* danger! All around! The air was charged with it. His heart pounded with it. He was excruciatingly aware of how vulnerable he felt with his genitals exposed. God, for a pair of Jockey shorts!

He stopped. He was looking at a locker secured with a Masters combination lock with white markings. His old gym locker. He didn't see how he recognized it, for it wasn't at all the same. In the Ferris locker room, the lockers were half-size—his had been in the upper row—this was full-size, like the ones in the hall. Still, he recognized the lock, recognized the dent in one of the louvers.

Clank clank clank. Iron footfalls coming into the locker room from the pool area.

Clank clank clank. More footfalls coming in from the gymnasium side.

With his left hand, because his right was numb, he attacked the combination lock, spun the dial two times right to ... To what? He concentrated, tried to block out his jackhammering heart, the clanking steps. He bent close till the white digits came into focus ... He remembered! He spun the dial two times to the right to twenty-six, lined the white mark up with the red dot, spun it back past eight and all the way around to eight again, then right to nineteen. He yanked down on the lock.

Nothing happened.

Clank clank clank. The footfalls were closer, louder.

He started to try the combination again, saw he was on eighteen, not nineteen, and moved the dial over a digit, yanked.

The lock clicked. He threw the door open, praying there was time. The sour gym-locker smell wafted out. He began chucking contents: socks, a green-and-yellow sweatshirt, a tennis racket . . . These he hurled out of the way, heedless of the noise he was making, panicking now. He thrust himself into the confining space, barked his knee on the steel. Inside, his heartbeat seemed huge. Twisted like a Hindu contortionist, his long head crooked sideways on one shoulder, knees bent, he tried to close the door with the insensate hand, couldn't. Couldn't with his good hand either. There was no knob or handle! He dug his nails under the edge of the metal, pulled, split his nail to the quick. In desperation, he kicked the door so hard it crashed against the next locker, flew back, and slammed shut.

Clank clank clank! They were in the aisle now. He tried to quiet his heart, still his breath, in case they did home in on sound. If they were equipped with heat sensors, he was gone.

Take it easy, he thought, realizing how seriously he was taking his situation. It's just a dream!

Yeah, but whose?

Goddamn you, Isidor Stark! Goddamn you, you son of a bitch! His thoughts raged. He realized—as he had half-suspected since the beginning of the dream—this was no ordinary nightmare. Was he being recorded even now, crouched in a high-school locker? The real or imagined feeling of being watched was unnerving. If he were just dreaming, he didn't have anything to worry about. Let them catch him; he'd wake up that much sooner—and he wanted to be awake more than anything else in the world right now. But if he wasn't dreaming, if this was a nightmare Izzy Stark had prepared for him . . . He recalled sanguine images of huge talons raking a ruined and bloody carcass. His stomach lurched.

Better safe than sorry.

The clamorous footsteps passed, receded, went elsewhere. Still he didn't come out, but kept his breathing shallow, his ears pricked. The cold that had paralyzed his arm, his shoulder, had spread to his chest.

Soon it spread to his other arm and down his torso to his legs.

He fell asleep.

★

Chet took the case down from the closet shelf, laid it on the bed, opened it, and cradled the gleaming sax in his hands. He put his lips to the mouthpiece and blew a kiss through the instrument. A note soft as a lover's moan. A gutful of bluesy jazz knotted his stomach, but it was late.

He lowered the sax, fluttered the valves. One felt stiff so he oiled it with the small tube he kept in the case.

Following the breakup of the Ames Band in 1951, he, Jase, and Lois—along with three other musicians: Harvey Burns, clarinet, Sol Epstein, bass fiddle, and Lawrence "Skeeter" Needleman, the piano man—formed a group called the Skeeters (after Larry, who wrote all the original songs they ever did and who was the bonding personality of the group). The Skeeters shared a passion for jazz and the Negro blues that was finding its way into white ears.

They'd played the clubs, caught the attention of a producer, and cut an album. Nineteen-fifty-two, the year Lois and Jase married.

In 1953, the second song on side one of their second album, the Skeeters' version of "You Drive Me Crazy," was featured on the *Hit Parade*. In 1954, they were on television again with "Don't Look, Baby," on which Skeeter's tinkling piano and Lois' husky soprano made perfect harmony. The Skeeters broke up when Lois got pregnant with Brenda.

The knock was so quiet he didn't hear it at first. When he answered the second knock, Jason stood at his door. Jase's face was road-mapped with worry, and something else. Fear.

"What's wrong?"

"May I come in?"

"Sure." Chet gestured toward the one chair, but when Jase continued standing, his forehead knotted, eyes narrowed as if trying to hold on to a slippery thought, he added, "What can I do for you?"

Jase stared at him a long moment, his mouth opened, closed. He massaged his forehead. "The TV," he said, looking close to desperation. "It happened again. You can remember for me."

16

"Casper?"

No answer. Cynthia, barefoot, with only Casper's shirt covering her nudity, padded into his office. He wasn't there. She yawned. Had he gone out? She didn't remember his coming back to get his clothes after seeing him leave the bedroom in the middle of the night. She did remember having restless dreams. A smile curled her full bottom lip. Sometimes, she could sleep like the dead.

She padded into the kitchen.

The jar of grape jam ruptured over the yellow tiles warned that something was wrong. The pile of refrigeratables—a carton of broken eggs, an exploded jar of Dijon mustard, half a pack of chicken franks, a half-gallon of milk, plums, cheese, sandwich meat—clenched it. The refrigerator had been emptied during the night. Even the wire shelves had been tossed with the food. Half a pizza crowned the affair. The pungent-sweet aroma of Heinz Hamburger dills wafted over all.

Why would Casper empty the fridge? She couldn't imagine a reasonable answer—not with the jumble of chucked produce blighting the floor.

As she reached for the handle, something cold and eel-like slithered through her guts. Her teeth and stomach involuntarily clenched.

Cynthia opened the door and screamed.

Having vacuumed the kitchen, Helen considered a second cup of coffee, but decided to head down and clean the basement while Izzy rested. He'd come to bed late and slept fitfully. She hadn't gotten much sleep herself.

She shivered as she stepped onto the hardwood basement floor. It was chilly down here. She wouldn't have paid the temperature any mind, after all she was down just for a quick vacuuming and a light dusting and it was always cooler in the basement than upstairs. What alarmed her was something else. There was a feeling . . .

Something was wrong.

She looked around, taking in the furniture, the television. As her gaze passed over the utility room door, the water heater roared to life startling her.

Stop it! You're spooking yourself, you nut!

Still . . .

Her gaze settled on Izzy's dreamatron. The feeling intensified.

She approached the instrument as one might a sleeping dragon—with fascination and dread. Taped to the mother-of-pearl console above the controls was the snapshot Izzy took with some of his fans.

The power switch was on, and one of the four Plexiglas ports was lit. Unlike old-fashioned cassette tapes, bubble paks contained no moving parts and, therefore, made no noise, so there was visually and audibly no way to tell whether it was active other than the tiny amber light that indicated a port was occupied. Whether the dreamatron was recording or broadcasting, she couldn't tell without accessing the computer.

Her gaze returned to the bubble pak. The light passing through the translucent material made the recording device shimmer iridescently. It was beautiful, yet it made her scalp crawl just looking at it. And when she touched her finger to the port window, cold and pain ran up her arm and through her body. In that instant, before she could pull her hand away, as she stood stunned and staring at the shimmering silicon wafer, a barrage of sensations and images assaulted her.

Later, she would try to separate the images and would eventually isolate images, smells, impressions of faces. Impressions of teeth, cold as ice, biting, stinging, tearing. Faces on fire, still biting and tearing. Sensations of smothering, of drowning, of burning. Pain and surprise and an unspeakable, all-pervading terror. Mouths open in shrieking incoherency, screaming their last. She couldn't hear with her ears, but she felt the deep vibrations in her soul. All this bombarded Helen's brain, hurtling like shrapnel across the landscape of her thoughts, in the time it took her to gasp and yank her finger away.

Suddenly, the cockpit-like instrument panel of Izzy's dreamatron assumed the semblance of a savage, hideously deformed face leering at her, the lighted dreamports on the right its four eyes, the double row of ivory keyboards left and center its teeth.

The power of the vision left her knees trembling, her heart pounding. She was shocked, unnerved. She pressed her hand over her heart, her clipped red nails bunching the front of her yellow sweatshirt.

She backed away from the machine, blinking the images from her eyes, turned, and fled up the stairs and out into the sunlit kitchen.

When Lois looked in on Jason after breakfast, he was sitting on the edge of his bed gazing fondly at the photograph he was holding. She recognized the five-by-eight in the gold-colored frame immediately, knowing at a glance what was missing from the top of the highboy and who the photographed were. After all, she had been dusting the top of that highboy for almost thirty years. This had been Junior's room, and the high-boy was part of the set they'd bought him when he outgrew his childhood furniture.

"Morning!" Jason said, looking up before she could speak. His smiling face beamed and she felt a warmth kindle inside her that she hadn't felt in too long. "Just thinking about the kids."

"So I see." She glanced at the picture, came over, and sat beside him. She hooked an arm in his.

The boy in the photo was six, his brown hair was tousled and he was missing a front tooth. The girl was five, blond, and photogenic. Junior wore dungarees and a blue-and-white-striped T-shirt; Brenda wore a yellow dress.

Now Junior was forty-seven, teaching guitar in a music college in Los Angeles, where he lived with the three grandkids and his wife, Sissy. Brenda was a nurse, divorced, living in Fort Lauderdale. She smiled remembering the tree house Junior built behind their house in Lyndhurst: a small platform made of mismatched boards and a canvas tarp slung over a length of clothesline strung between two branches. Clever boy, Junior. She shared the thought with Jason.

"Yeah, I remember," he said. "Has Junior called lately?"

"He called Sunday. He's thinking of getting out of teaching and getting a 'real' job."

Jason laughed. It was an old joke, like the old saying: "Those who can, do; those who can't, teach." Junior spent the 1970s and most of the 80s trying to get a musical career off the ground, playing with one group after another, trying to go it solo a couple of times, generally making enough to pay his rent and not much else. He hadn't done badly, all in all; he had gotten a lot of experience, and with the help of a college education, had gotten a teaching job.

"And I called Brenda last week. She was telling me how . . ."

"How what?" Jason asked when she left the sentence unfinished.

"How"—my God, why'd I bring this up?—"depressing her job is. She says there's a high mortality rate on her ward. You know, with the elderly making up such a large percent of the population."

"You've told me all this before, haven't you?" He took her hand.

Lois nodded reluctantly, regretted it immediately. Though he maintained a grin, his face slumped. Why can't I lie to him? It would make things so much easier!

She kissed his ear, laid her head on his shoulder, sighed, not bothering to try cheering Jason up with hypocrisy. "I don't mind repeating myself."

As soon as she said it, she realized that was a bunch of bull: lately, when she had to repeat herself, she got downright snotty. But Jason was kind enough not to mention it. So patient with her when she should be the one being patient with him.

"You know," she said, taking his arm, "I admire you, Jason."

"Go on."

"No, really. I've been the queen of bitches because I can't seem to cope with something *you're* going through. You're . . . You know what you are?"

"No, what?"

"You're heroic, that's what you are. Heroic."

"Bullshit," he said quietly, but he wore a lopsided grin and was obviously pleased.

She shook her head, looked him in the eye. "No bullshit. You're a brave man, Jason Carruthers." She kissed his cheek, stood, and picked up his socks and a T-shirt from the floor, took the stuff from the plastic clothes hamper.

"Oh, I was going to take that down," he said, returning the picture to the top of the highboy.

"That's all right. I've got it." She picked up the shirt draped over the back of the chair. "Is this for wash?"

He looked at it a moment as if trying to analyze what it might be she was holding. "Naw. I can wear it another day."

She held the cotton fabric to her nose, sniffed it. She lifted an eyebrow. "I'd say it's ripe."

He came up beside her, slipped his arms around her, and kissed her hard, crushing the shirt between them.

"Umm," she said when they broke contact. "Not bad." She traced his lips with her fingertip. "Why don't you come sleep with me tonight?"

"I'd like that." He rubbed the tip of his nose against hers, looked into her eyes, and sang in a false baritone:

> You.
> You drive me cra-zy—
> You
> drive me to drink.

His voice went low down on *"drink"* and she giggled.

> No matter what her name is Sue or Betty or Liz,
> all I can see is—
> you.
> No ifs, ands, or buts about it You
> dri-ive me
> nuts.
>
> You—

To his surprise and pleasure, Lois picked up her part on cue, just as she had years ago when Skeeter sang the male vocal, the old lyrics sweet and clear despite a slight deepening of her voice.

> You drive me cra-zy.
> But you,
> God, but you're so damned la-zy!

He laughed when she put her hand on her hip and gave him a critical look.

> No matter the time of day
> all you want to do is play.
> Yo-u
> dri-ive me
> cra-zy.

"Ha!" All smiles, Jason slid his hands up her bare arms to rest on her shoulders. "You remember."

"Who can forget being on the *Hit Parade*?"

"You've always been on my hit parade, baby," he said, palming her left breast.

She blushed. "Silly old man!"

"Younger than you." He laughed.

That jolted her. That's true, she thought. Though they were the same age, she was, more and more, the crotchety old lady, while he, with all he was going through, managed to remain a blithe spirit. And suddenly, unexpectedly, tears were welling and Jason was hugging her and her face was pressed into the bony hollow of his shoulder.

He held her lightly, let her cry. You learned your spouse's habits when you've lived with her almost fifty years. If he patted and consoled her, saying, "Now, now, nothing's wrong. It'll be alright," he knew she would grow distant and walk away saying, "Don't patronize me."

She pulled away, wiped her eyes. "I'm getting silly in my old age," she said. He was glad to see she was smiling.

★

When Izzy finally woke at noon, he found a note on the kitchen table in Helen's fluid script saying she had gone grocery-shopping. He had cereal: his fav, Quaker's Natural with raisins and dates. The box was low. He poured the last bowlful and looked disappointedly at the pile of crumbling stuff from the bottom of the box—the big chunks were gone—before smothering it in milk. He hoped Helen remembered to pick up more.

He put his bowl and spoon in the dishwasher and went downstairs. Soon as he dialed up the lights, he saw Helen had been there: the electric broom stood near the stair. Last night was a blur, and he refused to let himself think about it until he was seated behind his dreamatron, its gleaming control panel curved around him.

He'd gone to bed in a paroxysm of guilt and doubt, unable to stand the thought of what he might have done, his anxiety a nest of serpents squirming in his guts, writhing in his brain. Again and again, he recalled his phone conversation with Quent, remembered his horror and glee at hearing Quent's summary account of the teenager's death.

Lying beside Helen, staring into the darkness, eyes round, a scream caged in his throat, unable to succumb to the embalming folds of sleep until dawn paled the window, he'd warred with himself—his sense of self-preservation grappling with his horror.

Nösberger had been a threat—a serious threat—and he'd removed the threat. If Nösberger turned him in to the police and he had been incarcerated, he'd be separated from his machine, and, therefore, helpless against the machinations of his fans. His continued freedom was mandatory for his survival. He thought again how fortunate it was he had the taraxein. Though he didn't fully understand his fans' motive, he felt their malice. Even here, safe in his studio, he felt the chill of their stares, the collective malevolence of their thoughts.

Yet, what he had done and the work still ahead made his blood run cold. Squeezing his eyes closed, he vividly imagined his brains oozing out of his ears, his nose, his eye sockets.

Stop it! Put a zipper on it! Nail the fucking coffin shut!

He ran gloved fingers through his hair. You're falling apart! A few minutes ago, well-rested and with a bowl of cereal in his belly, he had felt super, sharp as a tack; now his guts were a bag of worms.

Checking the drawer on the lower right, he fished out the plastic zip-lock bag. He licked his lips. Just looking at the red-brown stains on the white blotter paper through the clear plastic made him want to tear a couple dots off and get them into his system. His palms were sweating and he was chewing his lip again.

Despite the side effects—the craving, the stomach cramps, the near miss with the bus—taraxein was fantastic! He was in love with the thrill of shaping dreams, no matter how many times he got frustrated or found himself at a dead end. But what had taken him half his lifetime to train himself to do—to concentrate to the point where he could construct and move images to achieve a continuous and logical flow—taraxein seemed able to accomplish within minutes. The drug gave him a heightened ability to hold and record an elaborate mental construct longer and in greater clarity and sensual detail than he had ever known. On taraxein, he wasn't always in control; often, it seemed that his monsters were on their own and he was just a watcher checking out the scenery.

He opened the zip-lock bag.

Zipped it up again. Put that shit away, man! He pushed the drug to the back of the drawer, closed it. "You're really hooked!" he said aloud, amazed at his reaction at just seeing the drug. It's still morning. Save it for later. You don't want to be ripped when Helen comes in.

Someone was banging on the back door.

Who in the world could that be? He didn't remember hearing Helen's Toyota roll up the driveway, but, then, he hadn't been listening and the Toyota was quiet.

The knock came again. Three times, a pause, and three times again. Thinking that maybe Helen had locked her keys in the car, he put on something he hoped would pass for a smile and went upstairs.

*

"Mind if I sit?"

"I . . ."

"Ahh!" Jason sighed as he sat behind the controls of Izzy's dreamatron. He patted the leather armrests. "An Eames chair, isn't it?"

"It is."

"I see you're working on something."

Izzy tensed as Jason's finger reached toward the occupied dreamport, but Jason was only pointing. Izzy took the elderly gentleman by the arm and gently lifted. "Sorry," he said, finding an appropriate smile in his repertoire. "It makes me nervous to discuss a work in progress. Bad luck, you know. Why don't we sit over here?" Smiling as neighborly a smile as he could muster, he escorted Jason to the sofa.

Jason smiled back, showing teeth as white and even as a young man's, and the gray that speckled his short-cropped, wavy brown hair didn't seem to have advanced in the three years Izzy had known him. His face, too, had aged well. He was handsome, distinguished-looking. Izzy bemusedly hoped his appearance would fare as well when he made the senior-citizens' league. Jason's eyes were clear and intelligent. All in all, he created an impression of a man fifteen years younger than Izzy knew him to be. Izzy felt, suddenly, an almost embarrassing pity for Jason and anger at the unjustness that a man so healthy in body, and with so creative a spirit, so full of life, should go soft upstairs. All those smarts and talent turned to Jell-O.

He felt guilty now for wishing he hadn't answered the knock when he'd gone upstairs and found Jason on his back step, dressed in a tan leisure suit and smiling like a Welcome Wagon. He'd almost been rude and told Jason that he was too busy to talk right now, but he was glad he hadn't had the heart.

"You said you had something you wanted to talk about," Izzy prompted.

Jason smiled and nodded absently for a moment while he watched the shifting patterns on the big wall screen. Finally, he said, "Yes," and turned his attention toward Izzy. "So, what are you working on?"

With a start, Izzy noticed something hooded and cloaked in the old man's smile. Something that wouldn't look at him directly, even though Jason was smiling right at him. *He's hiding something.*

Izzy started to repeat what he'd just told him about not liking to discuss a work in progress, but before he could speak, Jason said, "Oh, you've told me before you don't like discussing what you're working on. Forgive me. This senility business can be a real pain in the ass. Drives Lois nuts." He grinned, and for that moment, his eyes were so guileless and innocent that Izzy wondered if, perhaps, he'd been paranoid suspecting something furtive in Jason Carruthers' gaze. But, no, Jason had something on his mind. He hadn't come here to shoot the breeze.

"Kind of like a fetus, isn't it?"

"Huh?" Izzy said warily.

"A work in progress, I mean. Kinda vulnerable and subject to abortion while it's still cooking."

The mixed metaphor was gruesome, but Izzy got the idea. "Yeah, I guess it is. Well, I can tell you this much: I'm touching up my Halloween show."

"Halloween, you say?" Jason put his hand thoughtfully to his chin. His eyes drifted to the wall screen, to the shifting patterns of somber colors.

He's drifting, Izzy thought. *How advanced is his condition?* Was the old boy going to start rocking and drooling? He didn't want to see that. He liked Jason; in fact, he felt a genuine affection for him because of the hours they had spent together exploring and recording each other's collection. Izzy remembered his neighbor's genuine enthusiasm for old records and old movies. Jason had told him a hundred stories about music showbiz in the old days.

"How's Mrs. Carruthers?" Izzy asked, hoping to steer Jason off the subject of works in progress.

"She's fine, fine . . . Look," the old man said abruptly. "I've got to get straight to the point. I've been trying to remember what I wanted to talk to you about by repeating it over and over. And it's hard remembering and holding a conversation at the same time." He grinned. "I almost forgot, but that big TV of yours reminded me."

Izzy groaned mentally. Great!

"I asked Chet last night to remind me and he reminded me this morning."

"Remind you of what?" Izzy prompted.

Jason studied him a moment. And while he did so, Izzy thought he looked as clever-eyed and as sound of mind as he had ever seen him.

"My TV has been picking up strange signals," Jason said.

"Signals?" Izzy cocked an eyebrow. He didn't like the sound of that. "And you thought maybe you're picking up something I'm working on?"

"The thought occurred to me."

"What kind of signals has your TV been picking up?"

Jason screwed up his face in concentration, before he spoke. "I was watching a movie. Black-and-white 1950s science fiction, and suddenly, instead of the movie, I'm seeing something that's not in the film. This has happened before, but I can't remember the details."

Izzy nodded. He was getting antsy. His palms were sweating and he had an incredible urge to pace, to bite his lip, to excuse himself, to be alone. He did none of these things.

"You've seen the old Trinitron we've got," Jason said at last.

Izzy nodded. Big thing. Old console type in a heavy wooden cabinet.

Jason gestured at Izzy's wall screen. "Not as big as that, but the colors're sharp, the picture's as clear as when I bought it sixteen years ago." Izzy thought he was going off on a nostalgia trip and had already forgotten what he had come to tell, but Jason got right back on track. "Anyway, I'm watching TV, and all of a sudden there's this guy running butt-naked down this hall. Tall, long blond hair, bald on top." Jason was squinting, as if seeing what he was describing. His words gave Izzy goose bumps. "And there were others," Jason went on. "People, or something that looked like people, in black pajamas, and their faces were like silver mirrors. I could see myself when I looked at one and I was the same way. No face. Just this oval mirror."

Izzy's flesh crawled. Jason's set had picked up his transmission last night, perhaps, other nights as well. He couldn't believe it! He'd been perfectly content that—except for Nösberger, who no longer mattered—no one else knew of his experiments, and now, suddenly, he was learning someone had been watching all along. A witness!

"It was as if I was one of them watching this bare-assed guy disappear around a corner. We were chasing him." He looked at Izzy now, and Izzy thought that suddenly Jason looked his true age: his face, boyish before, was deeply creased, and his eyes had lost their youthful luster. Jason was afraid, Izzy realized as the old man said, "I think we were out to murder that fellow."

"What happened next?" Izzy's mind was racing.

"The movie was back on and the alien was killing a spaceman. Craziest thing."

"Yeah?"

"Anyway"—Jason looked as if he was finally getting to the point—"I was wondering if what I saw, if anything I've described, rings a bell. Could it be anything you're working on? You know, my TV picking up your signal?"

Had Jason seen everything he'd done? Damn! Of all the crazy twisted luck! "No. Doesn't sound like anything I'm working on."

"You're sure?"

"I'd recognize the scenario, believe me."

"I suppose you would. Look." Jason leaned forward, his brows raised in a just-between-you-and-me smile that did nothing to mask the wrinkles and worry lines that had surfaced during the conversation. "If it's something you're working on and you don't want to tell me, I'm not going to raise a fuss— even though I almost had a heart attack every time it happened.

"But Lois ..." He shook his head. The smile was gone. There was a warning in the old man's eyes. "She doesn't care much for the ol' gruesome grue and she's getting up in years. Who knows what that kind of shock might do to the old girl's ticker?" The smile returned. "So set an old man's mind at rest. Better yet, let's set Lois's mind at rest."

Ah, then. That was what had brought Jason Carruthers over. The elderly gentleman was referring to the scare Lois Carruthers received the night of his first experiment. Her involvement that night had been accidental, though fortuitous: from her revelation he had gained the first skeletal glimmering of his newborn talent, a glimmering made flesh by the dead man and the tracks.

Izzy decided the best thing would be to humor his neighbor. He smiled, spread his palms in a helpless shrug.

"I wish I could help, Jason, I really do. But I've been working the past three months on the dreamie I'm presenting in concert Saturday, and what you describe isn't part of it."

"You're sure?"

Izzy smiled. Humor him. "I'd know that all right, don't you think?"

Jason pressed his lips together, raised his eyebrows, and nodded. "Yeah." He slapped his knee and leveraged himself out of the sofa's clutch. "Well, I'll let you get back to work. Sorry to bother you, and thank you for being patient with an old crackpot's weird ideas."

"Don't worry about it. I enjoy talking with you. Stop over again soon."

Izzy escorted Jason to the stairs with his hand on the old gentleman's elbow. He couldn't wait to get him out of the house. He was antsy as hell worrying Helen might come in and invite Jason to stick around, and he didn't want Helen to hear Carruthers' story, especially with his muddy clothes sitting on top of that pile of laundry.

"Maybe you were picking up another channel," Izzy offered. "Do you have cable?" That's it! Confuse him! Feed him so many possibilities that, before he can begin to sort them all, he'll forget the whole matter. "I've even heard of cases where people have picked up on their television sets TV shows forty years old."

Jason considered this.

Izzy continued, "You know television and radio signals keep going, right out into space. And they keep on going. But some of them must bounce off objects—meteors, the moon."

Jason's forehead creased.

"With all the transmissions going on day and night, sooner or later somebody's antenna is bound to pick something up."

Jason was right with him. "Thanks for pointing out another possibility. A puzzle's always more interesting when there are alternatives. I'll bring it up when I see the professor. Just let me take a couple notes." He produced a small spiral-bound notebook and a pen from his jacket pocket.

For a second, Izzy thought Jason was referring to Dr. Nösberger and he concealed his shock.

"Professor?"

"I called Stevens Tech, physics department, and got this young fellow, a Professor Rejdak, on the phone. He seemed interested in my theory and invited me to stop by. I'm going to meet him at his office at"—he checked his notes—"this afternoon at four. What time is it now?"

Izzy, who wasn't wearing a watch, pointed to the gold-banded wristwatch Jason had obviously forgotten he was wearing.

"Oh." He shook his watch free of his cuff. "Almost one-thirty. Plenty of time."

He seemed interested. Professor Rejdak.

What was Jason getting him into? Was some hotshot physicist going to come snooping around asking questions? Was one thing going to lead to another, as it usually did, and the authorities learn about his connection with Dr. Nösberger? Jason, smiling and reaching out to shake his hand and thanking him for his time, had become one hell of a liability.

17

The shadow of the science building was a cold hand on the back of his neck, and Jason was glad to leave the parking lot and walk in the sun. Still, it was after five-thirty, nearing sunset and chilly even in the light.

The next corner was brighter, and he turned west so that the sun warmed his face and chest. An admirer of ornamental architecture, Jason began looking at the carved stonework over the doors and big windows and at the wrought-iron fences and gates of the brownstones he passed.

He stopped, stared down at the shadows of branches waving skeletally on the slate sidewalk . . .

Something he should remember, something half-formed, an uneasy image trying to focus. He closed his eyes, concentrated, tried to recall.

My car keys!

His heart leapt the way it always had when he thought he'd lost his keys or wallet; then he realized with relief that his keys had been clutched in his fist all along.

Shitfire! Walked right out of the parking lot and forgot the car. How the hell'd I do that?

He turned and started back past the brownstones. "If I were ten years younger, I'd kick your ass," he muttered to himself. "Out here freezing your tail off while you could be halfway home, nice and toasty with the heater on."

The image of his 1953 Buick Roadmaster convertible with its fat whitewalls and bright blue paint came to him, and he longingly pictured himself sitting on the sofa-wide front seat behind the big cream-colored steering wheel. In his imagination, he had the top up and the heater cranked, the airflow warming his feet and legs.

He held the keys out now, one of them extended eagerly between thumb and forefinger as if he were almost at the car, about to slip the key into the lock, instead of blocks away. But the street names weren't registering, and as soon as he turned down the busier, less sunlit street, they were forgotten.

Forgotten too was the memory of Lois dropping him off at Stevens Tech, promising to pick him up within an hour. Nor did the fact that he hadn't been behind the wheel in three years enter his mind. Jason breathed the air of a younger day nearly half a century before age and mental infirmity had fettered him, and spring entered his step and his spine straightened. 1953, the heyday of his musical career. He could almost hear the patter of his sticks on the skins as Lois's voice crooned from the Roadmaster's "selectronic" speakers.

A Latin beat pumping from the window of a passing car drowned his reverie. He turned and watched the yellow Isuzu pass, then looked down at the house key in his hand. Where was he going with his house key?

He looked around. Cars, pedestrians, storefronts . . . a single street lamp half a block up flickering on. Where was he?

He slowed, calmed himself by watching the sidewalk unroll, tried to make sense of the chaos, the cacophony of motorists and passersby and traffic lights.

What am I looking for? he thought, and his panic surged again. Then he remembered the tall Gothic chimneys that had cast shadows over the parking lot . . . a steep slate roof. He clung to the image as tightly as he clung to his keys.

He crossed at the corner, then took a good look up and down the busy intersection, but failed to glimpse the ornate red-brick chimneys or rain-gray slate.

He turned and started walking. After several steps he returned to the intersection and looked around again. What was I looking for?

As a young child, he had gotten separated from his mother in a shopping mall, and it had been like this, a time of confusion and panic, of terrible helplessness. The scene came back to him now, and for a moment he was that boy again, lost amid a sea of adult legs, of dress hems and trousers. The boy's panic rippled through him in expanding waves; he shrank under the intensity of it. Wondering why his mother didn't hurry up and find him, he began to cry.

His legs forced him past a Thom McAn's, a Blimpie Base, Gino's Pizzeria, a fish market with a stuffed blue marlin hanging in the window. It didn't matter now which street he took; he was lost. Shivering from the cold, miserable and confused, he stumbled along like a drunk, keys extended like a talisman, the other hand clutching the lapels of his jacket. The noise and motion of people talking, of cars going by, the visual clamor of all the signs over the shops and in the windows, added to the kaleidoscopic confusion pressing in around him.

He mopped the tears with the back of his hand, then scanned the corniced roofline of the buildings across the street.

What are you looking for? he asked himself, trying to prompt a revelation. He looked at his house key, looked up and down the street. He clenched the keys in his fist. "My name is Jason Carruthers and I live at Five Hamilton Place," he blurted.

"Thanks, bub. That's just what I was about to ask you."

Jason gasped at the tall policeman who had materialized beside him.

18

Nösberger dead!

Helen couldn't believe it. But class had been canceled, and Clora, who worked on the school newspaper, told her and others Dr. Nösberger had been found dead in his refrigerator, and found by one of the doctor's day students with whom, it seemed, he'd been living.

Something of a scandal for the school, she thought as her Toyota eased north on Tonnele Avenue, but for her, Nösberger's death had darker implications.

Because, once she'd heard the part about the doctor being found in a refrigerator, something clicked in her head, and her thought singled out one of the many image sequences she'd experienced in the basement—that of chrome-faced men pursuing a bald-headed man down a hall. Had that man been Nösberger? She hadn't seen the face, but standing in the classroom, listening to the startling news, she had been absolutely certain it was the doctor.

But how?

A possibility occurred to her as she drove: maybe Izzy had found Nösberger's face interesting and used him in a sequence he was working on. Still, she remembered the electrifying, razor-biting terror the imagery had evoked, the icy, dripping malice of the mirror-faced pursuers.

No, something was wrong, dead wrong. Call it intuition or whatever. And it wasn't just Izzy's personality and mood changes. It was something she had only the vaguest impression of—an impression of danger and of vast wings swooping toward her. She felt like a blind woman smelling a fire in a strange house: she sensed danger, sensed it growing, blossoming like some evil night flower, but she couldn't name it.

Dinner last night had been grim.

Izzy was in the basement when she returned from shopping. She started supper, something quick and easy, she didn't feel like hassling. She decided on fish cakes and French fries—crinkle-cut, Izzy liked those. Perhaps eating something he liked would lift his mood.

When she finished cooking, she called down for him to come up and eat. He'd growled from below, "I'm not hungry. I'll grab something later."

This infuriated her more than it normally would because of the anxiety she'd felt lately. Her strained nerves snapped and she shouted down to him that she had cooked for him and his food was on the table, and if he didn't damned well come up and have dinner with her, she was going to throw the circuit breaker to the basement—which, she realized as soon as the words left her mouth, was an idle threat since the circuit breakers were in the basement. Nevertheless, Izzy emerged a moment later, looking like hell.

Smiling vaguely, his gaze averted, he asked how her day was. He even kissed her hair and squeezed her shoulder before taking his seat. He was pale, dark circles under his eyes gave him a cadaverous appearance. His hair was lackluster, ditto his eyes, which seemed to stare dully at nothing in particular. His expression was haggard. Lines she had never seen in his face before had appeared overnight.

And he was still wearing the gloves. He obviously had spares; there was a soiled pair in the laundry. She hadn't seen his hands in days. When she asked him why he was wearing the gloves, he answered he was getting his image together for the tour.

She didn't mention the weird incident in the basement, nor did she ask him where he'd been the previous night. She wanted to talk to Dr. Nösberger first.

She wanted to look the Doctor in the eye and ask him if he had given Izzy any drugs and watch his reaction. She hadn't wanted to wait till the end of class, but hoped to catch him in the hall.

But Nösberger was dead.

"Izzy!"

Helen banged on the basement door again. Izzy wasn't answering. Where was he? She tried the knob again; the door was locked.

"Hello?"

Izzy's voice. Behind her. She turned. He stood in the arch to the dining room. He was smiling and his color looked good; in fact, he looked healthier than he had in days. His face seemed flushed with the vigor of life, very unlike his appearance at dinner. He appeared robust, relaxed as he strolled into the kitchen, one gloved hand hooked into a pocket, smiling needlessly and not very convincingly, his eyes taking in the kitchen walls and ceiling.

"You're not in the basement," she said, and felt stupid as soon as the words slipped out of her mouth.

"True," he said dryly. "Home a little early."

"Class was canceled. Izzy, if you're up here, then why is the basement door locked?"

"Oh, I've got something on the stove," he said cryptically. His grin became a smirk, the type her teachers used to tell the wise-ass kids to wipe off their faces.

She remembered the pak down there, remembered the flood of horror that had jolted her like a thousand electric arrows, and decided to plunge right in.

"Yes, I know." The pak, Izzy's personality changes, Dr. Nösberger's death—so many things she needed to discuss with him.

His blue eyes narrowed as he looked at her. His blond hair wisped his forehead. "What do you mean, you know?"

"I saw things down there this morning, Izzy." She nodded toward the basement door. "Things I can't explain."

The smirk returned—slyly, she thought. And this time she really did feel like slapping it off his face. She plunged ahead.

"'Real dreamie stuff,' as you would say. People screaming,

burning; winged horse-headed demons; mirror-faced men . . ."

He made a sudden move toward her, his expression threatening, his right hand balled in a fist. Shocked, she stepped back.

"You messed with it," he growled between bared teeth. His expression was feral, his nose wrinkled with anger, crinkled like a werewolf showing his rage. His face and ears darkened to a deep crimson. A vein throbbed in his temple.

"Mess with what?" She met his smoldering gaze head on.

"'Mess with what?'" he mimicked sarcastically. "You just said you had been viewing material I've been working on."

She felt herself getting exasperated. "Will you please listen? All I did was touch the window over the bubble pak and it was as if I'd stuck my finger in an electrical outlet. I just touched it and it was as if everything on the bubble pak went through my head at once."

"That's impossible! You had to have turned on—"

"It happened! Aren't you listening? When did I ever lie to you? You'd know it if I lied to you."

"No I wouldn't! Women can lie with a straight face because they have no consci—"

"Iz, do you hear what you're saying? You're generalizing and you're not talking rationally. Let's—"

"You're trying to change the subject," he snapped. "I asked you what the fuck were you doing spying on what I was doing?" His face was darkening, the vein pulsing.

"Izzy!"

She screamed directly into his face. That stopped him cold. He blinked as if she had slapped him; some of the flush drained from his face. But only for an instant, then he was full of snarling rage again, barely kept on leash.

"What?"

"Izzy . . ."

He was waiting, his stare withering. For an instant, she thought he looked dangerous, capable even of murder, and she shivered. She had hit a nerve she hadn't known existed.

"I know what you do is your business," she said, carefully choosing her words, "and I don't want to sound like a nag, but . . ."

"But?"

His eyes were cold, smoldering like dry ice. His expression unchanged.

Spit it out, she thought. "Have you taken any drugs lately?"

"Oh ho!" He laughed. The sudden transformation of his face was startling. He was sneering again, one eyebrow hitched condescendingly, his nostrils flared, his upper lip curled back from his teeth. The expression was so un-Izzy-like, so intense and terrifying, it was as if he had suddenly transformed into someone else, someone she didn't know and didn't want to know.

A stranger in the house! she thought. Which prompted another thought: Beware of strangers!

Sound motherly advice from her parents, teachers, and church, but what do you do when the stranger's the person you live with? The person you love most in the world? Under his gaze, she felt like a bug under a microscope.

"I mean it, Izzy. Have you been taking anything? Something's altering your personality and I have a right to know what. Even your perspiration smells differently lately."

"My what?"

"A chemical smell."

"Shit!" He looked at her suspiciously, as if she were making all this up.

She decided that now was the time to ask the question that was uppermost on her mind. She watched his reactions closely.

"Izzy."

"What?" He had started pacing. He stopped and waited, tapping a toe impatiently.

"Dr. Nösberger is dead."

Izzy turned and took two steps so that he was facing away from her when she saw the smile spread over his profile. The smile was creepy in view of what she had just said—and illuminating.

He knows something, she told herself. He knows something about Nösberger's death!

No, that's impossible! Impossible!

"What do you know about Dr. Nösberger's death?" she said. He whirled on her, the mask of anger back on his face.

"What do you mean what do I know? I know what you just told me! How was he killed?"

"Who said he was killed?"

"What? Are you playing with me?" His eyes were narrowed, his right hand was balled in a fist. She had better watch herself, but she had to know.

"You came in in the middle of the night. You took a shower. This morning I find your clothes—shirt, pants, socks, and a pair of sneakers—covered with mud on the bathroom floor." She watched his eyes narrowly. His expression didn't change; he continued to watch her impatiently, fuming, the vein in his temple throbbing. "Where were you last night?"

"Who are you working for?" he demanded, bashing his fist down on the table hard enough to knock over a salt shaker. "The FBI? I couldn't sleep. I went jogging. I fell down."

"Bullshit, Izzy!" She took him by the arm now, looked him squarely in the eye. "What's happening to you?"

"What do you mean what's happening to me?" He spat the words out, slowly, one at a time, between clenched teeth. "Nothing's happening to me."

"You're lying, Iz. Look at yourself! You've never spoken to me the way you have tonight. You've never looked at me the way you're looking at me now."

His hand clamped around her wrist. "How dare you call me a liar!"

"Don't touch me!" She shook his hand off, started to leave the room.

He grabbed her again, spun her around.

"Get off!" She slapped his hand.

"Where do you think you're going?" he growled. His grip tightened, bruising her arm. "I'm talking to you."

"Do you see anyone here who gives a shit?" she said, and slapped his hand again. He clamped down harder. "Ow! You're hurting me."

She thought she was doing the best thing. Her purpose was twofold: to loosen his hold and to knock some sense into him at the same time. So when she backhanded him smartly across the mouth, she never expected the reaction she got.

Izzy's head snapped back, his eyes ping-ponged to the right, and with a rage that forgot five years of living and loving together, his hands flew to her throat. But when he looked at Helen, actually looked at her through the red haze of his anger and saw her, his blood ran cold. He staggered back, keeping his gloved hands raised before him as if to ward off the devil.

It was no longer Helen he saw, but a demon in her skin. The Helen-thing's eyes were as bright and hot as molten chrome; a long, forked black tongue flicked out and licked over the serpent fangs.

He saw it now, in a blinding flash of realization. She's one of them! He groaned. She was talking, but he didn't hear: the roar in his ears was too loud. They had gotten to her! He felt himself evaporating under her chrome stare, shrinking under her serpent grin. Again, as he had at the Dreamacon, he felt as if his blood, his very life force, was being sucked out of him.

"Stop it!" he shouted, but the Helen-thing kept grinning, its eyes smoldering.

Then the thing's mouth opened and opened and kept on opening swallowing its face, its lips growing huge, floating redly in the dark. Helen's body gone, only the grotesque lips expanding like some psychedelic lava bubble teeth so white, snarling hungry teeth growing huge a forest of teeth and the vast meaty tongue wagging pervertedly, mouth swelling, enveloping him . . .

"Stop it!"

He swung his fist, struck the Helen-thing in the face as hard as he could.

Helen knocked over a chair on her way down. She realized what had happened before she hit the floor, but, for a moment or two as she lay stretched out, her swelling cheek pressed against the cool tiles, she was too shocked to move or speak.

Then the tears broke and she cried, "God damn you, Izzy Stark!" She started to rise shakily to her feet. She was staring through tears at the white floor tiles when he struck her again. The floor lurched toward her. One ear rang where he had slapped her down, the other side of her face stinging and aching from the impact with the floor.

For a moment, the room seemed filled with the buzzing of flies, the fluorescent bright as the sun, and she curled fetus-like, cringing, afraid he would kick her. But then she heard his sneakered footsteps moving away and rolled over in time to see him close the basement door.

"Izzy!" she screamed at the top of her lungs.

Tears ran her mascara, and her own face was now beet-red. The door remained closed. She pounded the floor with her open hand as she sobbed.

"Izzy!"

She got to her feet, steadied herself with the help of a kitchen chair until the room stopped spinning.

"You hit me!" she screamed at the door, her temper exploding. She grabbed the first glass object she saw—an unopened bottle of Dom Perignon she was saving for after his Halloween show—hurled it at the door. The bottle exploded in a shower of green glass and expensive silver droplets.

She went upstairs and packed a small suitcase. Ten minutes later, after a stop in the bathroom to clean her face, she backed her Toyota down the drive intending to go to her parents' house in Hoboken as Izzy sat at his machine chewing three hits of taraxein.

19

When Chet returned upstairs after seeing Dr. Leonard out, Lois's door was open and her light was on. He walked in and found her sitting on the edge of her bed in her pink robe and fluffy pink mules. She looked cold the way she was drawn in upon herself, her feet planted closely together on the white oval rug as if to keep warm, her fingers knotted tightly in her lap.

"He'll be okay."

Lois nodded, but didn't relax. She had recently given up tinting her hair, and now she was beginning to look like the grandmother she had been for over a decade. She looked frail, Chet thought, vulnerable—and beautiful, in spite of everything: an ethereal beauty that you just had to look at, because she might disappear if you looked away. Chet sat beside her and took her hand.

"It's my fault," she said. "I should never have left him." After dropping him off, she'd visited a fruit stand and a bakery while in Hoboken. She'd gotten stuck in traffic on her way back, and when she pulled into the parking lot and didn't see him waiting, she had gone in after him. A security guard directed her to the office of the professor Jason wanted to see, but the door was locked, the lights extinguished. Suppressing a welter of rising panic, she returned to the security guard, who, after a moment's reflection, recalled a man matching Jason's description leaving the building twenty minutes earlier. Lois ran out of the parking lot and scanned the street in both directions, but no Jason. She phoned the police, then drove up and down the streets searching for Jason before going home in frustration to await their call. Her gaze met Chet's. "He seemed so lucid this afternoon."

Chet lowered his eyes, bit his lip.

"What?"

"I think I know why he appeared so lucid."

"He's been overdoing it with his pills again, hasn't he?"

Chet nodded. "Dr. Leonard asked to see his medication. I showed him the bottle. It was nearly empty. Dr. Leonard said it should have been half full."

A hand fluttered to her temple. She shook her head. "I can't stand seeing him go like this, piece by piece. And God! I feel so guilty for snapping at him so often lately."

"It's not your snapping that hurts him, Lois, it's your coldness."

"I don't mean to be cold. It's just my way of detaching myself from something I haven't learned to deal with yet."

Chet patted her hand. "I know it. Jase knows it too. But Jase might not have much time left, and by the time you learn to cope with your fear of aging, he might be too far gone to recognize you."

She sat bolt upright, shook her head as if to deny his accusation, then her shoulders sagged. "You're right," she said. "I never used to think about death or age. It's seeing Jason losing his memory, realizing that life—one's whole life!—can be forgotten. Gone, as if it was never lived. That's terrifying.

"When Daddy died and years later when Mom passed away, I thought about death, about how awful it is that we have to be separated from our loved ones, about how vulnerable we all are." She was looking closely into his eyes, her forehead wrinkled, her brows knit. He nodded his understanding. "But lately I keep seeing Jason as a vegetable, spittle drooling down his chin, his eyes already dead. I know that sounds morbid, but I keep seeing him, when I think about it, as a corpse. Not neatly preserved and cosmeticized and dressed in his best suit, but like a cadaver on a pathologist's gurney, his mouth gaping, his body naked and stiff and emaciated."

She shivered. Her grip tightened.

How ironic, Chet thought, that Jase was able to see the human comedy in his malady, whereas Lois saw only the tragedy. It was important that she start accepting Jason's fate, because then, and only then, could she accept her own winter years and perhaps even enjoy them, instead of seeing them as a prelude to death.

Still, despite his own fairly stoical acceptance of the inevitable end and of human calamity in general, he shared her bitterness when he thought about his old friend's brains turning to lettuce while his body was still healthy and spry.

"I'm scared," Lois said. "And that frightens me, the fact that I'm scared. I'm not the weak-hearted type, but it's as if you look forward all your life, always looking to the next year, and the year after that, but you come to a point when you start looking back. And that's frightening, when you look forward and see nothing but blackness, and to take your mind off the fear, you find yourself looking back to your youth. You know what I mean?"

"Yeah, I find myself doing a lot of that lately."

"Then it's not just me getting paranoid because of Jason?"

Chet touched her face, the skin still smooth, nearly wrinkle-free. But for how long? Touching her, he thought of the wrinkles that would eventually map her features and sink her cheeks.

"No, it's not just you," he said softly. "Looking back, longing for what was, is natural, because, sooner or later, the future is beyond our control. Old age and death aren't things we can evade like taxes; there are no loopholes."

"Hold me, Chet."

He did so. Gladly. He chuckled.

"What's funny?" she asked.

"I was just remembering something I read a long time ago."

"In a kingdom far away?"

"Yes. England, to be exact. Medieval England. There was once a King Canute, whom the people thought so wise he could do anything. So one day he had his throne taken down to the seashore and he sat there, and when the tide came in, he commanded it to stop. Of course, it didn't and he got his royal feet wet, but he did it to make a point. The point being that human beings have to accept their limitations. They are neither immortal nor omnipotent."

"I know, I know." She patted his hand. "I'll try harder, I promise. It's just that he was always such a boy at heart. Still is. That was one of the reasons I married him, you know."

"Are you saying I was an old sourpuss, way back when?"

Her gaze, contemplative and playful, rested on him for several moments; then she smiled and said, "No, not hardly."

And, Lord, if Chester Brown didn't feel a stab of guilt, of betrayal at sitting here holding his best friend's wife. He knew, as his penis tented his pants, he ought to be getting up, saying good night, and heading down the hall to his room, ought to be putting distance between himself and temptation, but a heat had sprung up in his groin and was spreading to his face. Her perfume made his head spin.

Lois, too, must have felt desire, need, whatever it was that created this roaring stillness, for she didn't take her eyes off his and the intensity of her stare matched his own.

As her lips parted, as her eyes closed, as the blood roared in his ears, he was consumed with a tenderness he hadn't felt in a long time. He closed his eyes and they kissed, and in his mind's eye her hair was blond and her lips were red.

★

When Jason woke, he didn't remember a thing. He opened his eyes to a dark room. It took him a few seconds to realize he was awake. He was in his bed; he recognized every irregularity of its surface.

He turned on the lamp, went to the closet, took out the ancient smoking jacket Lois had given him for his forty-ninth birthday, put it on over his pajamas. He dug his feet into a pair of carpet slippers as frayed as the jacket's cuffs and left the room. At Lois' door, he paused, considered going in. Her light was on. He heard voices and assumed she was watching TV. But then his stomach rumbled and he decided he'd grab a snack.

In the kitchen, he got a Diet Coke and a Snickers bar from the fridge and went into the living room. As he sat facing the dead TV screen munching his Snickers bar, it occurred to him that he didn't have long to live.

Jason pondered the weight of that, the certainty. Oh his body might survive for some years, but not what was essentially him. A sadness bobbed in the hollow of his throat, but the memory of a happy and fulfilling lifetime stilled it.

When he died, Chet would look after Lois. He worried about her. It was the one thing that still hurt him, he realized. Not the fact that he didn't have long to live or that his capacity to recall day-to-day events was comparable to that of a carrot—these he accepted. But the thought of Lois (gorgeous, effervescent Lois!) ending her days in bitterness and fear—that hurt.

The blank screen wasn't a zooful of company, so he set his half-eaten Snickers on the coffee table next to his soda and went over to his film collection behind the glass doors of the wall unit. All current events, normal or otherwise, melted and ran and blurred daily for Jason into the oblivion of the present. And the present was perishable; only the past and its keepsakes remained vivid for him. And when he was in the living room, watching one of his old movies on the Trinitron, as he was about to, he was solidly in the past. It did him no good to try to keep up with a mini-series, the soaps, or current events; come next week, he'd find that he'd forgotten last week's installment. He'd even had to give up *Masterpiece Theatre,* except when it was based on a classic he had read long ago and admired enough to remember.

Only the movies stored from years of late-late shows and the songs that still ran through his head, recalling times when both his brain and his penis were a good deal firmer, gave him escape from the quicksand present. Thinking about the present made him paranoid, and paranoia was the rat gnawing in the wall, the termite undermining reason. Thinking about the present and how he was missing it, thinking about his fading concentration, his sweaty grip on day-to-day reality, weakened his resolve to enjoy the last of his awareness to the hilt. So he didn't allow himself to think, as Lois did, about the drooling moron his body would become when the lights went out. Lois used to say he was an optimist; when times were bad, he would still be scheming and dreaming. He had little optimism that his memory would suddenly, miraculously, be restored to him, but he was damned determined not to spend what precious little freedom of thought, of will, that was left him frustrated and depressed!

Skimming the labeled titles on the backs of the cartridges, an old favorite caught his eye. And from a small, cedarwood cigar box on one of the shelves, Jason removed a pair of 3-D glasses. A birthday gift from Lois in her zanier days.

Back at the set, he popped the tape into the VCR, donned the 3-Ds, settled into his rocking chair and hit the play button.

Jason recognized the underwater scene that appeared on the Trinitron. The film had started up about two-thirds of the way through. Not that starting at the beginning mattered anymore. When you knew the film as well as Jason, a scene or two evoked the whole; besides, the best scenes were toward the end. He picked up his Snickers bar and resumed munching.

The screen showed a tropical night scene: a small, brackish body of water, jungle vegetation coming right down to its edge. The Black Lagoon, looking every bit as sinister as its name. The only light in the scene came from a boat bobbing sullenly on the surface.

Underwater now. A dark shape moving through the seaweed toward the camera with surprising speed. The Creature!

The kiss inflamed Chet, and in his mind's eye, he caressed a handful of blond hair. His hand traveled over her shoulder, exquisite, smooth as satin, slipped down under her terry-cloth robe and captured one firm young breast, warm and soft through her thin nightie. The kiss prolonged, and she reciprocated, pressing against him, encircling him with her arms.

He kissed her ear. Her long nails trailed over his pajamas, raked lightly over his rigid penis. He groaned into the curve of her throat; her body responded with a grinding gyration of her pelvis. He felt her need, and it wasn't only physical.

The illusion that Lois was twenty-one again and so achingly young-looking and beautiful it took his breath away was so real that the image remained, hanging around her like a veil, a few seconds after he opened his eyes. Then she was sixty-seven and her face and her figure a little fuller, changed, yet the same.

No, not the same. There was more to love now. Not in the physical sense, but in the years of shared experience, in the conversations and the caring and sharing. So much more to appreciate after a lifetime.

Her breast was like hot silk beneath his hand. His testicles throbbed, a sensation he hadn't felt in a long, long time.

"I love you." His lips trembled, his breathing husky, the words barely audible. Somehow, he didn't feel silly at all saying that; it sounded right and long overdue.

"I know," she said, her blue eyes twinkling the way they used to when she was sultrily crooning a bluesy number into the microphone. "You always have. You and Jason. In one way or another, you've both looked after me all these years. I'm a very lucky woman."

Her mouth closed on his. They kissed, this time tenderly. And he realized, regardless of the ache in his pants, they weren't going to make love. It wasn't going to happen now after all these years.

The kiss ended; their lips parted.

"Lie down and hold me," Lois said.

He did, and she lay in the crook of his shoulder, her cheek nestled against his not-altogether-unfirm chest.

Her hair smelled like flowers.

Jason felt the old thrill of nostalgia and excitement. Now the camera showed the Creature head-on, and through the red and green lenses of the 3-D glasses, the Creature appeared to be rushing toward him, shark's teeth showing, its eyes alien and ancient.

The Creature's face filled the screen. Through the 3-D lenses, the infamous reptilian features seemed to be hurtling straight toward him as fast as the Creature's powerful limbs could propel it, gills pulsing, ancient eyes seemingly fastened on him.

Jason jumped at the sound of breaking glass, cleared his seat by two or three inches before coming down again with a jolt that set his hemorrhoids on fire. He blinked at what he saw, hands gripping the arms of his rocker until his knuckles were white. The salty smell of seaweed blew from the set.

The Creature, impossibly large for the thirty-two-inch Trinitron, was pushing its head through the shattered screen. A forked tongue licked hungrily over rows of reptilian teeth. Daggers of screen glass broke and popped off the reptile-man's scaled shoulders. The carpet was flooded.

A scaly hand, webbed and clawed, zoomed toward him. The action seemed to jump at him through the 3-D glasses, which he was too paralyzed to think to remove. Powerful claws dug into the soaked carpet. More jagged glass shards popped off as the nightmare emerged. The alien hatred pouring out of the Creature's eyes nailed him to his chair. The thing's teeth were bright in the dimness, its gills wetly gleaming.

Jason tried to rise, to flee, but he backpedaled away from the monster and ended up going over backward in the rocking chair, arms pinwheeling. He landed with a bone-crunching jar, cracking his head, the carpet absorbing some of the impact. The chair flopped over sideways as Jason scrambled to get his feet beneath him. But his legs were like water; they wouldn't respond and collapsed under him when he tried to rise. He started crawling, his panicked heart pounding.

Unable to take his eyes off the Creature, he stared over his shoulder as he crawled. The reptile-man appeared to be stuck, crested head and one huge green arm in the room, the other shoulder jammed in the now-glassless side of the opening. The heavy Trinitron console rocked with the Creature's struggles; brackish water trickled in as the monster thrashed, mouth open, rows of serrated teeth exposed as it silently roared.

Wood groaned. A section of walnut cabinet sheared off as the massive shoulder shoved into the room. Water poured in, surged across the carpet, and lapped against Jason's hands and knees.

The Creature emerged rapidly now, digging its claws into the sopping carpet, hauling its glistening body out of the Trinitron. Out and out it came, rippling sinew and gleaming scales, rising on its webbed feet.

The set was trickling now, the deluge spent. The living room had, itself, become something of a lagoon.

Jason encountered a wall and simply stopped, his overloaded brain unable simultaneously to watch what the monster was doing and to contemplate fleeing. Through the 3-D lenses, the Creature seemed to fly at him.

Talons ripped painfully into his shoulder, spun him around. The reptile-man loomed over him. A webbed hand closed over his face, 3-D glasses and all, and squeezed. The glasses gave way first, the tortoiseshell frames cracking, then splintering. A sliver tore the skin on his temple. Blood began to flow. Excruciating pain lanced like the biggest migraine in the world between his eyes, his nose bled as the powerful grip literally tried to fuse the frames to his face. Then the pain shifted to his temples as the Creature's talons broke the flesh and dug into the skull.

A second webbed hand crushed his windpipe. Held by his face and his throat, unable to release the scream howling through his brain, Jason was lifted clear of the floor as if he were a paper bag.

He clawed blindly at the impossibility, his nails raking its face. He kicked its scaled shins. He felt the damage in his throat, sensed he was beyond repair. His lungs burned from the lack of oxygen, consciousness swam. Then his skull finally gave way, cracking like the rind of a melon as the talons punched through to his brain.

Jason Carruthers died so quickly he had no last thoughts. Only an extremity of terror and pain . . .

And then, *nada*.

She lay in the crook of his shoulder. Her scent was the most intoxicating smell he knew. Gosh, it took him back. Nearly fifty years back.

Damn, where does the time go? The passage of half a century struck him like a dash of ice water.

Lois lay so still, the house was so quiet, that the loud crash downstairs jolted him.

"Jase!" Lois scrambled to her feet.

Chet was already moving toward the door. She followed.

More noise! A crunching. A gurgling. A wet splintering noise. The light at the head of the stair shone down into darkness.

"Jase!"

No answer.

"Stay here," Chet shouted and plunged down the stair. He hit the dimmer switch at the bottom and light flooded the living room. His jaw dropped.

Lois stumbled into him, screamed.

Chet took in the whole scene at once: the broken TV set, the overturned rocking chair, the water and Jason's body, sprawled in a sitting position against the wall, his head slumped forward onto his chest, his throat ripped open.

The smoking jacket Jason wore over his pajamas was red with gore. Chet's stomach lurched sickeningly and he tasted bile as he moved closer and saw that Jason's head was so badly crushed his nose was caved in and his eyes were pushed almost together so that they appeared to be looking into each other. An earpiece of the mangled 3-D glasses was embedded in the flesh on one side of his head.

Even as the realization slowly sank in that it was Jase sitting there dead, Chet froze. The hairs on his back crawled as he peered through the arch into the shadows of the dining room.

The killer's in the house!

His eyes snapped to the curtained, glass-paned door to the darkened foyer. Then back to the shadows of the dining room. He hadn't heard the front or back door open.

Lois showed no such caution. She fell to her knees beside Jason, cradled his ruined head against her breasts, looked up at Chet, helpless, tears running down her face, her mouth open as if sobbing but making no sound.

20

Helen stopped before her parents' house and put her hand on the wrought-iron gate. Fifty-six was the number in the lighted transom. It was one of the middle houses in a line of neat single- and double-family brick row houses. A few were painted white or yellow or red, the rest natural, some with their doors and yards and house numbers lit by porch lights, others dark. It was an old neighborhood, nothing fancy; there weren't any mansions, but the yards were trim, the sidewalks clean and well-lighted.

Her parents' house was white with a green door, the wrought-iron fence green to match the trim. Rose bushes (thornless) took up most of the tiny front yard.

As a girl, she had played hopscotch in front of this gate, drawing the familiar squares in chalk, replacing the lines after a rainy day. And she had played jump rope out here and in the small backyard that was half-cement and half-vegetable-garden. And up and down the block—in the front yards and behind the trees and cars—she and her friends had played manhunt and hide-and-seek and tag.

Allee-Allee-home-free-all!

The childish voices still echoed under these streetlamps, calling out through the early evening dusk, "First one to see the lights go on!" as, one by one, the streetlights began to flicker on.

The ghosts of the past murmured around her, haunted her as her fingers curled through the cool iron loops of the gate. Then she pushed the ghosts away.

She stared at the snug little house that swam like a mirage in the light of the two brass lamps on either side of the front door. She realized she was crying and wiped her cheeks with the back of her hand. Her left eye throbbed.

She sagged, leaned on the gate for support. She couldn't go in there with a black eye and face her mother and father, and she couldn't just stand here where one of them might look out and see her. She wished she could be in her old room upstairs sobbing silently into one of her mother's cedar-scented pillowcases without having to go through the lighted downstairs where they were probably watching TV.

She pushed herself away from the gate, away from the house with its neat garden and its warmth and memories, away from the questions that awaited her if she rang the bell. Away from her car, wanting to walk, to sort out the buzz of thoughts in her head.

Helen crossed streets, turned corners, not heeding where she was going, nor caring. She kept to the less-populated streets, avoiding crowds of teenagers still hanging out in front of closed-for-the-night candy stores and old men walking their dogs, terribly ashamed of anyone seeing her black eye. The thoughts, possibilities, doubts, fears, heartbreak, crowded in on her so that her thinking was strained and cracked and no longer able to follow a straight line. She tripped on a broken slab of sidewalk heaved up by a tree root, stumbled, then stood stock-still. She took in her surroundings, the tumult inside her head swept aside by the surge of apprehension that leapt to her throat.

She had wandered into a strange neighborhood, one she couldn't recall ever seeing before, though it was obviously within walking distance of her old block. No spruce front yards here; no porch lamps illuminating house numbers and trim façades. The street was as deserted as the oceans of the moon. No teenagers hung out on the sidewalks, no old men walked their dogs, not a single window or doorway in any of the dark, disturbingly narrow, four- and five-story apartment buildings showed a trace of light; and though she hadn't noticed it at first, every streetlamp on the block was out, except for the one under which she stood.

Where are all the people?

(Here's the church and here's the steeple.)

It's too early for them all to have gone to bed.

(Turn it inside out and here's the people.)

Another odd thing—the silence. The night had become impossibly, preternaturally silent. Not just quiet, which would have been unusual enough for Hoboken, but dead, ghost-town silent. Hoboken was a busy city. Even if this block was deserted, she should still hear the traffic noises from surrounding blocks: an occasional Harley ripping the night with its thunder, the far-reaching scream of fire trucks and ambulances, the whine and rumble of jets, Newark-bound, banking into the Pulaski Approach. But all she heard was the sound of her own breathing and of her small, amplified footsteps as she started forward again.

She left the dim circle of the streetlamp, feeling as if she were walking through a cemetery. Where is everyone? The night had changed: it was as if the fabric of reality had torn and she had unwittingly walked through the hole into the Twilight Zone. Where there had been no wind before, a surly breeze now blew dead leaves and newspapers sliding and skittering along the sidewalk and across the street. Even the sky had changed. She recalled it being starry when she was in front of her parents' house, but a cloud cover must have rolled in while she walked, for now it was dark and the only light on the block, literally, was the streetlamp she'd left.

Footsteps behind her! A scuffling, grating against the sidewalk. As if someone slow and ponderous with a game leg and heavy boots were following her.

She turned, gooseflesh crawling, and looked back toward the streetlamp. The sidewalk was empty. No one across the street either. Her gaze skimmed the darkened doorways. Nothing, as far as she could tell, but then again, she didn't have night vision and anybody could be hiding in the shadows of the parked cars or those benighted entranceways.

She started walking again, the clop of her low-heeled shoes loud in the unreal hush. She wished she were wearing sneakers, wished she were at her parents' house—questions or no questions.

Through her footsteps and the skittering of newspapers and debris the breeze herded toward her, she heard the sound again. A scuffling, a grating, as of heavy boots dragged along the sidewalk.

Scuffle, grate . . . scuffle, grate . . .

She stopped and looked back, but saw no more than she had before: dark, empty sidewalks and street, black skeletal trees, benighted doorways. Yet she experienced the definite sensation of being watched—not the blank, disembodied way the buildings seemed to watch her, but the scalp-crawling, physical sensation of eyes boring into the back of her head. A whimper escaped her throat and she started walking again.

Faster now, the *clop clop clop* of her heels echoing off the ghostly windows that observed her progress with the dead, vacant gaze of zombies. Her blood pounded in her temples, roared in her ears.

Shuffle, grate . . . shuffle, grate . . .

The pace was leisurely, far slower than her own; yet the sounds kept up with her, amplifying down the deserted street, fracturing the unnatural quiet with its abrasive loudness. She didn't look back now; she knew what she would see—nothing! And she didn't want to see anything either. She just wanted to get the hell out of this spooky neighborhood and find her way back to the Planet Earth.

She quickened her step, her heels . . .

. . . clacking noisily on the pavement as she hurried along, her footsteps echoing off the mute buildings.

He sees her clearly; his night vision is excellent. But even if he shut his eyes, even if he covered his ears, she would not be able to elude him; he would see her in his mind's eye, hear her with his mind's ear.

He feels her fear; it streams off her like sweat, heating and scenting the air behind her deliciously. He momentarily closes his eyes and lets his fantastically keen sense of smell lead him surely along in pursuit of his prey.

The left ring finger depresses a note in the upper register of the synthesizer keyboard. The note is just off the high end of human hearing and transmitted at such a frequency that his victim feels it vibrating in her spine rather than hears it.

Another Stark first, he thinks. Spinal soundtrack. In his alpha state, he smiles. The suspense, the rapport he has with his victim, her fear flowing electrically, icily, into him is an almost sexual sustainment, a prolonged ecstasy. And like an animal in rut, his inhibitions are clouded by lust, by excitement. The flesh of his scrotum tingles and crawls, the hair on his arm bristles, and a chill runs up his spine.

He feels the power of his creation, the gargantuan terror he conjures in his victim's brain, and at the same time he feels the leap of wild joy, of the exhilaration and anticipation of the hunter closing in for the kill.

Momentarily, he loses sight of her when she . . .

. . . rounded a corner, hoping to lose whoever (or whatever! the thought came unbidden) was following her, then broke into a run. She ran on her toes, trying to keep her heels from clacking, but it didn't do a lot of good. She thought about abandoning her shoes, but the broken glass that occasionally crunched and grated beneath her shoes dissuaded her.

She was on another block like the last, dark and dirty and deserted. Only this one was completely lightless. She wondered if Hoboken was suffering from a blackout. But, no, the one streetlamp had been on; the whole row would have been off had the power gone out. And that still wouldn't account for the total absence of people on the streets or the lack of sound coming from the buildings and the surrounding blocks.

The heavy scuffling grating footsteps had rounded the corner behind her and seemed very close indeed, though she had run almost half the block. A sheet of newspaper, ghostly white, sailed out of the darkness and wrapped around her legs like a live thing. She yelped with a sharp intake of air. Without stopping, she tore the thing loose—the mangled paper skittered away—and glanced back over her shoulder.

What she saw—or what she thought she saw—sent a stab of terror through her that slashed as deeply as a butcher knife. She caught only a glimpse of it—a silhouette, a shadow moving through shadows—and when she stopped running and nearly tripped in turning to get a better look, she saw nothing. It was gone, so she couldn't be sure whether she had seen it for certain. But for a split second, out of her peripheral vision as her head swung around, she could have sworn she had caught a glimpse of an impossible vision.

Black as the bottom of a well on a moonless night, velvet black, and moving, a shadow in the shape of a man, seven, eight feet tall, less than half a block away moving toward her out of the darkness.

She stumbled, her feet trying to do a 180-degree turnabout and run forward at the same time, but she caught herself. She searched the darkness, holding her breath, her eyes darting to the street, the trees, the doorways.

Did I really see something?

Yes . . . something. A shadow. A hole in the night. She shivered: the night was cold, her terror colder.

To hell with it, she thought and, half-running, half-hopping, yanked off her shoes. Scanning the dark sidewalk for glass, she ran for all she was worth.

Shuffle, grate . . . shuffle, grate . . .

The ponderous, lurching foot tread, amplified unnaturally, kept pace with her no matter how fast she ran.

She made another right at the corner onto still another dark, abandoned street. Ahead on her right, a long, decrepit-looking garage tall enough to park buses in took up part of the block. At the end of the leaning structure, between the garage and the first of the apartment buildings that took up the rest of the block, a black swath announced the entrance to an alley. Sprinting for the alley in a desperate rush to get there before the thing behind her rounded the corner, her foot came down hard on a piece of glass that deeply slashed her heel and . . .

. . . he feels the wild leap of his victim's surprise. As if a psychic ice pick flung end over end from her mind has plunged deeply into his, he feels his victim's pain.

It staggers him. Momentarily, the connection is broken as he mentally backpedals; then he is, again, seeing what his victim sees—the alley like a black maw rushing up to engulf her—and feeling with his victim the flaring agony she feels every time her weight comes down on her injured foot.

His victim plunges into the darkness and . . .

. . . as she had feared, the alley dead-ended. The side of the big clapboard garage on her right and the towering wall of a brick tenement on her left led her to a cul-de-sac. The alley smelled of garbage and urine. The smell of urine should have heartened her some—at least, it was a smell associated with human inhabitants—but she decided if there were any inhabitants in the tenement on her left, she would no more want to alert them of her presence than she would her pursuer.

A monstrous shape like a sleeping dragon rose out of the soupy darkness. She stopped, petrified, and bit a knuckle to stifle a cry of alarm. Then she saw that the shape was a steel garbage bin and a big stack of steel drums and wooden crates beside it.

She ducked behind the barrels. Just in time. The footsteps approached. Shuffle, grate . . . shuffle, grate . . .

Crouching on hands and knees, she looked out through the narrow gap between the garbage bin and a barrel. It was so dark in the alley the street seemed, at least faintly, illuminated. From where she peered, she could make out the dark bulk of a parked car.

Then a shadow, black as death, moved into her line of vision. She froze and held her breath. The gritty concrete dug into her knees, but she was afraid to shift her position, afraid her pursuer would hear and discover her.

She still clutched her shoes—in fact, she was leaning on them—but they wouldn't be much use as weapons. Her foot throbbed relentlessly. The first blossom of pain had been such a surprise that the pressure of the glass against the bone in her heel was more painful than the actual slicing, but now the pain was really setting in, throbbing, shooting bolts of agony up her leg.

She inched to the left to look around the other side of the barrel. Her head swam with the ripe corruption wafting from the garbage bin. A crate dumped in front of the barrels blocked her view. She raised her head until she could see over the crate.

At first, staring out between the barrels, she saw nothing. Then she realized she should be seeing something. Where was the parked car?

A velvety blackness spanned the mouth of the alley. The wind, steadily rising, suddenly whipped into a frenzy, sending dust devils of paper and leaves spinning off in all directions. One of these caught up sand and hurled it in Helen's eyes. Her vision blurred as she wiped her tearing eyes with a knuckle, all the while trying to see what was going on out there, terrified that her pursuer was already in the alley and sneaking up on her.

She was utterly unprepared for what she saw when her vision cleared. On the sidewalk in the mouth of the alley, on the slender strip of it that she could see between two oil-stained barrels, barefoot on the cold pavement, stood the figure of a young girl, perhaps mid-teens, her body naked, pale and lithe as she emerged from the blackness. The wind whipped her dark shoulder-length hair.

The girl moved into the alley, into the whirling dust devils, her feet pale in the starlight, for now the stars had come out.

I'm dreaming, she thought. Izzy knocked me out, and I'm lying on the kitchen floor having a nightmare.

Then she noticed the figure wasn't walking but floating toward her, gliding over the ground without touching it!

Something familiar about the figure.

Heart sledgehammering against her ribs, breath laboring under the flow of fresh adrenaline, her eyes traveled upward from the feet to the face.

Helen stifled a gasp.

Maria!

But how could that be? Maria was dead! Dead and buried and gone to heaven, if such a place existed! Or, at least, some-place where she was safe and happy and where they would be together again someday. Helen believed in an afterlife, had believed in it devoutly since Maria's tragic death. At twelve, she had been unable to conceive of an end of Maria; at twenty-three, she still couldn't. But this naked imposture wasn't her sister. This Maria's eyes were dead. In the afterlife, as she believed in it, it was the spirit (or mind-force with all its emotions, memories, loves, and hates that marked it as being a human spirit) that survived the mortal clay that aged and grayed and returned to dust. And if the dead did visit this world in human shape, then Maria would appear with a smile on her face and a blessing, or maybe with tears in her eyes because they had been apart so long.

The apparition stopped a few feet from the barrels. And now its cheeks didn't seem so pale and fair at all. Dark streaks marred her slender woman-child form, soiled her limbs, her torso, even, Helen saw now, her chin and around her mouth. The streaks looked like mud, but given this twisted nightmare, they were probably blood.

Something in its hand!

Helen broke the hypnotic fascination, tore her eyes away from that dead, smiling gaze, beheld the knife in the thing's grip, the foot-long blade darkly stained as if whetted in a recent butchering.

"Helen," the wraith croaked as if something were blocking its throat.

And then the thing that almost hurled her irrecoverably over the brink of madness happened: the creature's mouth opened and its tongue came out, chalky white, and slimy with the mucus of decay, and kept coming out, elongating, growing fat as a cow's. The mouth opened wider, and wider still; the throat swelled like a balloon; and over and down the bloated tongue spewed a horde of bugs—beetles and roaches and locusts and millipedes—cascading out of the darkness of the maw to the ground like a flood of crawling vomit.

Paralyzed with fascination and fear, unnerved and racked with nausea at the sight of her long-dead sister spewing forth a river of squirming insects, she didn't see the shadow racing over the ground until it was streaming between the barrels and swarming over her hands and bare feet.

Her scream rose louder than the keening wind. She stood, beating the clinging, crawling insects from her arms and the backs of her hands with her shoes. Beyond fear now, soaring on the frantically beating wings of hysteria, she backpedaled, almost running in reverse, stamping her feet down hard to shake off the bugs, oblivious to the pain that sledgehammered up her right leg every time she brought her injured foot down, and slammed up hard against a wall.

The apparition was coming toward her, its bloodied arms hanging by its side, the long knife dangling against a blood-smeared thigh. She was not walking, but gliding over the torrent of insects.

Unable to take her eyes off her sister's dead gaze, Helen slid along the wall to her left until she encountered the rough boards of the old garage and could go no farther. There, cornered and defenseless except for the shoes in her hands, crawling black drifts of bugs covering her feet and ankles, working their way up her legs under her slacks, the whipping, whining wind filled with the earthy clicking and scuttling of thousands of mandibles and insectile legs, she slowly slipped down the wall as she cowered before the thing-that-was-not-Maria gliding toward her. Then she was on her knees and the insects were swarming up her thighs.

The apparition, horrifying yet shockingly familiar, stopped before her. It no longer floated but stood on the concrete. Roaches, spiders, praying mantises, and beetles crawled up and down its legs, over its bloodstained belly. A long glistening snake squirmed out of its vagina and wound itself down one leg. A brown bloated smell of corruption cocooned Helen.

No! You're not Maria! I'm dreaming! Go away!

The pinch of beetles' claws, the furry slithering of spiders' touch was maddening. For the second time in two days, Helen experienced a mindless terror that stripped away a lifetime of reasoning. And for a moment, as she stared into the thing's grinning, dead face, the sensations and images that had leapt into her head when she touched Izzy's machine flashed through her mind, left an afterimage of a chrome-faced pur-suer that dissolved into Maria-yet-not-Maria's face.

Grinning, staring down at her, its face contorted into a mask of sadistic evil the real Maria would never have been capable of, the apparition raised the blood-stained . . .

*

. . . knife.

He sees and feels with an enlarged awareness. Sees what his victim sees—a tide of insects crawling up her legs; feels what his victim feels—her heart leaping against her ribs like some caged bird mad to escape. He feels his victim's terror, her cowering, hysterical horror.

Victim! You're thinking about Helen, shouts a voice he has forgotten, the voice of his conscience. Helen, damn you!

And at the shout, Helen's fear which he has experienced till now remotely, as part of a dreamie, stabs home like a stake through the heart.

His eyes fling open, breaking the psychic contact. He wakes from his alpha trance, kills the transmitting switch.

For a long time, he sits, panting, hands shaking, staring at the dim rectangle of the wide-screen TV on the opposite . . .

. . . wall to support herself, raised a hand to fend off the knife.

Her equilibrium lurched, pitching her forward onto her hands again, as the alley—the long gray wall of the garage, the brick wall of the tenement—wavered, then ran like watercolors, blurring . . .

. . . patterns of dark and darker, reforming, resolving . . .

She blinked. The alley was gone. She was on her hands and knees on a patch of hard earth circled by dry, rustling reeds. The sky was starry, and though she was chilled to the bone, she felt ten degrees warmer than she had a moment ago.

The sound of passing cars drew her attention. High above the rustling vegetation, supported by towering concrete pillars, a skyway spanned the sky. Below this, an ancient train trestle ran parallel to the soaring turnpike.

She sat, hardly aware of the cold seeping through the seat of her pants for the agony that flared in her foot. She still held her shoes. No insect carcasses clung to the soles. Though she still felt their squirming masses swarming over her flesh, biting, pinching, stinging, she was amazed to find no evidence they'd ever existed.

She inspected her foot. The starlight was too dim to see by, but there was a hole in her sock and the heel was sticky with blood. As this was no place to doctor it, she gritted her teeth and worked the shoe over the tender flesh.

A galaxy of stars exploded inside her head when she stood. She was in what looked like a park. Nearby, a street, complete with lighted lamps, passing cars, even a couple of pedestrians, ran under the turnpike and the train trestle and on up a hill.

Forcing herself to ignore the pain, she headed for the street.

21

Q.: Critics have complained that *Vampirophile*'s plot is predictable.

I.: Well, there are only so many endings to a vampire story. (He shrugs.)

Q.: Even when the vampire's really a human?

I.: That's true too.

Q.: You've also been criticized for concentrating solely on action and suspense and special effects and that your characters lack content.

I.: (Shrugging again): To paraphrase Alfred Hitchcock: the style is the important thing, not the content.

Quent leaned back in his chair and rubbed his tired eyes, hot from staring at the computer screen. He stretched, yawned, and looked at the clock built into the thermostat on the kitchen wall. He was surprised to find it was only a little after eleven. It felt like one in the morning; he was almost burnt for the night.

Quent's doorbell, mounted in a corner of the kitchen behind the fridge, burrred, as if it wasn't getting enough juice to ring. He stuck his head out the kitchen door and switched on the downstairs hall light so he could see who was there before pressing the buzzer to let them in.

It was Helen! What on earth . . . ?

Instead of buzzing her in, he ran down and got the door himself. She was limping badly when she brushed past him, mumbling "Thank you," her voice fatigued. And when she stopped at the foot of the stairs, putting a hand on the newel post for support and looked at him, he saw the black eye.

"My God!" he said, too shocked to think about discretion. "What happened to you?"

She ignored his question. "Would it be all right if I came in and sat down for a while? I really can't walk much farther."

"Yes, yes, of course!"

Quent ushered her upstairs, walking one step behind her, his hand hovering near her back in case she stumbled. She didn't seem to mind, and when she wavered at the top of the stairs and he caught her arm, she leaned into his support. Under his hand, her muscles trembled.

If her shiner looked bad in the hall light, it looked worse under the kitchen fluorescent. The flesh under her left eye was purple-black and puffy over her prominent cheekbones. She made no attempt to hide her face as he led her through the kitchen and into his tiny living room. Holding her arm, he helped her sit on the imitation-leather love seat.

"There's no use hiding my face," she said, taking his attention off her shiner by looking him in the eye. "I've had a rough night, I guess you could say."

I guess I could, he thought, but held back a torrent of questions leapfrogging over one another trying to get out of his mouth. "I'd say that's an understatement. What's wrong with your foot?"

As if he had reminded her, she removed her right shoe. The sock was filthy, the heel bloody. Quent lifted the foot and placed it on the coffee table atop today's *Jersey Journal*.

"Let me take a look at this." Gingerly, he peeled the sock off. The wound was small. Probably hurt worse than it looked.

"Do I need stitches?" she asked in a voice that sounded too tired to care.

"I don't think so. It's just deep enough to bleed a lot. Hold on, let's clean that up before it gets infected." He disappeared into the bathroom before she could protest.

They sat on the love seat: she with her foot, freshly bandaged

(Quent didn't have gauze so he cut up an old T-shirt), parked on the coffee table next to an empty brandy glass; he nursing the remains of a bottle of warm beer, not wanting to finish it but feeling like he should keep his hands busy. When he finished doctoring her foot, she had hobbled into the bathroom and freshened up and combed her hair. She looked better, calmer too, but her eye was just as black and her cheek just as swollen.

She seemed lucid, albeit tired, as her story unfolded piece by reluctant piece. But as the pieces formed a picture, he began to wonder if, maybe, Izzy had hit her harder than she thought. He watched for drowsiness, for lapses of attention or disjointed speech, but saw no signs of concussion.

She had split with Izzy, she told him right off while he sterilized her wound with hydrogen peroxide. Now here was a story worth some bucks to the supermarket set . . . if he were inclined to try to sell his soul to yellow journalism. He wasn't. He could see from the way she kept biting her lip and wringing her hands, she was torn up over their separation.

She described how Izzy had turned on her and struck her, how he acted like a deranged animal. "The funny thing is," she half-smiled, as if to keep from crying, "Izzy has never hit me before tonight. We've never even really fought."

She told him about Dr. Nösberger's bizarre death and how she suspected Izzy knew more than he admitted. "He appeared to be gloating," she said. She explained about taraxein and Nösberger's visit to Izzy's studio the very night a man was murdered and the strange footprints left in their yard. She voiced her suspicions that Izzy was taking drugs and how he was acting increasingly schizophrenic.

Quent's thoughts went back to Izzy's bizarre behavior at the Dreamacon. "Makes sense."

"You remember when Dr. Nösberger showed up Thursday?"

"Sure."

"Something happened between them that day. Izzy didn't tell me what and I didn't pry, but they argued. You remember how upset Nösberger was."

Quent nodded. Nösberger definitely had a gripe. "And now he's dead."

"Exactly." Her dark eyes met his, frankly, even grimly, and he caught a glimmer then, looking into those dark, worried eyes, of the depths to which her suspicions ran.

A chill swept over him. Did she really believe Izzy had consciously murdered her psychology professor? And if he believed her, what was the price for believing?

She told him about her pursuer, about finding herself in a deserted part of town she had never seen.

The details came gushing out, a torrent of words . . . her sister . . . the insects . . .

". . . And when I stood up and looked around," she said, "it was as if my vision was blurring. Everything wavered and"— she shook her head—"the alley disappeared."

"'Disappeared'?"

She nodded. "Look, I know everything I've said sounds crazy, like something that only happens in movies and dreams, but it happened. Anyway, the alley sort of shimmered and ran, and I was in a park and had no idea how I got there."

The terror—the kind of shocked, fearful expression people have on their face after a close call—never left her eyes as she told her tale. And his heart went out to her as it would to a lost child. He resisted the strong urge to put his arm around her, to stroke her hair and whisper, Don't be afraid. Everything will be all right.

His thoughts wandered to the first time he met her. Standing by her curio cabinet discussing her memorabilia. He'd been at once appalled and intrigued by the unexpected feelings he'd experienced. Feelings he'd chalked up to "lust at first sight." He'd felt like some moon-eyed, sweaty-palmed teenager. But it wasn't just a "crush" he felt sitting beside her listening to her story. He felt protective, caring.

And god damn you if you pursue that thought another inch, Mr. Quentin J. Hughes!

"Another brandy?" he asked. "I could use a refill myself." He indicated his empty bottle.

Her hand closed on his wrist, and he started at the jolt of electricity her touch sent up his arm. Her eyes were searching. "Do you believe anything I've said tonight?"

He thought: I believe you are in pain, physically and mentally. I believe Izzy hit you. And I believe—God help me—that I'm either falling in love with you or coming down with the flu.

"I know you must think you're talking to a schizo," she said when he didn't answer.

He met her gaze. "No, I don't think you're schizo. And, yes, I do believe you've had a very upsetting day." Upsetting? Jeez, if that wasn't fucking patronizing!

She sighed and dropped her gaze to the floor. "Maybe I *was* hallucinating. I don't know. It's just that . . ." Her eyes found his again. "You know, I've been with Izzy a long time now and I'm very familiar with his dreamies, and I could swear that I was experiencing his work."

Her wing-like brows were knit so that they looked like butting rams' horns over the bridge of her nose. But as much as he wanted to believe for her sake, he couldn't make the required leap of faith.

"Izzy was what—three, four miles away during this time?" he pointed out almost apologetically.

"That's right."

Her gaze didn't waver from his. Her expression told him she understood the contradictions but still believed Izzy had something to do with the nightmare she'd experienced. He, on the other hand, knew the limitations of the technology. The dreamatron had a limited range and was supposed to work only on those in an alpha state within the parameter of transmission.

"Okay," he said. "Let's say you're right and you experienced a dreamie miles from the dreamatron."

She looked relieved; her brow relaxed some.

"My first assumption would have to be that he's made some astounding modifications to his machine. Has he mentioned making any changes?"

"No."

"Received packages from an electronics company?"

"Not that I know of."

Quent shrugged. "He had to have changed something for what we're discussing to have taken place."

"There's another possibility," she said.

"What's that?"

"Maybe it's the dreamer that's changed."

22

Riiinng . . .

Heat rose in shimmering waves from the sea of glittering glass. The white sun was blinding. The glass clawed into his blistered hands, agonized his bloody knees.

Riiinng . . . riiinng . . .

No excessive gravity forced him down, none of his limbs were broken, nor was he hamstrung. It was as if that part of his brain that enabled him to stand or even to prop himself up on his hands had shut down, so that he was forced to crawl along commando-fashion, his stomach and genitals clearing the blistering glass by inches, his face taking the brunt of the rising heat as his shadow labored across the blacktop.

Riiinng . . .

He stopped, unable to go on, sprawled on the scorching glass in the middle of the vast intersection like a snake out in the middle of a highway, ready meat for the first truck-driving-cowboy to come along. His throat was parched. Wisps of steam rose from the glass as sweat dripped from his nose and chin. Gasping, he squinted and looked across the road at the candy store with the Coke sign in its window and the Dolly Madison ice cream sign with its familiar bonneted silhouette hanging under the larger blue-and-white sign announcing Annie's Sweet Shoppe, and he looked at the phone booth in front of the shop. So far away, so hopelessly unreachable . . .

Riiinng . . .

Helen was on the other end of the line, he was certain of it.

Helen!

He started forward again, gingerly, biting back the excruciating pain each movement brought, careful to keep the veins in his wrists clear of the glass. A jag of glass drove a wedge between the joints of his elbow, jabbed into his funny bone, and his tears dripped with his sweat.

The shadow of a cloud fell over him, then another, and another. The sky was darkening fast, the sun was hidden; already the glass felt cooler. He prayed for rain. A breeze sprang up, sifting the finer glass particles, Dolly Madison swayed, and the phone in the booth rang and rang and rang like a tolling of doom.

The sky grew dark as a total eclipse. The breeze became a wind. Annie's Sweet Shoppe and the smaller Dolly Madison sign below swung wildly now. Grains of glass peppered his face. Afraid for his sight, he closed his eyes. Under the keening wind and the crawling crablike scuffling of glass, the incessant phone clamored in the dark.

Oh, Helen . . . wake me, wake me . . .

The wind howled like a vast beast let loose on the world, a creature that knew only rage. The glass stung his skin. He felt the lacerations blossoming on his cheeks and the backs of his hands. He began to crawl again, adding new cuts to his already ragged palms.

Then a long sliver of glass pierced his eyelid and buried itself in his eye. The pain jolted him awake. Only the pain was in his stomach, not his eye.

He lay in his bed doubled up on his side, an excruciating cramp squeezing his guts. He couldn't straighten out. His whole body was clenched like a fist.

"Owww," he moaned as he tried to sit up and the pain intensified. "Helen!" As soon as he said her name, it all came flooding back: Helen's gone! She left me! And on the heels of that the brutal memory: Because I hit her!

Remorse, more brutal than the pain in his gut, swept over him. Now he forced himself to sit, and when he straightened himself out and the pain flared, he roared like a wild animal and punched the mattress.

She was gone and he had hit her!

He looked at her side of the bed: it hadn't been slept in, the familiar indentation in her pillow was missing. He got to his feet and, clutching his abdomen, made it into the master bathroom and sat on the toilet, thinking the pain was caused by constipation. He peed, but he couldn't go. As he recalled, he hadn't eaten much the day before.

He splashed cold water on his face, soaking his gloves. His head cleared a bit. The pain was subsiding. Collecting his clothes from where he had dumped them beside the bed, he dressed and went downstairs.

His mouth was dry. He went into the kitchen, turned on the overhead fluorescent, took a glass from the cabinet, opened the fridge.

The heavy-bottomed tumbler slipped from his hand, exploded when it hit the tiles. He backpedaled. The fridge door swung unmercifully wider, revealing the horror inside. The food, the shelves, everything was gone, and there was Dr. Nösberger, curled up inside, looking stiff and cold and gray and dead.

Resisting the impulse to flee, he reached out and slammed the fridge door. Three antique bottles rattled on top and a magnetic Stark note holder popped off the door. He opened the fridge again, just a crack—then opened it wider. The food was back: peanut butter, jam, wheat bread, milk, three foil-wrapped brownies left over from the batch Helen made Tuesday night.

Tears welled up and ran down his cheeks. He let them flow, not caring, only missing Helen and wishing he could convince himself that he hadn't hit her.

It's all your own fault, he told himself as he poured himself a glass of milk. He had been putting too much, everything in fact, into his art at the expense of Helen and their relationship.

He took his glass to the table and sat. He could still hear the phone's incessant ringing. It had been Helen on the other end; he had known that all through the dream.

He took a sip of the cold milk . . .

And spat it across the table! Gagging, he held the glass to the light. White worms squirmed in the milk.

He made it to the sink, retched down the drain. He didn't have much on his stomach to vomit—a thin stream of bilish fluid, followed by a few dry leaves. He washed the works— puke, milk and worms—down the drain, rinsed his mouth with cold water, and drank some, trying to rid himself of the feeling of slug-like bodies on his tongue.

As soon as the cold water hit bottom, the pain slammed into him like someone walloping his stomach with a baseball bat. And while he was doubled over, gripping the edge of the sink, he realized he was hungry after all—but not for food, for taraxein.

He salivated at the thought of the drug.

The blood is the life.

The craving became all-consuming. Just thinking about the drug's effects—the sense of immense well-being, the augmented concentration, the confidence—made the pain bearable.

He opened the basement door, flicked the light switch. Clutching his stomach with one hand and the rail with the other, he forced himself down the stairs. He made it to his machine and plopped himself in the seat. Immediately, he had the blotter out and was chewing four hits.

A while later, he stirred and realized he had been mindlessly watching the shifting blue-and-violet patterns on the wall screen. He blinked and took a deep breath, felt a roar in his ears when the breath turned into a yawn.

He felt much better. So good in fact he had forgotten the pain. Remembering now, he was grateful for the drug.

Hell, he thought. Maybe I *am* addicted. So fucking what? Other people were addicted to worse things—alcohol, nicotine—and didn't get any benefits but a shortened lifespan. His taking taraxein may have produced hallucinations and unwarranted fear, but it had also produced some of the most terrifying horror sequences he had ever experienced and had allowed his art to evolve into something new and exciting— and truly dangerous!

From the blood of schizophrenics . . .

A dreamie spun from schizophrenic nightmares! A "new wave" of dreamies! And, once more, the name Isidor Stark hailed as an innovator, as a prodigy, a genius!

His face glowed as he thought of it. The power of creation rippled through his skin, surged through his veins.

On impulse, he rose and went up to Helen's room to borrow her abnormal psychology textbook. He looked on the window seat and the wicker chair by the door, then searched the shelves; it wasn't there. Then he remembered she had been on her way in from school when they'd had the fight. He ran downstairs, and sure enough, there it was lying on the kitchen counter. He sat at the table and opened the book to the section on schizophrenia. He turned pages and, after studying again the illustrations of schizophrenic artwork, skimmed paragraphs until he found what he was looking for under the subtitle: "The Dreams of Schizophrenics."

Psychologists have long noted the similarities between schizophrenic hallucinations and a normal person's REM activity. Normal dreams are, usually, a loose-jointed episodic working out of waking wishes and problems, but in schizophrenia, dreams are symbolically self-centered and usually reflect the schizophrenic's anxieties. In acute schizophrenia, however, a malfunction occurs in the REM system producing a breakdown of the barrier that normally keeps REM activity out of waking time. This barrier, chemical in nature, has not yet been isolated.

In schizophrenia—in common with persons suffering from trauma or stress—a marked reduction of REM time is seen as the condition worsens. The lost REM time tends to bleed over into waking time. Psychologists now generally agree that the schizophrenic hallucination is a misplaced dream.

That's what's happening to me, he thought. My nightmares are bleeding over into waking reality as if taraxein has created a rift.

Farther down the page he read:

The dreams of a schizophrenic are usually bland, object- rather than people-oriented. As the condition worsens and the waking hallucinations become more and more intense, the few dreams he does have during his sleeping hours will often center on a single inanimate object. The object will usually reflect some wish or fear the schizophrenic has.

It occurred to him that the monster in his latest dream had been an inanimate object—a phone booth. He remembered the telephone ringing, the wind keening, recalled his certainty that it was Helen on the other end of the line, recalled his frustration at being unable to answer it.

Anger, abrupt and savage, flared through him, crushing the guilt that clutched his throat, and he swept the big psychology book from the table. It went sailing, leaves fluttering, crashed into the cabinet doors under the sink, and fell to the floor. He slammed his fist on the table. The salt and pepper shakers clattered over on their sides.

"Shit!" he growled. Yeah, he had hit her, but look what she had done to him. She had betrayed him. Sold him out like some fucking Judas. She had been spying on him. Snooping around his machine, seeing how much fucking mud he had on his goddamned sneakers. Probably watched him go out and come in that night too. Spying on him.

He thought of Nösberger curled in the fridge.

From the blood of schizophrenics . . .

Bleeding over into waking reality . . .

His eyes fell on the book lying face down, some of the pages crumpled underneath, and his anger dissipated. The spread-eagled covers, as he knew, depicted the most famous of Bosch's hellscapes. The garish red-and-black picture captivated his gaze. He rose and retrieved the volume and examined the covers closely under the kitchen fluorescent. His heartbeat quickened as he took in the fires, the blackness, the fish-and-bird-headed demons prodding and torturing their naked human captives, the roiling, powerful sense of insanity, of horror.

Chest swelling with inspiration, he took the textbook to the living room and the bookshelves near the sofa. He had only a vague glimmering of where his train of thought would lead, and he didn't try to force it. He was familiar with the muse and how she worked; how one thing would lead to another if he just trusted, and he'd end up with a synthesis that was greater than its parts.

He switched on a lamp, ran a finger over the spines of a dozen or so of Helen's oversized art books on the second shelf from the bottom and pulled the volume on Hieronymus Bosch. The dust jacket, like the psychology text, was predominately black and red.

An omen?

No, just the muse at work.

He sat and opened the book. Visions leapt from the pages: impossible anthropomorphic combinations of man and animal, and bird and fish, the wild glee in demons' eyes. He had always thought of Bosch as a master of the macabre, but now he looked on the five-hundred-year-old visions with new eyes, this time three-dimensionally, as if the garish hellscape actually stretched below, valleys and ridges and narrow fire-lit paths tortuously winding between smoky pits of boiling God-knows-what.

As the wings of his genius spread.

Encompassing all.

INFERNO

A dream is a brief madness and madness a long dream.
                                            Schopenhauer

23

After a chilly night, during which the Hudson filled with fog, and boats and ships called to one another like lost ghosts, Friday, October 30, woke unseasonably warm and soon streamers of mist rose fifty feet and more from the base of the Palisades like steam from a jungle.

The news stations Friday morning were rumoring that temperatures would mount into the upper 80s by midafternoon and probably drop no lower than 75 degrees that night. The eleven-o'clock news that evening would predict more of the same for tomorrow, accompanied by even higher humidity and generally putrid air quality. For the Halloween weekend, the metropolitan area was slated for a relapse into Indian summer. Not the Indian summer the words make you think of—autumn leaves glowing in multicolored splendor under a blue sky dotted with high white clouds, honey-gold sunshine pouring over all—but Indian summer at its hot and humid worst. The kind of muggy, uncomfortable weather that makes you wish you hadn't taken your air conditioner out of the window so soon.

By 12 midnight, Halloween, the hour at which Izzy's *Mystery Show* was scheduled to begin, and continuing through Sunday, the sky over the metropolitan area would be a hazy inverted bowl of smog holding in the heat and humidity.

The sudden change in weather would, as those who collect statistics on such things can attest, wreak havoc with some people's systems and would kill a few elderly and young folks with respiratory problems. A number of people would also fall victim to violent street crimes as tempers rose with the temperature.

But no way was the weather the major cause of death that Halloween season. Before cooler air blowing down out of Canada cleared away the oppressive smog Sunday night, giving Monday morning commuters a much-needed break, at least

370 people would die in Hudson County. But their deaths had nothing whatsoever to do with the weather.

While Helen slept in his living room, Quent lay awake, mulling over the things she had told him and listening to the foghorns.

Chester—who sat up downstairs in the living room most of the night with his old Ruger 10/22 Long Rifle braced across his lap, in case Jason's killer should return, while Lois slept under sedation—also listened to the foghorns. To his ears, they seemed to mourn for Jason.

Izzy, awake and working most of the night, neither saw nor heard anything but the vision taking shape in his mind.

That morning Izzy dreamed.

But before that, for much of the night, he had created.

Borne high on the wings of inspiration and three more hits of taraxein, he unleashed his imagination on the dreamatron and in less than six hours hacked out a rough draft of what he foresaw would be his most terrifying dreamie to date. All that remained was to beef it up and to tell Solly how he wanted the marquee to read.

He would substitute it for his *Mystery Show,* it was superior.

At last, run dry like a car battery when the lights have been left on overnight, he nodded at his dreamatron—and dreamed.

The dream was uncannily simple and perhaps the most frightening he'd ever had. He dreamed of an old-fashioned black Bell telephone, the type with the perforated dial. That was all—just the phone against a gray background.

And nothing changed. Waiting for the phone to ring or the dream to change was maddening, and the longer he waited, the higher his anxiety soared. The phone wasn't about to ring: it wasn't just dead in the sense of "out of order"; it was cold, mute and instilled with the aura of death.

Waking, he groggily reached out to shut the machine off, forgetting in his sleepiness about the automatic shut-off feature, and turned it on instead. Instantly, a barrage of startling images leapt into his head and he hurried to shut it off.

God, no, he couldn't handle that stuff before breakfast.

"Breakfast," he said aloud.

Wide awake now, he was aware his stomach was sore with hunger. He remembered his hallucination—the white worms in the milk—and his hunger diminished some.

Upstairs, he tried the Welch's grape jam, spinning off the lid and peering into the blue goo; the jam was alive with the maggot-like creatures. The jar went into the garbage.

Everything can't be contaminated, he told himself.

But then he saw the worms writhing beneath the plastic bread bag. A lone worm five or six inches long wriggled out from under the aluminum foil that covered a bowl of leftover something or other, worked its way along the bowl's rim for a centimeter or two, then dropped off and fell into the half-eaten bowl of Jell-O on the shelf below. A bag of Double Stuffs writhed on the same shelf, the plastic crinkling and crackling as roaches crawled within. He slammed the fridge door.

Someone had entered the house and planted the bugs. He had enemies. It could even have been Helen—probably had been, in fact! She had motive; after the beating he'd given her, she would be out for revenge. He had to consider all the food in the fridge poisoned.

Canned goods, then, he thought triumphantly, thinking he'd outwitted her. She couldn't contaminate cans. In the pantry, he found a can of chili. He salivated at the sight of the red can revolving on the electric can opener. His stomach noises started up a fresh symphony.

The rolling blade severed the last snip of metal and the lid came free. Gingerly, he removed the can from the opener and held it so that he could examine its contents without getting it too close to his face. The gelled, chili-red grease and meat sauce pebbled with beans looked okay. He shoveled the contents into a saucepan.

"God!" he screamed, and dumped the can into the pan on top of the huge gray slug that uncoiled in the grease. "This isn't happening. I'm hallucinating. There's nothing in this pan but chili."

Still, no way could he eat the contents of the pan. His stomach growled as he chucked the chili, saucepan and all, into the garbage.

Cold terror gripped him. Was he to be like Midas, unable to eat because everything he touched became uneatable?

His stomach growled as the fear crawled over him.

To take his mind off his hunger and calm his near hysteria, he went upstairs to shower and shave.

He couldn't take the water too hot; he was wobbly and shaky with exhaustion. His stomach, already knotted with hunger, shrank like wet rawhide under a desert sun with the stress of guilt and paranoia. Using his gloves like washcloths, he soaped himself up and stood under the tepid water for a long time, almost in a trance, letting the sound of drumming water replace his troubled thoughts.

He finished off his shower by standing under the cold water, gritting his teeth as gooseflesh shivered over his body. That washed most of the cobwebs down the drain, though the dull migraine of hunger still pinged like a ball-peen hammer in the wings.

Out of the shower now, dried, he wiped the fogged mirror with the towel. It immediately fogged over again. He had forgotten to put on the fan. He put it on now and currents appeared in the steam that had been roiling aimlessly before. The currents drifted toward the circular vent in the ceiling. Tenaciously, the steam clung to the mirror.

No matter. He didn't need a mirror to shave. He pulled the white-and-aquamarine can of Hair Off from the cabinet and smeared the mint-scented gel over his stubble. Waiting for the mask to dry, he counted to sixty then tugged at the edge of the Hair Off mask below his right ear. It resisted. He tugged again, harder. It hurt, but didn't come off. It seemed stuck, which was strange: Hair Off came off easily, more like Saran Wrap than tape. Had he let it stay on too long?

Gritting his teeth, he gave it the old heave-ho, and a long flap, from his ear to his chin tore loose with a sound like adhesive tape. In the patchily-fogged mirror, the strip of Hair Off looked like a flap of skin. He leaned closer. What he saw turned his bowels to ice water.

He held the flap closed while he toweled the mirror.

The glass was clear now. The Hair Off covering the lower half of his face was as green and cheesy as corpse's flesh. The eyes staring back at him from the mirror were incredibly blue against the blanched pallor of the face above the mask. He recognized the stark terror in his eyes. It matched the heartbeat thudding in his throat. He lowered again the thin flap of Hair Off and stared in shock at the horror beneath.

Flesh adhered to the plastic flap, leaving little patches of abraded skin down the jawline. It was as if the top layer of flesh had come off with the shaving mask, leaving a bloody, raw strip down the side of his face. And in the center of his cheek, the greatest horror of all—a quarter-sized plug of flesh was missing, a ragged, bloody hole through which he saw his gums and two of his teeth.

After gazing at the oozing wound for what seemed like an hour during which he died a dozen times but still stood, he tore his eyes away from the nightmare. Blood dripped into the basin, spattered the white porcelain.

"My God!"

He looked back at his reflection. The wound was still there, open, bleeding, though he tasted no blood! With such a wound, his face should have been in excruciating pain, but the only pain he experienced was the charley-horse-like cramp he was getting in his abdomen because his stomach muscles were so clenched.

Closing his eyes and gritting his teeth, he peeled the plastic down his chin and off his throat until, with a final tug, he freed the flesh-clotted mask. Without looking at his reflection to check the other side, he dropped the bizarre hide into the stainless-steel chute of the disposal and ran from the room. Though he told himself it was a hallucination, his hands were shaking and he was afraid of seeing again the soul-shaking sight of his teeth showing through the hole in his face.

In the bedroom, averting his face from either of the two mirrors—the dresser's and the one over the slate mantelpiece—he rummaged through Helen's drawer till he found what he was looking for: one of her silk slips, black and thin enough to be almost translucent. He dug through the closet until he found her sewing kit. Then, still averting his eyes from the mirrors, he sat on the edge of the bed and got to work.

He had done a neat job, he thought, catching his reflection in the white surface of the dreamatron. The black veil was unhemmed; he'd had a hard enough time threading the needle the way his hands were shaking. He had simply folded over one end of the big rectangle he had cut from the slip and clumsily stitched it down, then worked through a long ribbon also cut from the slip to tie around his head. For eyeholes, he'd lit a piece of rope and touched the smoldering end to where he figured his eyes would be.

He smiled under the veil, pleased with the image. It was all coming together. First his introduction to taraxein and his subsequent discovery of his newly gained powers. Then his vision last night and the extraordinary dreamie that had resulted. And now a new image. The black veil, hanging in soft folds from his hairline down past his chin and back over his ears and complemented by the black driving gloves, reminded him of Nathaniel Hawthorne's gothic classic, "The Minister's Black Veil." It was easy to see the image on T-shirts, red eyes staring out of the eyeholes.

He noticed that, although shadowed by the veil and only dimly seen in the pearly surface of his machine, he could see a bit of his throat showing under the veil. He bent closer, leaning over the controls, tilting his head up, letting the veil drop away from his neck so that he could see, dialing up the lights and peering down into the reflective surface to get a good look . . .

He froze, goggling at the minutiae of horror: the patches of putrefying flesh like gray-green sores, the spot of bony grill-work where his Adam's apple showed through the discolored flesh. Death was spreading.

He clasped the veil to his throat and shoved himself back in his seat, shivering as one would putting a hand into the guts of a maggoty animal. The image stirred a childhood memory.

When he was ten and growing up in Hoboken, he had, one day, heard a crash down the next block and had stopped what he was doing and had run down to see what had happened along with half the other kids in the neighborhood. When he got there, a crowd had gathered. A white ice-cream truck had hit an old lady. Her shopping bag spilled, her tomatoes had rolled under a parked car. The old lady was sprawled, her face bloody, one hand stretched out as if reaching for her glasses, which twinkled in the summer sunlight a short distance away. The top of her head had burst like an egg, spraying the blacktop with sluglike blobs of gray matter.

He remembered thinking, looking at the splattered brains before the policeman shooed him away: Why don't they pick it up? She might need that. It's getting dirty!

But the thing that disturbed him most—more than the thought of her brains soaking up the grit of the Hoboken Street—was what happened just before the ambulance arrived. The old lady's eyes became blank, fixed, no longer afraid or confused or anything. Then, as he watched, unable to look away, they fogged over as if a light had gone out inside. That's how it seemed: as if whatever lived in there had gone bye-bye and turned the lights out before leaving.

The incident had impressed him all these years. Whenever he needed to give a close-up of the face of the dead, he recalled the old woman's eyes. In a Stark dreamie, the dead always had fogged-over eyes.

His stomach growled, reminding him that he was running on empty. He had to eat; he would die if he didn't. Still, even though he knew, for the moment at least, that the worms and maggots were a hallucination, he couldn't bring himself to eat the food in the house.

What's to become of me? he thought despairingly, clenching his freshly gloved hands in his lap.

24

"Lois . . ."

She sat on the edge of her bed. In one hand, she held a picture of Jason, in the other, she clutched a brown threadbare sweater, one of Jase's favorites. How long she had been sitting there weeping, Chet didn't know. The police had just left—the second time. They were at the house a good two hours last night. The buzz of voices, the photographer's flash, the body bag were all a blur to him. Only the image of Jason's face remained vivid: his 3-D glasses crushed and dangling from his ears, his head smashed, blood streaming from his mouth, nostrils, ears, his eyes facing each other in a cross-eyed expression of horror.

Chet cleared his throat, tried again, "Lois."

She looked at him. Wet streaks cut glittering paths down her cheeks from her red-rimmed eyes to her jaw. He remembered holding her in his arms last night and thinking how smooth her features were, how youthful and wrinkle-free. Now lines had appeared everywhere, drawing up her features in a mask of weariness and sorrow, as if she had aged ten years in a single night.

He came to her, shrugged helplessly, near to tears himself, sat next to her on the bed, and put his arm around her, drawing her close. Questions hung in her eyes. Unable to say anything that could offer consolation, he said nothing.

"Ohhh!" A guttural sound, made deep in her throat, a sob, and he felt the sorrow of it, the bewilderment, the loss.

"Oh, God, Chet." She wept against his collar. "Jason can't be gone. Not my Jason! Oh, God, oh, God!"

He touched her face. The pain in her eyes was unbearable. And all he could do was hold her and smooth her hair. He couldn't even whisper that things were going to be all right, because things were *not* going to be all right, because Jase was dead and he wasn't coming back.

Downstairs, the bell chimed. Gently withdrawing, Chet went down and answered the door.

The bushy-browed man in the three-piece suit looked too intelligent to be a cop. "May I help you?" Chet said, annoyed the caller hadn't been deterred by the black wreath.

"Yes," the man said with a slight accent Chet couldn't place, though his tall, swept-back forehead and long curved nose suggested Slavic. "Forgive me for intruding. I see you've suffered a loss. May I offer my condolences."

"Look," Chet said, "we've got our hands full. Can I help you?"

"Of course. My name is Dr. Rejdak. Can you tell me if Mr. Carruthers is at home?"

Quent mopped his face with his handkerchief as he went up Izzy's walk. It was hot. Near eighty. Humid, crazy weather.

"I could swear, now that I look back on it, that I was experiencing his work," Helen had said, but he couldn't bring himself to believe Izzy had acquired the ability to transmit a dreamie three miles from Weehawken to Hoboken. Still, he'd as much as promised her he would keep an open mind. He wished he could get into Izzy's basement and spend some time alone with his dreamatron, see if he could find some modification that would explain Helen's bizarre experience. Otherwise, he would have to assume she had hallucinated the whole thing, and that could mean she'd been hit harder than she thought and she should be seeing a doctor, which she'd refused to do.

Another possibility occurred to him—not one that he took seriously, but worth a thought. He had heard that siblings—especially twins—as well as lovers and spouses, were more telepathically receptive to one another than, say, two strangers. But the accounts usually told of images individuals picked up at the moment something bad happened to a loved one. Nothing so elaborate or bizarre as what Helen described.

When Quent reached out to press Izzy's doorbell, a premonition of danger washed over him—and an almost visceral sense of repulsion, as if the house was trying to push him off the steps.

Not the house—its occupant.

He broke out in a cold rash as he forced himself to press the ivory-white button.

The door opened almost immediately—as if Izzy had been watching—stopped at the end of its latch chain.

"Morning, Quent." Izzy's voice. Behind the door. A little cold, certainly not glad to see him.

"Hi, Iz." Light from the broad transom flooded the foyer and through the crack Quent made out an umbrella stand and a portion of one of Helen's watercolors. Hidden by the door, Izzy was a shadow—a glimpse of shoulder, a sneakered foot.

"Did I catch you at a bad time?"

"Actually, you did. Concert's tomorrow night and I'm swamped."

"That's why I came over—the concert I mean. Thought I'd get a few comments before the show. I should have called."

"We'll have plenty of time to talk on tour."

" 'Tour'?"

"Sure, all expenses paid. You'll get plenty of material for our book. How's that sound?"

A week ago it would have sounded great. After last night . . .

"Sure, yeah, that'll work."

The door started to close. He put a hand on it, halted its progress.

"Iz?"

"Yeah?"

"How's Helen?"

A pause.

"She's sleeping."

Sleeping! Quent's temper, usually slow to arouse, boiled up.

"Tell her I said hi. And Iz?"

"Hum?"

"Anything to say to your fans before the concert? For the record."

"Sure." Izzy laughed and, for a moment, he sounded like the old Isidor Stark he'd known in high school. "Fan is short for fanatic."

"All right! And is it going to be a good show?"

"Good? The fans'll die when they see this one! *Ciao*, baby!"

"*Ciao*."

The door closed, clicked shut, followed by the sound of a deadbolt ramming home.

"Good luck tomorrow night," Quent called through the door.

She's sleeping . . . Izzy had lied so smoothly.

Maybe it's the dreamer that's changed.

Quent's blood boiled and he resisted the urge to lean on the doorbell until Izzy returned and to tell him that Helen was at his apartment right now with a black eye and what did he have to say to that?

Safe inside with a locked door between him and the world, Izzy looked out a window in time to see his neighbor intercept Quent halfway down the walk.

Mr. Brown looked excited as he called to Quent over the hedge. As he talked, he kept glancing at Izzy's house, his eyes searching the windows. The old boy couldn't see him: it was bright out and dim in here and he was watching through a crack between the curtains. The way Brown kept looking at the house . . . And now Brown pointed at him—or Izzy thought he did and stepped back farther into the dimness of the room. Quent, too, was staring at the house as he listened to the old man.

He's discussing me! Izzy clenched his gloved fists, licked his lips under the veil.

I asked Chet last night to remind me and he reminded me this morning.

My TV has been picking up strange signals.

. . . and all of a sudden, there's this guy running butt-naked down this hall. Tall, bald, blond hair.

Could it be anything you're working on?

Jason Carruthers had suspected much and had told Mr. Brown . . . How much had he told?

Now they parted, Brown moving toward his house and Quent heading toward the street. But when he reached the sidewalk, Quent veered left and went up the Carruthers' walk and accompanied Mr. Brown inside.

Quent hadn't known what to expect when Izzy's neighbor waved him over. He'd suspected something odd was up, by the way the elderly man's pale-gray eyes kept staring past him, searching Izzy's house. He introduced himself as Chet Brown and asked him to come inside. He had something important to ask him concerning Isidor Stark.

The black wreath on the door struck an ominous note.

Inside, introduced to a Dr. Rejdak, a physics professor from

Stevens Tech, and Mrs. Carruthers, he was seated, offered a brandy, which he declined, and soon learned why Mr. Brown approached him.

"I've seen you visit our neighbors' house twice," Mrs. Carruthers said. "Helen mentioned a writer friend of Izzy's was doing a book on him." She smiled when he looked surprised and explained, "Helen and I sometimes shop together. You are that young man, aren't you?"

Quent acknowledged he was.

"You went to high school with him, Helen said."

"Yes." Quent wondered when she would get to the point.

He was also more than a little curious about the sopping wet carpet and the smashed TV. From the look on Mr. Brown's and Mrs. C.'s faces and the tension in their voices, something unpleasant must have happened.

"Then you know him well."

"No, we were out of touch for years."

"But you've talked to him lately?" Mr. Brown asked, leaning forward in his armchair. Professor Rejdak sat impassive in the other armchair. "You're familiar with what he's working on."

"To an extent," he said, being purposely ambiguous, hoping they'd get past the questions and start explaining.

"What we're interested in knowing," Rejdak spoke up, "is whether or not Mr. Stark is doing anything differently in the production of his dreamies than he has previously. I understand he is an innovator in his field, that his sensory programs are ahead of the pack. Is he working with any new equipment?"

Quent thought back to the Saturday before last when he'd visited Izzy, remembered Izzy's pearl-white machine. He hadn't seen anything unusual about it, but then a new piece of equipment could be something as small as an expansion card or as immaterial as a program stored in the instrument's internal memory.

"Nothing I've noticed. Why?"

Mr. Brown proceeded to tell him of the grisly and inexplicable demise of Mr. Carruthers. During the telling Mrs. C. let go a torrent of tears that took her a while to get under control.

"When we got down here. The television was wrecked and

the carpet soaked," Mr. Brown added. "What I can't figure is where the water came from." He spread his palms and looked at the floor in a gesture of frustration.

"I'm sure I'm as much in the dark as you," Quent said. "More. What's Mr. Carruthers' death got to do with Isidor Stark?" Though, after his conversation with Helen last night, he had the nasty feeling there was a connection.

Rejdak picked absently at a piece of lint on his maroon tie. "Mr. Carruthers visited me at my office yesterday. He put a question to me: was it possible for his television to pick up images from his neighbor's dreamatron?"

Quent exchanged a glance with Mr. Brown. The older man nodded as if to verify Dr. Rejdak's account.

"At the time, I told him I'd have to give the question some thought."

"And . . ."

"And I've decided the possibility exists."

Quent sat forward on the edge of the sofa. This was a new angle. Suspending for the moment the buzz of questions and conflicting feelings concerning Izzy's involvement in the deaths of Jason Carruthers and Dr. Nösberger and his possible hand in Helen's walking nightmare, he concentrated on where this new turn would lead.

Dr. Rejdak's penetrating dark eyes, peering out from the bushy eaves of his brows, were fixed on his. "However, I don't think images from Mr. Stark's artistic experiments actually appeared on the television screen, but, yes, it is entirely possible Mr. Carruthers saw something."

"Go on," Mr. Brown said impatiently.

"The brain transmits and receives electromagnetic waves. It processes information in binary code much as a computer does. It puts out electromagnetic waves in the band between 1 and 100 Hertz. The dreamatron's modulator decodes the dreamer's raw data, divides it into discrete wavelengths corresponding to the various senses and transmits the wavelengths to the audience's sensory brain centers."

When Lois and Chet both looked like they were getting migraines, Rejdak tried again.

"The computer separates the thought information into sight, sound, smell, stream of consciousness, et cetera, and records it onto bubble pak. Later, when the dreamie's played, the signals representing the different senses are broadcast through amplifiers of the theater's soundless system on different frequencies. Did you know, for example, that the different sense centers in the brain receive and transmit information at different frequencies?"

Lois shook her head. Quent nodded—stereo equipment and the new dream recording and projection technology were his specialty; but he wanted the doctor to get on with it, so he said nothing.

"The auditory receptors of the brain, for instance," Rejdak said, "receive signals between three and five Hertz. This was learned in the early eighties when researchers, hearing accounts of people picking up radio signals from the air, experimented with deaf mutes and discovered they could bypass the ears. This led to soundless radio, audio systems, hearing aids, and dreamies. It was also discovered that not everyone processes sensory data on the same frequencies; hence the three-to-five Hertz range for sound. To get around this stumbling block and accommodate every member of the audience, the dreamatron covers the whole range of frequencies for a given sense by rapidly alternating the frequency of the transmission. In other words, everyone in the audience does not receive a given smell or sound or image at precisely the same instant but within nanoseconds of his or her neighbor."

"But Jason wasn't in the same building with him," Brown protested.

Rejdak smiled slightly. "There have been many accounts lately of people who live in neighborhoods around theaters picking up dreamie transmissions. By the way," the doctor paused and looked around at each of them, "did you know there have even been a few instances lately where dreamers have received impressions from audience members' minds?"

Mr. Brown looked at Rejdak as if he had three heads. "What?"

Rejdak nodded. "There have been reports. If true, they pose some interesting possibilities."

"There was a dreamer in England," Quent said, remembering something he'd read.

"Right," Rejdak said. "In Liverpool. One Alex Drummer to be precise. He played before a packed house of so-called *punks*. Seems they didn't like the show and their bad thoughts sort of collectively punched—" He jabbed the air for emphasis. "Anyway, he died of a cerebral hemorrhage. And some of the audience who spoke to the media proudly claimed they'd killed him and that was the way Liverpool dealt with junk."

"No shit," Quent said, then felt embarrassed when he met Mrs. Carruthers' gaze.

The professor smiled, showing dimples. "That depends on whether you believe what you read. I remain open-minded and mention this aspect of the dreamatron's interactivity with the audience only to get all the possibilities into the open. The dreamatron is interactive with the audience in other ways."

"How's that?" Chet wanted to know.

Rejdak explained, "The machine can be programmed to individualize a dreamie by isolating those signals that represent an individual's name and personal appearance, incorporating them into the dreamie and broadcasting them back into the audience. By alternating individualized signals at billionths of a second, literally thousands of individualized dreamies can be broadcast every second."

"Yeah," Quent said, "the villain whispers the victim's name and every person in the theater hears his own name."

"Exactly. Dreamies work both ways. It has been said that the dreamie is the closest thing to telepathy."

Telepathy . . . Quent recalled his earlier thoughts about siblings, lovers, and spouses being more telepathically receptive to one another than to strangers. Could it be, then, that Izzy's genius had found a way around the stumbling block of long distance.

Another thought occurred to him: perhaps taraxein had unlocked a telepathic ability in Izzy. "Maybe it's the dreamer that's changed," he remembered Helen saying.

"Telepathy," Quent repeated aloud.

"Um," the professor said.

Mrs. Carruthers looked unsatisfied. "That might explain Jason's seeing things on the TV, but what about the water, the footprints? What about my husband?"

"What do you mean?" Rejdak looked perplexed, but Quent thought he saw what Mrs. Carruthers was getting at. And he was astounded to hear someone voice the same suspicions Helen had shared. "Certainly you do not think your husband's picking up radio wave transmissions could have anything to do with his death?"

"I don't know." Mrs. C. shook her head, started to raise her hand to her face, lowered it to her lap. "I don't know." She looked at Rejdak. "But something happened to me last week that makes me wonder."

Mrs. Carruthers told him about the fright she'd had in the yard a week ago and about the footprints and the young man killed nearby. Then she asked Rejdak if, just for the sake of argument, he could think of any logical explanation that would support the notion that Stark was able to affect reality.

Rejdak sat thoughtfully rubbing his chin for a few moments. "Yes, yes, indeed there is," he said. Quent thought he saw a gleam slip into the doctor's otherwise inscrutable eyes. He had seen the look in the eyes of some of his more enthusiastic professors. Quent prepared himself for a lecture; his belt recorder was already running. "Only the rationale lies outside the known laws of physics. You're referring to mind over matter." The professor folded his hands in his lap, crossed a leg. "Otherwise known as telekinesis."

"You don't really believe in that ESP stuff," Chet said, leaning forward in his chair and looking incredulous.

Rejdak smiled. "I hesitate to use terminology so romanticized by the public, but in answer to your question, I neither believe nor disbelieve. I remain skeptical yet open-minded. However, there is too much professional documentation, too many reliable witnesses, to ignore the fact that telekinesis exists. The physics just haven't been explained yet."

When Brown came out again, escorting Quent and a guy Izzy had never seen before who looked like a foreign banker, or maybe a gangster, Izzy was upstairs in his bedroom watching through the big tinted window. He stood right in front of the window; he could see out, but they couldn't see in.

Tracking the trio through the viewfinder of Helen's Instamatic, Izzy got the chance he was hoping for. Halfway down the yard, at the head of the steps that led to the sidewalk, they stopped and Mr. Brown and the other guy talked. Izzy took a picture of the two. In a matter of seconds the picture developed itself and whirred out the back of the camera.

Quent appeared to be listening.

"They have filled his head with lies," Izzy said aloud, his voice quivering with anger. First Helen and now Quent! Traitors!

No, perhaps not Quent. Good old Quent! Though in high school they had known each other neither long nor well, he had developed an affinity for the man. Part of it was Quent's easygoing personality and attentive ear, but now that Quent was to be his biographer, his Boswell, his old schoolmate had become important in the scheme of things.

Someone had to live to tell the tale.

Still . . .

He squeezed off a profile shot of his old buddy just before Quent turned and started down the steps.

25

The first thing Quent saw when he returned home that afternoon, eager to tell Helen all that he had learned, was the note on the kitchen table. Neatly folded in half with his name inscribed on it in a pretty hand, the note was propped on the keyboard of his computer. His mouth, caught in the act of shaping Helen's name, closed. She was gone.

Pushing his keys back into the pocket of his cords and closing the door behind him, he went over and read the note.

Quent,

Thank you for your hospitality, your listening and your

understanding. Have decided to go to my parents, after all. I know there will be a storm when they see me, but I'll handle them, tell them Izzy's having a breakdown.

Please call me as soon as you get in. I'm dying to hear what you learned from Izzy.

Thanks,
Helen

And below this a number. Quent pulled off his coat and wasted no time punching the buttons on the cordless phone.

One ring. Two. A woman picked up.

"Hello?"

The voice, laced with anger, sounded pretty much as he imagined Helen's mom's voice would sound.

"Hello, Mrs.—" Embarrassed, he realized he didn't remember Helen's last name; it fumbled like a football on the tip of his tongue. "—Kalcanides."

"This isn't Izzy?"

"No, I'm a friend of your daughter's, Quentin Hughes. She asked me to call."

The sound of the phone changing hands. The older woman's protest. Then Helen's voice, muffled as if someone's hand partially covered the receiver, "I said I'll take it!"

"Hello?" Helen had the phone now. He detected an edge of anxiety in her voice and irritation at having to wrestle the phone from her mom. She's probably had a hell of a time of it with her parents today, he told himself.

"Hi, Quent here." He tried to sound chipper, though his mind was abuzz with things to say.

"Hi, Quent. Sorry about my mother." This in a lowered voice, as if she didn't want her mother to hear. He sat in his timeworn chair in front of his computer, pushed the keyboard out of the way so he could prop his elbows on the table. "She's the one I had to talk out of going over and punching Izzy's lights out. Papa wants me to sue Izzy for palimony."

An uproar started up in the background, voices arguing. "There they go again."

"How's your foot?" he asked.

"Better. I decided I needed some comfortable shoes and I have lots of old shoes here."

She did sound better, despite the squabbling in the background.

"Well?" she said after a moment's silence.

"Well, what?"

"Did you see him?"

Quent recalled the brief conversation through Izzy's door. "No, I didn't see him. He wouldn't let me in."

"You didn't get to talk to him?" She sounded disappointed.

"We shared a few words through your front door, if you can imagine that. He dusted me off pronto."

"How do you mean? Was he cold to you?"

"No, no. He sounded friendly enough. He was even apologetic for not inviting me in. He said he was busy getting ready for the show."

He didn't tell what he really said.

"The fans'll die when they see this one."

Which, in context with the subsequent discussion at the Carruthers' house, sounded diabolical.

"I asked about you," he said.

"Oh?" Her voice lowered, suddenly sounding very anxious. "What did he say?"

"He said you were sleeping."

"Sleeping?"

"Yep. That's what the man said. So maybe you'll take your father's advice."

The voice on the other end of the line grew cool. "I would never sue Izzy," she said. "Nor do I think I could ever really leave him."

"Then you'll be going back?"

"Probably. He's sick, Quent. Something's wrong with him and I won't desert him. I know we've never spoken the vows, but I've always lived by the words: 'In sickness and in health.'"

"But you can't go to him now; he's dangerous."

"I know that, I know that." He could hear the veneer of certitude that had held her together through a stressful afternoon with her parents crack. "I don't know what to do," she said. "I think I should call him."

"I don't think he'll talk to you, Helen. The impression I got was he wants to be alone. Anyway, that's not what I really wanted to tell you."

"What did you want to tell me?" she said.

Quent told her about Mr. Carruthers' murder. He kept it short, leaving out the gory parts, the stuff about the blood-stains on the Carruthers' living-room carpet or the fact that Mr. Carruthers' head had been crushed. No, he didn't tell her the gory stuff; she had enough on her mind and she didn't need the details that had made his own guts clench into a tight, queasy ball.

"Oh, the poor man," Helen said, then in a whispered voice that sounded like she had cupped her hand around the receiver, "Did Izzy have anything to do with Mr. Carruthers' death?" There was fear in her voice, the same fear he'd heard last night.

Good question, he thought. It was one he had asked himself. Mrs. Carruthers had seemed pretty keen on the idea, until Dr. Rejdak assured her otherwise.

"I don't know," he said. "I really don't. This is all pretty bizarre. According to the professor—"

"Who? Dr. Nösberger?" She sounded startled, as if she'd just seen the ghost of Elvis tuning his guitar.

"It's been a long day, Helen. And an informative trip. I guess I'd better tell you about this guy Dr. Rejdak I met at the Carruthers'."

"Dr. Rejdak?"

"Anyway," he said when he had summarized the conversation that took place in the Carruthers' living room, "what it boils down to, according to Dr. Rejdak, is there's a rational, scientific explanation for Mr. Carruthers' seeing things, but for electronic signals to leave material evidence like water and footprints is impossible."

"Is it impossible for my entire surroundings to change? Or for my dead sister to come for me with a knife?"

He shrugged, realized she couldn't see him shrug over the phone and said, "I don't know. I'm no physicist and my knowledge of electronics is mostly limited to stereo and VCR equipment. Look"—he shuffled her letter nervously on the table—"why don't you pick me up and we'll get something to eat, talk some more."

"With my face? Ha!"

Her laugh was humorless, and he remembered her swollen eye the night before, better by now, no doubt, but still dark and puffy with that bruised-meat look.

"You didn't mention me," she said, "or anything we talked about last night, did you?"

"No. Maybe I should have, but I thought it's the type of thing the press would love to get hold of."

"Thank you, Quent. Really."

This woman's unbelievable, he thought. He punches her out and she's worried he might get bad press! "That's all right," he said.

"Quent?"

"Huh?"

"You've been so kind already. But I have one more favor to ask of you."

"Name it."

"Do you have, or can you get, a ticket for the concert?"

"You still want to go," he asked, incredulous, "after what he did to you?"

"I have to."

Have to!

Great!

"I've got a bad feeling about the concert." He said it to discourage her, but it was true. He remembered the weird feeling he'd experienced on Izzy's stoop, felt a shadow of it crawl over his back.

His face was crushed . . .

The fans'll die . . .

"Me too," she said, surprising him. "But I've got to be there. Please."

What the heck, he thought. Give her the ticket. You've got two. She'll find one somewhere if she really wants one.

Voices were raised in the background. A man's first, shouting in rage: "Fuck him! His money don't give him no right—" A woman's broke in on the man's. They started a shouting match.

"Hey, I have to go," Helen said. "About that ticket—let me buy it from you. I'll come by tomorrow morning. What time is good?"

He gave in. He wanted her to feel comfortable talking with him. Christ, she needed him right now. With whom else could she discuss the things they had discussed without being considered a candidate for Sunnybrook? Besides, Gold Coast Magazine had sprung for two tickets for him to cover the concert and he didn't have a date. He'd figured on hawking the spare, but what the hell.

"About ten? Is that good?"

"Fine." She sounded relieved. "I'll see you then. And, Quent . . ."

"Yes?"

"Thanks for everything."

He started to say, That's okay, but she said "Bye" and he said "Bye" and the line was silent.

The funeral had been dismal and depressing.

It was hot at the cemetery, the traffic fumes from nearby Route 440 wafting over the plots. Deek's family's plot was on the other side of 440 from the old cemetery in the new section on what was formerly an automobile junkyard. Deek's mom had fainted when she went up to place a flower on the casket and had to be supported by Deek's aunt and his older brother Louie in his blue Marine uniform.

"One fucked-up day, wasn't it?" Jamie said. He sat turned around at his desk down the other end of the loft.

"Yeah," Todd said, closing the loft's trapdoor out of habit.

"Leave it open. Fred'll be by."

"Yeah, probably." Todd propped the door against the wall. Then, spying the small red-and-white Igloo cooler by Jamie's desk, "What's in the cooler?"

"Help yourself." Jamie turned out the suspensor lamp on his desk. "My pop gave it to me. Said, 'For you and the boys.'"

"Not having one?"

"I was waiting for someone to drink with."

"Wait no more."

Todd pulled a Bud from the ice and passed it to Jamie, took another and popped the top. After a refreshing pull on the can, he sat on the cot. He put his hand on the rough wool army blanket under which he had lost his virginity three nights before. Despite the day's proceedings, he felt a warm stir in his pants. At the same time, he remembered the look he had seen on Jamie's face, half-glimpsed the moment before the flashlight's beam blinded him.

Jamie hadn't gotten angry. In fact he hadn't said a word about the incident. Made believe it didn't happen. But Todd felt his friend's disappointment in him.

"What are you working on?" he asked.

"Nothing really." Jamie tossed his pen on the desk. "Doodling mostly." Jamie kicked off from his desk in his swivel chair hard enough for the wheels to clear the gaps between the floorboards.

"Try putting a motor on that," Todd joked.

Jamie grunted. "Shock absorbers more like it!"

Todd took a long, thoughtful pull on his beer while Jamie mopped his face with his handkerchief. Jamie pressed the cold can to his forehead.

"Don't feel well?"

"Headache's all."

"Jamie."

"Hum?"

Todd made a last-second attempt to think of something to say other than what he meant to talk about—it had been damned embarrassing. Get it over with. "About what you saw the other night."

"Saw?" Jamie lowered his Bud from his forehead, gazed inscrutably at the can as if he had X-ray vision and could see into the amber depths. "Nothing to see. You know I don't mind if you sleep over in the clubhouse. That's what the cot's for: to crash on when you work late on *Tentacle* or to get away from the parents, isn't it?"

Todd caught Jamie's sarcasm and didn't know whether to feel angry or humiliated.

But when Jamie looked at him, there was a twinkle of humor in his eyes. "You're not in love, are you?"

Jamie's totally uncharacteristic, out-of-the-blue change of subject had the effect of dispelling Todd's gloom. Coming from Jamie's mouth, the question might very well have been: "You didn't step in shit, did you?"

"No, of course not," he answered with the proper note of indignation. "I'm in lust!"

Jamie laughed, and he laughed along with him. Too much tension the past couple days. The laughter felt good.

"Just like you are with Miss Pinkham," Todd said. Last year, up until she got married and quit, Jamie had been rabidly in love with their fresh-out-of-college art teacher Miss Pinkham. Look serious and ask for help and you might get her to lean over you, give you pointers on your artwork for a memorable minute while you savored that mixture of perfume and raw female sexuality that set Miss Pinkham apart from the other teachers at Ferris.

Jamie waved him off, but he was grinning.

"Pinkham and Jamie sitting in a tree," Todd singsang. 'K-i-s-s-i-n-g. First comes love—"

"Shut up."

"—then comes marriage."

"You know," Jamie said, "you're an okay guy most of the time—good head on your shoulders, above average intelligence, some writing ability . . ."

"But . . ."

"But when you get silly, you remind me of someone's obnoxious younger brother making a pain of himself to get noticed." Jamie leaned back, closed his eyes, and stretched his neck as if he'd gotten a kink in it. Under the fluorescents, his face looked white. He removed his glasses and wiped the sweat with his handkerchief. "Is it hot in here?" he asked.

"Yeah. It's hot," Todd said. "But not hot enough to make you sweat like that." Jamie had complained earlier that he didn't feel well, and he had assumed it was because of the funeral. "You still don't feel well?"

Jamie dismissed the idea with a flick of the hand. "It's the weather. This Indian Summer. I wish it was fucking winter. Snow up to our asses!" His grin looked halfhearted.

You knew Jamie wasn't himself when he started cursing.

"Where's Fred?" Jamie changed the subject. "I hope he's got fucking weed."

Fred felt the knots in his stomach loosen as soon as he turned into the alley by Scatuorchio Funeral Home and felt the familiar crunch of dirt and glass beneath his combat boots. In the alleys he could think without feeling paranoid that everyone was watching him weave down the sidewalk with his six-pack under his arm. He inhaled the night air, smelled the weeds, the dirt, traces of oil, an occasional whiff of dog shit, and felt his head clear a little. Dog shit smelled natural in the alley, like manure in a cornfield, and somehow the smell and an occasional dead bird or rat helped preserve the illusion that, when he was walking the alleys, he was taking a walk in the country.

Along with the five beers he had consumed over the past two hours, he had downed a hit of acid, figuring Pop wouldn't know the difference since he had a beer with him; besides, what the fuck! After seeing Deek buried, he needed to put his head in a different cycle. The acid had done him just fine, made him feel reet and complete. He felt like Superman as he trod the broken glass under his feet. God help the mangy alley cat that ran under the heels of his combat boots tonight.

It wasn't just the acid and the alcohol, though, that made him feel this way—as hard as nails and mean as a cat with a hornet up its ass. He was angry—angry that Deek was dead, that, by now, he had about a ton of dirt on his chest and there wasn't a thing he could do about it. Pure, boiling, frustrated anger: the kind that had a head on it like a mug of beer. The acid only enhanced the anger, augmenting and harnessing it, till he felt like a walking dynamo, seething underneath but business-as-usual on the outside. Right now, he would have liked nothing better than to make mud pies out of the first dick-headed creep that looked at him sideways—unless it was smoking a joint when he got to the clubhouse. He dearly hoped Todd or Jamie had some cheeb.

The evening was warm and humid and Fred's white T-shirt was damp under his denim Lee jacket. Not bad out here in the alley; it had been putrid in his room, not a breath of air coming through the window. A gibbous moon only a day or two shy of full cast its hazy light over the garages and sheds that lined the alley. Fred stepped into the shadows on his right and relieved his bladder; then, zipping his fly and hitching the six-pack back under his arm, he continued on his way.

That morning, he had—along with three of Deek's brothers, his father, and his uncle—helped carry the coffin. It had been the longest day in his life. He had listened impatiently to the words of the priest, designed, supposedly, to solace the hearts of the bereaved, with clenched fists. After the funeral, he went back to Deek's house for the reception. The Cintrons had seafood delivered from a local restaurant to feed relatives and friends. Fred ate some shrimp and a little rice to settle his stomach and the three double shots of Spanish brandy Deek's dad poured for him.

Back home he moped around, thumbing through comic books and pacing ten minutes out of every twenty, looking and feeling miserable and making his mother, who also attended the funeral, cry all over again. Deek was a favorite with the whole family, as he was with most people who knew him. After dinner, which he hardly touched, his father visited him in his room with a six-pack of cold brewskis. His pop stayed to drink a beer with him, but left when he saw that Fred didn't feel like talking. Pop was A-OK. While other dads would have given their sons advice and pearls of wisdom—everything from "Keep a stiff upper lip" to "All things must pass"—his dad brought him a six-pack.

"Fuckin' A, Pop," he said aloud.

Once he was fairly well buzzed, he thought about going to Wanda's and getting laid. Problem was he needed someone to explain to him what it was all about: why someone like Deek, in physical prime, had to croak. Wanda wouldn't be able to answer that. So he stopped in the first bar he passed and bought a six-pack of Budweiser tall cans, ice-cold from the freezer, and headed for the clubhouse. Jamie and Todd would be there, and even if they couldn't give him answers, at least they were thinking the same questions.

Fred reached the end of the first alley, crossed Monmouth Street, and entered the alley by the Barge Inn. The lights were on in the bar but none of the regulars were out on the sidewalk. Fred realized that, had he not been so fried to think of it, he could have picked his beer up here instead of the My Way Lounge near his house and carried it a shorter distance.

This alley was as well-lighted as the last, except for a section just this side of halfway, where one of the lights on the telephone poles had been broken. The glass crunching beneath his boots, the ripe whiff of dog shit in his nostrils, Fred recalled all the times he and Deek had set the yard dogs howling for blocks around by baying like werewolves.

Suddenly, as if the smog had cleared, the crushed glass on the alley floor glittered like diamonds. He looked up. The gibbous moon, white as sugar, as cold and bright as fluorescent light, appeared magnified, as if he were viewing it through a telescope. Its Man-in-the-Moon features stood out in striking bas relief.

"Don't knock it," he said to himself. "Beats smog!"

Then, as suddenly as it had gotten lighter, the sky went dark. He looked up, saw black clouds boiling over the moon. The next instant, he was ducking from the hailstorm that had whipped up out of nowhere. Hail rattled like sheets of wind-blown sand on the garage doors and stung his face and forced its way down his collar as he hurried along, head bowed, eyes squinting. This was nuts! Fall weather around the metropolitan area could be unpredictable, but this was refuckindiculous!

Then it was bright moonlight again and the hail was gone. Once again, the ground glittered with broken glass.

The sound of running water ahead caught his attention. A familiar sound, one that he'd recognize anytime: the sound of someone taking a leak against a wall.

In the shadow of one of the garage doors lounged an assortment of criminal types dressed in what he thought, at first, were black leather jackets, but then one of the punks stepped into the moonlight and he saw that they wore black pajamas like the Vietcong in the old movies. And whereas he had thought the hoodlums were Hispanic, he now saw that their pale faces were vaguely Oriental. Their eyes were pools of black light as they glided toward him.

Fred attacked first. He didn't want to, but they quickly encircled him. Rather than let them all close in on him at once, he moved toward one of them as another came up behind him, and went into action. His size-thirteen combat boot came up, connected bone-crunchingly with the sternum of the gook in front of him, and even as the first foot descended, he pivoted, landed in front of an assailant who reached long yellow nails for his eyes. Fred ducked, kicked him savagely and squarely in the balls, and landed a right to the face, splintering bone. As his right foot, having completed its genital-squashing mission, came down, he whirled, throwing his whole body into the motion, and drove the heel of his boot into another assailant's ribs, hurling him into one of his fellows. They both went crashing into a garage door, rattling the heavy wooden panels. The first to bar his way was back now, rushing in, arms stretched wide as if meaning to tackle him—tackle him and then batten those lovely fangs that now glinted in the moonlight on his throat. Or maybe he preferred to jab a hole in his jugular with one of those nasty-looking fingernails. Claws raked his arm, fantastically gouging through his tough denim Lee jacket and slicing into his skin. He howled as pain raced up his arm, thudded into his brain. In backyards and apartments up and down the alley, dogs began baying and barking so it seemed to Fred he had stumbled into hell and was battling demons.

Ropy strands of saliva sprayed from between Fred's clenched teeth as he battled. His big bony fists were flailing hammers.

A hand gripped his left wrist, turning it to ice. Then the leathery yellow face that his right fist was about to smash into vanished, and Fred punched through empty air, the haymaker-gone-wild spinning him off balance.

What the . . . ?

He was alone in the alley, he realized as his adrenaline-charged metabolism slowly returned to normal. The moon was once again hazy behind a pall of smog, the glass no longer glittered at his feet. He grinned, realizing what had happened.

"Holy shit!" Never freaked like that on acid before. Must've been the combination of LSD and booze, he thought.

Shaking his head, he picked up the cans that had rolled this way and that when he dropped them and wrapped them in the torn bag. One of the cans he had crushed underfoot, emptying it outright, and another had popped its top when it struck the ground. Fred picked this one up and sloshed it; it was still half-full and he sipped from it as he hefted his parcel under his arm and continued on his way.

Panting like someone awakened from a nightmare, Izzy cut the transmission and shoved his chair back in a desperate effort to break contact with his victim. The fury of the fan's counterattack was so violent, so intense, so totally unexpected, Izzy had been jolted out of the dreamstate. Not only shocked, he felt battered and bruised and damn if a couple of his teeth didn't feel loose and his throat felt choked and throbbed with a dull, sore ache as if he had been backhanded in the Adam's apple. His balls felt roughly the same way.

He couldn't believe it! Never in a thousand years would he have guessed the transmission could work both ways, that his victims might fight back or that he could get hurt.

From being shocked, he was suddenly furious that the possibility existed; that his invincibility, his inaccessibility, might not be as complete as he thought made him seethe with unreasoning anger. He clenched his gloved fists until he felt the pulse of pain from his nails digging through the silk gloves into his palms.

Then, with a sudden expulsion of air, he forgot his anger. A thought had entered his mind. Did his victim actually physically hurt him? Or was it only psychological pain he felt?

He started to get up and go upstairs and look in a mirror to see if he had bruises, but he remembered his veil and the horror hidden beneath and remained seated.

Save Mr. Fred Whatever-his-name-is for another time, he told himself as his tongue jiggled a front tooth that may or may not have been loose. Right now he had other fish to fry.

26

The stars and moon were hazed with humidity, and though Lois couldn't see from where she stood by her roses, which grew alongside the house, blossomless and recently clipped back for winter, there would be fog on the river tonight.

When in bloom, these same roses perfumed the living room with a sweet attar. Only a month or so ago, Jason had commented on how sweet the roses smelled. Her eyes, which had been wet and dry off and on all day, teared again. Tears sprang so easily; every stick of furniture, every knickknack, curtain, even the refrigerator, which he was forever raiding and never gaining an ounce, reminded her of him.

Perhaps Chet was right. Maybe she should just clear out and head down to Florida along with the droves of other retirees. Maybe . . . But not until Jason's killer was caught.

The night was bitter with irony. One of the reasons they had not moved to Florida—besides the fact that she loved their house and was perfectly satisfied with living in New Jersey—was that Jason knew the house. Here Jason had his music and his movies, all thoroughly memorized. Jason had a memory for songs and movies that rivaled the photographic memory some people are said to have for text. He had lived in this house for years and knew his way around so well she was sure he could find his way with his eyes closed.

Dr. Leonard explained, when she asked his advice about moving to Florida, that at this "stage of the game," as he put it, Jason wouldn't be able to memorize a new telephone number, let alone find his way home in a strange city. "He's in great health," the doctor said. "Physically. Could live another twenty years."

Lois remembered the first time, there in the doctor's office, she'd compared that figure with another figure Dr. Leonard quoted her. The doctor had been straight with her. "I'm not going to mislead you, Mrs. Carruthers. You've got some hard decisions ahead. Though your husband might live in good physical health for many years, mentally he will be a vegetable in two to four."

Two to four . . .

Twenty years . . .

She had made a fraction out of those numbers that had hung in her mind so that she heard nothing that Leonard said for the next few minutes. She hadn't thought she'd be able to bear that—watching him drooling, decaying, shitting his pants. She and Chet had discussed nursing homes, never getting anywhere because the discussion quickly became unbearable.

And now decisions unconcluded could be left unconcluded.

Jason was dead!

Next door a window exploded. Startled, Lois looked up and saw a black shape erupt through a dormer window on the second floor of Stark's house, spraying glass into the yard and sweeping aloft on dark wings. Behind the first came another and another, a stream, a torrent of black creatures, erupting from the small aperture, winging skyward, a twisting swarm of monstrous airborne shapes, gaunt, damply glistening bodies flapping starward on long membranous wings. The night filled with a sound like sails slapping before a stiff breeze. The throng was so thick it seemed impossible that so many could fit through the small window or that they could all have fit in that one house. And now the stream stopped, as if a faucet had been cut off.

Upward and upward the column spiraled until the creatures became tiny, no more than a far-off cloud obscuring a few stars. Then, as she watched amazed, the cloud started growing again.

They're coming back, she thought.

Her eyes darted to the small dormer window. The house was dark, even the basement. Her eyes leapt to the sky again, to the twisting swarm hurtling toward her. The column crossed before the gibbous moon, the grotesque shapes hideous in silhouette. The creatures swooped. Down, down they plummeted, tar-black bodies glistening in the moonlight, which had grown suddenly bright, surging toward her, hundreds of hungry, predatory beasts set upon glutting themselves.

She stumbled to her feet, realizing she had fallen to her knees in her amazement, and ran—faster than she had run in twenty years—straight into a thicket of briars.

She turned. More briars. The thick, thorned vines surrounded her, hemmed her in. And they were growing! Before her eyes the vines thickened and writhed like a mass of pythons. The leathery creak of the vines lengthening, the machine-gun popping of sprouting thorns.

The tremendous flapping grew louder. Sobbing, she dropped onto all fours, hoping the briars would protect her. She looked up and saw the first of the horned, bat-winged creatures swoop just above the thorns. And now the scream that had been paralyzed in her throat erupted.

The thing had no face!

Chet, having changed out of the clothes he had worn to the funeral parlor, the suit seeming to have picked up the sickly-sweet smell of the funeral wreaths, was just coming down to look for Lois when he heard the explosion of glass next door. He ran to the window. At first, all he saw was that a small dormer window on this side of Stark's house had blown out. Then he saw movement in their yard to his left. He strained to see.

What was that crouched on the ground near the rose bushes? Someone was there! He opened the window, which had been locked because of the killer, stuck his head out.

Lois!

She was cowering on all fours, face in the grass, as if trying to make herself as small and inconspicuous as possible.

"Hey!" he shouted, thinking she was cowering from an attacker, but a quick glance around showed no one else in sight. He hurried out the front door, jumping off the steps onto the grass with a sprightliness that surprised him.

When he reached her, Lois was still cowering, hands behind her head, resting her weight on her elbows and forehead.

"Lois."

He touched her and she jumped. The face that swung around at him, expression wild and smeared with dirt, hair disheveled, was that of someone terrified out of her wits. He'd never before seen such an expression on Lois—or on anyone, except in movies. Her eyes were wide with horror, unrecognizing, and though her mouth was open for a bloodcurdling scream, no sound issued.

Then, as if a switch had been thrown, the crazy-woman expression was gone. Recognition came into Lois' eyes. Her lips moved; she seemed to be trying to say his name, but no words came out. He wasn't up to pulling her to her feet, so he knelt beside her on the damp ground.

"Lois, what is it?"

In answer, she looked skyward.

Chet followed her gaze. "Oh, no!"

His eyes saw the shapes wheeling like vultures overhead, spiraling down on myriad widespread black wings, but his brain refused to believe what he saw was there any more than it could believe in vampires or werewolves. Could these horned, faceless demons actually hurt them? Jason's final stare came to him, his eyes eternally crossed even now under the lid of his sealed coffin.

He scooped her up and amazed himself by making it all the way back to the front steps before tripping and spilling Lois onto the stoop. This time she helped him, pulling him to his feet and getting the door open.

Inside, she collapsed, shaking, into his arms. He comforted her, putting an arm around her and stroking her hair.

"You saw them, too?" she sobbed.

"I saw something. What did you see?"

"I saw . . ." Her voice trailed off, and though he couldn't see her face because it was pressed against his chest, he was sure she was staring into nothingness. She shook in his arms.

"It's him, isn't it?" she said. "Stark! What has he got against us?"

Before he could think of an answer, one of the living-room windows imploded; shards of glass whizzed halfway across the room and a taloned black claw reached several feet inside and slashed the air before withdrawing.

"Upstairs!" Chet shouted. He half-dragged her up to the

second floor. A window crashed in the front of the house, in Lois' bedroom. But they were moving down the hall, to the back of the house, to Jase Junior's old room, which Chet now occupied. Inside, he retrieved the Ruger 10/22 he had sat up with the night before. Then back out and up the narrow flight of stairs to the attic.

The attic was dark and full of old boxes, furniture, and somewhere nearby, Chet remembered, a rolled-up Persian carpet amid the nearly invisible litter of storage. What light there was fell through the two tiny dormer windows on either side of the house.

"Leave the lights out," he said when Lois reached for the switch.

Taking care not to trip over the ghostly objects his feet encountered, gripping his Ruger before him, he made his way to the dormer window facing Stark's house. He approached the window crouched, staying to one side, afraid he might be seen in the puddle of wan moonlight just inside the window. He eased one eye over the sill.

Outside, the neighborhood had mutated into a nightmarish scene. Above and between Stark's house and their own the air swarmed with hellish shapes. Through the throng, he could see Stark's gutted second-floor window. It was dark inside and appeared empty. He recalled what Rejdak said about it being possible Jason had picked up Stark's transmissions but impossible that such a transmission could have killed his friend. Well, what he was seeing now wasn't on TV and he hadn't just imagined the living-room window imploding: glass fragments had sprayed halfway across the room, showering the carpet and sofa.

Unless, of course, I'm dreaming, he thought. Maybe Jase is alive and there's nothing outside and no one named Rejdak visited and I'm just having a lousy night's sleep!

Still—afraid one of the things might smash the glass, he moved back a few paces.

Just in time! The window through which he watched the swooping, wheeling shapes suddenly burst. A horned head and a long muscular arm rammed inside, cruel talons slashed his sweater. Chet backpedaled, letting off two rounds as he did so. Though it was dark and the creature blocked most of the moonlight, at the moment of firing he got a look at the thing. And he saw, as Lois had seen and with the same shocked reaction, that the thing had no face.

Or almost none: though featureless, there was an impression of a monstrous visage lurking just beneath the whalelike skin stretched taut over eye and cheek and mouth as if ready to split at any moment and peel back to reveal a fanged, brimstone-eyed demon.

Two small holes appeared in the hideous visage and the thing wavered like a poorly received television image. The shape blurred, melted, dissolved; ectoplasmic tatters wisped, motes spun. And then he was staring through the gutted window at the winged horde blackening the sky, reminding him of the monkey legion that made off with Dorothy and Toto in *The Wizard of Oz*.

"They can be killed," he said aloud, refraining from whooping with victory only because he was afraid of drawing further attention.

"Something's downstairs," Lois yelled. Her voice was hysterical.

Keeping the rifle pointed at the window, Chet backed toward her a ways, listening. He heard the *thump* first, a sharp heavy sound like Long John Silver's peg leg clumping across a plank deck. Followed by a ponderous, distinctly wet-sounding noise, as if a giant dead squid were being dragged along the floor downstairs. He could hear the floor of the hall below creak under the weight.

Another of the faceless creatures hurtled toward the window. Chet fired a round and the thing veered off course and caromed into the side of the house below the window. Dream or not, the monster was solid enough for Chet to feel a tremor run through the floor. The crash against the side of the house was followed by the sound of breaking branches. Chet realized the thing had fallen into the rose bushes below.

Keeping the rifle readied, his finger on the trigger, he edged toward the window. He had to see. Two more of the loathsome mutants peeled away from the spiraling column and swooped at him. He tried to take his time and take proper aim, but his hands were shaking and in the back of his mind the sinister medley of noises in the hall below fragmented his concentration. He hit the first one and was rewarded with a glimpse of its wings crumpling and it plummeting to ground, but he missed the second and fell backward onto the attic floor when it seemed the thing was going to force its huge bulk through the undersized window. The thing caught the windowsill as had the first one he shot, and a taloned hand reached in and swiped at him as he fired. Chet felt fiery pain lance across his chest. In the same instant, the slug ripped through the thing's throat and the monster became a mass of swirling tendrils of grayish mist, dissolving as it fell away, vanishing.

Thrusting his head and the gun barrel out the window, he looked below. Nothing. But the rose bushes directly beneath looked crushed. Pain was a hot knife in his rib cage. When he pulled his head back inside, he put a hand to his side and it came away warm and sticky.

"Chet!" The emergency in Lois' voice made him forget his pain. "It's on the stairs!"

"Lock the door!"

"I can't! There's no lock!"

No lock. Right! Who but a nut would think to put a lock on the inside of an attic door.

He listened. Sure enough, the *thump*, followed by the ponderous wet dragging sound, had grown louder. The stairs groaned. A sharp *pop!* as if one of the risers cracked. A sliver of fear like a razor-sharp steel shaving ran down his spine and he suddenly realized how afraid he really was, how parched his mouth, how slippery his hands upon the 10/22's birch stock.

Lois was backing away from the door. Outside the destroyed window, winged demons flapped and whooshed by.

Thump!
Slosh-drag!
Thump!
Slosh-drag!

The hideous progress called up fantastically grotesque

images, and not knowing what could be making such a ponderous, preposterous sound made it worse.

With his attention torn between the stair door and the window, Chet's brain whirred like a tire spinning on ice, getting nowhere. The cold clutch of despair turned his bowels to ice water.

Then, clear as a picture, an image formed in his mind. The image of an electrical wire being struck by a bullet, snapping.

Cut his power!

Of course!

Chet flung himself at the window, fired into the featureless face of the closest creature, which dropped out of sight, and swung the muzzle of the rifle toward the front of Stark's house. Sighting along the barrel and hanging out the window, he traced Stark's electrical service line from the pole to the house. On this side, at the front corner of the house, the power cable entered a metal conduit that ran down to the basement. He followed the cable back out to the pole, a cold sweat trickling down his face and under his collar. He licked his lips.

There! On the crossbeam of the utility pole, at the juncture where Stark's power line split off and ran to Number Three, was a small white ceramic conductor. He lined it up in the V of his sights, leaning on the sill to steady his shaking hands. The white ceramic caught the streetlamp but was small and not exactly in range for a .22. Still, he was shooting long rifles and their trajectory was supposed to be flat for almost a mile. He fired.

And missed!

Shit!

He swung the rifle around and snapped off another shot at a winged shadow that swept past him.

How many shots had he fired? Six or seven or eight? The clip only held ten. God! Why hadn't he brought another clip? He had three. The other two were somewhere at the bottom of his closet. The rest of his ammo, he realized, was on the other side of whatever blocked the stairs. He had prepared himself last night for a single killer—not an army!

Lois screamed.

He spun, brought the gun to bear on the thing that stood in the open door.

He didn't know what he expected to see other than something huge and slimy, but when he turned and his eyes focused on the dimness beyond Lois, his jaw dropped in surprise.

Jason Carruthers stood in the door, his hand upon the knob, dressed in the ancient smoking jacket and frayed carpet slippers he had died in. His jaw hung crazily. Teeth were missing. His head was cocked at a ridiculous angle. His eyes, barely visible in the feeble light, stared at each other. His temples were pinched in like the crown of a hat.

Chet swayed, his knees nearly buckling. He looked at Lois between him and Jase. Her mouth was open, her jaw working as if trying to speak or scream. Then, before his eyes, Lois' whole body jolted, her mouth jerked wide, a gagging noise issued. She clutched her chest. The darkness spared him the terror in her eyes as she fell to the floor.

Heart attack! he thought.

Noooo!

He started to bring the rifle barrel around and blast this imitation Jason Carruthers, but remembered his plan and brought the white ceramic conductor into his sights.

And missed!

Two more of the creatures peeled off from the circling column and hurtled toward him. A siren was approaching. He forced himself to concentrate on the white object in the notch of his sights. He squeezed off the round, afraid, just before he was rewarded with the sharp report, that he had already emptied the ten-round clip.

A shower of sparks rained from the crosstrees of the utility pole. And the air was empty!

He whirled, brought the rifle to bear on the door. But Jason was no longer there!

"Lois!" God! Not Lois too!

He ran to her. She lay like a pile of old clothes in the dimness. She was breathing.

"You'll be all right," he croaked. His mouth was as dry as a dead cactus. Please, God, let her be all right!

The siren stopped. The double thud of two cops getting out and slamming the doors of the squad cars.

Ignoring the pain in his rib cage, Chet raced down the stairs to meet them and get an ambulance for Lois.

27

Halloween morning Izzy dreamed again of the dead black phone—mute, funereal, coffin-cold silence on the other end of the line.

He woke shuddering, standing in the kitchen in near darkness, wearing the same clothes he'd worn last night, with the phone in his hand. He had been sleepwalking!

But he had never sleepwalked—not even as a child!

He tried to remember and it came back to him. He'd finally passed out on the couch downstairs when the taraxein wore off.

An operator's impertinent reminder called his attention to the fact that he was still holding the receiver. He started to hang it up, but then the smell hit him, gagging him. He coughed, looked around. The back-door light fell through the kitchen window, but there were still plenty of shadows. He saw nothing out of place, and besides, the smell was gone and he wondered whether he had imagined it.

He hung up the phone.

He brought his hand up to wipe the sweat from his face . . . and stopped, remembering the sight of his face in the mirror yesterday. Had that, too, been a dream? Then he noticed he was no longer wearing the black veil he had so painstakingly manufactured from Helen's slip.

Maybe I never made a veil. Maybe everything—the veil, my face, the deaths, my hitting Helen—maybe it's all a dream! Or a hallucination!

He turned, praying this was true, feeling a growing surety, an exhilarating and expanding sense of positivism that it *was* so—that Helen was upstairs sleeping, her lovely body twisting the warm sheets and all was right with the world.

"Hel—"

The rest of her name froze in his throat. He was looking down at the white floor tiles as he turned, afraid of catching his reflection in the window or any of the other half-dozen or so reflective kitchen surfaces, and was startled first by the sight of a pair of blood-splashed carpet slippers. He backpedaled into the wall, banged his shoulder into the phone.

Then his widening eyes swept upward over the figure standing in the middle of the room, over the pajama bottoms, the eroding smoking jacket that hung on the mannequin-stiff figure. The hands, curled into arthritic claws below the black velvet cuffs, snared his gaze.

Hands look a little pale there, buddy! A little green maybe?

His heart skipped a beat. His eyes jerked to the face above the smoking jacket. The face was mutilated and as gray-green as early Renaissance paintings of Christ on the crucifix. Gangrene-green. Corpse-green. He had been holding his breath, so when he inhaled again, he was struck by the same overpowering odor he smelled before, only this time it didn't go away. Embalming fluid, his mind suggested.

His vision blurred, swam, and when it came back, white dots floated in the air between him and the apparition. It was Jason Carruthers' face, of course; he had recognized it instantly, though he had never seen Jason look the way he did now. The corpse's eyes were open, the whites were as hard and glossy as milk-colored marbles. A pair of 3-D glasses hung from one ear and his temples were caved in. The way his eyes faced each other above the ruined nose made him appear cross-eyed. And yet his eyes seemed to be focused on him quite clearly, rooting him to the spot. He was paralyzed. Terror petrified his joints.

I'm not seeing this! I'm dreaming!

His reason, scrabbling for purchase, clung to the thought.

I'm in bed. Helen's lying beside me. I'll jerk my foot and I'll wake up and she'll be next to me warming the sheets.

But that was too good to be true. The phone pressing into his shoulder too real! The eye-watering reek of embalming fluid dug oily tentacles up his nostrils into his brain.

"You're dead," he told the corpse.

228

The vision—even in his terror, he was convinced it was a vision, a hallucination, he was seeing—not a ghost—opened its mouth. There was grave mold on its teeth. And the grayish ichor that ran down the sides of its face in sluggish tides, streaming onto the smoking jacket's black velvet lapels looked hideously like something he'd seen leaking out of an old woman's head once upon a time in the middle of a sunny street.

Shockingly, the vision began to dissolve. Two of its yellowing teeth fell out, then three more in quick succession. Its upper lip curled back and split; the widening mouth hole spread like an ink blot over its face. The gasses that puffed off the thing no longer reeked primarily of embalming fluid, but of the more sinister effluvium of decomposition. Its eyes were gone, had shrunken to small, hard pebbles and then, perhaps, fallen inside the skull cavity. Now the mouth, the nose, and the eye sockets met and became one huge, gaping black hole. The stumps of its ears melted off. Clots of flesh that still clung to the skull, some with clumps of hair, flaked off; long white hairs and a flaky snow of dead skin dusted its shoulders. A faint smoke was seeping through the smoking jacket, rose like a miasmal steam from its arms and shoulders and collar and cuffs.

Now the smoking jacket, which hung loose on the emaciated corpse, fluttered like curtains in a breeze as threads unwove. The flesh underneath the jacket writhed and crawled hideously. The jaw, fleshless now, opened and closed as if trying to speak. More teeth pebbled the floor. The jaw fell off, shattered on the tiles. Tendonless, the thing's knees buckled. It fell backwards, arms flailing obscenely as if to catch itself as it fell. There was no expression of surprise. No expression at all—just a grinning, jawless skull. It toppled to the floor, a muffled clatter of dry bones. The parchment-yellow skull—what remained of it—darkened and crumbled into dust. The clothing fell apart. Izzy glimpsed vertebrae crumbling, wisping to dust. The hands had fallen apart and the individual bones flaked and turned to smoke. Like a balloon deflating as the gases escaped, the jacket and pajama bottoms flattened.

Before the final transformation into nothing, Izzy tore his

eyes from the horror. His neck cracked loudly with the force of the movement. He rushed blindly, wide-eyed with shock, into the dining room and, through it, into the living room, his sneakered feet pounding across the deep-pile carpet.

Something moved on his left and a needle of ice drove up his spine.

He stopped, thinking Jason had followed him. His eyes swiveled irresistibly toward Helen's curio cabinet, and when his eyes met those of the horror he saw in the curved glass of its door, the scream that had been frozen in his throat ripped out of his mouth.

Hands clenched at his sides, nails digging into the flesh of his palms, he screamed until his lungs were empty and only a thin dry wheeze escaped. The noise of his scream and the horror that filled his eyes drove every other thought from his head. The image no longer wore the smoking jacket and its eyes no longer seemed crossed, but the horror mask, with its gaping, wide-open mouth, resembled an earlier stage of the dissolution he had witnessed.

Then he realized with fresh shock that the features he saw in the curved glass door of Helen's curio cabinet—the peeling forehead, the gangrenous holes in the tight-stretched, bloody muscle, the yellowing teeth and section of jaw bone that showed through the gaping hole in its cheek, the wild staring eyes, alone of its features untouched by the ravages of decomposition—were none other than his own.

28

85 degrees at 7 p.m., 89 degrees at 8. The temperature had risen because of a low-pressure system that had settled over the Northeast, holding the smog and humidity in like a pressure cooker. Despite the oppressive heat and though most of the ticketholders were still deciding what to wear or out looking for something to heighten the experience, the crowd outside the theater had started to gather. WNEW was giving away two last-minute pairs of tickets to listeners, including a chauffeured

limo to drive you to and from the concert. All you had to do to win was be the first person to call in the correct answer to the question: "How many times was the word 'beer' used in this Miller beer commercial? Brought to you by Miller beer, maker of one hell of a fine beer."

Quent was about to ring Chet's bell a second time (the older man had insisted Quent call him by his first name when they had spoken on the phone earlier) when the door opened and he was yanked into the dark foyer.

"Did he see you?" Chet said, and Quent breathed a sigh of relief. The pale glow of a Moonlamp, a fat flashlight with a green dimming lens over the beam, snapped on as Chet closed the door.

"I don't think so. It's possible." Which was true. Izzy's front windows, which he had scanned as he hurried up the Carruthers' walk, were dark and Izzy could easily have been watching.

The living room was lighted by a single lamp, a three-way on its lowest setting. The lamp was on the floor behind the couch, so it did little more than give impressions of furniture, a staircase, the archway into the dining room.

"How's Mrs. Carruthers?" Quent asked as he followed Chet across the shadowy room.

"I saw her less than two hours ago. She was awake. But by God, she looked so pale."

New lines had road-mapped the old man's face in the past two days. His eyes looked tired and nervous.

"Doctor says she'll be able to come home in a week. Frankly, I don't want her anywhere near this place. I have lights on in the attic and in my bedroom upstairs," Chet said as Quent followed him to a window. The window, Quent saw as he got closer, was boarded up. "So if Stark does send us visitors, I hope they'll show up upstairs and give us time to run."

He believes it, Quent thought. He actually believes—expects!—Izzy to attack him. Fetch a couple monsters out of thin air and send them after Chet the way a movie mobster sends a couple of goons to waste someone who knows too much.

Chet had pulled two dining-room chairs up to the window and Quent saw there was a two-inch gap between the two pieces of plywood that boarded up the window at about eye level when sitting down. They sat.

"I talked to Rejdak this afternoon," Chet said.

"What did he say?"

"He said he found a frequency-jamming device, but he has to convert it to battery power to make it portable. He said for us to meet him in his lab at nine and he'll show you how it works."

"Me?"

"Yeah. You're the one with the sneakers—not to mention a ticket. You've got to smuggle it in. Rejdak says that'll be up to you. It's a little bulky."

Quent experienced a sinking feeling. "How bulky?"

"I don't know. We'll see."

"We don't really know that Izzy has killed anybody." Quent turned his palms up. "It just doesn't sound like Izzy."

"He hit Helen, didn't he?"

Indeed he had! When Helen came for the ticket that morning, her eye hadn't looked much better. He'd taken one look at the purple, bruised flesh, shot through with a hint of green, and his anger had welled up all over again.

Why should I defend the son of a bitch? he asked himself. Izzy deserved to have his legs broken for what he did to Helen. But he realized that underlying his anger were his feelings for Helen. Sure, he felt appalled over Mr. Carruthers' death and Lois' being in the hospital, but it was Izzy's hitting Helen that really ticked him off.

Trying to remain objective, he ran through a short list of alternatives.

One—there was at least one very clever, very bizarre killer loose.

Two—he was caught up in a case of mass hysteria.

Three—he was having a long bad dream.

Four—they were all on drugs—perhaps something in the air—and were all tripping their brains out.

"I know for a fact," Chet said, "the images, or whatever

they are, were coming from Stark's house. I conducted a little experiment." Chet told him about the faceless creatures that had darkened the sky, about the appearance of Jason's apparition—the "horrible things" he had referred to on the phone earlier—and how he had knocked out the power to Izzy's house. "Soon as I killed his power, the show stopped."

Quent didn't know what to think. Yesterday morning, by the clear light of day and with a professor from Stevens explaining at least a part of the mystery, it had been easy (and rational) enough to conclude that the killer was some maniac in a monster getup, but now, after observing Chet's face in the ghostly light of the one lamp across the room, he wondered if Rejdak had been a bit hasty in writing off the possibility of creating matter from thought via the dreamatron's radio frequencies.

Chet reached into his shirt pocket, produced a cigarette, lipped it, and dipped back into the pocket for matches.

"Did you know," Quent couldn't help saying, "that, in New Jersey, over twelve thousand people annually die prematurely because of smoking?"

Chet looked at him askance as he took a long drag on the Lucky. "Fuck it," he said. Smoke curled out of his mouth. "Excuse my French, but if I drank enough to calm my nerves, I'd be sloshed. And I don't want to be drunk if I run into any more of Stark's creations." He gazed off as if remembering. His eyes looked haunted. "I can hardly sleep. I keep seeing Jason's dead crushed face."

Quent saw the circles under the man's eyes—circles of sleeplessness and worry and . . . something else . . .

Fear?

"What the hell's going to happen?" Chet said so quietly Quent felt a chill between his shoulder blades.

"Hopefully nothing," Quent said.

"Hell, no! Something's going to happen. The dam's about to burst. Can't you feel it?"

Quent could have said, Yes, I feel it, but what he felt—what they both felt—was anxiety and anxiety was nothing but body chemistry, metabolism.

Still . . . Quent recalled the strong sensation of repulsion he experienced yesterday at Izzy's door (The fans'll die when they see this one) and wondered.

The device was almost done. All he had to do now was replace the faceplate and test it. A strange request from Mr. Brown this morning: did he think he could come up with a device that could block or neutralize a dreamie transmission in a theater. He'd answered, "Of course," not knowing Mr. Brown would want him to come up with the frequency scrambler by tonight. Still, the project had intrigued him.

Rejdak put down the screwdriver when the faceplate was secure. Rolling down the sleeves of his white shirt, he glanced at his watch. A quarter past eight. Mr. Brown and the other gentleman, Mr. Hughes, would be here soon. He'd completed the scrambler just in time. It had been a busy day and he hadn't gotten around to locating the device until late in the afternoon.

A shadow fell over him.

Turning to see what had caused the enormous shadow, Rejdak glimpsed eyes like twin pools of glowing yellow swimming in a craggy mass that gave the impression of a head, rough-hewn like the head of a stone giant. He also glimpsed what looked like an arm and a massive black hand that looked like chiseled basalt before the fist fell on him like a ton of rocks.

"Say hello to the *Queen Mary*," Chet said as the garage door rattled up.

At first, Quent saw a long gleam of chrome as the bumper was revealed, then he saw the stacked headlights and the gleam of more chrome; then the garage lights spilled over the acre-long hood of the antique Cadillac. The windshield seemed as big as a storefront window.

"'74?"

"'72. Get in."

The front seat was as long as a sofa. Chet popped the key into the ignition, pumped the gas once, then depressed it a tad. The huge Detroit engine coughed once, and turned over as if it had been sitting out in the freezing cold all night, though it was near ninety degrees.

"Humidity," Chet said above the stuttering engine. "It'll sound better. Takes nearly ten minutes to warm up sometimes."

"Ten minutes," Quent exclaimed, his heart sinking at the prospect of sitting here for ten long, excruciating minutes while he chewed his lip and acids gnawed at the lining of his stomach and perhaps something monstrous took place. Helen's face flashed before his mind's eye. God, she was going to be there!

"Don't worry. That's in winter," Chet explained. "It'll only take a couple of minutes today. It's only eight-thirty; show doesn't start till midnight."

Quent let out a sigh he hadn't noticed he was holding in. Izzy had just left. From the living-room window, he and Chet had watched him come out wearing an outlandish outfit. In sharp contrast to his all-white *Vampirophile* image, he wore black for tonight's show: black silk pajamas, black racing gloves, black sneakers—a black silk veil covered his face. Completing the image, a black Bentley limo waited in the driveway.

Chet let the engine rev a minute more, then tapped the gas, kicking the engine out of high idle.

The engine sputtered, died.

Chet tried again. *R-r-r-r-r-r.* The ignition ground.

"Don't worry," he said. "The *Queen Mary* takes a while to wake up, but once she's awake, she runs smooth as a Swiss watch."

Quent refrained from asking if that meant she ticked. Chet turned the key again. The starter ground, caught, and died.

The corpse lay on its back, face up.

Only it had no face!

The rest of the body seemed intact, though so splashed with gore you wouldn't think so at first. The corpse's head had been smashed flat. Not flat like in a cartoon where the guy gets crushed by a steamroller and looks flat and two-dimensional, but flat as in burst open, pulped, squished like a grape into a puddle of purple, gray and red hamburger meat tweeded with splinters of white bone.

The scene was shocking, and Quent, drawn by the need

to know what could have caused the spatters of blood that had dribbled down the wall and splashed into the aisle by the workbench, backed away as soon as he glimpsed the remains. The idea of checking for vital signs was not only revolting but totally absurd. A blind man could tell that Rejdak was dead just by smelling the blood, and for a sighted person staring down at the pool of gore and cranial fluid that ringed what was left of the head and upper torso, there was no room for doubt. Vomit bubbling unstably in his stomach, Quent tried to force his eyes (and his thoughts) away, but couldn't. The sight riveted him, convinced him of Izzy's powers. Doubt disappeared, vanished. Without doubt to cling to, he was terrified.

"Come on." Chet tugged his arm. "Let's get out of here."

Quent backstepped as Chet pulled him away. True to Chet's word, the *Queen Mary* had started after a little coaxing and had gotten them to Stevens Tech in fifteen minutes.

"Don't touch anything."

"Why?" Quent said, finally turning to keep from tripping.

"Because we'd never be able to convince the police that Izzy killed Rejdak with a dream."

"Dreamie."

"Whatever."

"Yeah, I get your point. Hey!" Quent turned, started back toward the atrocity, his gaze searching for the device they were supposed to pick up and which, Quent realized now more than ever, they might very well need tonight.

The fans'll die when they see this one.

Fan is short for fanatic.

It's a little bulky.

But the lab had been trashed. The detritus of smashed electronics littered the floor. Quent recognized the remains of two computer terminals amid the debris.

"Forget it," Chet said. "Let's go."

Quent didn't have to be urged again. He hurried out of the lab. Chet paused at the door to wipe their fingerprints from the knob.

29

Jersey City fire officials never found a cause for the blaze that gutted the historic Majestic Theater on that bizarre and tragic October night. No traces of a precipitant were uncovered and, strangely enough, individual fires seem to have sprung up in different parts of the auditorium.

By the following morning all that remained of the ninety-one-year-old brick building was a blackened shell and the marquee. Except for smoke smudges streaked by the firemen's hoses, the marquee remained untouched until the theater was razed and the site cleared a month later. Until the day the wrecking crew arrived and a crane ripped the marquee from the theater's façade and loaded it onto a dump truck, the marquee sported the title *Inferno*—Stark's final and greatest dreamie, if *greatest* is a measure of how real the dreamie is experienced by the audience. And below this the bitter legend:

Abandon Hope, Ye Who Enter Here

Quent lowered his gaze from the marquee, looked at his hand clutching the big chrome door handle.

Abandon hope . . .

The marquee was right. The two words echoed through his brain, through the static of tension and indecision, through the buzz of the crowd and the din of the unmoving traffic.

Abandon Hope . . .

And it was hopeless. With Rejdak's device smashed, what was he supposed to do? Jump up on stage and pull the plug on Izzy's machine?

"You okay?" Chet asked.

"Yeah, just cooking up a plan."

"Plan's simple: we go in, find the circuit breakers, and shut Stark down." Chet's hands gripped the wheel as he spoke.

Quent thought the elderly man looked dangerous. If his story about the attack on their house last night was true and if Izzy was responsible for Mr. Carruthers' death, he had every right to be. "Right. Except I'm going in alone."

"No way! I'm in this too."

"You've got a ticket?"

"I'll buy one."

"Concert's sold out."

"I mean on the street." Chet nudged his chin meaningfully in the direction of the gaudy partying crowd that overspilled the sidewalk. Chet had gotten to within half a block of the theater before becoming hopelessly immured in traffic.

"Whew! You're kidding. I heard tickets are going for a hundred and fifty. You got a wad like that on you?"

Chet fished his wallet out of his back pocket, opened it. "Twenty-three bucks and a stack of credit cards," he tallied sadly. "How much do you have?"

"Not enough. And scalpers don't take credit cards. Look, you stay outside and try to convince someone to stop the show. You look like a responsible person."

"Thanks."

"Welcome." But Quent found himself wishing the older man were wearing a suit instead of the cotton slacks and the Izod Lacoste polo shirt with the alligator on the pocket. He didn't look like a bum by any means, but the yellow shirt with the green alligator didn't make him exactly authoritative-looking either. His attire, plus his haggard, determined appearance, certainly wasn't going to convince Jersey City's finest.

Chet sighed. "Okay, we'll do it your way. Come on. I'll walk you." The one-time musician flicked a switch on his armrest and the door locks snapped open with a loud *click*.

As Chet opened the door and swung his legs out, Quent wriggled his own wallet out of his hip pocket to transfer the ticket to his front pocket, not wanting to flash his wallet in a crowd, even if he was carrying even less than Chet. Hurriedly, by the light of the streetlamp that fell through the windshield, he opened the wallet, peered in, *and froze!*

"Shit!" He punched the dashboard.

Chet, halfway out of the car, swung back in and slammed the door as if something were out there that would bite his feet off. "What's wrong?"

Quent stared at him a second before he said, "I forgot my ticket!"

"I'm sooo excited!"

Donna fidgeted on her beautiful bottom. She looked like a million dollars tonight, Todd thought, in her tight designer jeans and low-cut white blouse. He recalled the warmth and the weight of those globes in his hands Saturday night, the crinkled slipperiness of her nipples against his tongue. She must have put perfume down there between her breasts, because when he leaned her way—as he did now, squeezing her hand to show that he was excited too—her warmth and her exotic female scent floating up to him made him dizzy. And incredibly agitated! He hoped the lights went down soon, or he was going to be embarrassed. He crossed his legs.

Donna would be leaving in another week. He was trying not to think about that. He didn't like the knots he got in his stomach when he did.

Beyond Donna sat Wanda and then Fred.

Jamie's fever had worsened and he had broken out in a rash. The rash turned out to be chicken pox. After days of depression following Deek's death, Jamie's mood was glum when he learned he was going to spend Saturday night scratching his pocks. When Todd left him that afternoon, Jamie was still insisting he might go to the concert if he felt better. The only thing holding him back was he was so weak he couldn't get off the bed. Jamie's bad luck was Donna's good fortune.

"It's not going to be really gross, is it?" Donna asked, her breast warming his arm as she leaned toward him to whisper in his ear.

Todd smiled and shrugged. "Don't know. I haven't seen it yet. But once you're dreaming, you'll be too busy to think about barfing." Leastwise, I hope so, he thought. He leaned forward, looked past Donna at his buddy. "Pssst! Hey, Fred, wake up!"

Fred leaned forward and grinned broadly. "I'm awake."

Fred looked a little tipsy tonight, Todd decided. He had seen him worse, had seen him drive a hundred and ten miles an hour in a rattling old Chevy station wagon clenching a can of Budweiser between his teeth. He had also seen him, two years ago, fall backward out of the second-floor window of an abandoned house, crash through the roof of an old shed, and land in a pile of produce (the shed belonging to the guy with the vegetable stand around the corner), and exit without a scratch—his rear end soaked with orange juice, but unhurt, and with his pockets full of cherries and his T-shirt full of apples like eight or nine lumpy tits. And, of course, he had been grinning.

Fred was grinning like that now. He was here to have fun and fuck everything else. It occurred to him that his tall, big-knuckled friend might make a good soldier, if there was a war on, or a good mercenary.

"What happened to your eyes?" he said. "They're redder than Wanda's face after a day at the beach."

The corners of Fred's mouth drew into a broad, wise-ass grin. "I saw God," he said.

Todd laughed. Donna's bubbling giggle was crystal and silver in his ears.

"Does she have big tits?" Wanda stopped smacking gum long enough to get the wisecrack out.

Fred guffawed, drawing the irritated glances of the two girls sitting in front of him, and irreverently fondled Wanda's tit with the tip of his index finger. She slapped it away, but she was smiling.

Todd wished Deek were here. But they'd agreed Deek would have insisted they enjoy the show.

The houselights began to dim.

Todd took Donna's moist hand. "Ready?"

"Ready!" she said, squirming.

The houselights dimmed, darkness fell, and above the hushed murmur of the crowd, Helen heard the strong, relentless beat of her heart. She was so tense she still clutched her ticket stub in her clenched fist without being aware of it. She had been clutching it for twenty minutes. Too antsy to endure another half-hour her mother's open and unmerciful anger at Izzy or her father's belligerent silence. She had hardly slept the past two nights, yet she wasn't a bit sleepy.

This is how it feels to break up, she thought, opening her mouth and breathing shallowly to suppress the tears. She didn't like the feeling a bit—the constant adrenaline high that made her stomach burn like too much coffee and left an acidy taste in her mouth. She had lain awake most of last night, muscles clenched, pulse rapid, eyes wide open, listening to her heart beat.

The seat beside her was empty; she wondered if Quent was coming. She craned her neck to look up the aisle to her right. She didn't see him.

She'd tried calling Izzy several times during the past couple days—whenever her parents weren't around, and twice when they were sound asleep—but Izzy wasn't answering. Maybe it was just as well. He'd been working so hard. Maybe it would be better to wait until after the concert to speak to him. He was going through something. She had to give him time. As she sat there among all these people, it seemed unlikely, even foolish, to think that Izzy could harm anyone. And Quent was probably correct Wednesday night when he suggested she'd hallucinated Maria.

The curtains were parting, sweeping smoothly to the wings, revealing a lone white spotlight beaming down on what looked like a languidly smoking volcano. Then the white smoke issuing from the volcano began to billow and the crowd cheered as the lip of the volcano began to glow a smoldering scarlet.

Her heart leapt as out of the mouth of the volcano, veiled in black, Izzy and his gleaming machine rose into the spotlight.

"You what?"

"I forgot my ticket." Quent snapped his fingers. "When Helen came over this morning, I took the tickets out of my wallet. I left the thing on the kitchen table." His voice quavered, his emotions struggling between anger at himself and oh-shit-what-am-I-going-to-do-now panic.

Chet's hands were back on the wheel, as if it were a security totem or an oracle they might consult for directions as to what to do. The older man rubbed the plastic softly, as if polishing Aladdin's magic lamp.

Quent's gaze roved over the crowd that packed the sidewalks in front of the theater, picked out the uniformed policemen trying to unsnarl the traffic that now blockaded the thoroughfare like plaque in a hardened artery. There would be more policemen at the doors.

The din of the crowd, the blare of car horns, muffled by the Cadillac's closed doors, enveloped his thoughts, carried them along like leaves in a stream. Actually, he realized, it was just the opposite: time was moving fast, too fast, while he was sitting on his butt.

His gaze found again the marquee and its doomsayer scrawl:

Abandon Hope . . .

And above that the tall flaming title of Izzy's latest macabre masterpiece:

INFERNO

A classy title. One that conjured images of fire and brimstone and fates worse than death.

And Helen's in there.

Quent opened his door.

"What're you going to do?" Chet called after him.

"I'm going in."

Rather than climb out the driver's side and work his way around the double-parked cars and risk losing sight of Quent, Chet scooted over and piled out the passenger side and hurried after him.

"Hey, hold up!" Chet fell in behind him as they wove their way through the impossibly stalled traffic. "We need a plan."

The sidewalks on both sides of the street were jammed, pedestrians spilling off the curb. Hawkers who had set up shop along the curb out of a cardboard box or on the hood of a car or a bag hanging over their shoulders cried, "Get your T-shirts!" and, "Stark posters, right here!" The T-shirts (Quent saw all the familiar standards: the still-current *Floaters* with its dead bloated face and rotting hand breaking the surface, the older *Vampirophile,* Izzy in white-face, King of Ghouls) and posters were all from past concerts; no new T-shirt or poster was being released until the tour. A cop yelled at them to get back on the sidewalk, but they kept going and the officer paid them no further mind; there were too many people for them to be singled out. Only one lane was open, through which two officers at opposite ends of the block were alternately funneling traffic from both directions. It looked like everyone had decided to fuck the rules and party.

"Get your T-shirts!"

A hawker on his right held a black T-shirt with Izzy Stark's white face glaring at him out of red eyes. Though it had been a standard for over two years, it was as if Quent were seeing it now for the first time: no longer was the face simply Izzy Stark being playful with his fans; the smile had grown sinister, the red eyes glaring with madness.

"Come on." Chet pulled him along by the arm. "There."

Quent's gaze followed Chet's and he saw that, just ahead under the marquee, a broad strip of sidewalk was relatively unoccupied, the crowd held back by JCPD barricades. The ticketholders' line. Last-minute arrivals were being processed through the doors—tickets checked and persons frisked for weapons or bottles.

"I haven't played football in half a lifetime," Chet said, leaning toward him as they edged toward the open, barricade-lined strip of sidewalk, "but it looks like I might get to play tonight."

The absurdity of Chet's words momentarily took Quent's mind off the dread he was feeling. "What're you talking about?"

Pursing his lips, Chet nodded toward the head of the line. Quent strained to see what the taller man saw. Of course!

At the head of the line, between and flanking either side of the two open doors, were three uniformed police officers.

"If you see me tackle a cop," Chet said, "you run and keep on running. Get backstage, throw the circuit breakers. If it's locked, look around. Probably plenty of stuff back there. Maybe even one of those old-time fire axes hanging beside a fire hose behind glass: papers said they were fully restoring the Majestic, and that used to be a common item."

"You're not tackling anyone. You're not exactly immortal, you know."

"Exactly." Chet turned to him and Quent saw that the elderly man's expression was grim, jaw set, eyes determined. "I'm not going to live forever, but I'm not going to stand by and twiddle my thumbs knowing Stark killed my best friend and nearly killed Lois." He lowered his voice. "Something bad's going to happen. Can't you feel it?"

It still felt silly to think that Izzy had killed Mr. Carruthers—or Dr. Nösberger, or Dr. Rejdak—but it also would have seemed pretty crazy to think that Izzy had it in him to hit Helen. The image of Rejdak's pulped head formed a backdrop to his swarming thoughts.

The fans'll die when they see this one.

Maybe it's the dreamer that's changed.

Fan is short for fanatic.

And, of course, he did feel it, had felt it since they'd left Rejdak's lab. It was as if something was tangibly but inexplicably and unsettlingly changed about the air. Almost as if its constituent molecules had grown dense and electrically charged. The feeling—as invisible as the plague, and as deadly—emanated from the doors ahead of them. Under the marquee.

Abandon Hope . . .

He looked at Chet striding beside him, saw an elderly grim-faced man in better than fair shape, but no athlete. Then looked at the young policemen guarding the doors. Their chances seemed hopeless indeed.

Behind the gray JCPD barricades, the crowd partied. Quent didn't see any boomboxes, but music from at least four different radio stations bombarded his brain, bypassing his ears. There were soundless stereos in the crowd cranked beyond legal decibels.

"Tickets! Have your tickets ready!" a red-jacketed ticket collector shouted as he ripped tickets and returned stubs.

On impulse, Quent pushed his way past the ticketholders, advancing up the opposite side from the theater employee. Mutters and growls of "Hey, man! Watch it!" attended his progress.

"Police!" Quent barked at them without thinking, being out of ideas and reduced to impromptu. Miraculously, it worked!

Nearing the inevitable portals, he saw that all three cops were rookies. Glancing at Chet, he thought, Oh, shit! Here goes nothing! and repeated "Police!" for the young officer who held up a hand to stop them.

"Just a—"

Quent spoke, waving him aside before he could finish. "Make way for the commissioner!"

Chet played along beautifully: he gave the rookie the slightest nod and continued on.

"Evening, Commissioner." The redheaded cop stepped aside and touched the edge of his brim as they brushed past.

Out of the corner of his eye, Quent saw a man with a walkie-talkie moving toward them through the crowd. The rookie's head was turning. Then, miraculously, they were inside.

But not home free.

Not by a long shot!

The red-carpeted lobby, its walls decorated with framed posters of long-ago vaudeville stars, was relatively empty. No crowd to get lost in! He glanced back; Chet was right at his heels. The man with the walkie-talkie was conferring with the rookie; then he was hurrying through the door looking pissed, talking into his walkie-talkie.

"Hurry!" Quent urged needlessly and headed for the auditorium doors, thinking maybe it'd be dark in there and, maybe, he could make it to the stage, bust up Izzy's dreamatron before he got arrested. Maybe . . .

A hand fell on his shoulder—a strong hand, pulling him around, even as a booming voice bellowed, "Hey, you!" in his ear. Quent glimpsed a big beefy face, red with exertion and anger, the face of a bouncer in a bad mood.

30

And now it is happening. He refrains from raising his arms to acknowledge the sea of shouting, whistling faces in the orchestra and balcony and the ornate gold-and-red turn-of-the-century theater boxes. He pauses only until the applause subsides before getting down to business.

He lowers his head. The sudden act is punctuated by an abrupt change in lighting. The spotlight blackens, eclipses, and from the darkness at the back of the stage, a cross, twelve feet tall, of blinding red spotlights and outlined with smaller but equally brilliant white bulbs, suddenly, startlingly, flashes on.

The crowd goes wild.

The cross begins to pulsate, to strobe. The whole interior of the theater—seats, patrons, walls, ceiling—alternately flashes red and black. Through slitted lids, Izzy stares into the pulsing red light in the center of his control panel. The light pulses to the same rhythm as the dazzling cross. His breathing slows, the murmur of the crowd recedes.

The blinking ruby light fills his skull as though it were a goblet brimming with blood.

Donna blinked, yawned, remembered to close her mouth. She was impressed, excited: the flashing red light had hypno-tized her or something. So this is what a dreamie's like! So far, she liked it A-OK.

Todd didn't know how long he had been staring gape-mouthed at the stroboscopic cross, but his eyes were hot and dry from not blinking. He squeezed his eyes shut, but the blinding red cross was emblazoned on his retinas; he saw it superimposed on Donna's face when he turned to look at her.

She kissed him on the cheek. He was sure she had left a lipstick smudge shaped to her full lips, but he didn't care, he felt on top of the world.

"Look!" Donna bolted to the edge of her seat.

Todd looked. The volcano, atop which the black-veiled figure sat, was erupting. Or so it appeared. The lip of the volcano, glowing like the smoldering red of a cigarette tip, was overflowing, special-effects lighting simulating a lava flow. The smoke that had drifted up from the volcano all along, dyed scarlet as it rose before the strobing cross, began to billow profusely. More smoke jetted from fissures, a bloody steam rose hissing from the lava flow.

He noticed the draft that crept along under the seats, winding between the patrons' ankles. It stirred his hair. His eyes watered from its coldness. He worked his toes in his sneakers. His feet were freezing. Gooseflesh decorated his arms. The theater had grown cold—icebox cold—as if someone had turned the AC up full blast. And now he heard the whispering *whooooo* of the rising breeze.

With a *crack* like thunder, the ceiling split, exploding outward, instantly exposing the audience to a starless, overcast sky. Donna's nails dug into his arm. Todd instinctively pulled her to his chest and covered her head as best he could, expecting the roof to cave in on them.

But what went up did not come down. No deadly hail of wood, steel, plaster, and stone bombarded the audience.

"We're dreaming," Todd said, marveling. He had thought— and so had everyone else by the murmur that ran through the crowd—that the dreamie hadn't started yet, but for the roof to blow off the theater and nothing to have fallen down on top of us, we have to be under. He marveled at Stark's ingenuity. So this is the scenario. And we're the characters! Far freepin' out!

He looked over at Fred. Wanda was still staring open-mouthed at the figure on the stage. Beyond her, Fred was grinning.

"What do you think?"

"Fuckin' A!" Fred spoke too loudly, gave him a hearty thumbs-up.

This was something new, novel. Starting off with the audience in the theater, forming a continuum with reality. Todd looked around him. The dreamie was so detailed: he saw people he remembered seeing before the show began. Fol-

lowing the gaze of many of the audience members, he looked
up.

Out of the darkness above, unnoticed at first, then the eye
catching a flicker, a dim far-off glimmer approaching, drawing
nearer, as if something was hurtling toward him from a fantastic distance, descending from the velvety womb of space itself.
The plummeting glimmerings multiplied, became a horde of
winged figures illuminated by an eerie, flickering chiaroscuro.

He first thought the figures were nightgaunts. As he had
seen *Dreamquest* seventeen times, the circling formation of far-
off shadows was definitely familiar. But then, straining his eyes,
he saw riders on the things' backs.

"Nazgûl!" he breathed.

A dozen voices from the surrounding seats echoed him. He
thrilled at the sight. Tolkien's Nazgûl! What a stroke of genius!
Most of the audience probably was familiar with *The Lord of the
Rings*. Stark was using an old ploy: show the public something
they're already familiar with, and they'll accept it—hook, line,
and sinker. Then they'll want to swallow more. Lots more.
He did! Already a personalized critique of tonight for the next
issue of *Tentacle* was forming in his head.

Around and around the Ringwraiths flew high overhead,
the huge skull-headed horses sailing ponderously, impossibly,
yet gracefully gliding on powerful wings. And above them,
straddling their shadow-black mounts, the nine fallen princes,
gaunt and ghastly pale. The preternatural figures, horses and
riders alike, seemed to emit a pale chiaroscuro, an unholy
glamour.

The gelid breeze became a wind as the Nazgûl swooped,
cadaverous fingers twined in the manes of their spectral
mounts. Todd ducked and squealed right along with Donna
and Wanda as the lead Nazgûl's steed skimmed not five feet
over their heads.

"Fuckin' A!" he heard Fred shout.

"It's all right," Todd assured Donna. Grinning nervously, his
voice a little too high and thin, betraying his fright, he squeezed
her hand as the Nazgûl spiraled up again into the overcast sky.
"It's just special effects."

All around, people were rising, some having hidden under their seats. Todd felt an adolescent pride from not having done likewise. What next? he thought.

The Nazgûl, having risen in a graceful spiral all in a row like a gaggle of monstrous geese until they were again barely discernible as horse and rider, turned; their steeds, folding back their wings, shot earthward. The Nazgûl's return sent fresh quivers of excitement through the crowd, the air buzzed with voices.

Cold steel gleamed like moonlight as the riders drew swords and battle-axes. With a great *whooosh!* of air the shadow wings spread again, and like ground-skimming jets the skull-headed stallions zoomed over the heads of the theatergoers.

Steel flashed. And before Todd's startled eyes, four rows in front of him, a head, severed from a neck with a meaty *thwock* and pinwheeling a spray of blood, went sailing out of sight. The Nazgûl was past before the blood droplets settled.

A red streak diagonally slashed Donna's face. This time, she didn't scream, but dived for the floor. Todd joined her, his disbelief thoroughly suspended. Wanda joined them on the carpet. Glancing up, the nerves in the back of his neck singing with the threat of imminent decapitation, Todd saw the Nazgûl were again soaring skyward.

"Did you see that, man?" Fred said. Fred was still seated, grinning, looking a little white but otherwise nonplussed. "Hey, you guys look pretty funny down there."

Todd blushed, felt egg on his face as he tried to untangle himself from Donna and pull her and himself back into their seats. Stark had gotten to him but not to good old unflappable Fred . . .

There was blood on Fred's face. And on Wanda's and on Donna's and on his shirt.

Crraack!

Lightning erupted, eclipsed the blackness above, blinded him, blotted out the ascending Nazgûl.

The earth rumbled. The floor and seats lurched.

The rumbling didn't cease, but grew louder, the vibrations more forceful. The ground beneath Todd's feet swelled, tilted.

The metal frames of their seats groaned. Then a great rending noise, as of concrete splitting.

Crrrrraack!

People were screaming. Todd saw over the humped backs of the theatergoers on his right a new aisle open up zigzagging crazily through the orchestra swallowing seats and patrons in its path.

Dark, sulfurous smoke billowed through the fissure. The floor shook. Thunder crashed, crashed again. Lightning strobed, vied with the cross so that the smoke billowing up into the void into which the Black Riders had retreated alternately flashed red and white.

Todd ducked back down, suddenly—and irrationally, considering he had enough dreamies under his belt to know better— terrified that the Nazgûl would swoop out of the smoke.

Despite his terror, he grinned. Though three-quarters of his mind screamed out for him to wake up, the other quarter cheered and whistled applause at the ingenuity of Stark's latest monster hit.

Then the noise of rending, collapsing concrete swallowed up the noise of the thunder and the screaming crowd, and he realized he was screaming too as the floor dropped away like a sheet of thin ice and he pitched forward into the smoke.

Quent could smell the coffee on the cop's breath.

Then the cop's expression turned to surprise. The hand dislodged from his shoulder. Turning, he saw why—Chet, true to his word, had grabbed the beefy-faced uniformed cop from behind and was squeezing him in a bear hug.

"Run!" Chet roared louder than he would have thought possible.

He ran. There weren't many people left in the lobby. Glancing back, he saw Chet go down as the redheaded rookie who had waved them inside pulled him off the older cop. He stopped, started to go back and yell for them not to hit him, but they were already hitting him, and now the heavy-set, middle-aged cop was turning, running toward him, red-faced and angry, yelling for him to stop.

Sprinting for the safety of numbers, Quent hit the swinging double doors that led into the theater.

The shock of landing on rock rattled Todd's teeth and bounced his brains off the walls of his skull.

The impact should have been worse. Much worse. Considering the duration of the fall and the fact that he had landed on rock, he should have been squashed; yet he was hurt no more than if he had fallen off a chair. The fact that he still lived restored his faith in the unreality of the dreamie.

It's all in the mind, pal. Don't get a heart attack.

Noise, smoke, and confusion were his first impression when he lifted his head. The noise became the screaming of people in pain; the confusion resolved itself into a smoky darkness dotted with fire. Donna groaned nearby, and to his left he saw Fred looking a little stunned but grinning.

Sulfurous fumes clogged his nostrils, twined noxious tendrils into his lungs, and he bent his face near the ground to breathe better.

So what are you going to do, buddy? Crawl around on your hands and knees and choke to death? Or wait here until something worse comes along?

In an Isidor Stark dreamie, something worse always came along.

Donna blinked rapidly and coughed as a particularly acrid plume of smoke curled up her nostrils. She held her breath. All around was swirling dimness. There were yellow wavering lights here and there that might have been candles, but it was too dark and smoky to tell.

People seemed to be moving around her, coughing, calling out to one another: the buzz of an excited crowd. Fear in the voices. Beyond this she couldn't tell a thing.

She remembered she was holding her breath, let it out, breathed in. She coughed again, but then realized the smoke didn't really burn her eyes or throat; she had coughed because she had expected the smoke to choke her. Realizing she could breathe quelled part of her panic.

"Todd?" she said as a hand circled her wrist.

251

But the hand was slimy and cold, not at all like Todd's hands.

And then she saw the mottled lizard hide, the dry flap of scaly skin hanging from its cheekbone, the eye, like a pustulant bag of dead, unseeing jelly, hanging down on the yellowing, partially exposed cheekbone, the black tongue stiffly wagging.

Sitting on what looked like the floor of hell, having discovered he could breathe, Fred was pleasantly bombed, all reet 'n' complete, having recently made some discoveries about alcohol.

Actually, they weren't so much *new* discoveries as hitherto-unknown (to him) aspects of an old friend. In the days since Deek died, he had made two discoveries about alcohol: one, if he drank enough, he could reach a place in his brain where he had never been before, a place that was as cold and quiet as an empty deep freeze; and two, if he couldn't reach that icy plateau, alcohol made him want to fight. The latter stage was where he was tonight. To reach the former took a considerable amount of alcohol and a degree of solitude. Last night, stretched out on his bed with his shoulders propped up by his pillow after his parents had gone to bed, he had drunk over half a bottle of Pop's Johnnie Walker Red and he had attained that icy plateau where even his thoughts were quiet, before lapsing into sleep. He'd had a head and a half this morning, but the time spent lying on his back in his darkened room, his eyes closed to stop the ceiling from spinning, had been worth it.

Looking around, he dug the scenario. How far he had fallen he had no idea, but he had landed on his feet. His legs wavering ever so slightly from the six or seven shots of Southern Comfort he'd downed before the show, he surveyed what looked like a vast smoky plain. He couldn't see very far because of the greasy yellow smoke that billowed from what appeared to be pits of bubbling sulfur, but here and there through rifts in the smoke he glimpsed more sulfur pits spotted randomly about the dark terrain.

Not all the fires were stationary. For a moment he thought he glimpsed a column of bobbing torch fires like a string of fireflies in the night, thought he heard the tramp of marching feet, but then the wafting smoke closed over the unknown, leaving him to wonder.

Fred bent, pulled the thin pewter flask from his loose-topped engineer's field boots, spun the cap, and took a long pull. A Stark dreamie was a participation sport and he planned to burn off some steam tonight. He burped enthusiastically as he returned the flask to an inside pocket of his Lee jacket, giving his foot more freedom of movement for the upcoming adventure.

Donna screamed.

He turned around, saw the shambling, manlike creature spin her around, saw it raise in its other hand a barbed, three-pronged trident like the one the sea god Neptune carried. The thing's broad back was to him. Fred rushed it from behind, grabbed the trident as it rose over the creature's head, planted a foot in the small of its back, and shoved.

The heavy iron weapon came free in his hands.

The creature spun around, roaring. The wind from its lungs, like a blast from a freshly opened tomb, nearly felled him. The badly decomposed face was startling. He'd expected bestial furor in its features, not the blankness of its dead eyes. He grinned, admiring the effect. Then he was moving, a blur of long-legged action. He raced toward the nearest fire pit, the demon charging after him, the loose flaps of its cheeks slapping its yellowed teeth.

Near the edge of the pit, Fred rammed the butt of the shaft into a crevice, and the dead thing slammed into the heavy three-tined fork. Ducking its grasping hands, he threw his weight against the shaft, shoving upward with his shoulder. His weight combined with the beast's, momentum sent the creature up and over.

A satisfied grin replaced Fred's snarl when he heard the splash and subsequent hiss of the creature going under.

Helen landed on her side, shocked that she was still alive after a fall like that. Undoubtedly, Izzy had distorted the sense of distance. Hopefully, she was experiencing Izzy's virtual experience from the safety of her seat and none of this was real.

Having been the guinea pig for so many of Izzy's experiments, she was familiar with his smoke scenes and didn't bother holding her breath.

Why, then, was her heart pounding in her throat and gooseflesh crawling over her back? Was it because, for the first time in as long as she could remember, she wasn't sure she was safe? Was it her sixth sense warning her? Or the paranoia that led her to consider the ridiculous: that Izzy could have anything to do with killing anyone?

Whatever it was, when she heard the roaring and screaming issuing from the darkness around her, she crawled to the nearest rock and, despite the heat, pressed herself into a shallow niche at its base and tried fervently to become one with it as monstrous foot treads shambled by.

31

Quent burst through the door, his momentum launching him into the auditorium ... or what should have been the auditorium. He stopped and stared about in amazement. He looked back the way he had come, fearing the worst.

The door was gone!

His heart, already hammering from his encounter with the police, quickened with real fear.

He was in the dreamie, standing amid what looked like a vast smoke-filled plain. Ahead, in the direction he'd been facing when he ran in, a long horizontal streak of yellowish light slashed the blackness.

And now that his attention was focused on the yellow luminescence, he heard the screams.

Faraway.

Many-voiced.

Chilling.

He shivered.

Above and behind him was obfuscate night. He started toward the light. Which was where, he reasoned, Izzy probably was. And where the action seemed to be.

The fans'll die when they see this one.

Fan is short for fanatic.

Lightning doesn't have to strike for you to believe it exists, does it, Quent, old boy?

No, indeed it needn't, my man! Especially after viewing Rejdak's corpse!

Proceed with caution—that was the way to approach this. Assume, for the sake of survival, it's all true. Horrible things are happening and the worst is yet to come. The fact that he could breathe despite the roiling smoke was hardly consoling, considering the crawling dread that cloaked his shoulders.

The screams grew louder as he advanced.

Oh, Jesus! Why couldn't I have stayed home? he asked himself.

Because Helen's in here. And because you could no more stay away than you could skip breathing.

The pain that lanced his chest at the thought of Helen in danger quickened his step. People will die here tonight: best to proceed under that assumption. Though it was hard to believe Izzy was a killer, it was equally hard to believe, after seeing Rejdak, that those screams arising from the mystery ahead were special effects.

He stopped, listened.

Was that a footstep he'd heard on his right?

He squinted into the darkness, holding his breath.

Was that a bloated, fish-pale face he saw leering cadaverously at him out of the corner of his eye? A face that remained in his peripheral vision when he tried to look at it.

He shivered. Told himself he was imagining things. Moved on.

Ahead, the yellow glow grew brighter as he made his way through the dark; the luminescent band it painted against the black widened. He wondered at the source of the light. The screams sounded jarringly like the shrieks of torture victims he'd seen in movies, they grated on his soul like glass scraped across his teeth. He shivered again, as if he were out in a T-shirt on a bitter January night despite the oppressive heat of the dreamscape.

The earth opened up before him, and he was glad he hadn't been running. The land fell away, downwards and outwards, in a steep tumble of shadowy rock, revealing the source of the smoke and the fiery glow.

And the screams.

Horror assaulted Quent's eyes, tightened skeletal hands around his windpipe, as he stared out over the Boschean hell-scape. The first sweeping impression was of smoky distances, of darkness hole-punched with yellow fires from which sulfur-ous smoke rose in mushrooming columns, forming a shadowy canopy overhead. His heart leapt at glimpses of people herded between the fires. He fixed his gaze on one of the hulking shapes shambling along the fringe of the crowd. Then another. And a third. The last clearly visible standing in the light of one of the fiery pits.

Even as his mind reeled from the shock of seeing the gross demonic shapes lashing and prodding the herded humans, he saw what they were up to.

There, yellow-lighted by the bubbling brimstone, two shaggy creatures gleefully chucked a leather-jacketed punk into a fire-pit. And there, a toad-headed grotesquerie armed with a scimitar hacked at a screaming lizard lady. And farther away, so that he could barely make out what it was doing, an armless, wingless, crow-headed monster chicken-scratched the shit out of a red smear that once might have been human.

How much of it was "special effects"? And how much was real?

Are people really dying? Or is it all an illusion?

Staring at that red smear glistening wetly in the yellow glow of the sulfur pit, he recalled Rejdak's pulverized face, pulped like a grape after dropping a bowling ball on it, like a cantaloupe two minutes after being rolled out into the freeway traffic during rush hour, like a caterpillar that had wandered into a printing press.

Crouching down on his hands and knees as much out of a desire to make himself inconspicuous as out of fear of going over the edge, he examined the descent. In a way—though the only plants were briars growing out of crevices in the rock—

the cliff face resembled the Palisades below Izzy's house. In fact, as he peered into the gloom and his gaze came to rest upon a steep but accessible path leading down, he thought he recognized the path he and Izzy had taken Saturday two weeks ago. In spite of the fact that briars had replaced the mimosa and weeds growing on the Weehawken cliff side, he experienced a weird sense of *déjà vu*.

He made his way along the rim of hell until he was several feet above the path; then lowered himself over the side and hung by his arms, feeling with his toes until he found purchase on the narrow, sandy path. Then turned loose.

And started sliding.

Pebbles shot from under his sneakers. His arms pinwheeled. His hands grasped for the ledge.

He missed and spilled over the edge.

Quent came to, blinked, started as a shadow fell over him. His back ached as he rose on one elbow.

Vast, umbrellalike creatures with a myriad ropy tentacles dangling beneath, looking like the illustration of a Portuguese man-of-war he had seen in the *Encyclopædia Britannica*, moved silently and ponderously like great flabby dirigibles through the smoky canopy above.

One floated toward him, materializing out of the veiling smoke like a ship emerging from fog. Terror gripped him, froze him to the ledge on which he lay. The thing came directly toward him, veering neither left nor right, and though he could see nothing that resembled eyes, Quent was dead sure it was coming for him.

As it neared, he saw its pocked, gray flesh.

It's dead! he marveled, staring at the flabby, rancid-looking meat, the tentacles that had burst open in the process of decay. A dead husk borne aloft by Izzy's whim. His flesh crawled: somehow, a roving dead monster was always more frightening than a live one. Quent held his breath as it closed in. There was nothing of the sea in the smell of it—just the stench of rot, like ripe garbage, bloating toward him.

The smell was familiar. He placed it. *Floaters!* It was the same stench Izzy had used for the waterlogged dead in his gore extravaganza. Not exactly a consoling thought!

Now the thing loomed so near he could see into the holes in the great billowing wall of flab where the meat had rotted and dropped away. His hackles rose.

But before it reached him, it drifted down, a vast bloated island, the Hovercraft of hell. He sat up and leaned forward to see what it was up to. Its tentacles settled over a group of teenagers who appeared to be fighting off what looked like a couple of orcs. The victims' screams cut through the general calamity as the monster effortlessly rose, unhindered by its human cargo. Quent shuddered, averted his gaze, but the vision of tangled legs kicking below a mass of tentacles stayed with him.

Dread spurred him on. Sliding and scraping, he made his way down the greater part of the cliff face. Somewhere near the bottom gravity got the better of him and he skidded and tumbled down a rocky slope, stirring up a small avalanche. Gravel rained around him when the earth flattened and he rolled three times landing splayed on his belly.

He spat hot sand, rolled over, and got up, feeling the stings and aches of his cuts and bruises, which formed a background pain to the screaming in his knee. He cupped a hand over his kneecap. He'd torn his cords and the flesh was swollen, puffy. The slightest pressure made him wince.

Fractured something for sure, he thought morbidly.

Quent took stock of his surroundings, worried the noise of his fall might have attracted denizens of the hellscape.

Visibility down here sucked compared to what he had been able to see from above, but through the drifting smoke he saw that he stood on a rocky plain, a desert of stone and sand and yellow firepits, the tortured broken floor of hell.

Once again, noting the overall impression of the dreamscape was fire and darkness, yellow and black, he was struck with the similarity of Izzy's imagery with that of Bosch's hellscapes.

He was glad he was wearing dark clothes, sorry his face and arms were so white. He hadn't gotten much of a tan this past summer and he knew he must stand out like an albino at the Apollo Theater.

He rubbed his hands on the rocky ground, then on his cheeks. Nothing. He smiled grimly at the irony. In the real world there would be dirt, at least a sprinkling of sand. But, then, deadly though it might be, this was, after all, a dreamie, and, no matter how good a dreamer Isidor Stark was, no dreamer can create a world as complex, as minutely detailed, as nature.

He licked his lip, feeling exposed.

Which way to go?

His eyes picked out the line of medium-to-large-size boulders that followed the general curve of the Palisades on his right. It occurred to him that, perhaps, if he stuck to the boulders, he might find a door, get backstage.

Next to the adrenaline-charged dread that something awful might any moment pop out of the dark and gobble him up, the hardest part of infiltrating the enemy was running in a crouched position, a strain on his back and agony on his knee but safer than loping along with his nose in the air.

As he made his way from boulder to boulder, following the curve of the Palisades until the rocks abandoned the cliff and plunged into the hellscape, a seemingly endless parade of atrocities assaulted his eyes, delivering shock after shock until his brain reeled from the images.

At one point, he witnessed a black apelike creature with a grinning cow's head gleefully chuck a screaming teenager into a boiling sulfur pit.

Farther on, he saw a great bloated toad with the lower torso and kicking legs of a girl sticking out of a wide lipless mouth as big as the trunk of Chet's Caddy. A gruesome *crunch* reached his ears across the intervening yards, and blood squirted out the sides of the monster's mouth, soaked the white panties. The legs stopped kicking, hung limp, then disappeared, swallowed by the cavernous maw.

A young woman screamed and struggled as one demon pinned her down to the rock while a second ripped away the front of her clothing and speedily drove a stake through her heart. She continued to claw at her murderer's arm even as the black blood spewed out in jets. Still farther along, he watched horrified as a scaled, headless thing, a chrome-studded leather boy in each taloned hand, brought their heads together with a sickening *crunch,* then flung their flopping cadavers into the darkness.

As hideous as the images were, he admired Izzy's masterful handling of the appearance of death, of its sensual realism. The anthropomorphic demons Izzy had created, for the most part so obviously derivative of Bosch, surpassed the medieval master's creations precisely because of that sensual realism. The living dead. Literally.

His heart leapt at the sight of four leather-jacketed teenagers ganging up on a being that appeared to be something like a scaled lizard below and some sort of prehistoric bird from the wings up. But instantly, a giant rat the size of a pony tore into them, transforming the scene into a blur of tooth and claw and a spray of blood, squelching his momentary hope.

He glimpsed other groups fighting back. Should I help? he wondered.

No, he would help more if he stuck to the rocks and tried to get backstage, knock out the power.

And now he ran out of cover.

The last boulder, backlighted by the yellow glow, was at a distance from the others. It was large enough to hide him, maybe six feet wide and four high. Coming in low, he dropped quietly into its shadow.

Carefully, favoring his injured knee, he bent his head low to the ground and peered around the base of the rock.

Not twelve feet away on the other side of the rock, a monster in the shape of a powerful barrel-chested man with a rhino's head and the teeth-filled jaws of a pit bull chomped noisily on a fresh kill.

As if it sensed his presence, the head turned, a flap of bloody flesh dangling from its bull-like jaws. For a paralyzing fraction of a second, Quent found himself staring into shocking lambent red eyes, as wild with blood lust as a shark's during feeding frenzy.

He ducked, praying the thing hadn't seen him and knowing it had. As he dropped to the ground, his hand squished shockingly into something wet and hot. He recoiled, choking back the vomit, scrambled to his feet, realizing he had just sunk his hand into the still-warm intestines of a gutted corpse sprawled in the dark beside him.

The thing was moving toward him, tossing aside the headless cadaver as it broke into a massive lope, the flap of red meat still hanging from its jaws. The demon roared, spewing bloody gobbets of flesh.

Quent clawed his way free of the slippery corpse, scrabbled to his feet. His knee screamed as he forced it into action. He slipped in blood, almost fell. Then his sneakers dug in, and injured knee or no, he sprinted out from behind the rock faster than he had ever moved.

As if the devil was at his heels.

He risked a glance over his shoulder.

The devil was closing the gap.

Helen's blood pounded, a relentless surf, surging through her veins, throbbing in time to her pulsing temples. Something was definitely weird about this dreamie. She felt the difference in the raging hatred she felt crawling in the atmosphere like a live thing, a virulent animosity so overwhelming it seemed directed solely at her.

She'd played critic for so many of Izzy's dreamies, and the raw razor-edged hate she felt worming its way into the pores of her body was a new thing, unlike anything Izzy had ever done. Violence, yes! Izzy, in his imagination, could be as lethal as the most deranged mass murderer or human cannibal. But never hate. Izzy's floaters were only hungry, and danger and disgust dominated that dreamie. In *Vampirophile,* Albert, Izzy's albino vampire wannabe, was simply misguided. *Dreamquest,* which she personally felt was Izzy's greatest, was imbued with subtle sensations of loathsomeness and of a worming paranoia coupled with a heavy creepy-crawly dose of xenophobia. Not even in some of his wilder experiments that had never made it into dreamies had he demonstrated such virulence.

She hadn't moved. The crevice into which she pressed herself had become like a warm womb, too warm if she pressed her cheek against the stone. She only wished the womb were big enough for her to crawl into and hide from the nightmare shapes prowling by. Everywhere was night and fire. Shrieks of terror kept the air vibrating with horror. Crouching, pressing herself into the cloaking shadow, she felt relatively out of eyeshot of the huge things that lumbered, loped, and slithered past.

Once, out of the roiling blackness a bloodcurdling scream startled her, followed by the crunch of bone. Shaking with terror, it was all she could do to keep from crying and giving herself away as the hideous feasting continued. Then the munching stopped and she heard what sounded like a bundle dropped to the ground and the tread of something large and four-legged moving away.

A moment later, a long-haired teenage girl ran by in flames, screaming, lighting up the night around her like a torch, leaving in her wake a white, freeze-framed afterimage of horror that hung before her vision long after the girl vanished and her screams faded.

A pair of scaled three-clawed feet swung over her as something passed, the upper half of its torso obscured by smoke.

And then it happened. The last straw. The one that broke the camel's back. She bit her lip to keep from screaming, hugged the rock, body clenched, to keep from convulsing, but when the head, shoulder, and arm of a corpse dragged over her, the scream ripped out of its hiding place in her lungs and sliced the air like a siren's wail.

With a roar that might have blasted out of a Dolby soundless system—one of those that made your teeth vibrate—a horny, three-taloned hand swiped at her. She ducked, rolled, came up running, kicking up gravel with the thing hot on her heels.

The pit loomed close. Quent saw the individual bubbles through the steam—big oily-looking yellow bubbles merrily bursting, releasing as they popped noxious puffs of sulfur dioxide that, like the smoke, stirred his nausea but failed to incapacitate him.

The monster's stale, dead breath chilled his neck. Spittle

sprayed over him as its roar reverberated through his head like a blast of a diesel horn.

He dropped to his knee—his good knee—leaned into the monster's weight, hugged the ground (hot as a steam bath this close to the sulfur pit) to receive the weight, which arrived with the force of a baseball bat in the kidneys.

"Whooomph!" The air exploded from his lungs. Pain blossomed in his side. He was knocked over, skidded sideways to within a yard of the bubbling pool. The lip of the pit was scalding, blisters popped out on his right forearm and hand, and as he rolled clear, gasping in pain, he glimpsed the massive spread-eagle shape sail over him, arms stretched over its horn-snouted rhino head, its ruptured scabrous throat, as if the thing were diving into a swimming pool. He kept rolling, knowing—as he heard the satisfying *splash* of boiling sulfur raining down—that the edge of the pit would be flooded.

He slammed into a low ridge and lay gasping, his knee screaming for attention, his forearm something he didn't want to think about, and surprised as hell he hadn't been scalded to death.

He didn't wait to see if the creature would resurface. He scanned for cover and dove into the nearest shadow. He cracked his knee against the bottom of the shallow foxhole, driving pain like a steel spike up his leg. Everything went black, a blackness in which billions of stars swirled blazingly bright.

He flipped over on his back. And as his head cleared and he stared up into the roiling smoke, he thought, Oh, my God, the theater's on fire!

Then he realized he was still in Izzy's Inferno lying on his back in a hole looking up at the smoke canopy and listening to the screams of the tortured and dying. He felt about as safe as a turtle on a freeway. His shallow foxhole could easily become his grave.

He touched his arm, wished he hadn't.

He thought he'd laugh like hell if he woke up sitting in his seat and the whole experience—and that meant everything that had happened at least since Helen's showing up at his place Wednesday night—had been a dreamie after all. But then the image of Rejdak's crushed face flew at him like a bloody pie.

He peered over the edge of the depression. He hated to expose his head, but he didn't have a cornucopia of choices. The nightmare vignettes went on around him, heard but unseen.

A light broke through a rift in the smoke, caught his attention . . . not a yellow light, but white like a spotlight. His flesh crawled.

The rift widened.

Beyond the wall of smoke the ground sloped upward, then rose in a jumble of jutting rocks. And at the top of the pile, bathed in white radiance, sat the veiled figure of Izzy Stark, King of the Dreamies.

Quent glanced around. Darkness and light. Vague shapes moving like shadows. Nothing near. He pushed himself out of the foxhole and, struggling to his feet, ran toward Izzy, his knee creaking like a new shoe, pain spearing his leg.

A pall of yellow smoke passed between him and Izzy, closing the rift like a curtain drawn across a stage. But he'd seen the way. Straight ahead, the ground was fairly flat—if he could run faster and Izzy wasn't playing tricks on him . . .

A woman ran by, almost knocked him down. Her features were distorted with terror.

"Helen," he shouted starting after her.

And was instantly knocked to the ground by a loping ghoul, its huge ribbed head mottled yellow and orange like a pumpkin.

Even as he rose and staggered forward, even as he beheld the huge scales of dead orange-gray flesh hanging from its bald head, even as he realized the head wasn't really a pumpkin gone mushy with decay but a mass of tumors taking the form of pumpkin-like ridges, like some hideous Elephant-Man disease, knowing he would never reach her in time and, even if he did, he wouldn't do her a bit of good, he watched as the thing snatched her up and carried her to the nearest sulfur pit.

The pumpkin-headed demon stood on the brink of the pit, Helen's unconscious form lolling over its head, a deadweight that didn't seem to faze the thing. It lifted her higher, stretched its arms taut in the final preparatory movement to hurl Helen into the fire.

Too late! No way I can . . . Nooooooo!

His frustration transformed into fury as his eyes snapped to Izzy.

And in that instant of frustration and rage, his anger lashed out at his old school chum. He forgot that they had been friends, that they had gone to school together. He saw Izzy through the rifting smoke appearing like the Angel of Death in his black raiment. And in that instant, he saw—quite vividly, as if it were happening before him—himself wielding a blazing sword bathed in a silvery light, splitting Izzy's head open with a meaty chop like a pineapple on a butcher's block.

The hellscape blurred . . .

Izzy's mental construct rippled.

He saw seats. Rows of seats. Filled with people. A gilded theater box. Smoke curling from the wallpaper below the box. Burning seats. Burning people.

Something Rejdak said penetrated his amazement: ". . . the dreamatron is capable of interacting with the audience . . . Dreamies work both ways . . . the dreamie is the closest thing to telepathy . . ."

Telepathy!

"You can be fought, you son of a bitch," he growled between clenched teeth.

As reality shimmered again. Became unreality.

His eyes snapped to the bubbling sulfur pit as darkness closed around him. His heart leapt to his throat.

The edge of the pit—upon which the pumpkin-headed thing had stood, Helen uplifted—was empty!

"Helen!" he roared, heedless of the denizens of Izzy's dark.

Unbidden and uncontrollably, tears slid down his cheeks as he limped forward. And totally uncharacteristically of him, he felt a powerful urge to follow her, to plunge beneath the boiling surface, to feel the heat's searing kiss, for a moment before oblivion closed over his head and his mind went blank.

32

"Helen!"

Quent staggered toward the pit's shimmering edge. The soles of his sneakers grew tacky.

"Helen ..." he said again, barely audible now above the festive bubbling as he backed away, the heat and eye-watering fumes too much for him. He turned to Izzy to vent his fury, but a veil of smoke momentarily obscured the dream king.

I can't believe she's gone, he thought.

And it's my own fault! I gave her the ticket!

A nearby groan made him jump. A shape detached itself from the shadow at the bottom of a slight decline, like the shallow foxhole he'd taken refuge in before.

"Helen?"

He helped her to her feet. As she rose into the yellow light, he saw that she was dazed, disoriented. Her face was pale with shock, her eyes wide with fear. She was shaking, unsteady. But when he put an arm around her for support, she drew her hand back clawlike, and for a second, as her expression became ferocious, like that of a cornered animal, he thought she would dig her nails into his eyes, rip them bleeding from their sockets.

Then recognition dawned and she slumped into his arms.

"Quent! What? How?" She shook her head as if clearing it. Her brown curls danced around her pale face. Her shiner was a shadow of its former self.

"Come on. We're too exposed here." Limping, he led her away from the pit. "Look, I've got the key."

"Key? Quent, what are—?"

"Did you see anything unusual. I mean just before ..." He tapped a finger toward the glowing pool.

She shook her head. "No. I was sure I was going to be thrown into the fire. I blacked out. What happened?"

"Shhh." She was talking too loud. He was nervous as hell standing out in the open like this, and his knee needed a rest.

The heat was oppressive. God, I wish I were outside in January for a few minutes, he thought as he took her by the arm and, keeping an eye out for anything and everything, led her over to a flat rock and sat.

"I saw Izzy," he whispered when she sat beside him.

"Where?" She grabbed his arm. The reflection of distant fires danced in her eyes.

At that moment he hated Izzy for having this effect on her. "Over there somewhere," he said, purposely waving vaguely in the general direction of where he'd seen Izzy. She started to stand; he pulled her back. "Hang on," he hissed, his eyes nervously scanning the darkness. The suspense of what next, coupled with the effort of explaining to her, was killing him. In the back of his mind, he found himself wishing he could just lie down in an air-conditioned room and sleep. "Listen."

"I'm listening." She peeled his fingers off her arm and he silently cursed himself for being such a presumptuous asshole. He folded his hands between his knees. "Sorry."

She waved the comment aside. "Go on. Tell me what you saw."

"I saw Izzy. Then I saw you. And when I realized I couldn't reach you in time, I looked at Izzy and thought about . . ." Guiltily, he avoided her searching gaze. "Well, about hurting him. Then I was standing up in the theater and some of the seats were starting to burn. Then I was back here." He met her stare. She looked puzzled.

"And you think you . . . made something happen?"

"I do. Remember what I told you this Dr. Rejdak said about the dreamatron working both ways?" He didn't mention how Rejdak was spending his evening.

"Yes."

"I think that's what happened."

"Telepathy?" She looked dubious.

"Maybe not. Maybe it's the way the dreamatron works, like a gate that swings both ways. The point is we can fight him. I caught him off guard and jolted him. Maybe the two of us together can really hurt him."

Her eyes flashed. "Hurt him?" She stood, searching the

darkness. "I can't hurt him," she said without looking at him. The distant yellow light caught her high cheekbones, and for a moment he saw only beauty. With a pang, imagined or real, in his heart, he felt uplifted, poetic, the way one sometimes, especially as a child, feels uplifted at the moment of dawn or of sunset.

Breathless.

"Can't hurt him?" he said, showing more anger than he intended. "He almost killed you."

"But he didn't." Her eyes were flinty. His bad-mouthing Izzy was turning her against him. "And you forget what else you told me. That guy from Liverpool died from a cerebral hemorrhage." She shook her head and her expression softened. Now there were tears in her eyes. "I can't hurt Izzy." She searched the wall of smoke, but the curtains were closed. It was obvious her only impulse was to get to Izzy.

His impulse was to get her out of here.

"I didn't get a chance to look around much when the scenery changed before," he said, "but I think I saw an exit sign over there." He pointed.

"I don't want to exit," she said, surprising him. "I want to save Izzy before he hurts anyone."

"Christ, he's already hurt people." He was whispering so loudly he was almost shouting, but he didn't care. Whether people were dying tonight was a moot point. He had no way of knowing. But Rejdak was dead—that was one heavy-duty fact! And Jason Carruthers. And others. The red and gray and purple ruins of Rejdak's head hung before his vision like a garish painting. How could she be so blind?

She's in love. That's how! And not with you, asshole!

The smoke shifted, and once again Quent saw, in the near distance, Izzy sitting upon his rocky pile, playing his gleaming dreamatron, his eyes hidden behind his black mask like some blind pianist. Like some mad Phantom of the Opera pounding his moribund chords on his smuggled organ in the crypts below the city. The blankness of Izzy's veil lent him an atmosphere of inscrutability, of menace, that no human expression could have conveyed so well.

Movement out of the corner of his eye . . .

"Helen! Wait!"

She was running toward her lover. She didn't stop at his shout. The smoke closed between them.

He plunged after her into the wall of smoke.

"Whadaya say we have some fun, huh?" Fred leered drunkenly, gestured with his confiscated trident.

"I'm game." Todd grinned conspiratorially, not knowing what Fred had in mind, but juiced for action.

"Take the initiative," Fred echoed his thought. "Do unto others before they do unto you!"

"Amen," Todd agreed.

"What's cooking in that empty head of yours, Fred Spivak?" Wanda rapped her knuckles, none too lightly, on his head.

Fred laughed. "Ambush, Sweetcakes."

Wanda, a seasoned dreamiegoer herself, grinned at the prospect.

They came upon a long low pile of rocks. Leading the way, Fred crept up and peered over. Immediately, he backed off, squatted, and motioned for them to keep low. His grin was wolfish. Wondering what his friend had seen, Todd crept up beside him and took a peek.

Like the creature that attacked Donna, the man-beast munching on a great flabby human thigh not fifteen feet from them was a corpse. Though its maggoty flesh was pocked where chunks were missing, exposing teeth and bone, its jaws worked just fine. Abnormally wide and chocked full of shark-like teeth, its jaws reminded Todd of the Tasmanian Devil on the old Bugs Bunny cartoons. In the rapture of feeding, the beast's shriveled eyes had rolled back in its head. Its lower jaw protruded extravagantly beyond its upper, and twin up-jutting tusks extended from where its lower canines would otherwise have been. Rather useless-looking, unless they were for hooking into its victim while it fed to catch all the blood.

"All right, ladies," Todd announced in a whisper, crouching low at the base of the pile, "stay down and watch the show."

Donna blinked. "I think I lost one of my contacts," she said.

"Shhh."

"I'm not sitting back and watching no show," Wanda hissed. "I want in on the fun."

"All right, Sweetcakes." Fred's wide smile split his narrow face. "Come here." She did so, standing on a rock to peer over the ridge.

"See the beastie?" Fred asked.

"Yeah." She made a face. "Sounds like you eating."

Fred ignored the remark. "Think you can get his attention?"

Wanda smiled and licked her teeth. Todd thought she looked about as seductive as Olive Oyl. "Sure. But what if he decides to go around instead of over?" She pointed to the nearest end of the rocky barrier.

"You're being negative," Fred said. "Besides, monsters always take the shortcut."

"Do they?" Donna sounded impressed.

"Yeah," Todd joined in. "Dracula flies through your window, the Wolfman leaps over your hedge. Believe it. We're talking science."

"Go to it, gal," Fred said. "And when he charges, get out of the way."

"You just get out of my way, Wonder Dick."

Without further ado she scrambled up the wall. Fred pinched her bottom while helping her up.

"Yoo hoo," Wanda yelled. "Hey, sailor!" And as the beast looked, she whipped up her T-shirt and flashed her under-nourished tits.

The beast flung the thigh aside, roared, charged. Giggling her ass off, Wanda leapt down from the rock—and plowed into Donna, who had decided she wanted to see. Together they sprawled on the ground.

"Not a lot of class, but she's got balls," Fred said to Todd as, true to his prediction, the beast made a beeline over the rocks and Fred rammed the trident through its throat when its head appeared over the rim, severing its roar abruptly. Black blood gurgled out of the gapping maw. It lost its footing and went skittering back. The scrabbling of claws was loud from the other side.

Todd gave Fred a hand and together they threw their weight on their end of the iron shaft when the trident came to rest like a seesaw on the crest of the pile. The sudden upward jolt ripped its head off with a crack of vertebrae like the splintering of rotten wood. No more blood followed the initial gush, but a thick gray-green ichor oozed sluggishly from the raw neck stump as the corpse, arms flailing, spasmed backward out of sight.

The head, impaled through the throat, remained struggling on the business end of the trident. Its mouth was still open in a silent roar, its tusks and protruding jaw dripping blood, its shriveled eyes glaring hate. Quite animatedly—and quite undead—the head tossed and champed, struggling to free itself from the central tine, which had neatly skewered its Adam's apple.

Then, from the other side of the wall, clawed hands reached for the head. A headless corpse, reeking of blood, rose into view.

"It's trying to put itself back together," Fred said and yanked the head away.

The headless body was clambering over the wall. It flopped, half-fell, half-rolled down the clutter of rocks, smacking, bounding, and came to rest with a *whoomf.*

Right on top of Wanda!

"Aiiiiiii!"

Screaming bloody murder, her usual cool completely blown, Wanda beat and shoved at the thing sprawled atop her, but it was too massive to budge. So she beat it some more. Donna, who had found a stick, beat it too. Her eyes, big as saucers, forgot to blink.

On the other end of the trident Fred and Todd held between them, the head was straining to twist around to see, over a nonexistent shoulder, what its body was doing.

The headless creature grabbed at Wanda, but she was quick. Kicking and shoving, she wrenched out from under it and scrabbled to her hands and knees. Its talons clawed her calf as she scrambled away, tearing easily through her jeans and sinking redly into her flesh.

The thing rose, its massive shoulders hunched, its clawed hands clutching blindly before it, striking a classic monster pose. Even more awesome for being headless, it lumbered after Wanda, who was crawling on her hands and knees.

Fred, staring at the scene before him, failed to see what the head was doing stage right of his vision until it was too late.

The icy stream of mucus that spewed from the head's grotesque mouth caught Todd full in the face. Sputtering and spitting and wiping frantically, Todd let go the trident, leaving it in Fred's hands. Fred started to toss the trident and the head aside and run to get Wanda out of the pickle she was about to get herself into.

He stopped, realizing instantly that he had made a mistake in letting the head see where its body was going. He twisted the trident around so the demon couldn't see, but it was too late. The headless corpse, no longer lurching, launched itself at Wanda.

"Aiiii—"

And it landed on her with what looked like enough force to disable a fullback. The thing scrambled up before they could move and lifted Wanda to where its mouth should have been, but wasn't. The head impaled on the trident was chomping, its eyes rolled back in its head as if gorging.

Fred was stunned. And for a moment he forgot that it was just a dream, and reacted instinctively. For a moment he went that extra step in suspending his disbelief and reacted spontaneously in an explosion of berserker fury. He leapt into the air as if going for a high one on the racquetball court, raising the iron trident as high as his arms would stretch, and came down heavily, flipping the trident over before his sneakers *whumped* against the rock so that the head was skull-down, and smashed the trident against the rock like a sledgehammer.

The head exploded. Shards of bone and globs of rotten maggot-ridden brains shot everywhere. A rancid dollop of gore slopped onto Fred's forehead, ran into his eye; he wiped it off with a savage swipe of his hand, then whirled, trident leveled, ready to charge.

As the headless torso toppled.

It swayed for a second, one hand outstretched like the

mummy, the knees buckled, the hand dropped as the upper body slumped. As if in slow motion, it fell across Wanda's feet.

"Fred!" she screeched, scurrying out from under the thrashing torso.

Fred dropped the trident, was with her in a flash, pulling her to her feet. She's shuddering, he thought incredulously. He pulled her to him. There was none of her usual rib poking or kidney shots. Her skin was clammy. Shock? he wondered.

Naw! Not ol' Iron-butt!

"Freak, freak," he said, trying to cheer her up. "Don't tell me Stark got to ol' Iron-butt Wanda Lou!" He bunched up his arm, expecting the punch that Wanda delivered.

"What a man," she said in her best Olive Oyl voice, snuggling up to him.

"Aw, shucks, wuttn' nothing," he quipped back, making no effort to sound like Popeye.

Her face was sweaty. The little makeup she wore was smeared and her T-shirt was ripped at the collar, exposing her bony shoulder and the top of one small tit. Her small brown eyes, looking up at his, were as lascivious as her tongue. Holding her close to him, he suppressed the urge to rip off her clothes and take her right here and now.

But there was work to be done. And there would be plenty of steam left over for sex.

After the dreamie.

When it would be for real.

"Wait up!"

Helen was still ahead. Though limping slightly, favoring her right foot, she was still moving faster than he was and didn't slow when he called.

Distance was deceiving. Dreamlike, they seemed to be getting closer, but not enough to warrant all the running they were doing. Izzy's rock-pile keep had transformed into something of a low mountain. The ground was steep and strewn with boulders. They emerged from the smoke, and when he glanced back to see if anything was following, the yellow fires were below them. Now the way was lit by the white radiance surrounding Izzy. The boulders cast long shadows downhill. On the breezeless summit, Izzy was visible from the shoulders up, his black veil as unwavering as a flag on the moon.

With a small yelp, Helen stumbled and fell. In half a moment Quent caught up and helped her to her feet.

"Thanks," she said, panting.

He, too, was breathless. They leaned on each other for a moment while they caught their breath.

When he looked up, the landscape had changed.

Izzy was no longer visible. His rocky pile had vanished. And instead of the serrated edge of up-jutting rocks, the ridgeline of the low mountain ran level like the edge of a plateau. Furthermore, the steep slope was no longer bathed in the white light surrounding Izzy, but was lit in a red glow that turned the underbellies of the clouds a dark and ominous red.

"Oh, my God," Helen breathed.

He turned. She was gazing down the rock-strewn slope.

It took him a second to see what she was gawking at, to spot the two shadows flowing over the ground far below, rushing toward them across the smoky plain, following their footsteps, sniffing the ground. It took him another moment to make out their shapes, to see them as other than twin two-dimensional amorphous darknesses. Black as demon-shaped holes punched in the fabric of night, black as Izzy's veil, the huge bull-like heads hunkered down between massive shoulders.

Sparks and chips of granite flew as they hurled themselves up the slope. The beat of their hooves was the thunder of sledgehammers. Red, hate-filled eyes glowed like coals in an otherwise pitch-black night. The chill that ran up his spine was like an ice pick between the shoulder blades.

His thoughts raced! Running was useless. He whirled, looked upslope for Izzy. But the Dreamer was out of sight, over the plateau's edge, and the things would be on him before he made it to the rim. He searched for a rock, a stick, the jawbone of an ass.

Nothing!

While his brain spun its wheels, his hand took action and brought out his key chain, from which hung his penknife. He opened the knife; the tiny blade gleamed dull red in the light from the plateau.

Never in his life had he felt so pathetic.

As the bullheaded shadows neared, he saw that what he had taken for red eyes were really fires raging behind empty sockets. The same red blaze showed at their nostrils, and now, as they pulverized stone not forty feet below, their massive bull jaws swung open and a volcanic roar blasted like a hot wind across the intervening rock. It was as if the things were hollow, nightmare shells, filled with hell fire.

His knees shook, ready to fold. Dread lay in his stomach like the dead worm at the bottom of the tequila bottle. The penknife's plastic handle was warm in his sweaty fist. A glance at Helen showed him she was just as petrified. Her mouth and her eyes were shaped in big O's.

His mind whirred. Desperate thoughts flew by in rapid succession, like fanning through the pages of a book.

There has to be a way!

Dreamies work both ways!

That's it! Will against will! My mind against Izzy's!

But the fear . . . the debilitating fear!

He no longer had the element of surprise. And his mind was no match for Izzy's. Isidor Stark was a genius!

The thunder of hooves . . .

The debilitating fear . . .

He tried to picture himself chopping into Izzy again, but he was afraid. So paralyzed by the sight of the flame-filled maws, all he could do, as the creatures closed, was stand there with his mouth gaping.

Fire, water, earth, air . . . mumbled a part of his mind that hadn't given up.

There was always some way for the audience to defend themselves, to participate in battling the baddies. It was a mark of Izzy's style.

Goddamn it! There has to be a way.

Fire and silver!

Izzy's words struck him with the force of a slap.

But tell me, what are your own favorite weapons?

. . . fire and silver. Silver, like you said, for the werewolf . . . fire for everything else. Monsters hate fire.

And in the same instant, the image of himself wielding a flaming sword popped into his head, a vision so real he could almost feel the sword's magic thrumming through his hand, his wrist.

His penknife was glowing.

Quent stared at it in disbelief. The tiny blade shone white despite the red glare from the plateau. As if the light came from within the stainless steel. An opposing light.

And the blade was growing, becoming brighter and brighter as it lengthened and the tiny plastic handle swelled, filling his hand with a cold silvery mass. Ghostly white flames like nothing he'd ever imagined flickered along the blade's length, became dazzling, blinding, so that he had to squint at it through his eyelashes.

Fire and silver.

The keys and chain disappeared. A silver cross guard sprouted above his fist, a big round Viking-style pommel mushroomed from the heel of the grip. And as the blade grew and the fire brightened, became the dazzling white-hot fire of a burning magnesium strip, confidence and courage spread like cold fire up his arm, expanded across his chest, his shoulders, flowed into his head like a charged current, thrumming like the rails ahead of an approaching subway. And though he was too adrenaline-charged to notice until later, his headache cleared, his knee was still sore but his weight was bearable, and his burned arm no longer stung. The blisters on his hand and arm vanished, as if they had never been.

Sparks flew thick as the fire monsters charged up the remaining yards. The roar that boomed from their throats was the roar of erupting volcanoes.

Less than a dozen paces below, the ascent narrowed, flanked on either side by tall rocks. Leaving Helen where she stood, he ran down. As he anticipated, the creatures fell in line, one behind the other, as they entered the narrow defile. The first one burst through.

Black talons whistled toward him. Quent ducked, side-stepped, swung the fire blade. The point met with a satisfyingly meaty resistance, then tore free. The beast's momentum carried it past him, drove it into the rocks. From beneath the spasming monstrosity, a red glow spread as if it bled liquid fire.

Shocked that it could be so easy, worried that the first creature might rise again, Quent backhanded the blade at where he hoped the second creature's legs would be. But the monster leapt. The blade described a dazzling arc beneath its flight. It landed behind and above him.

Between him and Helen.

His heart slammed. He feared the thing would attack Helen, but it whirled, ebony talons slashing, red-glowing eyes and mouth flashing into view: a roaring furnace encased in shadow.

Like an ape leaping from a branch onto its prey, talons outstretched, bared to the fullest, ready to slash and crush and mangle, the monster jumped so fast Quent barely had time to react. He ducked, struck blindly, felt the deeply satisfying bite of his blade into something solid . . . but not fast enough: what felt like the tips of well-honed steak knives raked his left shoulder, narrowly missing the back of his skull.

For a blinding moment, pain flared so bright, so dazzling, that his vision blurred and he bit bloodily into his tongue. But only for a second, because the next moment he was blinking, wondering why he wasn't unconscious and bleeding to death even as he yanked the sword free.

The monster was down, facing away from him, slammed against a rock. Fire spurted like blood from its severed ankle. From the talons of the still-attached foot hung shreds of his T-shirt. With a roar that vibrated through the rock on which he stood, Izzy's creation began to scramble furiously up the incline, talons digging into rock, pulverizing stone.

"Oh, shit," Quent said, backpedaling toward higher ground. What, now?

Behind him, he heard Helen shouting for Izzy to stop it.

Though the moment of doubt lasted a fraction of a second, his fire blade dimmed. A snigger of fear wormed its way into his brain, ate holes into his confidence. Then he saw that the fires in the thing's eye sockets and mouth hole had dimmed, and he remembered that he had stopped one of them. If he could stop one, he could stop two. The fire blade rekindled.

Without warning and faster than he would have thought possible, the bullheaded nightmare drew its good leg underneath it and sprang. Fireblood streaming from its stump, it sailed over his head, out of reach of his slashing sword, and landed between him and Helen again. It flung out an arm. Having backed into a wedge in the rock, Helen screamed and averted her gaze. Talons raked her leg. Her scream rose an octave.

The shadow lifted its good hand to finish her off.

Quent bounded three flying steps uphill and, landing astride the horror, drove the sword through its back and out the front of its barrel chest. With a roar that jarred Quent as if he'd fallen out a window onto concrete, the monster rolled, dragging Quent, who was unwilling to let go the sword, over with it. Afraid the demon would crush him, Quent desperately wrenched the sword free. The blade left the wound reluctantly. Fire gushed from the creature's back and chest; liquid flames splattered like heart's blood over the granite and sand, rushed downslope in rivulets.

He backed away, panting, miraculously still holding on to the sword. The nightmare thing, trailing fire, rolled until it slammed into one of the rocks flanking the defile. The second demon, like the first, deflated slowly as the fire ran out of it.

Quent turned shakily to Helen. The sight of the blood flowing down her leg, painting the rock at her feet, jolted him. Her face was white, her eyes bulging. She stared past him at the collapsing husk of her attacker. Her pants leg was shredded and he could see, exposed between the bloody tatters, two ragged gashes that ran the length of her leg from hip to ankle. The bleeding was profuse—dangerously so—but she didn't seem to feel it. He knelt beside her.

What to do? Leave her and try to get to Izzy? Get her to a hospital? He had the terrible feeling that it was going to be too late: if the shock didn't kill her, she might still lose the leg. The wounds were too long, too deep, for him to stanch the blood flow with his belt.

Wisps of gossamer fire danced along the sword. Quickly, before Izzy got around to sending more trouble their way, he drew the blood-soaked denim of her slacks aside and laid the flat of the blade against the deepest gash, the one on the side of her thigh above the knee.

His stomach roiled, expecting the stench of burned meat, the crackle of crisping flesh, but neither happened. Helen jerked and he drew the dazzling blade away. Though her leg was still crimson with blood, the flesh beneath the blade was seamless. Not even a scar showed where the sword had touched.

Then he noticed her other wounds had stopped bleeding, and as he watched, the remaining gouges closed up, shrank, grew smooth and scarless, whole again. Gooseflesh rose all over his body as he watched the eerie healing process, like fast-motion time-lapse photography.

Helen groaned, reached for her leg, but her trembling fingers hesitated, afraid.

"It's all right," he said, and was pleased he didn't feel entirely like a jerk saying so. After all, he had just slain two demons and miraculously healed her wounds.

She touched her leg, massaged it, as if rubbing out the memory of her pain.

"Your sword . . ." She looked up at him, and he was pleased that something like wonder had replaced her shock.

"You saw?"

"Yes." She was shaking uncontrollably. "I was so afraid I couldn't move. Oh, God, Quent! I thought I was paralyzed."

He put a hand on her shoulder. "Stay put. I'm going up to look for Izzy." He nudged his chin toward the rim of the plateau, backlighted by the red glow.

"I'm coming with you," she said. He started to protest, but she cut him off. "Whether you want me to or not."

"Can you stand?"

She stood, tested her leg. "Good as new," she said.

Save for the copious blood that soaked her ruined pants and made her seem a candidate for the surgeon's saw, the leg did look as good as new. Again, the supernatural thrill he'd experienced watching Helen's gashes close surged through him. He scanned the rocky rim a half-dozen yards above. Isidor Stark's next trick was overdue. He scrambled up the remaining yards, pulled himself over the ridge top and gave her a hand up.

The three of them were alone. A glance around the broad circular tabletop revealed no hideous demonic bodyguards as Quent half-expected. In the center of the nearly level plateau sat Izzy, the black veil obscuring his boyish features. The nimbus of red light that encircled Izzy and his dreamatron dyed his black outfit and the mother-of-pearl console deep crimson. Only Izzy's veil maintained the untainted purity of its blackness.

Between Izzy and himself boiled the source of the blood-red light: a moat of what looked and smelled like boiling blood encircled the dream master.

Lightning flashed. The tableau strobed brilliant red for a half-sec. Strobed again. Thunder crashed, louder and louder. Lit by the dramatic crimson flash, backdropped against the roiling red steam that rose from the moat, inscrutable behind his black veil, Izzy appeared larger than life, an angel of death on a bloody space-age throne. Quent was torn between rushing Izzy and staying with Helen. He had a feeling—the charged air was pregnant with it—that something unpleasant was about to happen. The feeling flopped in his stomach like a large live fish.

The sky caught fire.

That was how it seemed anyway. Suddenly the sky flashed red and stayed red. Thunder continued to rumble and boom, and the light continued to vary in intensity, to flicker intermittent flashes of brightness, but the darkness no longer returned between flashes—the sky lit and stayed lit.

A rending *crraaack* announced the rainfall.

A red rain.

Big blood-red drops splashed colorfully as they exploded on the ground, instantly forming steaming red puddles, crimson rivulets.

And the reek! Gagging him, making him cringe in revulsion from the downpour that spattered around him.

Behind him, Helen sobbed. "Izzy! Stop it!" Then she was

spitting. "Blood!" Tears streamed from her eyes mingled with the blood running down her checks.

A rain of blood!

And he was untouched.

He drew Helen to him, raised the sword over their heads.

And Helen, too, was untouched.

The sword, he thought, marveling at the blinding white fire of the blade, the power thrumming in his fist, the glamour thrilling his body.

"Hold on to me," he told Helen, and she did. She buried her face in the crook of his shoulder. He squeezed her tight, hoping his torn T-shirt would absorb some of the blood. "Look," he whispered, "he's doing this to demoralize us . . . and to distract us. Don't let him."

She looked at him, blinking, her face smeared as if with some bizarre makeup, a gory Halloween mask. Her blood-soaked leg was no longer distinguishable from the rest of her. She looked past him at Izzy. "Izzy!" Staring out of the gore mask, her eyes brimmed with pain.

The rain stopped as suddenly as it had started. Blood steamed in puddles, streamed in rivulets. The red lightning too had ceased, and once again the plateau was lit by the vying light of the sanguine moat and the white flames of his sword.

Before Izzy could strike again, Quent released Helen and charged the Dreamer, his sneakers kicking up a bloody spray as he splashed through the puddles.

You can be beaten, he thought and hoped Izzy heard him.

The dreamie is the closest thing to telepathy.

Look out, pal—I'm coming at you!

Again he felt an icy chill, coupled with the strong feeling that someone was staring at him, peeking into his belfry. But it didn't matter with the glamour rippling through his nerves, the exquisite adrenaline-charged vitality surging through his blood.

Quent was close enough to glimpse a spark of blue through the veil's eye holes when the quake hit.

The earth convulsed, hurled him to the ground. He splashed chest and forearms into a pool of blood and stayed there, smelling the stench of the abattoir as the plateau bucked beneath him. The sword hissed in the pool; red steam plumed skyward. The rumbling stopped.

He glanced back. Helen was following him, running in his footsteps, her leg as healed as his, blood droplets flying from her limbs. Quent thought that, given the blood-soaked terrain, her gore-splattered appearance looked like a sort of grotesque camouflage. Seeing her like this angered him: once again he felt hatred seethe inside him.

And jealousy!

I can't hurt him . . .

Gritting his teeth and gripping the cool silver in his hand, he sprinted toward Izzy. A shadow fell over him. Something huge and dark and dead-smelling loomed overhead. A tentacle lashed toward him at waist level. He swung the sword two-handed without slowing. A fat four-foot length of tentacle flopped to the ground like a giant slug.

Then he was airborne, leaping the bubbling chasm, squinting his eyes against the terrific heat of the red steam through which he passed. For a moment, the blood reek was horrible, penetrating his nose and mouth even though he held his breath. The searing heat left him feeling baked dry from the inside out, as if he'd been plunged into a microwave oven; and when he landed, pitching forward, crashing down on his hands and knees, the rock burned his hands so that he lurched backward as he scrambled to his feet, nearly doing the very thing he wanted to avoid. Arms and sword flailing, he teetered wildly on the brink. Hot gravel rolled underfoot. A searing wind roasted his back.

He almost regained his balance. Almost. His left foot found traction, and he was lifting his right to thrust himself away from the brink . . . when the rock crumbled and gave way beneath him.

As he fell, his autonomic nervous system, anticipating the instant and excruciating pain of being boiled alive, sounded a red alert.

"NOOOO!" Helen screamed as she raced to the edge of the moat and saw Quent fall into the blood. Strangely, he made no splash as his body plunged beneath the surface. Too shocked to register this as significant, she saw only Quent falling backward, arms pinwheeling, into the bubbling inferno.

Was he dead?

Her mind shied away from the thought, not only for Quent's sake but also for Izzy's and her own sanity's—because, if true, then Izzy really was a murderer.

"Izzy," she shouted at the top of her lungs. It didn't come out as loud as she'd wanted; she was short on spit at the moment.

Across the moat, Izzy looked at her and she could see a familiar yet alien glint of blue through the eye holes.

A sharp pain lanced her brain. Like a sliver of glass. Like a nail from an electric gun. An icy pain. Incapacitating. Unbearable.

Izzy's black-gloved hand snatched the veil away. She gasped and raised a trembling hand to her lips. His moldering flesh was like onion peel clinging to dried-up, jerky-like muscle and yellowing teeth and bone. Lips, nose, most of the cheeks were gone, so that his was the skeletal grin of a rictus. His irises were still blue—and quite undead—but the corneas were glowing red, as if filled with boiling blood. His peeling skull was almost hairless, his expression that of a beast about to plunge its muzzle into the red meat of a fresh kill.

She screamed. And continued to scream as the rock beneath her feet crumbled and she pitched forward after Quent into the boiling moat.

33

On this infamous night, the ticketholders were not the only ones to sample Izzy Stark's wares.

Walls, building—no matter. Radio waves penetrate people too.

Across Grove Street and down a block in City Hall, a night-watchman named Joe Hanley, who was catching a few winks upstairs on the bench outside the Department of Licenses, burst into flames. By the time William Grimes, a fellow watch-man, responded to his screams, there was little left by which to identify the smoking husk, except for the number on the blackened badge.

The incident might have been coincidental were it not for the fact that five other persons—three teenagers, one adult, and a two-year-old in her crib—all sleeping in the neighborhood of the theater, burst into flame the same moment.

Quent stood there, furious, staring up at the ceiling of frothing red high up the granite walls of the tunnel, wondering how he was going to get back up there.

Worrying what Izzy would do to Helen.

The bubbling red appeared to be flowing. He was amazed that he was still alive, that he wasn't suffering third-degree burns from head to toe, that he hadn't even broken a leg in falling the sixteen or twenty feet from the glowing bloodstream that had proved only a gimmick, after all.

He looked at the fantastic sword still clutched in his hand; the flow of fluorescent white lit the tunnel.

A splash overhead caught his attention and he saw Helen falling toward him. He moved the upraised sword in time to keep from skewering her. With his free arm, he grabbed her around the waist to break her fall. Her plummeting weight staggered him. Her chin cracked against his collarbone, the click of her teeth loud in his ear, and they both went down in a heap.

Her lip was bleeding, he saw when the stars stopped spinning. The sword—fire and silver—thrummed in his hand. Helen lay atop him, quite still, breathing but unconscious. Lying there beneath her, he shook the sword at the bubbling ceiling, squeezed his eyes shut, and pictured himself hacking Izzy to bloody pulp.

Helen groaned. She was struggling to rise.

He sat up, lifting her with him. "Helen."

"Quent?" She rubbed her chin, worked her jaw. Her white teeth gleamed in the sword's diamond-white light, none broken.

Holding her, his arm around her for support, Quent felt a stirring of a very unplatonic protectiveness that made him feel foolish and presumptuous yet proud at the same time. He stood, helped her to her feet.

Right and left, two corridors led into darkness. The boiling red ceiling roofed only the section in which they stood.

"Which way?" she said.

Quent faced one of the walls. "We both fell facing this way. So, assuming we're really somewhere near the stage, the door should be to the right and then to the left."

"Let's try it," Helen said.

Of course, in a realm where time and space distorted to the dreamer's whim, who could say if left was left and right was right? Extending the sword before him like a beacon, Quent took Helen's hand and led her into darkness.

"Wow!" Donna said. "Wait'll I tell the kids back home."

Todd was pleased. He'd been worried that maybe he and Donna weren't so compatible, after all; he couldn't see going steady with anyone who didn't like dreamies. But after seeing her whaling away at the headless corpse with that stick . . .

"You're turning out to be a regular little barbarian, aren't you?" he said.

Donna grinned. "In my blood, I guess. Life's a bitch." She waved her stick. "This is good practice for the real world."

Todd shifted the iron trident to his other hand. Fred had given it up in favor of the switchblade he'd pulled from his boot. Unfortunately, the realism of Stark's dreamies had its disadvantages too; he wondered if maybe Fred's generosity in parting with his spoils of war didn't have something to do with its weight.

"Ow!" Donna grabbed her foot.

"What's the matter?"

"I broke my heel. Damn." Then she giggled. "Who would've ever thought you could break a heel in a dream?"

"Anything can happen in a dream, Sweets. Here, let me have your shoe."

She started to remove the broken shoe.

"No, the other one."

But it's still good."

"I know. Let me have it."

She handed him her good shoe. Resting the trident in the crook of his arm, he broke off the heel and returned the shoe.

She smiled sadly. "I guess that is more practical. I bought them for tonight."

Todd grinned "Your shoes aren't really damaged. Remember? We're still sitting in the audience and your shoes are still new and both your contacts are in your sexy blue eyes." He kissed her and she squealed.

"What a man!" she echoed Wanda, and kissed him on the cheek; and then, in a quieter voice, "I'm going to miss you."

A lump rose in his throat. He'd been trying not to think of that. He stopped, looked into her eyes. "Will I see you again?"

"Sure, sure," she said, but he didn't think she sounded so sure. "And I'll write. You'll write back, won't you?"

"Write back?" He snorted. "I hope you've got a big mailbox."

"Hey," she said, squinting into the smoky darkness, "we lost Wanda and Fred."

The sword was dimmer now—ghostly, sputtering milkily like a dying flame—and shorter.

And why shouldn't it dim? After all, it wasn't really a magic sword. After all, it was only a penknife . . .

And suddenly, after all, it was.

Only a penknife.

The light dimmed dramatically in the labyrinth, and he found himself holding the little knife, blade open, in his hand, the one-and-a-half-inch blade protruding from one end of his fist, his keys from the other.

That's that, he thought wearily. It seemed as if they'd walked a few miles already without getting anyplace. The phosphorescent glow from the gray cavern walls was dim, but it was good enough to see Helen's downcast expression as she stared at his penknife.

"Don't worry. It'll be there again when we need it." He wished he felt as confident as he sounded.

"I hope we won't need it," she said.

"Me too," he said, but he didn't think there was much chance of avoiding further confrontations. He was being negative, he realized. And why shouldn't he? He had witnessed the most gruesome murder scene imaginable, had been chased by cops and monsters, and now he was lost in what seemed like an endless labyrinth.

"Think we're backstage yet?" Helen asked, stooping to pass under the low ceiling. "Seems like we've been walking forever."

He detected no sarcasm in her voice. "We're moving in dreamtime," he said. The answer to how they could seem to be walking for hours when the whole concert wouldn't run much over an hour and a half didn't just suddenly pop into his head; he—and probably a few million others—had been marveling at that trick for years.

"We've got to treat this as real and keep moving. And I don't just mean *moving* as in *walking*. I mean *doing*."

She pushed an errant wisp of hair back. "And what are we supposed to—"

She was slipping, stumbling. She reached out to grasp the wall, and recoiled with an expression of shock and disgust. She looked at him, her eyes wide, frightened.

"Quent?"

"What's—" Her hands slid into his; one of them was slimy.

"The walls," she said. But he was already looking, staring at the palely glistening slime that covered the walls and ceiling of the tunnel. And the walls themselves—no longer rough phosphorescent-coated granite—had taken on the appearance of a kind of leathery flesh-toned hide, livid with raw sores from which oozed a rancid, yellow-gray pus that collected in puddles like the one in which Helen had slipped.

"Ugh!" Helen shivered with loathing. Quent felt his stomach churn. He tasted bile. "Let's go back," she said.

"We should keep going." He spoke between clenched teeth as he tried to breathe steadily, though the air was fetid with sickness and decay. "I've got a hunch the closer we get to Izzy, the worse things will get."

Helen nodded. She waved her hand under her chin as if trying to fan the stench away. "That makes sense. What, now?"

What, now? indeed. "Well, we agree we're in the Majestic

Theater." She nodded. "Then all this must be a façade." He waved expansively at the corpulent walls. "And if Izzy's will created the façade, our combined wills ought to have an effect on it."

She looked dubious.

"Look, you've got to believe we can affect the outcome of this dream. There's got to be a circuit-breaker box or a fire alarm. If we can't cut off his juice, then, at least, maybe we can get the fire department in here."

"How do we get to the fire alarm?"

How, indeed? he thought as he folded and pocketed the penknife.

Will . . .

"It has to have something to do with concentration and will." He looked at a wall of the tunnel, at the dribbling ooze. "Put your hands on the wall," he said, turning to meet her gaze.

"Are you kidding?"

"No, I'm not kidding." He was anxious, desperate to get out of this maze. "Look, this is not real." He slapped a wall, producing a sound like that of a hand striking a thick slab of rancid fat. Mucus splashed his arm and pants; a convulsive shudder rippled through the flabby meat. Real or not, the labyrinth wall certainly felt real.

"Awk!" Helen covered her mouth with the back of her hand, the one that hadn't touched the wall. He had to give her credit: a lot of people—male and female—would've barfed already. Helen had a strong stomach to have gotten this far. He guessed she had to, living with Izzy.

"Concentrate on feeling the wall." Repressing a loathing that slithered over his flesh like a swarm of lizards, he demonstrated. "The real wall. Ignore what you see and smell. Feel for the wall."

She closed her eyes and, visibly shuddering with revulsion, reached out and placed a hand on the opposite wall.

"Maybe closing your eyes is a good idea," he mused. "At least it cuts out Izzy's visuals. Keep them closed."

She opened them. "But what if we get separated?"

"Right. Here, hold my hand and feel for the wall with the

other. Close your eyes." They started walking, slowly, Quent exploring one side of the tunnel, Helen the other. "Remember, all this is an illusion and our will to survive is as strong as his will to destroy us."

At first, nothing happened. Quent inched along, eyes closed, barely breathing, trying to cut out some of the appalling smell, concentrating on feeling the wall underlying the illusion, but feeling only putrefying flesh beneath his hand. He had been in the Majestic before but never backstage, and he couldn't decide whether to try to picture a brick or concrete wall or a plaster one.

He decided to picture neither, but to concentrate on the idea of firmness, of flatness, of the unyielding solidity of the theater wall.

Still the texture beneath his hand remained leprous, the tactile sensations ranging from thick slime to a honey-like stickiness to scaly patches like psoriasis on a grand scale. The topography rose and fell, undulating and wrinkled and hideously cankered. He tried to ignore the nausea that was trying as friskily as a puppy to bubble out of his mouth, tried with all his might to concentrate only on touching the wall—the *real* wall—on feeling its solidity against his palm: cool or hot, rough or smooth, but real!

An image suddenly came to him. A vivid image of a brick wall. Dark-red brick. Old brick. Cool brick—cool, at least, to his sweating palm.

He opened his eyes, expecting to see what his mind had seen, but beheld only the crusty nightmare of the labyrinth wall.

Helen had stopped when he stopped. Her eyes were open, questioning.

"Brick," he said.

"Huh?"

"It's brick. The walls backstage are brick. Picture a brick wall, imagine yourself touching it."

Brick, she thought, closing her eyes, trying to see and feel the texture of brick.

If to think is to be, she thought, then, perhaps, to think is also to do. But the thought went spinning away.

She continued walking, trailing her hand over the leprous flesh. But as hard as she tried to picture a brick wall, she kept seeing Izzy's image, veiled in black, superimposed on the grid pattern of red rectangles.

Fred heard Todd shout his name and Donna shouting Wanda's. He glanced left; Wanda was gone. He'd been daydreaming, watching a movie in his head wherein he stood like Conan on a log spanning a bottomless chasm fighting off legions of the dead, his broadsword a red blur cutting the air in figure eights.

He slipped his hand into his pocket, ran his thumb over the switchblade's plastic handle, smiled. Sure as certain, their shouting would summon up something nasty. Something was sure to hear and come running . . .

. . . or crawling . . .

. . . or lurching . . . slithering . . . flopping . . . hopping . . .

"Wanda?" he whispered, glancing around, his dark eyes catching the yellow glint of a fire not far away.

No answer.

He mentally shrugged. Well, you're on your own, kid. Meet'ya back at the ranch. He started walking cautiously back in the direction he thought he'd heard his friends' voices.

A rumbling noise grew up out of the distance. The ground trembled. Two cold white eyes, bright as spotlights, rushed toward him. He hit the dirt, tried to blend in with the ground, hoping whatever the fuck was bearing down on him would pass right on by. It sounded too big for a switchblade.

The rumbling passed, receded as abruptly as it had begun. He stood. Dust was settling. Before him a low ridge, a dirt embankment blocked his way. Mounting it, he noticed the tumultuous groans and shrieks of the damned had vanished; the smoky nightscape was quiet now, except for the crunch of his boots on the gravel.

Then he saw the dotted white line.

He grinned. Hot dog! A highway! He marveled at the neat pattern of pale dashes stitching their way through the darkness and realized what the monster that been too big for his switchblade was.

Across the two-lane blacktop, two hobo types stepped out of the smoke and onto the road. Looking none too healthy, they were dressed in filthy rags, their faces scruffy and badly decayed. They were grinning toothily, and by the way their fingers were working as they headed toward him, he didn't think they wanted to ask him for directions.

A rumbling grew out of the darkness, the road trembled. White high beams slashed through the smoke. Fred flagged frantically as the tractor-trailer cab hurtled his way.

Gears ground. Brakes squealed. The big truck downshifted, screeched to a stop. It sat idling on its massive wheels like some huge beast taking a breather. Kicking up gravel from the shoulder, Fred lit for the passenger door not five yards away. A glance over his shoulder told him his yellow-fanged, shaggy-headed friends wanted a word with him; they were kicking up some gravel of their own.

His foot was on the steel step. He had the door handle in his hand. He wrenched it. The door was locked. He couldn't believe it! He slammed the handle back and forth, madly trying to rip the door off by its hinges.

A pale hand came into view through the window and popped the lock with a flick of a finger.

Fred whooped with glee, back in control, ecstatic now that he had an avenue of escape.

The driver's face stopped him. One foot inside and one on the running board, he froze, surprised as if someone had kicked him in the balls for no reason at all.

Deek smiled at him, his black eyes piercing under his barbarian bangs.

The hand on his calf decided him. A thumbnail punched a hole through his jeans and sank into his flesh, opening a rivulet of blood that ran into his boot. The muscle squeezed so hard it felt as if it were going to burst like a water balloon. Hanging on to the seat and the door, Fred roared and kicked the thing viciously in the face. The thumb popped out of his leg with a wet plopping sound as the derelict flew backward, arms flapping like an upside-down bird, all the way across the shoulder and over the embankment.

The truck was rolling now, gears grinding under the floor of the cockpit, the engine revving. The other boogeyman, no longer grinning, made a grab for him. He planted a heel in his eye and heard a satisfying crunch. But by now the pain in his thumbnail-stabbed calf was shooting up his leg to his spine and points north. Excruciating. Hauling in his injured leg and slamming the door, he faced Deek.

Lice were hopping in his fur vest, maggots gliding through his hair. The death's-head decal on his chest, crosshatched by the vest's rawhide laces, had flaked off like old wallpaper as the flesh had decayed. So what if Deek was dead? His old buddy had just snatched him out of trouble, hadn't he? He was smiling and had his eyes on the road. He had his hands on the big wheel and the shifter. So what if he stank like a road-squashed cat after a couple of days in the sun? The dreamie would be over soon, the loose ends wrapped up one way or another. What the hell . . . Truth was, he missed Deek.

"Hey, Stiff—pun intended—what time is it?"

"Cheeba time, Daddy-O," Deek said, keeping his eyes on the road, his voice crackling like a sandpapered record. Not that there was any road to see. Outside, the yellow-gray palls of smoke swirled by as the truck sped through it. Visibility didn't extend as far as the end of the hood.

Deek pulled a bone out of the ashtray and punched the cigarette lighter. "Sense, pal," the corpse croaked. "Real ass-kicking shit!"

Fred laughed despite the pain in his leg. It was good to hear Deek's voice, even if it did sound as if he were speaking through a paper bag filled with sand.

Deek took a long toke, passed him the joint, but when Fred reached for it, the cigarette was no more: between Deek's moldering fingers was a slimy white worm. Fred grinned despite the nausea that squeezed his intestines even as Deek singsonged the words.

"Freak, freak!"

A white worm, a sister to the one in his hand, tentatively poked one end out of Deek's ear, decided it liked it better inside, and retreated. Grinning, Fred flicked the worm at his dead pal—it missed and left a smear on the windshield—and wiped the slime on his jeans. "Whew!" He waved the air. "Stinks in here. Your mama still feeding you rice and beans? Man, I always knew you would end up one big fartbag, and now look at you."

"Takes one to know one, Peckerbreath," his undead friend quipped back.

"That's my sidekick, Deek, all right!" He was amazed. Stark had been exposed to Deek for such a short time, yet he had captured Deek's humor so well.

The pain in Fred's leg was a throbbing agony, an ice pick lodged in the base of his spine. "Hey, how about a slug of Southern Comfort?" Fred pulled the flask from his Lee jacket and had to grab the dash because Deek was braking hard and down-shifting like a motherfucker.

"Wha—"

He managed to get his head up from between his knees as the truck squealed and bucked to a stop. The highway was empty as far as the limited vision permitted him to see. He turned to ask Deek what was up, but Deek was swinging out of the cab, hopping down onto the blacktop.

Fred piled out his side and, limping painfully and waving the smoke out of the way, hurried around the front of the truck . . .

And dug in his heels as he rounded the fender on the driver's side.

Beside the idling truck, hand on the handle of the open door, stood a headless man. Where the head ought to be was a gaping bloody hole, an open portal onto his torn larynx and splintered vertebrae. The stump of his neck, spouting blood, wasn't neat, as if the corpse had been axed or guillotined, but ragged, as if the head had been ripped off.

The creature wore a fur vest laced with rawhide thongs.

The face on the chest—no longer the grinning death's-head—was Deek's. As Fred watched, the face swelled like a balloon, grew round, distorted like a face in a fun-house mirror.

The face was crying. Blood-red tears ran down its muscular stomach. The gaping mouth moaned darkly. Fred stood staring as the creature walked up to him, its eyes glistening like black pools, its gaze mesmerizing, as it grinned at him from behind the crisscross of laces like a prisoner behind bars. Fred failed to notice until too late that it held one hand behind its back.

"Deek," he said in disbelief. "What the—? Unnnn!"

The stiletto came around in a blur, its six-inch blade slicing Fred's T-shirt and abdominal muscles, spilling his intestines over his belt.

Too late, Fred swung his own knife, but being headless, the thing ducked easily. The creature's blade moved in for the coup de grâce.

Fred collapsed to his knees, too busy trying to hold his intestines in to bother supporting himself. The creature's mouth stretched into a sinister variant of Deek's lopsided grin. Its tongue was a coil of intestine as the blade sank into his right lung, grated against a rib.

Immediately, a feeling like air bubbles expanded in his chest. Suddenly it was hard to inhale.

Fred sucked wind. His surroundings shimmered, the air vibrated, the lurid yellow glare off the sulfur fires faded, then the smoke and the darkness became one as he blacked out.

Quent was concentrating so hard he was unaware he was squeezing Helen's hand until he noticed the pressure of her own hand squeezing back. He concentrated on feeling the cool, dry texture of a brick wall, on seeing the redness of the bricks.

"Iieee!"

"What?"

Her shout and the sudden knuckle-grinding squeeze she put on his hand jerked him out of his concentration. His eyes flung open.

Her arm was buried almost up to her elbow in the wall, as if the wall was swallowing her. Her eyes were huge. She looked more than a little sick when she withdrew her arm. "There's a hole."

He touched the slime-slick wall near where she pointed, felt the yielding, sore-dappled flesh. Then, though he saw flesh, his hand slipped into nothing. Vanished! "Jumping Jesus!" He withdrew his hand. Slowly, he reinserted it, watched bug-eyed and impressed as a kid watching a butterfly emerge from a cocoon for the first time, as his fingers and then his hand disappeared.

Sweating profusely, his scalp and arms and shoulders crawled with gooseflesh; he was scared shitless, for he was almost dead certain that his hand would encounter something in there and maybe he'd lose it.

He was in past the elbow now. Sweat ran into his eyes, trickled down his collar, as he felt around.

Nothing.

And then he felt it. He went for broke, sank his arm in up to his shoulder. Resisting the wave of dread that tried to force him back was like trying to stand up in a strong current.

The cool, flat, slightly rough rectangles of mortared brick were a shock, a surprise, and an absolute tactile joy to encounter. He moved his hand to the right as far as he could, patting along the wall, then to the left. His hand bumped against something. Feeling it, though he couldn't move his arm far enough to encompass it all, he estimated the object to be a metal box with a glass front. The box was far too long to house only a phone. In his mind's eye he pictured a large coil of gray . . . and something else. A flat metal bar hung on a chain from the side of the box.

"Helen?"

"Yes?"

"You weren't thinking about a fire-alarm box, were you?"

Her eyes darted to the wall where his arm looked as if it sprouted from the cankerous hide. She looked at him questioningly. "Yes. Why?"

He smiled, took the metal bar, and smashed the glass. No sound reached him through the rancid flesh, but he felt the bar going through the glass, the glass exploding, showering. He raked the bar up and down, from side to side, knocking out the shards he imagined protruded from the steel door frame. He reached in.

She gasped at the sight of the fire axe Quent pulled from the wall. He held it up between them and they both examined it as if it were a relic from a lost civilization. The axe looked brand-new, the red paint on the wedge-shaped head was unscratched, the edge keen.

Behind them, from the direction they had been heading, in which direction Quent had predicted things would get worse, things got worse. A loud, wet dripping noise, as of a big dead fish being smacked against the fleshy wall, reached his ears. Followed by a heavy dragging sound. The noises repeated. Repeated again. Again. Something was coming their way, around the bend not far ahead.

Slap . . . drag . . . slap . . . drag . . .

They gasped as one when something large and dark whipped around the corner, smacked wetly against a wall, and clung there. Followed by the ponderous dragging sound. The thing that bunched on the wall like a huge slug looked like a tentacle, gray-black as smoke and glistening wetly.

A second tentacle whipped around the corner, smacked against the wall, and clung.

Slipping out of Helen's grip, Quent hefted the axe and laid into the wall opposite the mysterious hole, rationalizing that if one side were close to a wall in the real theater, then the other side must be more open. A long gash appeared. He and Helen were splashed with sickly yellow-gray ichor. His gorge rose as a thick wet band striped his face. He lifted the axe again.

Helen screamed. The long, tapering end of a tentacle encircled her waist, was pulling her toward . . .

A black mass filled the tunnel ahead where it turned. And now that he got a better look at the thing, he noticed the sound he had taken for the buzz of his own frantic thoughts was really the noise of a boiling mass of flies. His eyes snapped to the tentacle wrapped around Helen's waist—it, too, buzzed and writhed. His scalp crawled. Helen beat hysterically at the appendage. Flies swarmed up her arm.

Quent jumped to her side, hacked the tentacle. Despite the fact that the monster seemed to be composed of a multitude of individual organisms, his efforts were rewarded with a meaty *whock,* which led him to think there might be something more substantial underneath the layers of insect. From the gagging stench that lifted off the blob, he wouldn't be too surprised if the thing was another of Izzy's animated corpses.

Flies flew from the furor of his assault like fat droplets of black blood, but wave after wave of undulating insects rippled down the length of the tentacle, filling in the wound, replenishing the limb.

Quent redoubled his efforts, moving along beside Helen as she was dragged inexorably toward the monster. Amid the red blur of his anger, he imagined he was laying into Izzy, and the axe head, dripping black fly parts, began to glow. A thrumming, rejuvenating current coursed up his arms, through his body. Exhaustion and doubt ran off him like rainwater as the glowing axe head brightened to a white, icy brilliance. The light lit the tunnel garishly, reflected blindingly off the silver handle.

Grinning, Quent renewed his assault. Helen's advance stopped, the insectile horde unable to fill the growing gap fast enough. Popping, instantly crisping fly bodies rained like black popcorn thrown by a hellish and invisible audience.

The limb severed. Helen, suddenly free, snapped back as if she'd just won a tug-of-war where the opposition had let go of the rope. Sobbing and shaking hysterically, she swatted the fat crawling insects from her face, her clothes, her hair.

There was no time to comfort her. The tentacled thing still blocked their path, and where there was one tentacle, there were others. He pulled her back up the tunnel to where he'd already laid into the wall and started chopping.

Charring flesh sizzled and smoked, a choking stench battered his senses, hot fluids spurted the front of his shirt, his neck, his face. He hacked in a frenzy, his arms a blur, the axe a *whoosh* of white light as it rose and fell. The gap widened, opened . . .

Onto a smoky darkness.

A ragged, running wound, a gash maybe five feet long, opened onto . . .

Where?

"Come on." He pulled Helen toward the opening. "Go through."

She hesitated, revulsion battling with her determination at

the thought of squeezing through that foulness that flapped like some abhorrent Freudian vagina image.

A tentacle whipped around her ankle. He severed it in a single chop, burying the blade in the floor.

"Go on!"

She didn't need further urging. Keeping her head down and closing her eyes, she passed through the fleshly gate onto elsewhere.

"Fred?" Wanda whispered.

For all her usual outward boldness, her flippant aggressiveness, she was afraid. She found it more fun to act as Fred's cheerleader than to actively engage these half-rotten monsters. The way the monster's head had swiveled around on the trident had unnerved her unlike anything she'd ever experienced in a dream.

This dreamie's weird, she thought. It wasn't like she was herself experiencing the dreamie through the eyes and senses of a character. It was as if she *was* the character! It was one thing to see the flesh of a fictional character rip open, see its blood gush all over the place; it was something else, however, to see these things happen to your own body. Dreamie or no dreamie!

Damn it! I'm lost! she thought.

She was turned around in this nightmare and didn't know which way to go. Wondering if she should call louder, she turned . . . and jumped!

Her heart leapt to her throat. Out of the dark, two squat, powerfully built batrachian hybrids hopped toward her, ornate scabbards slapping their glistening backs.

She had just enough time to jump back out of the way when the one with the turtle-like beak reached her, reared on its powerful hind legs, and curling its webbed hands around the haft, drew out a long gleaming rapier. The blade sang as it sliced the air. She sprang far enough back to avoid having her throat laid open by the blur of steel, but she raised her hands, held them out before her as if to ward off a blow, and the cold steel kissed her flesh. Three pinwheeling, red-trailing blurs toppled in the wake of the rapier, and she was staring in horrified disbelief at the spurting stumps of the index, middle, and ring fingers of her left hand.

The second creature, the one with the bug eyes on the sides of its head, landed in front of her, reared, unsheathed its weapon.

Screaming mindlessly, Wanda pressed her face against the sandy rock and covered her head with her hands.

Abruptly, as if they had stepped out of an alien dimension onto the Planet Earth, Quent and Helen found themselves backstage. The walls, indeed, were brick. Looking back, he saw no trace of the tunnel.

He almost smiled at his success. The corners of his mouth started to curl as he turned to share the victory with Helen.

But the smell . . .

The air reeked of sulfur and something else . . . something hideous. The clamor of the fire alarm was deafening.

"My God," Helen said, her eyes wide with horror. "That's not . . . ?" She shook her head, as if to negate the possibility.

My God, his thoughts echoed Helen's words. His head turned as hers did, to face the stage door, down at the end of the corridor, past the dressing rooms.

Smoke was curling underneath . . .

Helen ran toward the door. Quent took off after her.

"Helen! Stop! Don't open it!"

She touched the steel surface, recoiled, clutching her hand.

"Fire's right on the other side," he gasped, coming up beside her.

There were tears in her eyes when she looked at him. "I've got to find Izzy."

The acrid smoke foaming under the door was thick. He coughed and pulled her away. "There's a door on the other side of the stage."

Racing back the way they had come, Quent saw the big glass-fronted case on the wall, the thick coil of canvas, brass-nozzled hose, the glass shattered onto the floor and into the case. The axe shimmered in his hands, rippled with boreal lights.

The second door was open. In the wings, the stench hit him viscerally, like a steel-toed boot to the solar plexus. His gaze paused only an instant on Izzy, garbed in black, hands playing over the controls of his machine atop the platform behind the volcano set. Only an instant. Then his widening eyes were drawn inexorably toward the flames. Helen, too, stood aghast.

Flames licked high from the orchestra seats and raged up and down the curtain and wall on stage right. One of the once-gilded boxes—the one nearest the stage on that side of the auditorium—had become a crematorium: four charred cadavers sagged in the blackened remains. Victims caught dreaming. Similar charcoaled horrors sat or slouched in seats all over the auditorium.

Unlike the breathable smoke of Izzy's Inferno, the dark clouds billowing up from the smoldering seats and curtains and bodies, filling the girdered space above the stage, were suffocating. The smoke clawed Quent's throat, burned his lungs. He coughed it out only to replace it with more. Motes of white light danced in his vision.

Perched atop a broad hydraulic cylinder behind the foam volcano, Izzy played on, oblivious to the flames. The platform supporting Izzy and his machine was maybe a dozen feet above the stage. A ladder led to a smaller platform about halfway up that would be level with Izzy when he descended.

Coughing and shouting for Izzy to wake up, Helen was on the ladder in an instant.

The controls that operated the lift consisted of a metal box attached to the steel column. There were three buttons—up, stop, and down. Quent punched the down button and the platform started to descend. Helen waited at the top of the ladder, and when Izzy drew level, she leapt onto the platform.

Glancing up as he ascended the ladder, he saw Izzy turn when Helen put her hand on his shoulder, the black veil rippling in the breeze of his movement, saw him backhand her across the mouth, heard the crack of knuckles sharp above the roaring flames, saw her stumble backward, teeter at the edge, fall. She landed hard, flat on her back.

"*Damn you!*" Quent charged onto the platform, the axe

radiant with the heat of his fury as he raised it over the Dreamer's head. The black attire might have enhanced the image of mystery and charisma, but at the moment, with the curtains collapsing thunderously across the front of the stage and the stench of burned flesh scorching his nostrils, he saw Izzy as monstrous.

And then Izzy did become monstrous.

As the Dreamer faced him, the black veil wisped, disintegrated, blew away, and Izzy's face, barely recognizable save for the short mane of blond hair, was hideously distorted. His brow had thickened, and muzzlelike, his lower face jutted, teeth and gums showing as he leapt, seized him, lifted him. Quent cried out as talons that burst like miniature switchblades through the fingertips of his gloves punctured his arm. In his terror, Quent dropped the axe. The horror slammed him down on the planks. His head and shoulders hung off the platform as the Izzy-thing pinned him and reached for his neck. Quent grabbed the creature's wrists and tried to force the hands away. The blade-like talons protruding from the gloves glimmered in the firelight. But the Dreamer was stronger and the talons sank toward his throat. He was weakening, his arms quivering. He tried to work a foot under Izzy's chest and shove the horror away, but his legs were leaden.

Instead of skewering Quent's throat, the monster shoved his head back with the heel of its hand. Back and back Quent's head bent, until he was seeing the burning auditorium, the smoking cadavers, upside down. He felt drugged . . . hard to think . . . his body wasn't responding.

Pain shoved a sliver of glass under the base of his skull and an awful grating in his neck snapped him to. Panic gave him strength. He rammed his right foot under the demon's chest and heaved. Up it went, monstrous, teeth-filled visage contorted with rage, fire eyes bulging with surprise as it went over, crashing to the stage below, landing on its neck with the same sickening crunch he'd imagined for himself.

Quent rolled over in time to see the creature disappear—no slow fade, just there it was and there it wasn't. He shoved himself to his feet and, swaying dangerously, blinked the stinging smoke from his eyes. Izzy, slumped facedown over the controls of his machine, appeared unconscious. The axe no longer glowed. Quent picked it up and, grasping it in both hands, advanced.

"Izzy?"

The black-clad figure didn't move. Not knowing what to expect, Quent raised the axe.

Nothing happened. The Dreamer slept . . . or appeared to.

Without warning, Quent's legs gave out and he dropped to his knees. The axe slipped from his hands and he doubled over, racked by nausea. With a horror verging on tears, he realized he was succumbing to smoke asphyxiation; if he didn't get out of the theater quickly, he was a dead man.

Unable to stand, he crawled toward Izzy, reached up, and pulled him out of his seat, all the while groggily wondering how he was going to carry Izzy and Helen both out of the theater when he couldn't stand.

His hand found the ladder and he swung over the edge, placed his foot on a rung, swung the other leg down. Then, gripping the top of the ladder for dear life with one hand, he grabbed Izzy by the shirtfront and dragged the Dreamer's unconscious body toward him with all his remaining might.

And fell.

The breath slammed out of him, his skull cracked the stage and darkness took him.

Todd woke into a nightmare.

It was raining.

At first, he thought it was part of the dreamie—the screaming, the rain, the flames and smoke, the mind-boggling, roaring confusion—but as his head cleared, he realized the theater was burning and the rain was water from the sprinkler system.

He was on his feet, moving. Donna blinked at him—big baby blues flashing a desperate semaphore as they were pushed along with the crowd surging toward the theater doors.

"Todd?" She blinked as she had in the dreamie, as if she really had lost a contact. Tears ran down the rounded baby fat of her cheeks.

"Stay with me," he shouted above the combined roar of the flames and the crowd. But she had his hand in a death's grip and wasn't about to let go. Smoke billowed over them. Todd caught a lungful and was blinded by a coughing fit. When his vision cleared, they were in the lobby, borne along with the crowd toward the sidewalk visible through the open doors.

Fred and Wanda were nowhere in sight. He would later recall, sitting in the quiet of his parents' kitchen listening to the drone of the refrigerator in the hour or so before dawn, going over and over the night's tragic events, trying to make sense of it all, that the last thing he remembered from the dreamie was getting separated from Fred and Wanda.

When they emerged from the theater, the night was filled with sirens and flashing red and blue lights. White-shirted attendants carried burn victims to waiting ambulances. Before the night was over, it would take four National Guard trucks from the Armory to clear out the bulk of the bodies, and a search team would be sifting through the ashes for days.

In the fresh air, Donna found her voice. "Where's Wanda?" Her eyes showed her fright as she futilely scanned the crowd.

Todd climbed onto the hood of a parked car and stared out over the heads of the people. Moaning injured awaiting ambulances occupied the hoods of some of the other parked cars. Firemen in smoke apparatus carried or supported a last few victims; otherwise, the sidewalk in front of the marquee was clear for the fire department to work. He looked for Fred's head sticking up above the crowd in the street or behind the police barricades to the right.

He didn't see him.

He was about to climb down and get Donna farther away from the burning theater, when he saw Wanda, alone, wandering as if in a daze, drifting along with the stragglers toward the police barricade.

He jumped down, grabbed Donna's hand, and edged his way through the pedestrians.

"Wanda," he called as he neared, but she didn't seem to hear. Her eyes were wide with shock.

"Wanda!" he grabbed her arm, turned her around.

"Are you all right?" Donna was asking, but Todd saw the damaged hand, the blood trickling from the stumps of her three missing fingers. "Oh, my God," he cried, and pulled out his unused handkerchief. "Where's Fred?" he shouted as he bound the hand.

The mention of his name roused Wanda from her daze. She blinked, her forehead creased as she looked at the people around her. Failing to spot Fred, her eyes returned to the doors under the marquee of the Majestic.

Two stories above, flames curled from under the ornate cornice.

The pain was excruciating, a white-hot branding iron lodged in his chest.

Rain pelted his face, filled his ear.

Disoriented, foggy-brained, Fred realized he must have blacked out as his surroundings reassembled from the darkness. The smoke and the screams of the dying still surrounded him, but there were differences. His face was parked at eye level against a carpeted floor and he was staring point-blank at the metal leg of a theater seat.

He turned to rise. The pain inflated his head, crossed his eyes. A fit of coughing knocked him down again. Red droplets spattered the carpet. Jesus, he thought, I'm coughing blood! His chest hitched like a fish lying too long in the sun.

Panic struck him, slapped him so hard tears sprang to his eyes. I'm dying, he realized. He suddenly saw that fact with cold, clear certainty. He was lying in a burning theater, dying, and everyone was too busy trying to save themselves to bother with him. And some low-blow cocksucker had stabbed him while he was dreaming.

Fuckin' coward!

Then he realized what was happening, and a broad grin spread over his face.

Freak, freak!

Fuckin' A! Hell of a trick. Make the audience think it's woke up, only it's still in the dreamie. No one had done that yet. Stark had snuck in a fast one.

Too bad, Deek. You missed one hell of a blowout show!

The thought of Deek missing the show saddened him. The sadness was worse than the pain. He slipped his fingers into his jacket, brought out his flask. His hands trembled as he tried to twist off the cap. And when he did get it off, a coughing fit made him almost spill the contents.

Insidiously, a numbing cold had crept over him, and as he tried to raise the flask to his lips, he dropped it and the remaining shot or two sloshed out as his face hit the floor.

He didn't need the drink, after all. He had reached that cold painless plateau without it.

Red lights danced in the smoky blackness.

Fire . . .

And the stench!

The theater . . . burning . . .

The memory brought a panic that woke Quent's mind, but was insufficient to rouse his lethargic limbs as he tried to push himself to his hands and knees. Gravity seemed to have quadrupled. His limbs had no feeling.

He got his arms under him, squinted into the smoke. Flames consumed the curtains. Izzy lay beside him, unconscious or dead.

Another heap lay beyond Izzy.

"Helen," he croaked, and wished he hadn't. He pressed his forehead to the warm oak and his vision blurred as his body was racked with coughing.

Keeping his face close to the floor, where the air was nominally better, he began crawling toward her.

Shadows fell over him. Dark figures backlighted by conflagration. Two goggle-eyed, pig-snouted monsters stepped out of the smoke. One of them bent over Helen; the other strode toward him.

My God, it's not over! More demons! What did he have to do to end the dream? He looked for the axe, but it was beyond his reach, leaning against the cylinder.

And then he realized the shape bending over him was a raincoated fireman wearing goggles and an oxygen mask, and he was swept by an immense relief unlike anything he'd ever felt. Then he was being lifted, dragged to his feet, hauled along with one arm over the fireman's shoulder.

Helen, too, was lifted. A third fireman appeared and bent over Izzy.

Another rending crash over on stage right. The flames, having climbed the wall on that side, licked across the ceiling. Quent caught a lungful of smoke as he stumbled along. He blacked out for a minute as his coughing fit produced a flock of white stars that circled his head.

Emerging from the side entrance around the corner on Montgomery Street, the fireman crossed the road and left him propped against a parked car when he nodded he was okay. A fireman laid Izzy on the sidewalk, ripped off his veil, and clapped his oxygen mask over the Dreamer's nose and mouth. Helen was placed beside him and her rescuer likewise transferred his mask to her face. She was breathing, Quent saw with relief.

Staring up at the flames, he was vaguely aware of the flashing emergency lights of ambulances and fire trucks, of the noise and confusion of the surrounding mob that the police were having difficulty keeping back. He gratefully inhaled the night air—hot and full of the stench of incinerated flesh though it was—and his head began to clear. He watched the tall flames dance on the roof of the historic vaudeville hall, watched the smoke billow under the cornice, watched the arching streams from the firemen's hoses piss ineffectually into the inferno.

Helen was moving. She pushed aside the oxygen mask and bent over Izzy's unconscious form.

"Izzy! Izzy, wake up," she sobbed as she cradled his head.

A paramedic bent beside them. Quent moved closer. The Dreamer's face was twisted in the throes of nightmare.

A horrendous crash overwhelmed the noise of the crowd and the fire engines, and Quent turned in time to see the roof of the Majestic cave in. Sparks and flames shot high into the night.

Epilogue

... We are such stuff
As dreams are made on, and our little life
Is rounded with a sleep.

—Shakespeare

"Eastern Airlines Flight Eighteen to Atlanta is now ready for boarding at Gate Thirty-three," the lady in the brown Eastern uniform announced by the door that led to the enclosed boarding ramp. "Have your boarding passes ready, please."

Helen pulled her ticket from her purse and examined it.

"That's not your flight. You've still get ten minutes," Quent said, checking his watch. They were seated in the boarding area for Gate 34.

"I know. Just nervous." She stared out the big window at the refueling jet for a long moment.

He stared at it too, resentfully. In a few minutes it would take her out of his life. Oh, sure, he'd see her when he could find an excuse for a visit ... for a while anyway, until they drifted farther apart. Sad as it made him feel, maybe that was best. Izzy, after a year in a coma, was still the center of her attention—probably every waking moment—and as long as he was around her, other women were invisible.

"God, it's so unfair," she said. Her gaze met his. She looked tired, but beautiful despite the circles under her eyes—poignantly beautiful today because of the emotions her moving stirred in him. "I'm going to miss my house."

"I thought you said your condo in Washington has a fantastic view," he said, trying to get her to see something positive in her moving—even if he couldn't.

She sighed. "I'll miss the river and the Manhattan skyline."

Quent repressed a sigh of his own. "You're still going to push for the court order."

Helen twisted the strap of her purse in her lap. It was a

frustrating subject. Her petition for the CIA to release Izzy from the Walter Reed Army Hospital in Washington, D.C., to which the Company whisked him to seclusion a few days after the story of the Halloween tragedy went national, had been tied up in the courts for most of a year. Quent remembered the horror in Helen's voice the day she called to tell him Izzy had been "kidnapped" by the feds. It had taken her two months just to get permission to see him. Just last week, the Third Circuit Court of Appeals upheld the government's right to hold Izzy "in the interests of national security," as the Company's lawyers put it.

"Yes," she said, "I'll appeal, even though my lawyers say it doesn't look good." She looked down at her lap, twisted her purse strap some more. "God, I wish Izzy would wake up. You know, the doctors tell me he could wake up anytime . . . or he may never wake up. I want to be there when he wakes up." She smiled at him and there were tears in her eyes; the smile was brief. "I worry, Quent, I really worry."

"I know, Helen."

"You know, every time I fly down to check on him, I always examine his scalp." Her hands were trembling; she lowered her voice. "I have nightmares about them opening up his brain to see what makes him different. And there's no way I can tell if they're injecting him, because he's on intravenous and they can hook up anything to that system.

"I know I sound paranoid, but I can't help it, not with the magazines and TV and, worse, those checkout-counter newspapers speculating on why the CIA is holding Izzy."

He knew what she meant, and it was largely his fault; the rumors had died down for a while, but then his book, *Shooting Star,* came out, and the circus started all over again.

He glanced at his watch. A lump rose in his throat . . . less than five minutes till boarding. "I got a letter from Chet yesterday," he said, not wanting to spend their last moments together in gloom.

"Did you? How're the newlyweds?"

"Fine. They love Florida and they had a great time in the Bahamas."

Helen smiled ... a genuine smile that touched her eyes as well as her lips.

"Chet said they've started a band."

"No."

"Yeah. Chet's playing saxophone and Lois is singing. Got together with some of their neighbors in the retirement village. Chet said they put on dances at the community center."

"That's great. They're adapting."

"Yep." Quent remembered how happy Chet had been at the wedding. At Chet's request, he'd flown down and served as best man. Quent was happy for his friend—and more than a little jealous of his felicity.

"Is the autograph tour still on?" she asked.

"Yeah. I'll be autographing copies of *Shooting Star* in twelve major cities. I'm also scheduled for *Good Morning America* and the *Tonight Show*."

"Sounds exciting."

"You mean exhausting," he corrected. And it was: he'd already autographed at Rizzoli's and been interviewed on Manhattan radio shows. "It's a strange experience, people wanting your autograph because you knew someone famous."

"Now you're famous."

"No, I'm just the guy who told the story—with your help, of course. It wouldn't have been much of a book without your help. I know it was difficult for you."

She nodded. "Yes. But I don't know how I would have gotten through the year without your keeping me busy. Thank you."

"Eastern Airlines Flight Fifty-six to Dulles International is now ready for boarding at Gate Thirty-four," the overhead speaker announced, and Quent's smile slid off his face. "Please have your boarding passes ready."

"I guess this is it." She glanced at the line and he drank in her profile, painfully aware he wouldn't be seeing her for a while. Her exquisite cheekbones, her haunting dark eyes ...

I know, he thought. I'll fly down soon and write an eyewitness account of how Uncle Sam is treating the once King of the Dreamies. Maybe help get Izzy transferred back to New Jersey.

He saw her to the line, and when it was time for them to part, he hugged her and kissed her cheek. Then she disappeared into the boarding ramp, leaving him staring at a vacuum that had suddenly opened in his life.

"That it?" grunted the tall, leather-faced man in the serge suit.

"That's it," said the plump doctor in hospital whites holding the vial of clear liquid to the light. A smile lifted one corner of his pencil-thin mustache. "Synthetic taraxein. The ultimate hallucinogen. Twelve times stronger than the organic."

Colonel Milner's frown contrasted with the doctor's smug grin. "You're not giving him too much, are you?"

Dr. Amory shook his head.

"We don't want him to die—not with the attention the media's giving us."

"He'll be fine."

On the bed, his mind tenuously bound to insensate flesh, the Dreamer slept. An IV tube needled into his left arm. Two more tubes punctured his neck. A breathing tube connected his trachea to a respirator and a CVP line dripped a saline-and-potassium solution. Under the harsh fluorescents, Stark's skin was alabaster white, his lips nearly colorless. His head was shaved. The soft hiss of the respirator and the rhythmic blip of the heart monitor were the only signs of life.

In addition to the life-support and monitoring equipment, fine wires ran from electrodes on Stark's scalp to a compact, stainless-steel dreamatron on the patient's left. The machine was set to record but not to transmit.

"How's the recruiting going?" Amory asked, plugging the vial into the CPV tube.

The colonel snorted, a gleam in his cold blue eyes. "Fine. With dreamatrons illegal, the kids born with the talent need an outlet. Of course, the money is attractive—they will be among the highest-paid soldiers in the world. An elite troop. Imagine a whole battalion of Russians swept by paranoid hallucinations. Imagine the havoc as they turn their weapons on one another."

"Yes ... Well, by the time you get the first batch trained,

we'll have the perimeters of the synthetic taraxein mapped out."

"We'd better." The colonel's eyes grew flinty, his gravelly voice tight. "The KGB's recruiting potentials. They can't be far behind."

The luminous green blip on the heart monitor suddenly quickened, interrupting their conversation.

Dr. Amory's lean mustache stretched above a fat smile. "Showtime," he said as the Dreamer's eyes began to dance.

About the Author

When I was a boy walking in the Georgia woods, I thought wouldn't it be nice if I could will music into being. Create my own soundtrack to fit my mood. I grew up. The idea matured. I thought wouldn't it be nice to create movies by imagining them into some new technology so they could be streamed directly into your head, or performed before live audiences so that spectators could experience the "dreamie" vicariously from the perspective of the viewpoint character of his or her choice. Ah, but what if the dreamies get out of hand? What if they spill over into reality and the Dreamer's imagination is on the dark side and he is, perhaps, not quite sane?

Me? Living in the hinterlands of western New Jersey with my darling wife Roberta, riding my bikes and writing full time since retiring from teaching English.

] BLACK AMBROSIA Elizabeth Engstrom   40550-8 $16.99
Angelina offers you eternal peace—at the cost of your soul!

] NIGHTBLOOD T. Chris Martindale   40549-2 $17.99
A Vietnam vet they couldn't kill—against a vampire army that cannot die.

] THE PACK David Fisher   40552-2 $16.99
Bitter winter, and the dogs of summer have grown hungry . . . and vicious!

] LET'S GO PLAY AT THE ADAMS' Mendal W. Johnson   40534-8 $16.99
Tonight the kids are taking care of the babysitter . . .

] THE NEST Gregory A. Douglas   40530-0 $16.99
A dry rustling filled the night-time woods as they swarmed in their
millions to attack.

] WHEN DARKNESS LOVES US Elizabeth Engstrom   40531-7 $16.99
In the lightless depths of an underground labyrinth, unseen creatures
lie in wait, cold skeletal hands stretched out in welcome . . .

] THE TRIBE Bari Wood   40532-4 $16.99
"Marvelous... Wonderful suspense!" – Stephen King

] THE SPIRIT Thomas Page   40533-1 $16.99
A nightmare story of man against monster that will make your blood
run cold!

] THE REAPING Bernard Taylor   40534-8 $16.99
The seeds of evil have been sown, and the time to reap the harvest is
nigh!

Lightning Source UK Ltd.
Milton Keynes UK
UKHW042344110820
368051UK00002BA/257